D1856183

The Battle for the Freedom of Oz

Glinda, Oscar and Wickrie-Kells raced south, knowing that this coming battle held even greater dangers for them than the previous battles. This was not a matter of helping one side to win and making the other lose. If either side crushed the other and kept a large portion of their armies, the entire land would remain at risk.

The only way to obtain a victory for their cause here was to ensure that both Witches lost completely and lost equally. How could they possibly ensure that? Glinda and Oscar were only two people.

Yes, they were only two people, Glinda smiled grimly, but those two people were a *sorceress* and a *wizard.*

The Witch Queens

The Hidden History of Oz, Book One

TARL TELFORD

The Hidden History of Oz, Book One: The Witch Queens

Published by Emerald Engine Studios
Cover art by Tarl Telford. All rights reserved.

Copyright © 2012 Tarl Telford
Guide for Parents © 2014 Tarl Telford
All rights reserved.

ISBN: 0615667872
ISBN-13: 978-0615667874

DEDICATION

To my red-haired wife, Aimee, who believes in my dreams.

CONTENTS

Section Two: The Boy 82

Section Three: The Witches 117

ACKNOWLEDGMENTS

Many thanks go out to all of those who have written in Oz before me—L. Frank Baum, the original creator of this faerie land, and those who have followed in his footsteps, faithful and otherwise. And to those who have made Oz the ultimate American fairy tale, bringing new generations along the yellow brick road, into the ream of dedicated fans, you are appreciated.

Gratitude and thanks to those early readers who offered constructive feedback on the first drafts of the story.

For my family, who reads and listens, those who have always believed in my writing ability, and in my dreams of making a living as a writer—thank you.

The greatest appreciation to my wife, for listening to my dreams day after day and year after year. You are the everlasting heart and inspiration that makes these stories real.

And to you, dear reader, for picking up this book and discovering the power and adventure of dreams, thank you.

INTRODUCTION

Every land has its history. There is that history which is celebrated, and that history which is hidden.

Every generation rewrites its fairy tales to give meaning to world that they live in. That is why we see so many re-imaginings of Grimm's fairy tales in books, movies and television. The stories lend themselves to reinterpretation in new settings and times. *The Hidden History of Oz* is a series that takes the original vision of Oz, conceived by L. Frank Baum, and imagines it with the darker tones prevalent in today's times, but it also adds a clear explanation—a requirement for a thorough dissection of history and events.

The Hidden History of Oz began with a project that required me as a writer to annotate *The Wonderful Wizard of Oz*. As I researched and pulled apart Baum's text, I found quite a few loose ends. There were stories and histories introduced, but never explored or mentioned again. My overarching questions as I explored were WHY, followed closely by WHAT ELSE? So I poked and prodded and dug and researched. I found that even Baum didn't keep a clear chronology throughout his works. Despite all of this, Oz has been loved by generations. The world primarily knows Oz from MGM's 1939 movie, *The Wizard of Oz*. I hope to make it very clear that *The Hidden History of Oz* is *not* related to that movie in any way, shape or form.

The Witch Queens is a prequel to the novel, *The Wonderful Wizard of Oz*, written by L. Frank Baum in 1900. Every attempt has been made to stay faithful to the original source material and create a solid backstory for the characters introduced in the original story. Please bear in mind that this prequel is specific to *The Wonderful Wizard of Oz*—not any of the successive novels by Baum or those who came after.

This story attempts to fill in many of the gaps left in fictitious historical references made by the original author in *The Wonderful Wizard of Oz*. There were many stories told in that book that were never referenced again. Connections are drawn based on available information from the original work. While there are inconsistencies within the original body of Oz novels, this author attempts to reconcile historical occurrences and character histories to craft a solid and entertaining story. Any discrepancies between this story and the many stories currently existing in Oz canon and beyond are strictly the responsibility of the author.

The story of the Wizard coming to Oz has been wondered at and explored in various media. Until this story, all such stories sought to build more on the fanciful history. But Oz is not all rainbows and lollipops. As with all good stories, there are shadows. Thanks to the light of good, we can see these shadows. They are not overpowering to the world, or to the characters.

Oz is powered by dreams. How many generations have dreamed Oz more and more wonderful? Now we find out why.

It is the hope of the author that the reader may find enjoyment and dream a little bigger as they journey with Glinda, Oscar and their friends.

Tarl N. Telford, July 2012

©Tarl N. Telford, 2011. Except as provided by the Copyright Act, no part of this publication may be reproduced, stored in a retrieval system or transmitted in any form or by any means without the prior written permission of the publisher.

THE GIRL

1 THE LIFE OF GLINDA

Glinda was destined to one day become Glinda the Good, the most powerful sorceress in all the Land of Oz, but today—with her sixteenth birthday still several weeks away, and her parents doing what parents naturally do—Glinda wanted no part of being good.

From the top of her tousled red hair to the bottom of her bare feet, every freckle, every flared nostril, every narrowed glare identified her clearly as her mother's daughter. Her red hair was unique in all the land, shared only by her mother—the Red Sorceress. Glinda could do nothing without it reflecting on her parents. That reflection was ever her curse. Glinda's mother, Gayelette, kept her daughter as a slave in the tower near her palace. Not a slave, exactly, except in Glinda's mind, but Glinda's red hair bound her to her life as surely as shackles.

Glinda was always alone, or she felt very much alone, all the time. Her home was a tower in the shadow of the great Ruby Palace in the northern lands of Oz. Here she lived away from her parents, lost in the companionship of her books, and ever cursing her imprisonment. Even though her tower door was open, and stairs led down to the ground (pointed away from the Ruby Palace, no less), she was trapped. She could come and go as she pleased, but mostly she didn't. She had plenty of food and nice clothing to spare, and she had a voluminous library of books, but there were always strings attached to the gifts from her frequently absent parents—Glinda was expected to abide by four specific rules. The rules were as follows:

No leaving the tower after dark. They didn't trust her. The shutters were locked at night from the outside. How could they even manage to do that? It was more than forty feet off the ground to get to her window. Neither one of them could fly. The locked shutters prevented Glinda seeing the Ruby Palace at night. Although, sometimes light peeked in through the cracks in the shutters when the night was full. It was a mystery, and they wouldn't even allow Glinda to try to solve it.

Stay out of the Ruby Palace. What was in there? Nobody was allowed in. But Glinda was family. Why wasn't she allowed to go in? And there was a corollary to that rule, too.

Do not disturb your mother while she is working. Her mother was always working. The Ruby Sorceress was probably the most powerful person in the entire land, but she was too busy to pay attention to what was right under her own nose. She didn't care one whit about her daughter, so why should Glinda try to care about her mother? This rule hadn't been difficult for several years. Once Glinda had discovered the magical worlds within books, she didn't care any more about trying to get close to her mother. It didn't bother her at all. Not even a little. Most of the time.

Be the person you are destined to be. This was the one that frustrated Glinda the most. How was she supposed to find her destiny if they never let her do anything? It wasn't fair that she had to be exactly what they wanted her to be. What if she wanted to be something different? What did her parents know about destiny anyway?

That was it. Those were the rules that made her life a living prison. Glinda counted down the days until she would be an adult. Her sixteenth birthday was approaching. Though it was still several weeks away, it could not come soon enough. When that magical day came, she would finally become an adult and she could rid herself of all the shackles that bound her to childhood. She could at last be free of all the things that, to her parents, made her a child. She would be a woman in their eyes. But the one thing she could never be rid of was her red hair. It was a shining beacon to everyone, proclaiming exactly who she was—Glinda, daughter of Gayelette, Queen of the Ruby Palace. Even to people Glinda had never met, it was perfectly clear who she was. It was a known fact throughout the entire Land of Oz that there were only two people that had red hair. Of these two red-heads, only one of them was young.

Only one was young. That was not actually true, as they were both young, and they certainly appeared so. It was true that Glinda was only fifteen—that was undisputed. Gayelette, however, was older, though how much older nobody seemed to know. She certainly did not look old enough to have a fifteen year old daughter. Once she had bragged to Glinda that they would very soon be the same age and they would look like sisters.

It was said that Gayelette had discovered the secret to stop aging. Naturally, all of the women were envious of her, but Gayelette never paid them any mind. As the years of her life passed by, Gayelette had grown more and more reclusive. She did not associate with the people of the North Village or even those of the larger lands of the North. She kept her confidences and her attentions strictly to visitors who came within her personal residence. This house was constructed of strong stones and surrounded by an equally strong stone fence. This house sat nestled in the hill at the base of the Ruby Palace. Visitors to Gayelette's home ranged from merely mysterious to the outlandishly exotic. Witches and fantastic travelers from the far reaches of Oz sought out the Red Sorceress for her knowledge.

All of these types of exotic folk congregated here this time of year—the one time that all magical enemies and purveyors of the esoteric arts could come together—in the shadow of the Ruby Palace, at the Abracadabra Bazaar.

It was for this once-a-year event that Glinda was preparing today. Despite her mother's clear instructions that she was to keep her hair straight for the event, Glinda spent over an hour curling and teasing her hair. She was almost sixteen, and she would not be told how she could or could not fix her hair. She wanted to make a bold statement when she went out. Her hair would be remembered today. Glinda, not her mother, would be the star today.

The door to Glinda's room in the tower was closed. She didn't want anyone sneaking in and telling her that she couldn't do what she was doing. She wanted it to be a surprise. Oh, she looked forward to seeing her mother's face. Glinda spent the morning curling her hair and making it just right. As she finished the last lock and teased it into place, a shimmer in the mirror drew her attention. She looked behind her in the mirror. There was another red-haired reflection just behind her. Only this was older—an ageless beauty. Her mother, Gayelette, Sorceress of the Ruby Palace, forced a tight smile at her daughter's reflection in the mirror.

"Your hair is different than I had planned. You have time to straighten these curls before the bazaar. You are my daughter. You must look the part."

Glinda glared at her mother but said nothing. Then she slowly turned on the stool. "Why?"

"You are my daughter. I expect you to look like it today."

"But that doesn't make any sense. I don't want to always have to be like you want me to be. Why can't I do what I want to do, just once?" Glinda protested.

"Your dress will be here within the hour. It is lovely white. It is a good color for today. I expect that you will like it."

"I was going to wear my green dress."

"You must learn to rise to expectations, Glinda." Her mother declared. And that was final. Gayelette tapped her heels together three times and she was gone.

Once Gayelette had gone, Glinda was free to be angry. She hurled her brush at the place her mother had occupied mere moments before. She screamed angrily and stomped her feet. Then she threw herself down on her bed and clutched a pillow to her chest. "I am not what everyone expects! I'm not, I'm not, I'm not!"

It was during this fit of teenage tantrums that the dress was delivered. The knock at the door was met with a scream and several shoes being thrown. The dress was hung neatly outside to wait for the princess to calm down.

It only took an hour.

Glinda emerged from her tower room wearing a beautiful *green* dress. Her red hair was exquisitely curled and teased for greater volume. She looked narrowly at the white dress hanging by the door. She lifted one of the sleeves and ran her fingers over the lace and embroidery. It was a lovely dress, but it was not *her* choice. Therefore, it would stay where it was, and Glinda would go out, of her own choice, to face the world on her own terms.

2 THE MAGIC BAZAAR

Glinda crossed the fields below the Ruby Palace. The deep red palace glistened in the midday sun. It was an ancient moment frozen in time. The palace was an eruption of molten ruby thrusting upward toward the sky, caught forever in a frozen fountain. This ruby fountain sprang from the rock and solidified. Over the centuries it had been carved and shaped into the wonder that it now was. There was no other place like it in all of Oz. It was a magnificent creation frozen in time. For those who saw the Ruby Palace for the first time, it was a moment that would last forever. This was the legacy of Glinda's family—it was exactly the kind of the thing that Glinda had no intention of dealing with.

She walked along the river, heading toward the fields south of the North Village—the town where the Abracadabra Bazaar was held yearly. There was once a better name for the town, but they changed it before Glinda was born. Nobody would ever tell her, even when they would talk with her, what the name had been, or why it had been changed. It was something to do with her mother, she was sure.

She saw the long lines of travelers coming up the brick road to the fair grounds. Everyone was hurrying to get through the gates. The assembled multitude grew larger by the minute. Folks were flooding in, hoping to get a good position to view of Smith & Tinker's latest invention, and to see the upcoming show on the stage. This year promised to be the best one yet. Glinda entered the bazaar and immediately turned left, walking down a narrow alley between two rows of stalls. She was delighted by the sounds and the smells—so many wonderful things that she didn't have in her tower—and she momentarily lost track of her surroundings.

Glinda rounded the corner and bumped into a taller woman. This woman had long dark hair and golden eyes. Her face was lined with what Glinda easily recognized as magic lines, testifying that she was a witch. She wore a long black overdress, accented with blue embroidery, and a rich blue underdress, displaying glyphs and scintillating gems. Her dress gave the impression of a dark shell cracking to reveal the magic hidden inside. The blue color signified that she was from the East, from the land of the Munchkins. Glinda realized in the half-second it took to regain her balance that this witch was Kalinya, Witch of the East.

Kalinya scowled and raised her hand to strike down this foolish girl who would dare bump into her. Then she dropped her hands to her side when she recognized the red-haired girl. Kalinya's magically-lined face softened into a reasonable imitation of a smile. "Ah, Glinda, sweet child. I love your hair. Gone feral today? Where-are we off to in such a hurry? Lost your mother, by chance?"

"No. I know where she is." Glinda responded, pushing past the witch. "I have to go."

"Of course you have to go. You always have to be her little shadow, don't you?"

Glinda stopped short and slowly turned around. Her eyes blazed with angry fire at Kalinya.

"Or do you?" Kalinya prodded.

Glinda's burning glare made little impact on the older witch. Glinda said, "I know who you are. You are the wicked witch, Kalinya."

Now Kalinya smiled a genuinely wicked smile. Her golden eyes laughed at the red-haired girl. "All the way from the mysterious Tall House in the lands of the east. And you are Glinda, the puppet princess of the Ruby Kingdom."

"I am not."

"Oh, you most certainly are, Glinda. No one else has that red, red hair."

"I am not a puppet."

"Are you trying to convince me…or yourself?" Kalinya mocked. "As long as you live in the shadows, you will never shine." Kalinya saw Glinda's defenses crumble and she pushed her attack. "Now if you were my daughter…"

A commanding voice, cold as steel, sliced through the air behind them. "Kalinya."

An involuntary yelp escaped Kalinya's lips as she leaped around to stand next to Glinda.

From twenty steps away, Gayelette, Queen Sorceress of the Ruby lands of the North, stared icy daggers at her foe. "I have warned you about talking to my daughter."

Kalinya wrapped her dark sleeve around her wrist and regained her composure. Her gold eyes darkened and danced up mockingly to meet Gayelette's gaze. "Oh? So *now* you assume maternal responsibility? Isn't that just the wickedest thing? When this fine, upstanding young woman, perfectly able to abide and, *perhaps*, even prosper in the outside world, decides to have a perfectly innocent conversation with a *powerful* witch, you come to snuff out her light? Tut, tut." Kalinya clucked at Gayelette. "And you call me wicked." Kalinya slid past Gayelette and smirked at Glinda. "I'm sure we'll be seeing a lot of each other, dearie. Smith & Tinker have some tantalizing goodies this year."

Gayelette looked narrowly at Kalinya as she slunk past. Then her eyes went to her daughter. "Are you all right?"

"I was doing fine, Mother." Glinda's eyes dropped to the ground.

"Look at me when you are speaking, Glinda."

Glinda's eyes burned, but she forced them up to meet her mother's steely gaze. "I did fine without you."

Gayelette crossed the distance between them in a heartbeat. She lifted one of Glinda's wild curls. "So I see."

"I can do my own hair, Mother." Glinda protested.

"And you can dress yourself, too. I specifically requested the white gown for you today. And you disappointed me."

"Why shouldn't I disappoint you? You never tell me anything. You go off and I don't see you for days or weeks at a time. Then when you finally show up, it's *Glinda do this*, or *Glinda wear that.* I'm sick of it."

"I am doing what is best for you. Glinda, you have no idea what I am going through for you."

"I would if you told me!"

Gayelette's face hardened into a cold mask. "You are a presumptuous daughter." She took hold of Glinda's arm. "Come with me. We'll get your white dress."

"I'm not going back there." Glinda twisted her arm, but she didn't pull away.

"We don't have much time, Glinda. Come. Now." Gayelette ordered.

Glinda followed for two steps and then finally pulled her arm away. "Why?"

Gayelette appeared to blur for the barest fraction of a second. When Glinda pulled away, Gayelette stumbled, as if the ground shifted under her feet. She turned on Glinda, her red hair blazing like a torch in the sunlight. "Today is more important than you know. There is the Convocation of Witches very soon. I will not have my best presentation upstaged by that rock-tosser, Kalinya."

"So this is about you? This has nothing to do with me? I'm not going."

Gayelette turned to face the distant tower. "Don't be daft. Come with me."

"What is your problem with Kalinya? Why is she afraid of you?"

"Everyone is afraid of me." Gayelette said, matter-of-factly. Her impatience was evident. Her feet tapped quickly as she stared down her daughter.

Glinda's eyes darkened. She planted her feet stubbornly on the ground and refused to move. "Why?"

"Kalinya is a witch. She cannot be trusted. You cannot trust any of the witches, Glinda. They only want what is inside your head." Gayelette stepped toward Glinda, extending her hand.

"Why?"

"Because it is full of secrets."

"But aren't you a witch? Should I not trust you?" Glinda's stormy blue eyes flashed between distrust and delicious fascination.

"*Sorceress*. Not witch. Big difference. And I already know your secrets, so of course you can trust me. I know what is in your head because I put it there. You see, Glinda, unlike the witches, I actually *create* and do *things*. The witches just toss around magic like it was stuffed cats. Kalinya, for example; Glinda, don't ever trust that shifty-eyed rock-tosser. Those yellow eyes might promise power, but they are dead as amber."

"Well, at least she has two eyes. I heard somebody say that there's a witch with only one eye." Glinda brushed a curl out of her eye, stealing a glance at her mother's face. Even though she refused to take her mother's hand, she was glad that her mother was actually talking to her.

"That would be Ondri-baba. She is Kalinya's unfortunate younger sister. Unfortunate in that she does not have the beauty, the brains or the ruthless subtlety of her sister. All she has is a deep hatred and jealousy. Where she is not clever, she is mean and cruel. You are lucky that you don't have a sister, Glinda—she would have been exactly like that."

That statement dropped Glinda's rising heart down into her stomach. She could not hide her disgust and disappointment at her mother in that moment. Gayelette noticed the change and cocked her head to the side curiously.

"Yes. If you had a sister, she would have been horrible to you. You are a beautiful girl, Glinda. You are smart and you are determined. Once you realize the magnitude of what you have inside your head, you will be on your way to being a powerful sorceress."

Glinda opened her mouth to say something, and then closed it, when she realized she didn't have any response to that. So much for her mother talking to her. Conversation was only about Glinda when it was convenient. Any other time, it was about Gayelette.

"And her one eye, it's magic. A curse from the Queen of Dreams. I will need to make a visit to her to examine that someday. It is fascinating how someone so powerful can be so absolutely ignorant of what is right in front of them." Then Gayelette turned on her heel and walked. "Come." She ordered.

After several steps Gayelette turned around to reprimand Glinda for her slowness. But the girl was nowhere to be seen. Gayelette walked back to where Glinda had stood. "Glinda?" She called softly. Then the tempest raged in her eyes. Furious, she turned toward the distant Ruby Palace. Gayelette clicked her heels three times and she disappeared.

Glinda ran among the stalls, weaving in and out of the baskets full of wares from across the land of Oz. Rich smells filled the air, but Glinda ignored all of that. She was otherwise occupied with a heart full of strange storms. She wanted to go back and take her mother's hand and be there with her, but at the same time, she wished that she would never see her mother again. She heard her mother call once, but she ducked into a tent and scooted behind some crates. If her mother really wanted to find her, she could. If she didn't...Glinda didn't even care. Not at all.

Outside the tent she heard the excited chatter of the people as they passed by on their way to the central stage. The time for the Convocation of Witches was rapidly approaching. This was one of the most exciting events in the Abracadabra Bazaar. Each of the Witches in the land produced a trick or an invention, in Gayelette's case, that was intended as a public display of their power. They boasted of their great power and tried to outdo the others.

It was a show of power, but it was primarily to stoke the egos of the participants. This was a debate of sorts, with the participants displaying magic and showmanship instead of verbal jousting. Other participants were allowed a rebuttal, so that no one was left without a voice. It was great fun for the people to watch the most powerful people in the land belittling each other and showing what to them was unimaginable power.

A loud voice sounded over the chatter of the crowd, silencing them all. This was a voice they recognized, but it was of a magnitude that they had never before heard. A man's voice, full and robust, sounded with a little bit of tinny reverberation. "Thank you, ladies and gentlemen, for gathering at the main stage. To begin this year's Convocation, your esteemed guests, Smith & Tinker, I being Mr. Smith, have two things by way of announcement. One, as you can hear, my voice is amplified greatly. This device is called the mega-trump-o-phone. So all of you in the back can hear clearly when your hostess, Gayelette, brings out her show-stopping scion of amazement!"

And the crowd roared.

Curious, Glinda crept from her hiding spot behind the crates. She peeked out underneath the tent flap to see if the way out was clear. Glinda lifted the flap several inches and froze. There were cream-colored skirt hems right in front of her face. Shapely ankles in sandals shifted impatiently.

Someone was waiting right outside the door, so Glinda could not move. She lowered the tent flap slightly so that she was hidden in the shadow.

Soon the clanking of metal—the clanking of a dozen metal key rings jogging quickly—approached, and the ankles visibly relaxed. Glinda listened from the shadows.

"So what was the great hurry, lassie? Y'couldn't wait like the others? There're plenty of goodies to go around." This male voice was thin and danced with a restless brogue.

The female voice, low and husky, replied, "I have no desire for trinkets. I believe that you, Mr. Tinker, know how to suitably impress a lady? I have a lovely mirror, and it shows me truth, but I want the reflection to hold. My mirror holds a reflection, and lets me see deeper than peering eye can see, but there is more. I want the reflection to *really* hold."

The brogue whistled in amusement, "I believe I understand." There was the noise of clanking keys and bits of metal as he dug deep in his coat pocket. The clankery stopped when he pulled out a small something. "For the Witch who wants the perfect face."

Glinda lifted the tent flap just a little bit higher to peek out and look up. At this movement, Mr. Tinker glanced down, seeing the girl with red hair. He lifted the item up and away from her view, drawing the witch's gaze with it. The item was a small, blue glass vial. "I hold in my hand a very rare and precious unguent, what has been called by mystics from the Land of Ix, *Imaginary Paint*."

Imaginary paint? Glinda mouthed silently.

"It becomes what it is intended to be. It can be yours for a very reasonable price. I am certain we can come to some sort of arrangement."

The witch with shapely ankles took Mr. Tinker's arm and led him away from Glinda's hiding spot. She had not seen the girl. *Thankfully.* Glinda peeked out of the tent to see the shapely witch and Mr. Tinker walk toward a nearby intersection. She perked up her ears to hear the witch's final words before they rounded the corner.

"*... paint someone else's face ...*"

3 THE CONVOCATION OF WITCHES

Elsewhere, on the main stage, Mr. Smith demonstrated the most unique item in his wagon this year—Sandy Servants. "Here I hold in my hand a small hourglass, about the size of what you'd use to time an egg. Simple. What could it possibly be? Flakes from a jinni's scalp? Scrapings from a dragon's teeth? Dried tears from a chromatic cloud? Enough guessing, I'll tell you. Inside this hourglass is magical sand from across the burning wastes of the Deadly Desert. Inside each one of these vials waits a fully-extant servant, ready to do your bidding, for *one hour*, and one hour alone."

Mr. Smith unscrewed one end of the hourglass and poured the sand over his hand and allowed it to fall to the ground. Rather than falling as gravity would dictate, the sand flowed and shifted like spastic putty. It formed itself into a whirlwind and rose up to the height of a man—the same height as Mr. Smith. It pushed out arms and legs and a head with very flowing and rudimentary features.

"Dance, Sandy Servant." Mr. Smith commanded, and the golem began a slow shuffle. The audience gasped in amazement. This was life, or something very much like it, not the normal fare for this audience. This shuffling was akin to strange sorcery. A few gasps quickly gave way to excitement.

This was a presentation of the caliber that the witches would present in their Convocation, not Smith & Tinker. Normally, Smith & Tinker had been the purveyors of springs and things and magical jumpers. The toys and trinkets were amusing and entertaining, like a carousel was amusing, even though there was really nothing new. This was far more than anybody had anticipated. They ooohed and aaaahed.

"I gave you a command to dance, Sandy Servant. Lift your feet and dance." Mr. Smith poked at the golem with his finger. As his finger made contact with the magic sand, the features became more distinct, even starting to look like Mr. Smith.

The golem picked its feet higher and danced a fast jig. Its features became more distinct as the dance grew faster. There was no doubt that this thing was acting on its own, rather than miming Mr. Smith. Mr. Smith danced beside it, differently, just to prove that he was not controlling the creature.

"These Sandy Servants are good for one hour before the sand must be re-corporated in the vial. The hourglass is its mind, if you will, and it needs to rest before you put it to work again.

"I've got plenty of vials here, a whole cart full. Get 'em while the sand is still hot from the desert."

While many of the audience were duly impressed, very few pulled out any kind of money to buy any of the vials. The primary audience for these types of products was not the gathered crowd, but the users of magic.

Three witches pushed forward, jostling with each other for the lead position, to communicate with the Mr. Smith in hushed tones.

Glinda watched from the back of the crowd as the witches talked with Mr. Smith. Glinda recognized Kalinya in her electric-eggshell-cracked dress. Next to her, the short, stout witch in metal must be Ondri-baba, her sister. The third Witch had an obviously shapely figure, swathed in a cream-colored dress. That must be the one that Glinda overheard talking with Mr. Tinker. Glinda strained but she could not see what they were saying. Mr. Smith nodded and closed the crates of vials. He spoke to the audience, though they were not interested in buying his wares. He had an image to maintain, in his role as salesman. Then he switched roles to Master of Ceremonies and put his stovepipe hat back on.

"Thank you, lovely ladies, for your purchases. The rest of you rabble, hold steady as our other honored guests make their way up to the stage. Then we will begin this year's Witches Convocation."

The crowd cheered. Jugglers and tumblers leaped up on the stage, entertaining with whirling sticks of fire. The audience gasped as a tumbler tossed in a whole pie in the blazing blur of motion. They shouted in surprise and appreciation as a third juggler stepped into the middle of the whirling flames and caught the pie. He danced the pie in and out of the fiery rods. Then his hands fumbled. The pie slipped. And went right in the face of one of the jugglers!

The bumbling juggler grinned sheepishly, and then took a deep bow. The pie-face took a wild swing, missing the bowing bumbler. That left the last juggler trying furiously to keep all seven flaming rods in the air. Which he did marvelously. The audience cheered.

The entertainers cleared the stage, and Smith and Tinker announced each entrant in turn as they walked up the stairs to the main stage.

The Witches made their way up onto the main stage. There was Kalinya, clothed in black and blue, from the land of the East. As she walked up the stairs, she lifted her skirts above her feet so that Glinda caught a glimpse of her striped stockings.

She was followed by her shorter, stockier sister, Ondri-baba. She had a noticeable hunch—probably from the heavy decorative collars she wore— so she walked slightly stooped over. The audience grew silent as Ondri-baba took her place on stage. They were all watching for a glimpse of the witch's magic eye. Her luminous silver and green eye darted this way and that, seeing horrors unseen to anyone else. When she stood in the shadows, the slight glow from her magic eye cast a greenish pallor on her face. It made her look like the walking dead. With Ondri-baba, every look and sideways glance was a grimace of anger or disgust. She was ugly because she chose to be.

This contrasted sharply with the next up on the stage. She was young—older than Glinda by a few years—but still much younger than the previous witches. *Locasta* was her name, Glinda heard somebody say. The girl glanced around at every sharp noise. She was drawn toward Kalinya like she was a doll on a string. On the top of her head she wore a big floppy hat with the brim drooping down below her shoulders. She wore a white dress with a black and blue cape, to identify her as Kalinya's apprentice. The cape had similar cutout designs as Kalinya's dress. The most apparent difference between Locasta and the other witches—other than her age—was that her face was not yet lined with magic, like the others. She had a certain normalcy that the others could not project. Of all of the witches, only the apprentice, Locasta, wore a hat.

The next up on stage was Mombi. She was beautiful compared to the other witches. She walked slowly, drawing every expectant eye to her in her form-fitting, cream-colored dress. She didn't appear to have the same magic lines on her face as the others, but Glinda was unconvinced after hearing the secret conversation about imaginary paint. Mombi took her place, and she lowered her eyes to look down at the stage. Then she slowly closed them. When her eyes flashed open and she raised them to the crowd, she was practically glowing. Her lips curved into a practiced smile. She extended her hand, and everyone in the crowd was in her grasp. There was a studied radiance that illuminated from her, drawing every eye to Mombi. But the warm smile didn't extend into her eyes. There was a hidden mystery there—her face was a painted mask—but the crowd didn't care, Mombi gave them a show.

Then Gayelette walked up the stairs, carrying herself with a regal bearing that none of her competitors could match. Her red hair was shone radiant against her white dress. Her face was young and fresh, not scarred by magic like the others. She was as young as she had always appeared, for Gayelette was the eternal sorceress. As she crossed the stage, the gravity of her persona quieted the crowd. Gayelette would not be won with cheers like Mombi. She commanded a respect, even if it was motivated in part by fear.

Then the crowd turned to the stairway to see the last entrant. But the stairway was empty. Concerned murmurs rose. There was clearly the expectation that one more person should come up those stairs.

The voice sounded over the mega-trump-o-phone. "Yes, ladies and gentlemen, the staircase is empty. One of our favorite faces will not be joining us today, or ever. Sonadia, the Witch of the South, is dead."

The audience gasped in horrified denial. Up on the stage, Kalinya just smirked.

At the same time as the announcement, Glinda's father, Quelala, pushed toward the crowd toward her. He was a handsome man with a closely-cropped beard. He was tall, with blue eyes and a large forehead. He carried over his head a folded white bundle, raised up where it could not get accidentally dirtied. He saw Glinda's curled red hair and reached out to embrace his daughter with one arm. "Glinda, there you are. Your mother gave me this dress to give to you. Please change into it."

Glinda blanched at the thought. "I don't want to wear it. Then I'll look just like her."

Quelala looked down at his daughter and forced her eyes to meet his. "Glinda, you are your mother's daughter. This is a very important day. Our time is very, very limited here." He kept glancing up at the main stage, where Gayelette was stepping up to the front. "I need you to do this, right now."

"No."

"You see that girl up there? She's wearing a white dress."

"That's not a girl, that's your wife."

"The other one. *Locasta*. Do you know what that means? That means that she is being announced as an apprentice. She is being introduced as one of them up there. Do you get that?"

On the stage, Gayelette addressed the audience. She reviewed the affairs of her kingdom in the north and the bountiful harvest this year. She spoke of her studies and the continuing need for vigilance as the time in Oz passes by, drop by drop. She watched as Quelala pleaded with Glinda and even handed her the dress. Quelala pointed to the stage—not to Gayelette, but behind her—spoiling the surprise for Glinda. Then Glinda's face showed comprehension. She snatched the dress from her father. But it was too late. Gayelette's face hardened as she saw her daughter panic. There was no more time for games.

So Gayelette concluded her address. "–For my demonstration this year, I was to have a grand surprise, which you would have all appreciated. But it is clearly not ready. And so I exit, leaving you to the fine entertainment of the Witches." And she walked off the stage.

Glinda paled. She was frozen in shock and embarrassment. Even if nobody knew that she was supposed to be Gayelette's surprise, *she* knew. The look of disappointment on her mother's face burned indelibly into her memory.

Quelala reached out to put his arm around her, but Glinda shrugged him off. She thrust the white bundle back into her father's hands and ran away.

Up on the stage, the Convocation of Witches continued. Each witch demonstrated their great talent. Mombi ran her fingers through her long dark hair and it suddenly turned blonde. She danced around, changing her appearance and becoming this and that. She knew how to work a stage. Without a word said, she had the audience ready to eat out of her hand.

Ondri-baba demonstrated her walking hut. It was a strange contraption, really. It was a very normal, or rather, a very shabby hut on first glance. It had metal plates in strange places, with plaster work covering some cracks. But then at Ondri-baba's command, it rose up on spindly legs and walked around. This was the most impressive thing that the short-memoried audience had seen all day, and Ondri-baba looked poised to win. When she was challenged by Kalinya as to whether or not her house could jump, she prickled at the challenge. She commanded, and it jumped. But on the second try, it jumped too high and broke one of its legs. That effectively removed Ondri-baba from the Convocation competition.

Kalinya smirked and introduced her apprentice, Locasta. This was the first apprentice among the witches in more than ten years. The surprise cinched the title neatly for Kalinya. Without the competition from her chief rival, she soundly trounced the others on the stage. To add the final touches, Locasta demonstrated her talking hat that gave oracular advice.

With all of the excitement and rivalry demonstrated up on the stage, the crowd was quickly distracted from the missing participants.

In fact, there was only one person—Quelala—who noticed the missing redheads, and he was not certain which one to go after. So he did as he always did, and he followed after Gayelette.

4 THE SECRET OF RED HAIR

In the Council Hut owned by the Elders of the North Village, Gayelette sat at the table, writing. The front door burst open, and Kalinya breezed into the house with all the air of an unwanted visiting relative. Though Locasta was following closely behind, Kalinya slammed the front door in her face and latched it shut. "I won. Handily."

Gayelette continued writing without glancing up. Kalinya postured and attempted to regain control of the situation, which was quickly becoming awkward. Finally Gayelette finished her writing and delicately placed the quill back in its stand. She capped the ink bottle and then linked her fingers below her chin. "You don't belong here, Kalinya. This building is reserved for Gillikin Counselors or practitioners of the sorcerous arts. You are *neither*. Please leave."

Kalinya glanced around to ensure that all of the windows of the room were closed. "I know you have discovered something, Gayelette. Something profound. You are researching something that nobody else seems to know anything about. You are amassing *power*." She lingered on the final word.

"And you want a taste." Gayelette said. It was not a question.

"I want it all!" Kalinya slammed her palm down on the table in front of Gayelette, disturbing the inkwell. The quill slowly fell over. Gayelette picked it up and set it back into position.

"You know nothing of my work. What I do here is not for you, but for the entire land."

"*Poppycock*. You want power so you can control others." Kalinya snarled.

Gayelette stood from her seat, and Kalinya involuntarily backed up a step. Though her skin was young and beautiful, Gayelette's eyes were old with the wisdom of several lifetimes. She narrowed her gaze at Kalinya. "Control others? You think I want to control *others*? Why would I waste my time trying to control *people*? You speak of *power*? You know nothing of power. You are bitter because you are nothing but a rock-hurler. You throw things. What power do you possess? Can you stop the sands of time? Can you turn back the wrinkles from your face? Can you bring back the dead? *That* is power."

Kalinya's golden eyes glowed with envy. "Teach me."

"No."

"Teach me!"

"No." The word was barely a whisper, but the implied threat cut through the room like a razor.

Gayelette reached for the ruby pendant around her neck and Kalinya flung out her hand, throwing Gayelette across the room into the hearth.

"TEACH ME! Or I will destroy you!"

Gayelette arose. She crossed the space between them in less than the blink of an eye. She stared at Kalinya, nose to nose. Gayelette's red hair glowed with power. Kalinya trembled before her, both in rage and fear.

A slight age crease appeared in Gayelette's face, next to the corner of her mouth. Using this level of power always aged her slightly, but it was necessary in this case, to teach the impertinent witch a lesson. "You know nothing of power." Gayelette snarled the words in Kalinya's face.

Insulted, Kalinya raised her hands for another assault, but Gayelette grabbed Kalinya by the wrists. Gayelette's hands glowed around Kalinya's wrists as the life flowed from the wicked witch's hands into the Ruby Sorceress.

The age line disappeared from Gayelette's face.

Kalinya fell to her knees. She wailed in horror as she looked at her gnarled hands. "What have you done?"

"You will never strike me again." Gayelette spit on the floor. "I have taken five years from your hands. They will heal in time, but they will grow old before you. They may even fall off."

Kalinya glared up at Gayelette through angry tears. "I would have humbled myself to become your apprentice. I would have given everything I have to learn what you know."

Gayelette smirked. "Humility has never been your mask, Kalinya. But I will humor you. *Dreams*. No one in all the Land of Oz dreams. I want to know why. I search. That is what I do."

"I don't understand. What is '*dream*'? How do you know…?"

Gayelette grabbed Kalinya by the hair and dragged her to the door. "The words are enough."

She cast open the door and threw Kalinya by her hair to the ground outside the house. Locasta, Ondri-baba, Mr. Tinker and a number of other bazaar attendees watched in surprise. The witch who had easily won the Witch's Convocation this year was unceremoniously and indelicately dumped on her face.

"You are not worthy to serve me. I already have an apprentice." Gayelette said.

Locasta ran to her mentor and helped her rise to her feet. "What happened to your hands?"

When Kalinya turned around to face Gayelette, she was gone—completely gone.

Down by the river, far away from the bazaar grounds, Gayelette and her husband, Quelala, walked hand in hand.

"You didn't have to humiliate her in front of her sister." Quelala chided. In the distance, their Ruby Palace rose against the afternoon sky.

"I will not have her interfering with my work. I was writing. If Glinda is not ready, I have to document my work. If it cannot be master-to-apprentice, mother-to-daughter, then it must be pen-to-paper."

"You will have time to write when you are old. Right now you are still young." Quelala brushed a red lock of hair from Gayelette's cheek. "You are always young. Let us be young together. Let the ghosts care for their own curses. Glinda is not a child any more. She is thinking thoughts that are not fit for a child to deal with. She needs a mother."

By the riverbank nearby, two Gillikin women, clad in cloaks, gathered rushes.

"Glinda is getting older." Gayelette admitted.

Quelala agreed. "While you work in the Ruby Palace, I have sat on the tower steps many nights, sitting, worrying about her. Worrying that the events of that full moon night so long ago haunt her. She has not forgotten that night. I have heard her cry out in her sleep."

"She…she dreamed?" Gayelette wondered aloud.

Quelala grimaced. Those were not the words he wanted to hear from his wife. "Her memories are not gone. We don't know that she dreamed. How could such a thing even be possible?"

Gayelette's face lit up. "That is wonderful! We must bring her into the palace again."

Quelala stopped and placed his hands on his wife's shoulders. He looked deeply into her green eyes. "Gayelette. My only love. My ever beautiful queen. You are a powerful sorceress. Perhaps the most powerful the land has ever known…"

"Perhaps?"

"Yes. Perhaps." Quelala smiled quickly. "But you are more than a sorceress."

"I am *THE* sorceress."

"You are a mother."

Gayelette was silent for several moments. "I have a daughter. She will be a powerful sorceress. I have taught her. She has dreamed."

Quelala corrected her. "WE have a daughter. She is nearly sixteen years old. She is growing up alone. Our daughter needs a mother."

Gayelette smiled and nodded. "She will. Tonight. Tonight I will be her mother. I will bring her into the Ruby Palace. It does not matter that the other witches do not know. I will proceed with my plans. Glinda will learn at my side what it means to be a sorceress."

Quelala unsuccessfully tried to force a smile. "That is not exactly what I meant."

"Shh." A rustling behind them drew Gayelette's attention. Now there was only one Gillikin woman pulling rushes from the riverbank.

"It's nothing. A woman gathering reeds." Quelala looked to see a shadow out of place behind the reeds. *Was it one of them? One of his friends that he had promised to protect from Gayelette's wrath?* He could not allow Gayelette to investigate. Even if he wasn't sure it was one of them, he quickly shrugged and gestured off to the distance to divert Gayelette's attention. "I will go find Glinda."

Gayelette could hardly contain her excitement. "Yes. Find Glinda. I will prepare the Ruby Palace. Tonight is a night that will change the world." Gayelette picked up her skirts, and in the blink of an eye, she was gone.

Elsewhere, Glinda sat on a fence eating a cob of corn. The afternoon sun decided that it had just about had enough of this day and started its journey toward the far horizon.

"Glinda…" Kalinya whispered from behind Glinda, startling the girl. Glinda jumped off the fence. Her cob of corn dropped to the ground. Glinda glared backwards, and quickly picked up the corn. She turned around, blowing on the cob and brushing off the dirt. "That wasn't nice."

Kalinya stepped halfway out of the shadows of the cornfield. Her hands were held carefully in the folds of her dress, concealing their unnatural aging.

"What do *you* want?" Glinda glared.

Kalinya stepped forward and reached out her gnarled hands to take the dirty cob of corn from Glinda. She flicked her fingers and magically thrust all of the clinging dirt from the half-eaten cob. "I only want you to be happy." She held the clean corn out to the girl.

Glinda took the corn and rolled her eyes. "I am happy." But teenage sarcasm soured her voice.

"Are you? I think I know otherwise. I can see that there is something you want very much. Your mother is so disappointed."

"So now you're the fortune teller. I thought that power belonged to the stupid hat." Glinda turned away and discreetly tossed away the corn. She did not want anything to do with what Kalinya's withered hands had touched.

Fury roared in Kalinya's eyes as she raised her hands to smite the girl. Her gnarled hands wove intricate battles in the air as she struggled to hold her silence. She forced her hands down behind her back and gritted her teeth as Glinda turned back around to face her.

Glinda climbed back up on the fence. Then she cast a glance at Kalinya. "Why do you…no, that's not what I want to ask. Never mind."

"Speak, child. I do not have all day."

Glinda chose her words specifically to match how she felt at that moment. "When my mother talks of you, she calls you a wicked witch. She never says anything good about you. Calls you a rock thrower. Why do you let her do that to you?"

Fierce emotions raced across Kalinya's face—shock, anger, hurt, betrayal—until control forced itself back into position. "Gayelette is powerful." She held her hands up in the evening light. "I am a witch. From your mother's high throne, she may well call me wicked, but answer me this, child, she speaks of me. Does she ever speak of you?"

Glinda's eyes shot to Kalinya's face, but she could not read what lay behind those golden orbs. She studied them, searching for a scrap of something that she could call truth.

Kalinya continued, "I am who I am, and I am what I am. Can you claim the same for yourself? Who are, you, Glinda? Do you even have a name? Or are you simply, the '*daughter of the Sorceress*'?"

There it was—that scrap of truth that Glinda searched for. She thought that she wanted the truth, but with this truth, she would have gladly preferred lies. Angry tears welled up in Glinda's blue eyes. She swiveled her hips and dropped off the fence and stepped into the cornfield behind her. Kalinya scrambled to the fence, seeking to regain her position in front of Glinda's face. "Do you want to be you mother's apprentice? Aren't you curious about your own potential?"

"My mother will do what she wants. She always does." She bitterly spit out the words.

Kalinya reached out to Glinda, "Now if you were my daughter…I wouldn't treat you as a stranger. You would be loved. You would be treasured, as a tender *dream…*"

Glinda jerked away from the withered, outstretched hand. "I am not a dream. I am real. *REAL!*" She pushed through the cornstalks into the lengthening shadows. The insulting words stung even after their echo died in the air.

"Come back, child. I don't hate you, Glinda."

Glinda whirled and glared at her. "You will, Witch. You *will* hate me. You will hate me even more than you hate my mother."

Glinda left the cornfield and headed toward the river, which led toward her tower.

"What a pretty girl." An old crone, dressed in a black cloak and leaning on a cane hobbled up to Glinda. A reed dropped on the ground behind her. "Your hair is just lovely. Where can I get hair like that?" The crone reached out and twisted a lock of Glinda's hair around her finger. Glinda jerked her head backward, disgusted.

"Ow! You pulled my hair."

"A thousand apologies, my pretty, pretty pet. I was only trying to touch your hair and you pulled away."

"Get away from me."

"Oh my dearie, you misunderstand me. I was not trying to—"

"I don't care what you were trying to do. Nobody touches me."

"You have a loose hair sticking out." the crone reached for her hair again, but Glinda stepped backwards, smoothing down her hair. "That's not it. Here, my dear," The crone dug into her bag and pulled out a large silver mirror mounted on a finely engraved handle. A mystical sheen glistened on the mirror's surface. "You can see your whole face in my mirror. There, now you can fix your hair."

Glinda looked in the mirror and smoothed her unruly hair back. "Thanks."

"A pleasure, pet."

Glinda turned to walk back toward her tower, rising up against the setting sun. The crone turned the mirror away from the departing girl. Glinda's reflected face still showed in the sliver mirror. The *old* woman stood up straight and pulled out the white hair growing from her head. Long dark hair instantly replaced the old.

"Thank you my dear. My witch sisters will thank me for borrowing your face." Mombi was no longer a crone, but a passing shadow of normal. She unfurled her fingers to reveal their subtly-won prize—five strands of Glinda's red hair.

Mombi put away her silver mirror and wound the strands of red hair around her fingers. She ran her fingers through her dark hair. With each stroke, her hair became more and more red until it matched Glinda's color exactly.

5 THE SECRET OF THE WINGED MONKEYS

While the sun dropped lower, first resting on, and then sinking into the distant mountains, Glinda's heart sunk deeper in her chest. She stared out the window of her tower. The Ruby Palace was a constant reminder that Gayelette was there, and Glinda was here.

Nothing profound happened today. Unless you count the profound failure that Glinda had become. Her mother had wanted her to be up on that stage with her. All it would have taken was wearing that white dress. But she never explained anything. She just expected Glinda to act.

Glinda's head was usually filled with stories of great and noble actions, but today those tales of daring-do let her down. Courage didn't mean what she thought it meant. She thought that courage against oppression always paid off. She stood up to her mother, so why wasn't that rewarded? She stood up for her own freedom. So why didn't she feel free?

Glinda pulled a short red leather jacket from her closet. She untied the sleeves and they fell to the floor. She slid the jacket over her shoulders and looked at herself in the mirror. *Ready for adventure.* But where was it? Adventure was out there, and Glinda was in here, in the tower.

Even the other witches saw that Glinda wasn't free. They expected her to be like her mother, too—the daughter of the sorceress. Now Kalinya was coming in to try to cozy up to Glinda, probably just to get to her mother. What was so special about the sorceress anyway? None of the questions had any answers. And none of the answers she had made any sense.

Above Glinda's tower a dark winged shape flapped by, chattering nonsensically words that sounded like, "Witch hair, witch hair."

In the nearby sparkwood forest, Kalinya impatiently drummed her gnarled fingers on the black bark of the sparkwood tree, raising tiny points of light in the deepening darkness. The moon had not yet glanced above the horizon. Melodious insects happily chirped their evening songs, grating on Kalinya's nerves. *She should not have lost her temper at the girl. Glinda was the only way to get to Gayelette. If she could not get Glinda to join her, there was no chance of forcing Gayelette to reveal her secrets. If only the sorceress had explained her cryptic secrets further. What was a dream? How did Gayelette know what they were? How did she know that nobody in the Land of Oz had a dream?* These questions irritated Kalinya's mind as she waited for her co-conspirator to rendezvous.

From the shadows, Mombi cleared her throat, directing Kalinya's attention to her. Mombi stood cloaked head to foot in her dark cloak. The cloak skirts were still wet from her earlier espionage and disguise in the reeds. "Your hasty actions will betray you in the end."

Kalinya looked down at her withered fingers and clasped her hands together, keeping them still.

Mombi gestured, "Let us go deeper into the sparkwood forest. There is much to discuss, and little time. We must be in position before the moon rises."

Kalinya led the way deeper into the wood. They arrived at a sheltered spot beneath a large tree. This place was previously chosen for its seclusion. They were out of the sight of the stars, and no one could see them. Kalinya gestured at a branch above them, and it cracked and plummeted downward. As it hit the ground, the force of the impact caused the branch to spark and burst into flame. "Now we can see."

"At least you are not afraid of the dark like your sister." Mombi murmured. "That makes all of this much easier. Not jumping at shadows or seeing things that are not there. Her eye may be powerful, but the curse makes it worthless, in my opinion."

"Gifted, she said it was. Gifted to her by something, but she never got around to telling me what or who, for helping a foreign queen. It doesn't matter. She is useless to us. What news do you hold for me, Mombi?" Kalinya growled. She never liked to be reminded about her familial relationship to Ondri-baba. It was a sore spot that would not heal, not yet, but soon.

"It appears that Gayelette is opening the Ruby Palace for Glinda this evening." Mombi began. She gestured with her hands, imitating exactly Gayelette's grandiose flourishes which she was famous for. Physically, Mombi was a good match for Gayelette, mimicking her mannerisms and idiosyncrasies perfectly.

"We need to get inside the palace and find what she is doing in there." Kalinya snapped a sparkwood twig, then threw it from her. Her fingers knotted as she furiously tried to work out a plan.

Mombi reached out to take one of Kalinya's gnarled hands and worked the fingers loose until they relaxed. "Tut, tut. You should really moisturize more. Your age is showing."

Kalinya yanked her hand back from Mombi. "That witch stole five years from me. What she took, I will shake out of her. I will throw her into the sky, or drop a house on her. I will drop the entire Ruby Palace on top of that sanctimonious sorceress. Smash her into tiny little rubies."

"The path of action does not require violence to be effective. There are other ways to influence outcomes."

"Diplomacy sickens me. You are always making eyes at people. Winking and telling secrets. You will never—"

"I gave you the time and the place. You tried violence and...look at your hands. There are times that words can win more power than magic."

"I need to get into the Ruby Palace tonight."

"I heard that Gayelette tossed you in the mud."

"It surprises me that you were not cheering her on. You have switched allegiances so often; I rarely know which of your guises to believe anymore. Who are you today, Mombi? Is this just more of your mocking trickery?"

"Trickery, yes." Mombi pulled down her hood, revealing gorgeous red hair. "But mocking," She smiled a beautifully convincing smile, "We shall see who is mocked."

Kalinya stared at the incredible transformation in the other witch. Mombi's hair was a little bit longer than Glinda's hair, and it was straighter right now, but it was exactly the same shade of red. "Your hair—"

"Lovely, isn't it? I'm going to keep this color. I can see that it might be very beneficial someday."

"So you've got her hair. Then what? You are not a fifteen-year old girl. That body you are so proud of, that will not fool a sorceress."

"No. For that, I will need your help." She pulled a corset from within her cloak. "You'll need to pull it tight." Kalinya was only too happy to oblige.

Mombi gasped as Kalinya tied off the laces. When she regained her breath, she pulled the silver mirror from within her cloak. It shimmered as it displayed the face of Glinda on its surface. "A face that a mother could love." Mombi carefully removed the reflection from the mirror, peeling the film back and then arranging it on her own face. The magic paint conformed exactly to the contours of Mombi's face, turning it into Glinda's face.

"There is only the matter of clothing now." Kalinya smiled as she began to see the plan unfold.

Quelala whistled as he ascended the first tier of stairs to the tower base. "Glinda? It's your father. May I see you?" He held the bundled white dress in his hands. He tossed it back and forth, planning on hanging it back up in the tower.

Above him, a shadow moved in flickering candlelight. A door slammed open somewhere above.

"Thank you. I'm coming up."

Glinda lay face down on her bed, kicking her feet absently. She still wore the red jacket. She faced away from her father as he entered. A storybook lay open next to her, revealing Glinda's actions of the last several minutes.

He laid the dress over the back of a carved chair by the door. "I brought the white dress back." Quelala said. "You will look very pretty in it. Very much—"

"My mother's daughter?" Glinda finished her father's sentence. Her blue eyes flashed with hurt.

"A princess." Quelala continued. "You have had a rough day. You should have been told about the bazaar. I am sorry. But it was humiliating for your mother to walk off that stage like that. She was counting on you." Somehow those words didn't seem to help Glinda at all. Quelala sat down on the bed next to his daughter. She scooted away from him to the far side of the bed.

"Your eyes are getting stormy. Something is bothering you."

Glinda flopped over, turning away from him.

"But I'm sure you don't want to talk about it right now. Well, I was going to save this for your birthday in a few weeks, but this might be a better time." He tapped on Glinda's foot. "Hey, Glinda, could you at least let me see your pretty blue eyes?"

Glinda huffed and rolled on her back. She opened her eyes very wide for one moment and then closed them again. She purposely did not meet her father's gaze.

Quelala smiled.

"As a boy in this area, I ran around the forest a lot. Even then your mother liked to control things. Which she's very good at. I'm sure you've noticed." Glinda rolled her eyes beneath her closed lids, but that didn't stop Quelala from continuing. "I found some secrets that your mother didn't like. I'd like to share some of them with you." Glinda's eyes opened, just a little. Quelala pretended not to notice and continued. "Your mother is older than I am, so she didn't have the same view of fun things as I did. I found the most fun secret you can imagine. And it's still around, but don't tell your mother, otherwise we'll both be in big trouble. And I mean BIG trouble. You have to promise me."

Glinda's eyes were wide open now. She sat up and crossed her legs, leaning toward her father. He was offering her a real promise. Just something between the two of them. A conspiracy was being offered to her. Glinda was not quite so close to adulthood yet that she didn't still have a great deal of childhood curiosity left in her. The adults in her life had not managed to educate it out of her. She saw the same curiously rebellious twinkle dancing in her father's eyes.

"You are a young woman now. You are not a child. There are some things you need to know about your mother. She wants to see you tonight, and there will be a lot of questions you have. I don't want you to be afraid. But all of that can happen later. Right now, I've got a secret." He reached into his shirt and pulled out a silver whistle. "This," he began, "is a Silver Whistle. Every king or queen of the animal tribes has one. It controls their people. There are whistles that control wolves, crows, probably even bees, but this one," he leaned in toward Glinda conspiratorially, sharing one of his greatest secrets, "controls something much better."

Glinda's eyes danced with expectation. "What does it control?"

"I'll show you." Quelala leaned out the window and blew three quick bursts on the whistle. "Come on. Let's go downstairs. They are all very anxious to meet you. I have been telling them that they would get to meet you finally. They have been waiting for this moment for weeks now."

Glinda's excitement over the surprise was only matched by her father's anticipation in giving it. He was a boy again.

All around the tower came flapping and chattering in the darkness. The stars were blotted out by shapes flying through the sky. Some were the size of dogs, and others were nearly person-sized. Glinda reached out for her father's hand as the tribe of Winged Monkeys landed all around them. A silver-furred one with a jester's hat as a crown landed and bowed his head deferentially to Quelala, who returned the friendly bow. The monkey turned to Glinda and said, "I am King Klick, ruler of the Winged Monkeys. It is our pleasure to finally meet you."

Mombi and Kalinya hurried toward Glinda's tower. The full moon was starting to peek above the horizon and soon it would bathe the landscape in silver light. They had only a very short time to infiltrate the girl's tower and retrieve the appropriate clothing to complete Mombi's disguise as Glinda.

The distant base of the tower came alive with dark moving shapes. The flock of shadows chattered as they circled the tower, passing in front of the open window at the top to reveal the shape of a person with wings. Then they flew off toward the far horizon, away from the rising moon. Neither witch could dwell long on this strange event, for the moon peeked its first silver edge above the hill.

"I will go up alone." Mombi with Glinda's face said. "If she is up there, I will demand to know what she is doing with my face. If you hear screams, come up. Otherwise…I will handle it."

Kalinya crouched at the base of the tower, back behind the staircase. Mombi with Glinda's face hurried up the stairs to the landing and into the open door. Kalinya looked out at the rising moon. The Ruby Palace glowed red in the silver light. She clenched her fists in angry anticipation. Staring, she watched the lights in the palace turn off, one by one, yet the glow remained. Every night it was the same, the palace glowed as Gayelette conducted her strange experiments. Nobody knew what went on inside. But tonight would be different. Tonight the door would be opened. Tonight, Kalinya would force her way into Gayelette's confidence. Even if she had to destroy the girl, Glinda, or rather, Mombi to do it.

Footsteps on the stone staircase signaled the approach of Mombi-Glinda.

"This dress was lying right next to the door. I didn't even have to look. But I had to paint the silver mirror again." Mombi-Glinda was clothed in the richly embroidered white dress. Even with the tightly-cinched corset, Mombi's shapely form filled out the dress in ways the tailor had not anticipated for a fifteen year old girl. She whirled her cloak over her shoulders. "It's a little bit tight."

"Keep covered." Kalinya said. "Even if Gayelette has not paid attention to her daughter growing older, I don't think she's that ignorant."

Mombi laughed. "It looks good on me. Better than on her. Even though I am...her."

Kalinya grumbled under her breath. Mombi was flaunting her beauty, even though it wasn't all hers. At least the face was not hers. Of the actual witches, Mombi was the prettiest and the least affected by magical lines. It gave her the most infuriating of all reasons to brag. She could in all honesty say, *I'm prettier than you*, and she would be right.

Of all the witches, Mombi had the most physical of magic. She had focused her talents on transformation, which made her a valuable ally, or a potentially deadly enemy. No matter which side Mombi played, she filled her role with utmost gusto. She was a born actress, as if such a role could make a living in this magical land.

"Come on." Kalinya growled.

Mombi-Glinda skipped down the stairs and followed Kalinya into the silver light.

In the far away skies, Glinda screamed in excitement as the wind rushed through her red hair. The cool night air swept over her freckled face. She was high in the sky, dancing among the stars. Winged Monkeys held her tight, and then let her go, screaming and chattering right along with Glinda.

The giant moon cleared the horizon and rose into the sky to join them among the laughing stars.

Glinda and Quelala raced through the sky on wings of night. Quelala laughed like he was a boy again. Glinda looked over to see her father carried by King Klick and another large monkey that wore an eye patch. She had never seen this side of her father. She smiled as she realized that here, in this moment, like never before in her life, she fit in. She screamed as the monkeys carrying her tossed her high into the sky, only this time they didn't catch her like the other times before.

Glinda plummeted toward the ground. All around her the monkeys chattered in anticipation. Then they grasped onto her arms and dove toward the ground.

Moonlight reflected on the prism lake as the dark cloud of chattering monkeys streaked toward its surface. Glinda's feet skimmed the surface of the lake, shattering the silver moon into a million little waves. The monkeys laughed and hooted happily. Glinda's blue eyes shone brightly for the first time she could remember.

Outside the entrance to the Ruby Palace, Mombi with Glinda's face stood nervously. Part of it was an act, like an uncomfortable teenaged girl, and the other part of it was sheer terror from walking into the lair of the enemy. She calmed her breathing and stepped into the light.

Kalinya stood off to the side, just out of sight to anyone on the inside.

"Glinda, come in, my daughter." Gayelette's voice called from inside the Ruby Palace.

Mombi with Glinda's face glanced nervously over at Kalinya, who gestured her in.

"That dress looks lovely. You are certainly growing up."

Mombi with Glinda's face stepped across the threshold of the Ruby Palace. She didn't know what to expect. A shimmer passed through her as she entered into a different world. Her breath caught in her throat momentarily, and her eyes swam with colors, not all of them natural, and then she was through. She smiled in relief. She had crossed the greatest test.

"Don't be shy, my dear. You belong here, with me." Gayelette stepped away from a reflecting mirror to face her. "I had no idea you were growing up so fast."

Mombi-in-disguise smiled uncomfortably. She shrugged.

"Come here. There is so much that I want to show you." Glinda reached out and took Mombi-Glinda's hand and pulled her past the reflecting mirror apparatus into the shadow of the orrery. The orrery was a moving model of the planets and stars. What would normally be found in a planetarium was found here, for Gayelette had to calculate times and seasons for her experiments.

"Watch your head," Gayelette cautioned, "these orbs can move fast."

The moonlight crept through a mid-level window to spill onto the floor. It approached the reflecting apparatus. This signaled the countdown to the grand experiment.

"I believe in dreams." Gayelette began. "They are things, just like you and me. They cause changes, just like you and I can cause changes. But nobody can control dreams. And the deepest mystery for me is, *why don't people in Oz dream?*"

Mombi-Glinda's attention was drawn to the far corridor. Strange drifting shapes crossed from one shadow to another, always drawing closer and closer to her. Her head cocked to one side as she stared. The shapes were not imaginary, but they were not solid, either. They seemed not quite real, and at the same time seemed too very real to ignore.

"And so I started my research many years ago, after I was visited by the Queen of Dreams. She came after your father and I were married. I wanted to know how she could have power over these mythical things that nobody can control. She guided me to discover..." Gayelette followed Glinda's gaze over her shoulder to the drifting things. "Pay no attention to them. They're just curious about you. It's been years since..." Gayelette snapped her fingers as an idea came to her. "You know, I just had an idea. Do you want to meet your grandmother? We've got a few minutes before the moon hits the reflectors."

Far away, at that very moment, Glinda tumbled to the ground in a broad meadow more than a day's walk distant from the Ruby Palace. The purple grass glistened in the starlight. She laughed as she sat up. Her father laughed also as he rolled to the ground. King Klick jumped on Quelala and they wrestled around like two rambunctious little boys. Then King Klick tousled Quelala's hair and jumped backwards. Quelala howled and jumped after him. The silver monkey jumped into the air and hovered just out of reach as Quelala leaped up for him. "Go, then." Quelala laughed, "I like my hair messed up."

King Klick laughed aloud and flapped off to join his people on the far side of the meadow.

"It warms my heart to see you happy, Glinda."

"They're monkeys, right? How did you meet them?"

"When I was young, I lived in the south part of Oz. It was the only place I can remember at that age, but it never felt like home. When I met your mother, or rather, when your mother found me, I came north. She was busy in the palace even then. As a boy, I explored the forests all around. I met the Winged Monkeys. We have been friends ever since. Your mother did not like them one bit. She called them scamps and rascals. And they were. They like to have fun and get into trouble. It almost cost them their lives one time. Almost doomed the entire tribe to extinction."

"Really?" Now Glinda was really interested. This was like an adventure out of one of her books, only it was her father telling his story.

"That's right. It was on the day we were married. Your mother had made me a fine cap of gold. I was going to pick it up to wear for the wedding ceremony. I had on a very nice velvet suit. It was the nicest suit I had ever worn. Now I thought it was a bit much, but your mother liked it, so I wore it.

I was walking next to the river, the same river you walk by every day, heading toward the Ruby Palace, when the monkeys saw me and thought they'd have a little bit of fun. Generally I wouldn't mind, but it was my wedding day, and I was very anxious as it was.

"They swooped down and picked me up. I laughed and asked them to carry me as my friends to the Ruby Palace. I wanted them to be a part of the festivities. But Klick always loved jokes, and he and his band dropped me right into the water.

"Naturally, I was pretty upset. Klick called down to me, *'Swim out, my fine fellow, and see if the water has spotted your clothes.'* What was I supposed to do? I swam to the shore and pulled myself out."

"Were your clothes ruined?" Glinda asked, spellbound.

"Yes. But, unfortunately, your mother was looking out of one of the towers of the palace at the time, so she saw what happened. She had tolerated the monkeys before, but this was supposed to be *her* day—her wedding day, you know, it's supposed to be all about the bride. And they had ruined it for her. The wedding was postponed until every last winged monkey was rounded up. I tried to tell her it was a joke, but you know your mother's temper.

"When they were all before her, Gayelette had their wings tied so they could not get away. She said that they should be dropped in the river just like they had dropped Quelala."

"But that's horrible." Glinda protested.

"King Klick knew it was more than that. He knew that his people would drown in the river if their wings were tied. He pleaded for his people. I put in my voice also—they were my friends. Finally your mother relented, but she forgave only on one condition—that the Winged Monkeys would ever after that time do three times the bidding of the owner of the Golden Cap. That was to be me." Quelala stopped, growing pensive. "I did not want them drowned. But sometimes I think that the enslavement that they live under isn't much better than if they had drowned."

Glinda asked, "But isn't it better to be in slavery and alive than to be dead?"

"The dreams a man has must be his own." Quelala replied.

"But dreams aren't real."

"Dreams can mean aspirations; the things that you want to come true in your life. Dreams can also be the imaginations or visions in the night when you sleep. What I am talking about is aspirations. Nobody wants to be in slavery, but many people find themselves there. They wake up and wonder what happened. There are many kinds of slavery. If you are not free, from anything—if you cannot choose the way that you want to live your life—you are a slave."

"Then I'm definitely a slave." Glinda plopped backwards onto the ground.

"If that is so, then you need to fix it." Quelala leaned over to look in his daughter's eyes and nodded. "Fix it."

"How did you get free, Father?"

Quelala smiled sadly. "There are some chains I cannot break. My word is one of them. I am a slave to my honor. But I wear those chains with pride."

King Klick hooted above, circling. That reminded Quelala to get back to his story. "It sounds like the monkeys want me to finish. So King Klick gave me the whistle to call them, as a token of his gratitude. So I have the Golden Cap and the whistle. I call them and I control them, though I have never had to use the charm to get them to do anything. I hope one day they'll do the same for you." He smiled. "They are my friends."

Glinda ran her hands over the flowers of the meadow. Many of them had their heads bowed for the night, but there were other orchids that began rising as Glinda touched them. As she watched her father, Glinda furrowed her eyebrows, deep in thought; *this was a side of her father she had never seen before.*

The moon peeked above the tree line, sending a silver shaft toward them. Quelala grabbed a handful of the flower buds and pressed them into Glinda's hand. He took her hand in his and raised them high into the air. "Watch this." As the moonlight hit the orchids, they burst into full silver-tinged bloom. Their bright blossoms glowed in the moonlight. The shaft of moonlight stretched over the whole meadow, and all around them exploded in all of the magical colors of night. Glinda stared in awe. "Night blossoms." Quelala said, smiling proudly at his daughter's expression of wonder.

Suddenly Glinda pulled her hand away and wrapped her arms around Quelala's neck in a big hug. "This is the most beautiful thing I've ever seen. This is wonderful, *Daddy*."

Quelala's eyes brightened. "You haven't called me *Daddy* for years."

Glinda drew back and looked up at her father's handsome, beaming face. "It's different now. Now that…this." She gestured all around her, intending the meaning of the whole night.

Silhouetted against the moon flapped a single shadow. In the distance, yet approaching quickly, faint screeches could be heard. *"Witch hair, witch hair, witch hair."* Then all the monkeys were suddenly screeching the message.

"Witch hair?" Quelala asked, looking at Glinda.

The band of Winged Monkeys took to the sky, circling over the top of Quelala and Glinda. The messenger, a small monkey, chattered quickly to King Klick, who dropped to the ground in front of Quelala. "He says that a witch stole hair and is in the Ruby Palace."

"That doesn't make any sense."

King Klick huffed and chattered and screeched at the smaller monkey, who chattered back excitedly, pulling the fur on the top of his head for demonstration. "A witch has hair to get red."

Glinda reached up and touched her hair.

At that moment the ground shook, knocking Glinda off her feet. Quelala pulled her back up, and then the next wave hit, knocking them both off their feet. All of the monkeys who had landed leaped into the sky, screaming incoherently.

"That came from home!" He started running in the direction of the great noise. "Your majesty!"

But King Klick was already there with Brutus the eye-patch monkey, sweeping Quelala off the ground and into the air. Behind them, Glinda shrieked as she was plucked off the ground to follow after them.

Beneath them, the meadow of rarely-blooming night blossoms shuddered as tremor after tremor shook the flowers. As quickly as it had brightened into all the colors of the night, it darkened. The meadow, so brilliant for a moment, returned to its darkness, and wept silent tears as the petals dropped to the ground.

6 THE DESTRUCTION OF THE RUBY PALACE

Just a few minutes earlier, at the front gates of the Ruby Palace, Kalinya threw open the door and brazenly challenged Gayelette, "Your secrets will be mine!"

"Get out! You do not belong here!" Gayelette shouted at the approaching witch. She stepped in front of the girl with red hair, "Glinda, stay behind me."

Nearby, the swirl of phantasms crept closer to the moonlight checkerboard pattern on the floor. Mombi-in-disguise glanced around nervously and inched away from Gayelette.

"Your experiments are fascinating. They are watching." Kalinya observed. "How do you trap the ghosts in the mirror? Were they ghosts before you trapped them?" Kalinya stepped forward, her golden eyes searching everything.

"Last time was a warning, Witch. You are not my pupil. I have an apprentice. These sorcerous arts will not be yours."

Kalinya cackled sarcastically. "You have no apprentice! I am the first witch in more than ten years to take an apprentice. When I was young you had no apprentice, and you looked the same as you do now. You lie, Gayelette. You lie like a storybook mirror. You never age." Kalinya held up her withered crone hands. "You don't age like everyone else does. Your secret to aging will be mine."

Kalinya waved her hand and a mirror apparatus on an armature creaked as it shifted in response to Kalinya's magic. The telekinetic powers that Kalinya wielded may not have been sorcery, but they were a great threat to the precision of Gayelette's experiments.

"These apparatus have specific configurations. The experiment requires precise alignment." Gayelette warned the wicked witch.

"Apparatus? Don't you mean *apparati*?"

"So the witch reads her dictionary? I don't have to dumb it down for you." Gayelette snapped.

"And just what is this experiment? Is it about dreams? Is it about these ghosts flitting around?"

The moon crept higher, extending its light closer to the mirrors.

"These ghosts exist out of time. Making the unseen into physical form is the experiment. Your moderately impressive knowledge of hurling rocks will not help you here, Kalinya. I require specific magical assistance. That specific knowledge has been passed to my apprentice." Gayelette turned to the red-haired girl, but she was no longer next to her.

Mombi-disguised-as-Glinda shot Kalinya a panicked look, but Kalinya studiously ignored her.

"So you catch these dreams in your mirrors and make them physical. That's the secret? That's the experiment that you cannot share?" Kalinya thrust her hand out and scattered the gathering ghosts. "I will have your secrets, whether from your mouth..."

Gayelette turned to look for Glinda, but she was no longer anywhere near her. "Glinda, get back!"

But Mombi-as-Glinda panicked, and she walked quickly toward the door. Kalinya reached out with her magic grasp, and Mombi-Glinda jerked like a rag doll and was magically drawn in next to the Witch.

Gayelette watched in horror as Kalinya reached out a withered hand and magically lifted the red-haired girl off the ground by her throat. Mombi-disguised-as-Glinda gasped and struggled for breath.

Gayelette looked at the moon's light, now reaching the golden mirrors. Behind her, the orrery spun through its myriad revolutions. *There was still time to make adjustments.* She stepped quickly to the mirror and adjusted its position, catching the moonlight. The silver beam bounced from the first mirror to the second, to a third, on through dozens of strategically placed mirrors. A web of silver light sliced the air into pockets of aether.

"I will kill her, Gayelette!"

"You will let her go." Gayelette demanded, but her eyes stayed on her work.

Mombi-Glinda's eyes bulged as she choked, struggling for air. Gayelette finally turned her attention to the red-haired girl whom she believed to be her daughter. "P-p-p-lease" Mombi-Glinda croaked. Then the girl's eyes rolled back, and her body went limp.

Kalinya cocked a leering eyebrow at Gayelette. "What will it be? You have this pretty little dream catcher all around us. I have your little pretty."

The ghosts began a spine-chilling howl as the moonlight artificially penetrated deeper into the castle. Everywhere the light pierced one of the phantasms, the ghost froze in its place. The focused moonlight wormed through every visible portion of each incorporeal form, giving it greater distinctness. With every passing moment in the dream catcher, the phantasms were becoming more real.

The Ruby Palace shuddered as great energies welled up from beneath the surface. The tremors drew Kalinya's attention, and she dropped Mombi-Glinda to the floor. "Interesting. What do you have down there?"

Kalinya moved in the direction of an open stairwell, where a beam of light flowed downward. A keening cry echoed up from the ruby staircase. Every one of the phantasms raised their voices to join the wail. The entire palace was filled with both light and ethereal cries.

Kalinya quickened her steps toward the stairwell. Gayelette took three steps with the magic silver slippers and magically she was across the room, blocking Kalinya's path to the stairs. She caught Kalinya by the arm and pulled her backwards. The two women struggled in a slow dance for control, as both of them tried to lead. In an instant, the spell was broken, as Kalinya pushed Gayelette backward into the silver beam. Gayelette's back arched as the cosmic power shot through her.

Kalinya contorted her hands, reaching out with her magical grasp, and the orrery crumpled downward, knocking several mirrors out of alignment.

Gayelette screamed and kicked out at Kalinya. Her slippered foot glanced off of Kalinya's arm, doing nothing. In *order to use her magic, she would need to make contact, skin to skin.* So Gayelette kicked the silver slippers off her feet. Kalinya caught the flash of silver as the slippers hit the ground. She dove for them, her clawed hands reaching out to clutch their prize, quicker than a hungry vulture seizes carrion.

Then she screamed as Gayelette's bare foot smashed down on her hand.

Gayelette glared down at Kalinya, her red hair glowing in the silver light. The entire Ruby Palace coursed with silver energy, inside and outside. It flowed up the columns and lit up the night sky, challenging the moon for brightness. But Gayelette could not move from her position. She was stuck like an insect—pinned in place. The silver beam shot through her and allowed only the movement of her limbs.

The wicked witch, Kalinya, looked up from the ground toward Mombi-disguised-as-Glinda to plead for help. The red-haired girl had managed to rise to her feet, despite the trembling floor. She looked at Kalinya, but there was no sympathy in her eyes. She pulled out the silver mirror and held it in front of her, capturing the reflection of the two women.

"Glinda!" Gayelette called, "Help me destroy this madwoman!" She stomped her bare foot down on Kalinya's arm.

Kalinya screamed as her arm withered under Gayelette's bare foot. "Help me!" she cried to her comrade, reaching out with her free hand. She tried to use her magic to pull Mombi-Glinda backwards, but the blinding pain coursing through her body prevented her. She could not focus. And then it was too late.

Mombi-Glinda backed away toward the entrance. Then she turned and ran, disappearing into the night.

Another tremor shook the palace, dropping large alchemical devices down from the upper shelves in the chamber. Kalinya mustered her strength and swept her free hand, propelling the heavy mirror armature into Gayelette, knocking her backwards and pinning her against the wall. The malformed dreamcatcher net now pierced the walls of the palace, creating great glowing cracks in the ruby masonry.

Kalinya slowly rose to her feet and stepped out of her boots. Her striped stockings stood in stark black and white contrast against the ruby floor. Then she slid her feet into the silver slippers.

Below her feet, the castle trembled again. The disembodied screams grew louder as the shaking increased. Kalinya tilted her head to bare her teeth at Gayelette. "After all of the good you have done, it comes down to this. A trapped rat in your own pretty, pretty maze."

Great chunks of masonry fell all around them, pounding the ruby floor, striking scarlet sparks into the silver air.

"There is a great charm on these silver slippers—the slippers that I now own. Is there anything else I should know?" Kalinya mocked.

Gayelette winced as the tremors rocked the mirror apparatus to pinch her further, shooting pain up her side. "Line of sight." She gasped, "They only take you line of sight." Gayelette lied. She ground her teeth to keep from crying out to her enemy.

"I see. You see? Line of sight." Kalinya sneered. "And don't worry about Glinda."

"Don't hurt my daughter."

"I will teach that red-haired wench a lesson she won't soon forget. I will teach her to run from me. Oh, how she will run."

Gayelette closed her eyes and forced a deep breath. She summoned up all of the remaining power she could will and cried out in the ancient faerie tongue, *"Let these ruby walls their age regress, and the cause of life forgotten bless. Out of time once, twice, thrice and ageless. Let the doors be locked in blind duress. So to stay 'till the truth enkeyed through silent book, the graven martyr shall death overlook."*

The entire Ruby Palace groaned as it shrugged off its foundations and began shivering like a child with a fever.

Kalinya yelped and ran toward the front entrance. One, two, three steps, and she was outside at Glinda's tower. She collapsed to the ground at the edge of the forest. Then she looked back at the shuddering palace glowing brighter and brighter until Kalinya had to shield her eyes. And then she slumped down to the ground in fits of giddy laughter.

They could see the bright glow of the Ruby Palace as soon as they cleared the tree line. No matter how fast the Winged Monkeys flew, the palace seemed no closer. After several minutes, the blur of the glowing castle sharpened, and they could see the Ruby Palace shaking and shuddering. "It's going to fall!" Glinda screamed.

"No!" Quelala shouted. Then the Ruby Palace shrugged up off its foundations and became brightly translucent. A single point of light, brighter than all the others, seemed to look out through the walls toward them, meeting their desperate gaze. "Gayelette!" Quelala cried.

Glinda hit the ground only a few seconds after her father, but it was clear that they were too late. The Winged Monkeys had all turned back from the glowing Ruby Palace, except those brave few carrying Quelala and his daughter. Even those four quickly fled after their charges had reached the ground.

Just as they hit the ground as the entire Ruby Palace exploded in light. It twirled like a top, growing brighter and brighter, then the light grew impossibly bright and the palace disappeared. The attendant thunderclap flattened trees all around and left a quivering crater in the stone, at the edge of the canyon. The first thunderclap knocked Quelala and Glinda backwards into the river. The riverbanks protected them from the second blast, which flattened the trees all around the palace grounds. The ground heaved for several more minutes. As they stopped, finally Quelala was able to climb out of the river. He scrambled toward the empty hole in the sky, leaving his daughter behind.

"Gayelette!" He shouted again and again, but there was no answer. The terrible silence was the only thing worse than the scene of desolation before them.

Tears flooded from Quelala's eyes as he ran helplessly along the edge of the crater calling for his wife. A dark ruby pool, looking more than anything like glistening blood, down at the base of the crater bubbled three times. Then it flowed down into the ground and disappeared.

Above them, the silver moon moved on its charted course, paying them no mind. Glinda slowly approached her father. Tragedy was romantic in the storybooks. That was all she knew. But this numb shock was unlike anything Glinda had ever read about.

Quelala was on his knees, digging at the ground, moaning incoherently like a wounded beast. His fingers closed around a large chunk of ruby and he leaped to his feet. He held out the ruby like a poisoned thing. He grasped his forearm with his other hand and walked to the far edge of the crater. There was a cliff. His steps came haltingly, as the ruby commanded his entire attention. *Everything was gone. The ruby brought life, and now the ruby took life. What was dropped out of time must now be dropped in time.* Tears flooded his eyes, and he held the fist-sized ruby out into the silver air. *One step, and everything would be right again. So much lost. One step.* The stars blurred as the angry, tired tears flooded by did not spill over onto his cheeks. Silver streaks winged nearby. *Probably the monkeys. They would be just has happy to see me gone.*

"NO!" The scream behind him turned Quelala around. The tears clouded his eyes, but he saw Glinda run past him. When he turned unsteadily around, the red-haired girl stood between him and the cliff edge. Her eyes were filled with angry tears. "I won't let you. You have to stay here with me."

Quelala stepped forward. "I have to go."

"No you don't. You have to stay. Please, just stop. That's all. Just come with me. We'll go. That way. You don't know what you're doing."

"Get out of my way. You don't belong here."

Still the Winged Monkeys circled, waiting, watching.

Quelala turned his gaze back to the fist-sized ruby and shuffled forward. Glinda ran to him and dug in her feet. She pushed him backwards. The ruby fell from his hand onto the ground as Quelala stumbled backwards. Glinda fell with him as they tumbled backwards over the edge of the crater.

It was not a long fall, though the grade was steep. But this drop was not nearly as dangerous as the nearby cliff. Glinda caught her hand on an outcropping. She pulled herself up and scrambled back up to the top. Quickly she traced her steps and found the fist-sized ruby. She put the gem in the pocket of her skirt to hide it from her father.

A groan nearby echoed in the aching silence as Quelala pulled himself out of the crater. His forehead was bleeding, but his eyes were free from the shocked glaze. He sat on the edge of the crater for a long minute and stared into the emptiness. Glinda slowly approached, but her father paid her no mind.

Quelala pounded his fists into the hard ground and cried out in lost desperation. When the scream faded into the shadows of echo, he forced himself to stand. "Gayelette." He whispered.

"Father?" Glinda softly called to him. "She's gone. It's all gone. Please, Daddy, it's dark."

"I can't see her. I reached, I could see her hand. She was reaching out, but I couldn't…"

Glinda stepped back and shook her head silently. She reached out her hand, but her father would not see. She dropped her hand and wrapped her arms around herself, shivering. Her eyes were wide open, and cold tears flooded over her pale cheeks.

"Who? Who could have…? How? Oh, how could this happen?" Then he heard Glinda's teeth chattering. He turned to recognize his daughter behind him. "Your mother, Glinda…Gayelette...she wanted to show you. She was going to finish…her mother—your grandmother—was…tonight was going to be the last time…"

Glinda timidly approached. Her lower lip quivered as she tried her best to see her father's face. It was darkened with dirt and blood and pain. Quelala looked down at last to his daughter and saw her pain. He composed his face into rigid mask and opened his arms. Glinda collapsed into them, sobbing. Silently Quelala screamed at the uncaring silver moon.

In the distance, damaged and unsteady, the top floor of Glinda's tower crumbled into itself and collapsed into the base.

Beneath the ground, the bubbling ruby river, drawn by the inexorable pull of the Giant Hourglass—hidden away in the mountains of the North—flowed backwards on its course. With the Ruby Palace gone, and the balance of time severed, the ruby blood of Oz flowed back to the next-most-powerful location—the *Giant Hourglass of Oz*. The backwards force of the powerful river burst out of the cliff face, showering heavy rubies as the liquid petrefacted in the air.

The untimely hail of precious gemstones pounded down on the Giant Hourglass, knocking it from its super-slow-motion turn upside-down to a working position with its bottom flat on the ground. The flow of red rubies inside the hourglass started immediately, flowing from the top down into the bottom.

The guardians of the hourglass—tall, spectacle-wearing giraffe-men, looked at each other in worry. *"It is too early. It is days too early."* they said. *"The Day of Reckoning is not yet passed. And now death is returned to Oz."*

7 THE DESTINY OF KING OZ, THE SEVENTEENTH

In the center of the Land of Oz, in the Valley of Emeralds, lay Central City, the capital city of the central lands. Central City was the home of King Oz, ruler of the Emerald Lands and the surrounding countries, by virtue of Lurline, Queen of the Faeries. She who had enchanted the land in ages long past, gave rulership into the hands of her descendants. They governed through the centuries and built notable cities and monuments, some of which were long forgotten, but others which were still standing today.

The most famous landmark in Central City was the Grand Tower, which rose high above the landscape and could be seen for miles and miles in every direction. It could even be seen rising above the hills leading into the valley. This was the pride of Central City.

Tall shafts of emerald thrust out of the hills, creating a natural barrier into the valley. Some said that these were green shafts of lightning, frozen by the faeries as a symbol of power in these central lands. Others said that they were walls of a forgotten city, the only reminder of a war long past.

The people of the Emerald Lands trusted in the protection of their Emerald Fence, as they called it, and bothered little with an army. Of course, King Oz had his private army that protected the Grand Tower and stood outside the family palace, but that was purely ceremonial, and numbered fewer than forty guards. The last wars had ceased two generations past. The time for peace was here, so there was nothing to fear. So the soothing words of the politicians said, and the people were satisfied.

Central City was comprised of large buildings in the center of the Emerald Valley. These buildings had been designed by architects whose names had been forgotten before the forest had been planted. Ancient buildings had more modern additions. Newer buildings were built atop broad bases of older markets. Nothing of the old had been torn down, only built around. In some areas, the city grew organically, much like a gnarled olive tree. The winding and twisting paths wrapped around the centuried architecture like stone jewelry.

The Family Palace stood at the base of the Grand Tower. It was called the Family Palace because there was only one family that had ever ruled these lands. They had always ruled from the center. There was no need for any other name. It was a tradition that had lasted for twenty-two generations. Today's momentous events portended no evidence of changing that rulership. The sun was rising majestically in the west and the whole day felt as if was going to be unforgettable.

Nearby, a clear river sparkled as it wound its way through the valley. This was the center of the land—the center of the world as far as the royal family of Oz was concerned. Everything that needed to be said was said from Central City. The people supported the royal family and upheld their every word. Their lineage was specifically chosen by the immortal faerie queen, Lurline. The ruling monarch could not die until they reached their chosen time. It had been proven that they were immortal. The current king was Oz, the Seventeenth. His father had been Oz also, but he was the Sixteenth. His grandmother had been Ozma, the Fifth.

It was the tradition for the ruler to name the heir to their throne heir either Oz (if the baby was a boy) or Ozma (if the baby was a girl). King Oz had only recently married, and had no heir as yet. The previous King Oz had two sons, the eldest was named Oz, after his father, and the younger was named Pastoria, after a great uncle that spent most of his days picking doughnut flowers and waltzing with flutter byes. To say that great-uncle Pastoria was crazy was inaccurate; to say that he was lazy and cared nothing for reality was more accurate, but it was still an understatement. The younger Pastoria was given his name to motivate him to greater heights of accomplishment. It did *not*. In fact, he lived down to every expectation made of that name.

The sun rose bright on this Day of Reckoning. Today was the day that the king would prove his valiance and immortal status, securing once more the love and goodwill of the people. The Day of Reckoning only occurred once or twice in a ruler's chosen lifetime. It was a secret known only to the ruling members of the Royal Family and their direct heir on which day the Day of Reckoning would fall. Unknown to the people, it always came during the turning of the Giant Hourglass. This was once in a generation, or about every twenty years.

This was the first time that this king had come before his people to demonstrate his divine rulership by mocking death. For his death-defying feat, King Oz, the Seventeenth, had chosen to step off the Grand Tower. A great ceremonial "X" had been painted for his landing spot at the base of the tower. The royal band played a lively tune in front of the entire assembled city.

Atop the Grand Tower King Oz tucked his golden hair into a specially made swim cap. He was well-known for his perfect hair and did not want it blown out of position on the long fall down. In the top archway of the tower, Pastoria absently chewed on a doughnut flower as he watched his older brother make final preparations. Pastoria was dressed even more flamboyantly than the king. He was adorned in peacock-inspired finery. With little to do with his time, and an entire kingdom at his disposal, Pastoria fancied himself the best greatest hope for the entire land. While his brother ruled, he would be the one the people loved. *And how could they not love someone as finely-dressed as Pastoria? For a finely-dressed person such as Pastoria could distract the poorly-dressed masses from their own squalor and give them fancies to pass their time.* It was Pastoria's duty to the people to look good.

"Suppose, brother, that the swim cap does not hold your hair perfectly in place? How shall you explain the fashion disaster to the people?" Pastoria picked at a sprinkle caught in his teeth with his little fingernail.

King Oz didn't even cast a glance backward at his brother as he pulled on his golden gloves with a diamond set in the cuff. "I shall tell them that today I feel that the wind in my hair bodes well for the future of this nation. May I live long and prosper exceedingly."

"A fine, fine sentiment. The poets shall write your wit as art on the walls of every building."

"And you, Pastoria? What shall you say at the base of the tower, as the Day of Reckoning draws to a close?"

"I think I shall take a nap. I have a perfectly delightful book of clever rhymes that I shall read before I descend to partake in the festivities."

"It shall be well. Our father taught us well that the Day of Reckoning must fall on certain days and at certain times. Otherwise the Giant Hourglass .... I shall tell you the secret this evening, the secret that rests with the kings of Oz. A man can only die when the blood of Oz is flowing." King Oz stopped and smiled. "But I distract too long. My people await. Brother, I will be waiting at the bottom." With that, King Oz, the Seventeenth, stepped off the tower to his destiny below.

At the same moment, in the northlands far away, Quelala rose at daybreak. He had slept on the top of the steps, overlooking the place where the castle had stood. He watched as long as he could, but he could not battle the weariness forever. Sleep had come. He rose and looked into the ruins of the tower. Glinda was sleeping on her broken bed. She had surrounded herself with as many of her books as she could gather.

The night had passed. Time marched on. They did not have the power to stop that. Looking around at the destruction, it didn't appear as if they had much power at all. Forces beyond their control had caught them up and erased those things that they loved. The land was bare and hurting. The fallen trees and desecrated tower could not hide their pain.

The ivy that had before blanketed the tower walls had blown off, leaving the broken tower stripped bare. It rose like an upthrusting bony finger accusing the sky. Inside, all of Glinda's bookshelves were fallen, chairs were broken, and her personal items were strewn everywhere. Those that escaped the ruin of the tower speckled the landscape. They had blown out the window when the magical explosion scarred the land.

Quelala stretched his arms out to embrace the sky, but the sky was cold and bare and unfeeling. There were no clouds. The sky did not embrace him back, and he was still alone. Behind him, Glinda was still sleeping. Dew hung thick as tears on the stone steps as Quelala descended into the cold sobriety of this new morning. The angry shock of the previous night was replaced today by a cold, numb emptiness. As the soft shadows from the rising sun crept uninvited into the crater where the Ruby Palace had proudly towered, Quelala stared out into the distant depression. He did not even turn as Glinda's shoe scuffed slickly on the stone step. She descended to sit next to him. Glinda wrapped herself in a white blanket to ward off the evils of the unforgiving morning.

"She's gone, isn't she?" Glinda sat down on the bottom step.

Quelala forced a nod. His throat was choked with silence. He could not yet form words.

"What are we going to do?" Glinda asked. She was still not quite awake, as if she could ever fully awake from the events of the night. It was a cold morning, providing no comfort. The night was one that had pounded into their emotions like bent nails into wood. The bitter nails scarred everywhere they were pounded, and they did nothing to secure belief or trust. Outside those scars, Glinda's lone thought, much like her foggy breath, was ragged and hoarse.

Nearby, a ruby throne glinted in the morning sun, drawing Glinda's gaze. Quelala cleared his throat and wiped his eyes free of tears. "We are going to take a walk in the garden."

Quelala led the way. He walked quickly. Glinda struggled to keep up with him.

The garden was Quelala's pet project, because he did not frequently assist inside the Ruby Palace. His responsibilities with Gayelette's research had been limited, although they were vital to her work. That left plenty of time for him to develop other interests. One of these was the garden. It was a beautiful collection of plants from all over the land. The garden was peculiar in its shape—that was by design. Instead of flagstones, the garden had a sandy path around the central area, with an encircling garden around that. The ruby throne sat in the center of the mixed red and purple flowers at the north end of the central garden. Glinda ran her fingers over the throne as she circled it. She sat down, and the throne hummed beneath her, glowing slightly.

Quelala took note of this and said, "It knows you. This garden holds a secret. Where you sit now is the throne of leadership. Your mother sat on that throne for many years. It holds power to give you a long life."

"I feel like I'm sitting inside a map." Glinda said.

"That's right. I intended it to be a map." Quelala managed to smile sadly at his daughter's long-awaited recognition of his work. "This garden represents Oz and the surrounding lands. See? There are many lands within Oz, and many outside. It is important to have a map ready and growing."

Glinda got up and walked to the center of the garden, where lovely green flowers grew, surrounded by a green picket fence. "These are the Emerald Lands." She said, "That would be Central City."

"That's where *you* are going." Quelala said. "It is time."

Glinda looked up sharply. "You mean, where *we* are going."

"No, Glinda. Where *you* are going. I am regent over this kingdom. Your mother was queen. In her absence, I must govern. There is much to be done here, and much to explain. I have no answers, but the people will require something. You should go." Quelala pulled out the silver whistle out of his pocket and blew a quick tune.

Within moments, flapping wings heralded the arrival of King Klick. "My friend, Quelala, I come at your request."

"Friend Klick, I am greatly troubled by the devastation that an enemy has produced upon my family's kingdom. I seek to understand what villainy has obtained power. Please convey my daughter to the Valley of the Swift Horses. There you may confer my instructions to King Zephyr, the wind stallion, that Glinda is to be carried to Central City in the Emerald Lands." He paused and took a long breath, "I regret that I cannot be but formal. My wife is…gone."

King Klick bowed formally. "It shall be as you wish." He turned to Glinda and asked, "Princess, are you prepared?"

Glinda shook her head. "No, Daddy. Don't make me go. I'll stay here with you, where it's safe."

Quelala took his daughter's face in his hands. "Where I am is not safe. I love you dearly, but it is not safe. That is why I send you away to safety. Whatever villain did this may come back. I will find answers and send for you. Speak to King Oz. Your mother's name will get you far in this land."

Glinda frowned at that. The reminder may have been well-intentioned, but it was not welcome. She kicked at the green picket fence and glared at the green flowers.

Quelala saw the growing storm in her eyes. "You have read many fairy tales, Glinda. They have been your nightly companions for years. You have loved grand adventures of young heroes journeying over mountains and streams to battle vile foes. If this is your adventure, I pray that your only foes be political ones. You are a princess, and one day you will rule. You were intended to be at your mother's side last night. That was her plan. But I...your destiny—"

He stopped short and kissed Glinda on the forehead. "My blessing goes with you."

He paused, searching for the right words, but then decided otherwise. "There is more that I must tell you. Soon. But not now. The Golden Cap is your legacy." Quelala quickly returned to the Ruby Throne and pulled back a flagstone at its feet. There, in a stone box rested a cap made of spun gold. It was garnished with a circlet of diamonds and rubies. Quelala paused and reverently pulled it out. King Klick watched with great interest as Quelala reached in to the stone box. Quelala looked up at Glinda before he placed the charmed cap on his head. The Golden Cap contained a great power. It made Quelala into something more than he had been before. Wearing the Golden Cap made him look the part of a king.

Glinda recognized for the first time in her life that her father was made to be a ruler, with a queen at his side ... only now he stood alone. "There is a powerful charm associated with the Golden Cap, Glinda. I will tell you. Someday soon. For now, remember the things that I have said. Remember what your mother has taught you. You were her daughter in every way and she trusted you."

Glinda dug in her pocket and pulled out the fist-sized ruby. She pressed this into her father's hands. "I don't want to go."

"I have this ruby to remember—to remind me. I won't jump. That much I promise you—I won't jump."

Suddenly a shockwave hit the garden, thrusting up flowers by their roots and flinging them into the air! Glinda was launched into the air, shrieking in fright. King Klick was airborne in an instant, catching Glinda's hands and arresting her fall. He shouted, and in a moment, two other monkeys were at his side, launching from among the shadows of the fallen trees. One of them, Brutus, looked back ravenously with his one good eye to stare at the Golden Cap on Quelala's head.

Quelala whirled around to see a dark-cloaked shape skipping inhumanly fast across the shadows toward him. Silver glinted on the figure's feet. *No!* It couldn't be. *The Silver Slippers!*

Kalinya stopped at the edge of the garden. "Your precious queen put up little fight. She cried for mercy at the end. I expect that you will whimper exactly the same." Kalinya mocked Quelala. Then she wiggled her feet and disappeared.

"Daddy, *NO!*" Glinda tried to wiggle out of the tight grasp of the escaping monkeys.

"Get her to safety!" Quelala called to King Klick. He did not turn around. Quelala gritted his teeth as he focused on the rapidly flitting figure and the Silver Slippers. She was flitting all around the garden, never in any place for more than a second.

Suddenly she was in front of him.

"You have a throne, but no queen." Kalinya mocked.

"Your life is the only payment that will balance the scales, Witch. I will take that payment now." Quelala growled.

"Foolish, considering I am the most powerful witch in Oz now. I have the Silver Slippers." She skipped behind the throne. Then she thrust her hands upward and the Ruby Throne disappeared into the sky. "And you now have neither *queen, nor throne.*"

"What goes up must always come down, Kalinya. Not even you are immune from that." Quelala slipped the chunk of ruby into his pocket.

Kalinya cackled. She skipped all around the garden, tossing up bunches of blossoms as she ravaged the landscaping. "I can throw you away at any time."

"And yet you don't." Quelala set his feet and clenched his fist. He exhaled slowly. It had been years since he had been in a fight with a witch, and complete attention was required. He stretched out his hands and called upon the charm of the Golden Cap.

Kalinya darted around the garden, ripping up flowers and decorative shrubbery alike. She cackled in glee as her target closed his eyes, in apparent defeat. Then she felt a strange, insistent pulling at her throat, which traveled down into her heart. It was a relentless pulling, the likes of which she had never before felt.

And then she was right in front of Quelala!

He grabbed her by the arms, pinning her fast. She stamped her feet three times and she was behind him. Quelala whirled and reached out, drawing the witch in again. Such was the power of the Golden Cap. Whatever the wearer desired, it had the magic to bring it to them. In this case, Quelala would not let the witch escape to follow after Glinda.

They engaged in a bizarre dance of attack and escape, parry and riposte. Once Kalinya broke free and thrust out her hands to hurl fallen trees and stones after the distant fleeing monkeys, showering them with debris, but narrowly missing them with the larger hurlings.

Their dance took them around the entire garden. At last Quelala had them where he wanted them—the shadow patch in the garden where dark vines grew. The moment that their feet stepped into the patch, the vines twitched in anticipation.

Quelala drew in Kalinya to a tight embrace and stepped backwards into the vines. Though her hands clawed at him, scratching him deeply, he held on for the sake of his daughter. Kalinya screamed like a banshee as the black vines entangled her and lifted her off the ground. Quelala stepped free from the vines as they wrapped tightly around the witch.

"What have you done to me?" Kalinya demanded, gasping as the vines tightened around her waist, constricting her breath. Her arms were pinned to her sides, preventing her from magically flinging anything.

"You destroyed my garden." Quelala wheezed, his breath coming in ragged bursts. "I brought you to the one place in Nonestica where you can be imprisoned."

"No-o-o-o-OOOOO!" Kalinya screamed, trying to kick her feet, but they would not touch, so the teleportation powers bound in the Silver Slippers, would not work.

"I warn you to stay away from my daughter. I am sure that you will find a way to break from the vines. The Kingdom of Dreams is not so easy to escape, you can be sure." Quelala walked back toward the crater. "If I could reclaim the Silver Slippers from your feet, I would, but their charm prevents me from doing so. There are only two ways that you would have claimed the Silver Slippers. Either you pulled them off of my wife's dead feet, which I doubt. Or she kicked them off for some reason, and you took them. Either way, I find your lies repugnant. My wife would not beg you for anything. Neither will I."

"You can't leave me here." Kalinya protested, convulsing angrily.

"Shall I stay to watch you die? Should I exact every ounce of vengeance I deserve? Shall I wait for the Silver Slippers? I know those vines will hold you at least until evening. I have business in my kingdom to manage. I may return then, or I might not. Nevertheless, I warn you, Kalinya, stay away from my daughter."

Kalinya screamed and struggled, but the vines only wrapped tighter. She cursed and spit at Quelala's retreating form. She screamed until she could not see him anymore. The sun rose higher and higher, but despite the direct light over this corner of the garden, the shadows strangely grew darker.

8 THE GIRL NAMED WICKRIE-KELLS

The Winged Monkeys flew with Glinda for well over an hour, when they descended into a purple valley. Horses of blue and purple and green ran gracefully all around the valley, manes and tails flowing behind them like mist trailing clouds. This was the Vale of the Swift Horses. The largest of the horses, a deep midnight-blue stallion, reared up on his hind legs at the approach of the monkeys. He whinnied at the herd, which broke away and ran to the other side of the valley. Zephyr, king of the Swift Horses, trotted over to Glinda and King Klick.

"Greetings, Zephyr, High Horse of the Swift Ones. I present to you Glinda, daughter of Gayelette, Queen Sorceress of the Ruby Palace." King Klick inclined his head to the stallion, gesturing to the red-haired girl.

The Stallion genuflected, kneeling gracefully before Glinda. "I am Zephyr. It is a singular honor to meet you, Princess. Your mane is the color of your mother's."

"Thank you." Glinda curtsied to the noble equine. "My mother is …" Glinda's brows furrowed, fighting the whirlwind of emotions.

King Klick saw her discomfort and hopped up in front of the stallion. "She is to be taken to Central City in the Emerald Valley, to speak to King Oz. Quelala requests that you are to take her."

Zephyr stamped his hoof and neighed, nodding his head. "If you are ready, Princess Glinda, I will take you now."

Glinda rode on Zephyr's back as he galloped upon the wind. Zephyr told the story of his people.

"The swift horses rode on the wind, they only lighted down to the ground to feed on the morning dews, or to run in their sheltered valleys scattered across the land. Many times we are invisible, appearing as wisps of movement in the clear air. Sometimes, Princess, when a random breeze seems to blow on the back of your neck, that is the passing movement of swift horses. We have watched you often.

"This morning, it was only because you arrived in the valley during second breakfast that we were visible. A few minutes later and we would not have been seen. Also, if King Klick had not been with you, the swift horses would have made their escape. The horses only stayed because they knew that the Winged Monkeys were trustworthy.

"The Swift Horses came from far outside the Land of Oz. There are many herds throughout Nonestica. Our herd was chosen by the faeries for their strength and speed. The faeries brought us as companions after Lurline enchanted the land. For a time, everything was well, and we enjoyed frequent trips back to our homeland. Then the Witch Wars separated the lands after destroying the inland sea. Few of the Swift Horses ever made it back across the deserts to the land of Ev. This single herd of swift horses is all that is now left in the Land of Oz. So we roam the land, stopping at sheltered valleys to feed and rest."

"There are times when the clouds reach down to touch the earth that we can ride the clouds across the land. Sometimes we gallop down into the rain."

Glinda wondered at that. "I thought so. Sometimes I imagined I saw horses when the lightning flashed."

"You may have." Zephyr whinnied. "Lightning is great sport for us."

"So you can really ride on clouds? I thought they couldn't hold anything. They look solid, but they can disappear into the sky."

"Clouds can be made or unmade. There is more to a cloud than meets your eyes. Someday you will see."

"I can make clouds. My mother taught me a spell to make clouds."

"Clouds are good friends to have. They can be trusted." Zephyr said.

"There are some other incantations my mother taught me. I can make hats change shape. I can turn hourglasses upside down. And then I can make clouds. Some sorceress, huh?" Glinda looked glumly at the ground speeding below them.

"The power that a person holds in them is not limited to the things that others know. If you were to become only what I have told you, then you would be only a *listener.* You would wield no power beyond what I have allowed you. Glinda-girl, you are more that what you limit yourself to be.

"As you search the winds inside your heart, you will find the clouds touching the earth and you will ride the greatest winds."

They sped along toward the central lands, leaving Glinda alone in her thoughts to ponder what winds rushed inside her heart.

In the Emerald Valley, it was afternoon before Pastoria emerged from the bottom door of the Great Tower. He was expecting fanfare and festivities, but he was sorely disappointed. All of the crowds were gone, there was no music, and an air of solemnity hung over the place. Contrary to his expectations, only the royal Butler awaited him. The Butler rose to attention as Pastoria opened the door.

"Your Majesty," the Butler began.

Your Majesty? But the royal title was only reserved for the king. Why would Pastoria receive that honorific from the king's man?

The Butler continued, "There has been an accident."

Zephyr and Glinda arrived at the gates of the Emerald Valley in the middle of the afternoon. A guard dressed in emerald green stopped them outside the great green pillars. "Hold. All traffic into the valley has been halted. There has been a great tragedy. You will have to wait outside the valley."

Glinda said, "This is Zephyr, King of the Swift Horses. And I am…Glinda." She left off the royal identifier, much to the surprise of the horse, who shook his head in dismay. "You have to let us in."

The guard shook his head sadly. "I have been given my orders, and I will not let you pass. There are greater problems that we must deal with here than you can possibly imagine."

"I can imagine very great things." Glinda said solemnly.

Zephyr nudged Glinda away, and trotted a few steps to speak with the red-haired girl privately. "I must return to my people. If there truly is this great evil coming that you have spoken of, I must defend my people when it comes to our purple valley."

"But who will I go to? Where? How?" Glinda bit her lower lip, and then she hugged the horse around the neck. "Thank you for bringing me here. Even if I don't know where here is."

"You know where here is. Now you must realize who you are. Believe in yourself, Glinda. You are the daughter of a queen, and you are a growing sorceress. You are beginning a great adventure that may change everything that you once knew." And then the midnight-blue stallion galloped away to the north.

Glinda walked to the top of a nearby hill where other barred travelers were gathering to watch a peculiar congress of crimson peacocks. A stately procession of the deep red birds entered the natural amphitheater and arranged themselves into two wings—one on the left and one on the right—each facing the speaker's mound in front.

For an hour, Glinda watched the peacocks warble their self-important speeches. Then she met her first friend. Another girl her same age came over and sat down next to her. "I'm Wickrie-Kells."

"I am Glinda. So, do you come here to watch the peacocks?"

Wickrie-Kells was taller than Glinda, with long brown hair and amber eyes. She wore her hair tied back in a long braid. She smiled and said, "Hmm. Most days, yeah, I do. Sometimes I come to watch the people. I found you, didn't I? I haven't seen you here before."

"I'm new, I guess."

"You'll like watching them for a while. Everybody that comes to the capital, here, does. They watch the parading and the showmanship. It's something to talk about."

Wickrie-Kells told Glinda everything she knew about the crimson peacocks. Every day the peacocks would go up to the hill and make their warbling speeches. This had been going on for longer than anyone could remember. First one peacock would strut up to the top of the speaker's mound, spread his feathers and make his speech about the good that was most required for others. Then another would go up there to take the place of the first. Eventually, most of the peacocks had their say. They would take a vote, and they would adjourn until the next day.

For several hours, Glinda and Wickrie-Kells sat and watched the peacocks. The birds' speeches were very impassioned. It was clear that they were saying very important things, even if Glinda could not make sense of a word they were saying. Actually, it was not that Glinda could not understand their words; it was that she could not understand how such words strung together with such verbose proliferation could mean anything at all. So she decided to ask.

"What are they talking about?"

"I think right now they are pontificating about how the other peacocks that sent them there are so proud of sending them there and how they have a responsibility to behave proudly so that they can be proud some more." She shrugged. "You're not from around here. I can tell. Most people who come here get finagled into watching at least one or two sessions. It's part of why the birds do what they do. The peacocks just need to be admired." She pointed at the one strutting slowly to the top of the hill. "He's the leader of that group on that side. He's been doing this a long time. See where the sun is right now? And he's going to make his point right now."

This peacock was a deeper crimson than the others. It was clear that he had been to the top of the hill many, many, many times. He glanced at the position of the sun and began his speech. The peacock warbled just as the red rays of the sun caught his tail feathers, blazing red and shimmering multicolored light over the entire assemblage. They all applauded and warbled congratulations on his speech.

"But it wasn't the speech at all!" Glinda protested. "It was his posturing. He timed it just right to make his point."

"And *my work here is done.* It only took you one day. Most people never even learn that much." Wickrie-Kells agreed, smiling proudly.

As the sun descended, the blood-red peacocks adjourned for the day. They all congratulated themselves on another job well done.

"You never told me your name." Wickrie-Kells nudged Glinda.

"I did once. You must have forgotten. I'm Glinda."

"Just Glinda? Come on, you have to be more than just Glinda."

Glinda's eyes grew stormy and she fought against the welling sadness, anger and disappointment of the last thirty-six hours. She was Glinda, but she was more, according to other people. She was her mother's daughter. She was the daughter of the sorceress. She was the prospective apprentice of the most powerful sorceress in the land. She was the red-headed princess in the tower. In fact, the very thing that she wanted to be, the thing that she claimed to be, was the one thing that she could not be—just *Glinda.*

The mixed emotions flooding through Glinda's eyes startled Wickrie-Kells. "There's a lot more to your story, I can see that. I can also see that there is more to Glinda than who you are letting yourself be. Come on, I'll take you back to my house. My father will be glad to have another face to see at the supper table. Mother has been gone for more than week visiting her great aunt-four-times-removed in Munchkin country." Wickrie-Kells stood, and then she helped Glinda to her feet. "I am certainly glad I chose to sit next to you instead of anybody else. You have *interesting* written all over you."

Glinda went with Wickrie-Kells down past the guard and down into the Emerald Valley. He made no argument when they passed. Either the situation had been resolved that had kept Glinda out before, or he knew Wickrie-Kells and accepted that Glinda was now okay to enter. In the valley, everyone they passed was unusually somber. When Glinda commented on this, Wickrie-Kells answered quietly, "The King died this morning. He was supposed to be immortal."

"I don't understand."

Wickrie-Kells explained, "Our kings don't die like normal people do. They don't get old and snore off to faerie land. They don't get in accidents. They are supposed to be better, more perfect than us. We took it for granted that King Oz was going to live forever." She shrugged her shoulders, more to dismiss the looming questions than to answer them. "Everything that we thought was true is being questioned now. People don't know what to believe. The King's brother, Pastoria, is going to be King, but he's got a lot to do to make people believe that he should rule and be king. But what other option do we have?"

Wickrie-Kells pointed the way to a small cottage on the outer ring of the twisting city. "*There.* It's not large, but it's warm at night, and my father sings wonderful songs."

Glinda said softly, "I need to see the King. My father told me to see the King and tell him what happened." Glinda repeated, more to herself than to Wickrie-Kells, as if saying it out loud would make it more real.

"The King is gone, Glinda. You can't see him. Nobody can see him until the funeral, and then we only get to see him from a distance. We're not like them." Wickrie-Kells opened the cottage door for Glinda. "We cook our own food and tell our own stories. Tonight, m'lady, you dine with the peasantry."

Glinda spent a wonderful evening talking and laughing like she had never laughed before. Every night before this one she had taken her dinner in the main room of her tower. Usually her father would join her, but many times she would dine alone. Always at dinner, the conversation had struggled, usually ending in awkward silence, punctuated by stifled burps. Here, though, there was never a break. Wickrie-Kells and her father enjoyed the new company and they enjoyed each other. And their burps were not stifled at all. *A thankful sign of a good meal* was their explanation.

Wickrie-Kells' father was a portly man, with a full beard and laughing eyes. His name was Tjorn, pronounced Tee-yorn. He said, "I wanted to change my name to Bjorn tomorrow, but then that might be confusing to everyone else because I would have to tell them that I wasn't Bjorn yesterday." He snorted and shook with laughter.

"He loves to tell that joke. It is not often that we get a new face at the table, but every time we do, Papa tells that joke."

When Glinda told them of the destruction caused by the wicked witch, Kalinya, of the Ruby Palace, they were appropriately angered.

"No one here has that kind of power. Papa, do they?"

Tjorn frowned and looked seriously at Glinda. "If what you say is true, and I do not doubt your word, young lady—you are nothing if not from high breeding. You ate your stew like a true lady of the court. Ah, I was once in the court of the King. I was a storyteller for King Oz, the Sixteenth, the one before the most recently deceased king."

"Why are you not there now?" Glinda asked, naively drawn in to the web Tjorn was spinning.

"It is a long story, but no, no, no. It would be of no interest to a girl such as yourself. You are probably only interested in handsome princes…and this story does not have any of those. So we will talk of other things."

Wickrie-Kells watched her new friend as she begged to hear the story. She had fallen right into her father's story web.

"Please. I have never been outside the shadow of the Ruby Palace. Tell me your story. What was it like being in the King's court?"

"First, we will hear your story. Then, perchance we have light in our eyes left, we shall discuss my adventures, such as they were, in the court of the king."

Glinda began with the memories she had growing up, how her mother was always too busy to be with her, but never seemed to give her the freedom she wanted. So Glinda lived her childhood in books. She liked to imagine that she was destined for great adventure, instead of being a princess with an overprotective mother. She told of flying through the air with the Winged Monkeys.

"I've never seen a Winged Monkey." exclaimed Wickrie-Kells.

"I will show you…someday." said Glinda.

Tears filled her eyes as she related the destruction of the Ruby Palace with her mother inside. She left out the part about her father and the cliff. That was family business, and there was no need to share that burden just yet. After the sun rose, the palace was still gone. There was no visible perpetrator, but Kalinya, the wicked witch, showed up and tried to kill both Glinda and her father. Her father stayed behind to protect Glinda as she escaped. There was no way that she could get away from the Winged Monkeys to stay with her father. Then the king of the Swift Horses carried her to the Emerald Valley. And that is what led to Glinda waiting outside the valley with the crimson peacocks. She sniffled as she concluded, and she folded her hands on the table.

Despite the unfinished tragic ending to the story, Wickrie-Kells expressed optimism. "There has been an accident in this valley, and there was an accident in your land. Something big is happening. And we're the only ones that know about it. There is no way to gain entrance into the royal Family Palace until after the funeral of the king. But after that, with the inside scoop that we have, I'm sure I can get you in. My uncle is Butler to the king. I'll take you to see him right after the royal funeral."

9 THE CROWNING OF A NEW KING

The funeral preparations comprised the better part of the week, for the death of a king was not a common occurrence in the land. The people were not prepared to face the questions that were now asked of them, so they busied themselves in the physical funerary preparations.

Finally the day of the burial came. Trumpets sounded from atop the Grand Tower as the funerary procession wound its way from the Family Palace, down the winding road to the river, and from there it climbed up the hill overlooking the great Grimmpill Lake. This hill was where the dead were buried. The lake was named Grimmpill because of the cemetery on top of the hill. The Grimmpill Graveyard held the remains of all of the rulers. The first rulers were at the very top with their families. The succeeding rulers were further down, being buried in concentric circles around the hill. The common people were currently buried along the path leading to the hill, on the far side from the river. King Oz, the Seventeenth, was buried halfway down the hill, alone, for he had only recently married and had no children. Glinda and Wickrie-Kells both looked, but they did not see the royal widow anywhere. Tjorn suggested that Pastoria removed her from the picture so that she didn't detract any attention from where it rightfully belonged—on him. From everything that Glinda had learned about the ruler of this land, that made sense.

Pastoria saw this funeral as a fitting capstone on his brother's reign. The funeral was modest. Some expenses had been spared. This was a capstone on a short monument dedicated to King Oz, the Seventeenth, *long* may he be remembered (today). For all of his brother's good deeds and wise rulings, nothing significant had happened during his time as king. That milquetoast era would very soon be over. A new dawn was breaking over all the land. King Oz the seventeenth would be buried. The sun would set on the reign of all Oz and Ozma, and it would rise on the Pastorian era.

Kind words were said over the funeral breakfast. A day of mourning was proclaimed by Pastoria. One day would certainly be enough to recount and commemorate all of the (few) things his brother had done. This announcement was quickly followed by another, more exciting announcement—tomorrow we shall celebrate the coronation of Pastoria. Which, Tjorn wisely said, had been the plan all along.

The decorations and festivities had already been prepared, so there was very little additional preparation required. The only thing remaining to do was to gather the powers of the four corners of the land into the central lands. Witches or Sorcerers from the four corners of the Land of Oz were required for each coronation. This bound the powers of the kingship into the central lands.

Four witches were already on hand for the funeral.

It was at the funeral when Kalinya spotted Glinda in the crowd of commoners. Glinda's red hair naturally stood out in the crowd. As soon as she saw Kalinya turn in her direction, Glinda moved to leave. She wanted to avoid a public confrontation, if at all possible. Glinda and Wickrie-Kells turned and walked away from the people. They rounded a large crypt, and headed quickly toward the bottom of the hill. But in a heartbeat, Kalinya was right there in front of Glinda.

"The lost daughter of the sorceress, helpless and alone. How are you, Glinda, darling?"

"I have nothing to say to you." Glinda turned away and Wickrie-Kells stepped in between her friend and the witch.

"Glinda is not alone. She's got me. I know who you are, and you will not win."

Kalinya waved her hand and brushed Wickrie-Kells aside. She continued, her eyes fixed on Glinda. "You are how old now, fifteen? I imagine that your birthday is not far away. I seem to recall the announcement for last year's hullaballoo came around this time. That means approximately one month until your sixteenth birthday. Join me, and all of your youthful indiscretions will be forgiven. You can be my apprentice. I will be the mother you never knew. I will have time for you and we can discuss all the things you have in that pretty red head of yours."

Glinda stepped forward, setting her jaw defiantly. "And if I don't?"

"I will destroy you, just like your mother."

In a blink, Kalinya was gone. Somehow, she had harnessed a similar power to Gayelette. Glinda gasped—she didn't realize that she had been holding her breath. Wickrie-Kells laughed and hugged Glinda. "You are amazing. You've got a witch that threatened you. How can you be so amazing?"

But Glinda didn't feel amazing. She didn't feel like she knew anything. If only she knew more about her mother's secrets. If only she had paid more attention…then, just maybe she could have represented the North at the coronation.

As it was, Glinda watched the coronation from a safe distance. It took place at the top of the Grand Tower. Pastoria invited the witches to hold the four corners of the crown. The Witches were there to act as the ceremonial faeries of the coronation. Pastoria did not care who they were, nor where they were from. The four Witches had roles to play, and Pastoria expected them to play those roles. He had even provided appropriate gowns for each corner of the land.

The magic scroll with the ceremonial words had been opened and each Witch was expected to read her part and promise powers from each land. The witches were essential to the coronation because the scroll was written in a red ink that was invisible to those who did not know the ways of magic.

The ceremony began:

Kalinya intoned, "From the East, where the sun sets, I pledge the remembrance of the sun's golden light, which keeps the memories of the day long into the dark of night."

Ondri-baba pronounced, "From the West, where the sun rises, I pledge the delight of knowledge, which springs upon the waiting like the first rays of the morning sun."

Mombi, standing in for the Sorceress of the North, promised, "From the North, where the time flows through all of Oz, I pledge the flow of time moving forward, and the secrets of the kings of the past to guide this new ruler."

Locasta, who stood in for the Witch of the South, cried out, "From the South, where the warm winds bring storms and rainbows, I pledge the refreshing of the land, which brings the bounty of all the harvest for the king's wise use."

The promises concluded, and each witch placed one hand on the crown as they lowered it onto the waiting head of Pastoria.

As the Witch standing in for the Sorceress the North, Mombi breathed the final pronouncement upon the new king. "As the kings of the past have shared their breath with you, let your breath never cease so long as the rubies flow. At their pause, let your divine kingship take hold."

Then Mombi raised her voice to cry to the people below the tower, "Behold, King Pastoria, may his reign be unique in all the history of Oz!"

Beyond the base of the Great Tower, near the river, Wickrie-Kells turned to Glinda, "You should be up there, representing the North. It was your right. You mother was the sorceress and queen."

"I wouldn't want to be up there with those witches. I don't trust any of them." Glinda sighed. She picked up a pebble and tossed it into the river. "I'm just a pebble. I might make a little splash, but watch, time just flows on like the river. In order to make any sort of difference, any sort of splash, I'd have to stop time."

"Enough pebbles can change the course of a river. You just need to keep splashing."

"Do you think that the king will really listen to my story?"

"Of course. You know what nobody else out there knows. I mean, except for that witch. But the king will believe you. I'm sure of it."

The festivities lasted for three days and nights. The Grand Tower was lit so completely with lights that it became a beacon through the dark. It drowned out even the moon's light, making it possible for the guards at the entry to the Emerald Valley to play cards without a lantern. The bright light all night long was a demonstration—Pastoria was showing his power over all that had previously stood untouchable.

When the visitors to the Emerald Lands had departed, and the witches had gone, Pastoria retired to his throne. He permitted his Butler to begin scheduling his meetings. Up first on his schedule was a girl from the lands of the north with a very sad story.

Glinda quickly told her story to the uninterested king, pointedly detailing the betrayal of her mother by Kalinya.

"Your story, if it really is yours, is quite potentially a very sad one." Pastoria began. "However, if you bothered to notice, there was an actual, real-life witch from the North placing *this* crown on *my* head. So I am inclined to doubt your true facts in this matter."

Glinda fumed. "Mombi was *not* from the North. She has nothing to do with the North. My *mother* was the queen and sorceress of the land."

"The squabbles and petty in-fighting in other lands do not concern me or my kingdom. We have matters of decorum to concern ourselves with. You see, we have a responsibility to be civilized, while the rest of the land—"

"As regent over the Emerald Lands, you have a responsibility to take the lead in matters of right and wrong." Glinda demanded. "You must take action against those that have destroyed my mother's kingdom. You must stand against the villains that have threatened the peace of Oz. You *must*."

Pastoria laughed. "I must? I *MUST*? I am the king. You do not understand, young lady. I mustn't do anything. I may *do* as I wish. And those *villains*, as you propose, those wouldn't happen to be the hands that laid this crown on my head, would they? Consider how that would look—the newly crowned king declaring war on the very magical foundation that creates his kingdom?

"No, no. I will not disturb the cradle that holds this newly born kingdom. I will rock it gently and let it sleep forever. My kingdom is *not* my brother's kingdom. You see, he was born to rule, and there is no doubt that he would have been a good king, just like all of the other Kings Oz and Queens Ozma. Nothing special about them except their number. But then you get to me, twenty-third in line from Lurline's blood, from the original Ozma, and yet who am I? I am Pastoria. I was not born to rule, yet here I am.

"Destiny has taken a strange side road, and fate has fallen asleep at the bridge. The work I do is not maintaining the twisting city with the big tower. No. I am chosen to do a much greater work." He gestured offhandedly, "My kingdom is just the beginning. I have *great plans* for these Emerald Lands. Maybe someday I'll get up to your north lands, but that is much, much lower on my priority list."

Glinda stared in disbelief as Pastoria stopped in the middle of his speech, got up off his throne, and walked to the front of the line of the scarlet peacocks. He led them through the sunbeam checkerboard pattern on the floor, to the roosts at the far end of the antechamber. At the head of the procession of peacocks, Pastoria fit the pompous, self-righteous mold of their monarch exactly. When all of the peacocks were settled in their roosts, Pastoria returned to his throne. He picked up a fallen scarlet tail feather and carried it ceremonially, as a scepter, to his royal seat, where he returned to his speech directed at Glinda.

"I have no word other than yours that your kingdom is destroyed. If I send people there, what will they find? Will they find death? Destruction? A hole in the ground? Will they find everything as it has always been? What assurance do I have other than that of a girl that there even *are* villains in the land? I have none."

"But that's not fair. You are supposed to be good. You have to call people to task and make them do the right thing. You have to. It is your job."

"For who is it right? For *you*? You are a foolish girl, acting out of spite. There is no question that your mother, Gayelette, and Kalinya were rivals. What proof do you have to offer me that your mother did not send you here to turn me against Kalinya? My people look to me for guidance—I am their king. They look to me for deliverance from the sorrow brought by my brother's untimely death—I am their king. I have no desire to draw them into a conflict from which there is no purposeful exit—I AM THEIR KING.

"I will not enter into war with an unknown opponent for an unproven ally." He cocked an eyebrow at Glinda. "You are my ally, are you not? I am your king."

Wickrie-Kells took Glinda's arm and nudged her back toward the entrance. "We should go."

But Glinda refused to budge.

Pastoria snorted. "You are defiant to an art. I have given you every single, reasonable opportunity to graciously retract your request. So let me absolutely clear, so that your juvenile mind can understand. This is not my war. You misunderstand who I am, young lady—"

"Princess." Wickrie-Kells interrupted.

"Oh, pardon my lack of manners. I was unaware that a coronated King needed to give proper obeisance to a *lesser* princess. I am your king. And you have just wrung out my last good grace. Begone."

At a signal from the king, the Butler entered and showed the two young ladies out. He mopped his brow nervously with a handkerchief. "I have stretched my hands out far enough for you, Wickrie-Kells. Do not come to me again. The king has no desire to engage in this squabble, however *dire* you may think it to be. Now go, and do not return. Tell your father it will be some time before I visit him again. We must let the king create new memories to replace these bad ones you have brought."

They left the palace and followed a path outside of the Central City limits. Glinda and Wickrie-Kells walked along the river, down the path that snaked into the nearby forest. Above them, the afternoon sun peeked down through the trees. They came to a circle of boulders in a clearing next to a pool of still water fed from an underground source. Though it was near the river, the water in this pool looked different. It made the entire glen feel different.

Then Glinda heard a rustling above them. Leaves dropped in their path. Glinda glanced up to see a silver winged monkey looking down at them.

"King Klick." Glinda waved greeting.

King Klick dropped to the ground to walk next to Glinda. "There are chatters that your emerald king does not wish to offend the witches. That is why he refuses you."

"It's so frustrating. Why doesn't anybody believe me?"

Wickrie-Kells took Glinda's hand. "I believe you."

"I know. But you, you're not an army. You can't help me."

Determination set in Wickrie-Kells' face. "I will help you, Glinda."

"Thank you, but—"

"But nothing. I am going to help you. If we can't get help here, we'll go to other cities. I have a cousin in Yellow Castle. That's where the Winkies live. They are known to be a very curious people. If you can't get them to be interested in your story, you won't get anybody."

"Your friend is right, child-Glinda." King Klick said. "My people know terror as much as anyone—the terror and fear that one feels in the face of death. My people have known that, and I have known that for them. The disbelief practiced by your kind is strange to us. How a human can exercise such doubt, in the face of honesty, is a skill not known among the Winged

Monkeys. We are friends to your father. It is because of this friendship that I come to you today. Your father is not to be found. I have searched, but there is no scent of him in the regions. Perhaps he is hiding. Perhaps he is not wanting to be found. It is as if he disappeared from the land. I do not know. I inform you from a need for courtesy."

"I thank you for that, King Klick. I do not have the loyalty from you that you swore to my father. I hope that you support my goal to return to my father."

"That, I will do. Any effort beyond the return will require the consent of my people. I am a good king, but I am not as wise as my father was. I cannot see where this conflict with the witches will lead. I will not engage my people in a war that may destroy them. But for your return to your father's side, I give you my word."

King Klick flew up to the branches in the tree and looked back. "I will convene a council at this place tomorrow, before sunset. If you desire to witness, you may come."

The next day, as the afternoon came, Glinda and Wickrie-Kells again followed the river down to the circle of boulders among the trees. As they arrived, a female monkey, Beriyel, showed them to a place next to the river where they could watch. They were not allowed to sit up front, or even among the tribe. Though they had been invited to witness, they were, after all, still strangers.

The Winged Monkeys congregated, some dropping from the sky, some through the trees and others along the river.

Brutus made a strong entrance, skimming the river and circling the boulders before dropping down to the largest boulder, just to the right of the head stone. He seated himself proudly, with his head held high. His one eye glared out, daring anyone to challenge him.

Circling high above the trees, King Klick watched everyone gather. Then the silver-haired monkey king dropped through the trees to enter at the back of the tribe. After he ensured that everyone had arrived, King Klick walked among his people. Many reached out to touch him as he walked by. He acknowledged all who caressed him with the deference of a kind father, though he was father to only four of the assembled monkeys. Others rolled their eyes in disgust as King Klick took his rightful place at the head of the tribe.

He looked down at his people and waited for everyone's attention to focus on him. When the silence had come, he spoke. "We gather today in council to determine the future of our nesting grounds. Our home has been ravaged by the witch, Kalinya. There is still room in the forests to make our home again."

Glinda and Wickrie-Kells watched as several of the monkeys shifted in irritation. These monkeys were impatient and waiting for something to happen.

"I have received reports from our scouts who have been to the North Village. The people of the North did not even see them when they landed on the rooftops and window sills. Where a month ago we would have been chased away by brooms, we are now ignored. The people in the village have been overheard to say that they are happier now that the Ruby Palace is gone. There are no strange things in the night."

Wickrie-Kells whispered to Glinda, "Were there strange things at night?"

Glinda shrugged. "I don't know. My tower was locked every night. I never could see out. Some nights there were red lights that came from the palace all night long, but I never knew what they were. They were always gone in the morning."

King Klick continued, "If we return to the North, we will have peace with the people. We will be in a position to help when the man Quelala calls. We will be able to help the girl, Glinda, as she seeks to restore her kingdom."

Brutus raised himself off of his boulder, and some of the other monkeys twitched in anticipation. He struck his chest and said, "We have no place with them. We are free now. Quelala has not used the charm, and he said he would not. We are free now. The Red Witch is dead. We have nothing to fear." Brutus glowered out of his good eye at the silver monkey. "We are a free people. We do not owe loyalty to any human—not *anymore*."

King Klick warily watched his one-eyed rival warily. The impassioned speech was not directed at the king, but at the tribe. "Have a care, Brutus. You do not speak for the tribe." The king turned to the assembled Winged Monkeys, perched on all levels of rocks, branches and trees surrounding the river, and spoke frankly to them, saying, "We faced extinction at the hands of the Red *Queen*. Her life was long, and we *feared*. Even before her marriage to the man Quelala, we feared her wrath. It was our own short memory that endangered us. For our sake, the man Quelala risked his happiness in speaking for our survival. We do not take such oaths lightly."

King Klick continued, "We swore that oath to the Red Queen that we would obey the owner of the Golden Cap. You remember, those who were there, that each of us placed a hair in the magic flame. Since then, there has been no stranger to join our tribe. So each one that swore, not only pledged themselves, but their children, and their children's children by virtue of the hair they burned. We are bound. Let it never be said of us that the Winged Monkeys break their vows. We may be playful and love mischief, but such is our nature. To lie is not *our* nature. We are *not* liars."

Affirming hoots sounded through the assembled tribe. Glinda looked around. There were still some who stayed silent. These appeared to be the well-groomed, adolescent winged monkeys. Monkeys of status within the tribe. They looked to Brutus for his response.

Brutus hopped down from his rock and circled around King Klick, glaring at him with his good eye. "Do you not remember the oath you swore when we lost *our* queen?" A murmur of disapproval rumbled through the tribe. This was forbidden to speak of, yet Brutus brought it out. And this was done in the open, with strangers among them. The breach of etiquette was as great as the challenge to the kingship.

"You swore, O King, that you would do all in your power to bring her out of the Ruby Palace. To restore our queen to her proper place. And have you? I say, *you have not.*"

King Klick jumped down from his seat on the boulder and roared in the face of his challenger. "She was *your* queen, but she was *my* mate. Your loss pales in comparison to mine. But *I* rule here, not you. She was MINE. This tribe is MINE." He bared his teeth and beat his chest, rising up to his full height. Unwilling to back down, Brutus rose up to his full height. He was taller than King Klick, and broader by a shoulder. The two males roared and beat their chests, never letting their eyes move from the other's. They were locked in a battle for the kingship of the tribe.

Glinda started forward to try to stop the fight, but Beriyel jumped in front of the girl and held up her hands. "It is forbidden. You must not."

Glinda watched helplessly as the two large males circled about each other, each looking for a weakness to exploit.

King Klick twitched his left wing, drawing Brutus' attention for a split second. In that split second his right hand shot out and snatched the eye patch from off Brutus' head. He leaped up to the top of the head stone and held up the eye patch, shouting in victory.

Brutus glared at him with both eyes exposed—one dark and vicious, the other white and milky, unseeing. He dropped down to all fours and backed away, taking his place on his rock. His angry eyes never left the silver-haired king.

Glinda and Wickrie-Kells looked at each other uncomfortably. The alliances they had planned on for their army had been fractured. King Klick appeared to support them, but there were factions within the tribe that clearly did not. This first battle may have been won, but the war was a far from over.

10 THE CONFEDERATION OF WITCHES

The next morning, Glinda and Wickrie-Kells left the safety of the Emerald Valley and headed west. Wickrie-Kells wore a woven poncho, embroidered with her family crest—a crowned oven. Her family had been breadmakers in generations past. Their talented family had split, with the bakers moving west into the land of the Winkies. The portion that remained in the Emerald Lands maintained their connections with the royal household, eventually serving as entertainers and storytellers.

Wickrie-Kells believed in story. "There is amazing power in believing that a baker can slay a dragon. It makes me believe that I can do anything, too." The simple logic was impossible to argue with. That faith made Wickrie-Kells an amiable companion on their journey.

They followed the river out of the western end of the valley and passed by Lake Grimmpill. Central City held nothing more for them in their decision. They headed toward the rising sun in the west, with trust that they would find answers among the Winkies.

The Winkies were a people known for their wonderful metal workings. Their metallurgists were renowned throughout the entire Land of Oz for their finely tooled metal artistry. Everything from swords to lamps to wagon wheels, those that were Winkie-made were the finest in the land. In every Abracadabra bazaar held by Smith & Tinker, they always featured metalwork from the Winkies in the West. Glinda even had a filigree hair comb that her father bought for her three years ago.

With hope in their hearts, they set forth on their way. Wickrie-Kells put on a cap to keep the sun out of her eyes. She pulled it low, making Glinda laugh. That simple gesture, making Glinda laugh, helped the red-haired girl rise above the disappointment of the Emerald Valley. Wickrie-Kells taught Glinda some songs that she loved. The sounds of music echoed over the hills as the girls traveled across the green land.

Outside the shadows of the green pillars, another meeting was taking place—a Confederation of Witches. Organized by Ondri-baba, this meeting took place on the North side of the Emerald Lands. Ondri-baba saw the others coming from afar with her magic eye and she had tables laid out with good things to eat—pastries and fruits of all kinds.

Mombi was the first to arrive. She came from the direction of Central City, walking, which was a very unusual tactic for a witch. Commoners walked, witches did not. Mombi had been the last one of them to leave the coronation. It appeared that she had not truly left at all.

Her hair was back to its natural dark brown, so dark as to be almost black. Her face had reverted to its own shape and form. Her dark eyes held shadows that flitted back and forth like reflected ravens. She said little as they waited for the others to arrive. She slowly savored a plum, but warily watched the horizon.

"Fate plays cruel tricks on the unwary." Ondri-baba said, chuckling to herself. "You're as wired as a cat on a waterwheel." Ondri-baba trundled like a turtle, clothed in her metal collars and extravagant ruffles.

"I am waiting. That's all."

"Of course. Want to see the magic sand?" Without waiting for an affirmative answer, Ondri-baba pulled out one of the hourglasses purchased from the Abracadabra Bazaar a month ago. "These sandy servants can do much more than Smit 'n' Tinky said."

She demonstrated the results of her experimentation with various designs for the sand—molds in which to pour the magical grains. She laid out several finely crafted metal molds. As she poured the sand from the hourglass into the molds, the sand took the form detailed therein. One became a tiger, another became an armored warrior and another a bat. The bat didn't fly very well, but it could glide.

Mombi watched this display of power silently. Even as Ondri-baba cackled with glee at her creative use of these clever weapons, Mombi schemed inside her head. She was watching the other witch give away all of her secrets and strategizing how to use this information. Ondri-baba was not clever, but she was fierce. Mombi feigned disinterest, but inside her mind, the wheels were spinning about how best to use this to her advantage.

Then suddenly, Kalinya and Locasta appeared. They appeared out of nowhere, as Kalinya was now wont to do. Locasta looked sick and she had to sit down. She pulled off her wide-brimmed hat and fanned her face.

Mombi and Kalinya had avoided talking at the Coronation, but now they could avoid each other no longer. The witches locked eyes, and it was clear that there was no love lost between them. Mombi kept her feelings veiled. She said nothing, but she spit the plum pit out on the table. Kalinya was nowhere near as subtle. She directed her words to her apprentice, Locasta, but it was clear that her remarks were directed at Mombi.

"Look at that, my apprentice, there is the true guise of the two-faced schemer. She can wear the face of an angel and the face of a devil, sometimes in the same day, but her heart is as dark as raven's wing."

"And that, Locasta, is your first instruction," replied Mombi, "in how your master operates. In any scheme, the greatest danger is not from your targets, but from your accomplices. You never know when they might forget who they are dealing with, or what promises they might have made."

Locasta raised her pale head to look from one face to the other, not quite understanding. She took shallow breaths and blinked quickly, trying to make sense of the situation. The history between these women—witches, they must be referred to as witches, not women—was deep and bitter. Magic had taken a toll on their appearance, and it was clear that they were not normal women. Rivalries may exist among normal women, but for those who had entwined their lives with magic, rivalry ran as deep as blood itself. All the Witches carried themselves differently than the common women. These were no common women, yet they did not choose to be noble, not in any sense of the word. They were *changed* by the magic they had woven into their lives.

Ondri-baba bustled between them, breaking their icy stare. "Enough, you two. Whatever bad blood was spilled is dried away like sand. You are here because *I* asked you to come. This is *my* convention, and I will not allow either of you to disrupt my plans."

Two days passed—two days of traveling north and west across the green prairies of the Emerald Lads—and then Glinda and Wickrie-Kells happened across a brick road. It was made of fine yellow brick. It led from the south and turned so that it headed directly west. That made the going much smoother for them, and they happily continued on their way. The road passed by fruit trees and fields, which provided fresh food to supplement the bread and cheese that they had packed in their knapsacks.

It was on the third afternoon of their journey that they encountered a peculiar creature. On the western horizon, racing toward them with a speed far faster than any person could run, the creature appeared to be gliding on the road. As it drew closer, they could see that it appeared to be made of metal, but it looked alive. The creature had myriad brass metal fittings so it glittered in the sunlight. At the end of its limbs, instead of hands and feet, there were wheels. The click-clack as it sped over the bricks became audible as it drew closer.

"What is it?" Glinda asked Wickrie-Kells.

The other girl shook her head. "I don't know. I've never seen one before. My father might know, but…do you think it has a name?"

Glinda scoffed, "It's not a person, silly."

The creature skidded to a halt in front of them. It worked its lower jaw a few times to loosen it. Then it spoke. "Are you Glinda?"

Surprised, Glinda made a little curtsey. "Yes, I am. What are you?"

"I am a Wheeler. My masters made me, and they sent me to you to request your presence at a secret meeting tonight."

Wickrie-Kells narrowed her eyes suspiciously. "And who are your masters?"

"They are the great and wise inventors called Mr. Smith and Mr. Tinker.

"That's fine. I suppose…but how are we to get there?"

"My masters provided a means for you to travel quickly. To run like a wheeler. In the pouches on my back, there are slippers with wheels. Put these on your feet. There are tethers linked to my back. Hold on."

The girls did as the wheeler instructed and put the wheeled slippers on their feet like skates. They put their shoes into their knapsacks, so that they wouldn't get lost.

"I was instructed by my masters to remind you once more. *Hold on.*"

The girls were nearly jerked off their feet as the wheeler leaped forward. They quickly gained their balance and screamed in excitement as the wheeler picked up speed.

They sped over hills and through fragrant fields of blossoms. Always, always the road clacked under their wheels. This was more exciting than anything Wickrie-Kells had ever experienced. Glinda had slightly more experience with this type of speed—both with the Winged Monkeys and with the Swift Horse, Zephyr—but it still took away her breath with the speed at which they were traveling. She laughed out loud at Wickrie's screams of delight as the wind blew through their hair.

A startled bug flew up in front of the wheeler's face and his eyes followed the bug—he did not see the curve in the brick road. Their momentum carried them off the bricks and sent them tumbling into the flowers. Glinda laughed out loud as she pulled flower petals from her hair. She looked at Wickrie-Kells, who laughed back at her. They looked back at the wheeler. It was lying completely still in the grass beyond them.

"What happened? Is it…?" Wickrie-Kells clapped her hands over her mouth.

Glinda crept over to the wheeler and prodded it. No response. "That doesn't make any sense. It worked there..."

"Did it break something? An arm, a leg, its head?" Wickrie-Kells shook the Wheeler's shoulder. "Hey, Wheeler, are you all right?"

Glinda pulled the wheeled slippers off her feet so she could stand normally, and grabbed the wheeler's leg and pulled it back toward the road. "The leg isn't coming off, so it isn't broken. Something can't just be working one second and be not working the next. If it was alive, it would have at least twitched. I told you it wasn't a person." Then she had an idea and looked at the brown-haired girl with an excitement in her eyes. "I think it's *magic*."

Wickrie-Kells grabbed the arms and lifted them. They managed to half-carry, and half-drag the metal wheeler back on to the yellow brick road. The moment its arm touched the yellow brick, it twitched. Glinda took this as a sign that they were on the right track and heaved the rest of the wheeler on to the road. It clicked and whirred and buzzed to life, climbing up on its feet again. Glinda jumped for joy and clapped her hands. "It works!"

Wickrie-Kells shook her head, amazed at the cleverness of her friend, and the adventures they were having together. For a girl like her, these last two weeks were the stuff of legends, and yet their adventures were just at the very beginning.

At that moment, many miles down the road, the witch Mombi arrived at the camp of Smith & Tinker. She rode in on a large sandy steed—a heavy horse made of two hourglasses' worth of sand. She had pushed herself hard, riding for an hour at a time, and then walking, to allow the sand time to recharge inside the hourglass. Mombi had ridden through the night, sleeping only two hours, so that she could arrive at the location of Smith & Tinker before they left. Ondri-baba had seen them from far away with her magic eye, and she sent Mombi immediately to deliver a message. She unfurled a parchment and presented her credentials.

"I come representing an alliance of witches. My purpose is to deliver warning." Mombi watched closely as the two men traded glances. "There will be war. You are hereby forbidden to engage either side through counsel or through supplying magical arts." She handed over the scroll.

"The sandy armies are under the control of Ondri-baba, and she has claimed the West as her own. Do not interfere."

Mr. Tinker smiled at the dark-haired witch. "Mombi, you are not the same person I knew, once, eh? You have a certain *difference* about you. Have you done something different with your hair?" Then he turned to his companion, Mr. Smith, and listened as he read the parchment.

"It says that anyone who is not directly surrendering to, or allying with, Ondri-baba will be destroyed." Mr. Smith cocked an eyebrow at Mombi. "*You, too?* You are her ally?"

Mombi's eyes shifted under Mr. Tinker's inquisitive gaze, and she looked away. "I am an ambassador."

Mr. Tinker scoffed at that. "You've more than one face, *girl*."

Mombi looked up, startled. For the first time in years, someone called her, '*girl*'. Despite her pleasure at the flirtation, she only smiled wanly. "I am a *Witch*. My face is lined with magic. I am not young like I once was."

Mr. Tinker nodded in mock approval. "Time is an enemy to almost everyone. So, hmm. I think I see your dilemma. Wait, *no.* I've got it. So there isn't any *mirror* that might make any difference in *who* you see?" Mr. Tinker let his words sink in. He could see the wheels in Mombi's head furiously turning.

"The way I see it, you have a choice here—be the villain, or become invisible. Ondri-baba can make other things invisible, but you...Mombi; you have the skill to become invisible."

"Perhaps we've said too much." Mr. Smith posited. "She has to be going." He rolled up the parchment and held it out to Mombi. "Thank you for the message, missy. Tell your queen mum that she won't be hearing from us no more. We're leaving this land. Crossin' the sands and looking for fertile fields to paint and tinker. We're actually on our yearly trip across the sands to Ev. Lovely place, Ev. It's beautiful this time of year."

Mombi left them on foot. The sandy steed could wait until a later time. She had a great deal to think about—her mind was racing. Without explicitly saying so, Smith & Tinker had given her an escape—a path out of this coming war.

With the sun setting at their backs, Glinda and Wickrie-Kells arrived at the camp of Smith & Tinker. Mr. Tinker greeted them first. "*IgNob* has returned, with our esteemed guests, as ordered. Welcome, treasured guests, to the temporary domicile of Smith & Tinker, *artificers extraordinaire*."

Mr. Smith showed the girls into the main tent. "We're pleased to have you with us. I see IgNob found you. I trust the ride was a thrill?"

"Yes, Sir." Wickrie-Kells beamed.

Glinda nodded agreement. "It was *soooooo* fast."

A table and chairs dominated the center of the tent. Food was cooking on a portable stove, and a lantern hovered above their heads, suspended on a rotating wheel. Mr. Smith gestured to the wheeler, who stopped and peered in the door of the tent, "IgNob, you're excused. Go eat with your brothers."

The wheeler, IgNob, bobbed his head up and down and rolled around the back tent, where a brick loop had been built. The road remained clear, but the wheelers had constructed a patio with a nice path connecting to the power of the brick road. It was there that they had their own tent. Clanking and whistling sounded in the evening as IgNob joined the other wheelers. Bright light inside the tent showed the rolling creatures silhouetted inside, *eating*, whatever that meant for a creature of that sort.

Glinda didn't remember any wheelers at the bazaar, and she mentioned this to the inventors.

"We have our ways of keeping things hidden. Just because you don't see a thing don't mean it's not there." Mr. Smith sipped from his mug.

Mr. Tinker chimed in, "Also, sometimes you'll find the things not seen are stronger than those that are."

"It, I mean, *he*, didn't work when we ran off the brick road." Wickrie-Kells said.

"That is an astute observation." Mr. Tinker remarked, pointing with his eyebrow over his mug. "Why do *you* think that was so?"

Glinda spared no hesitation before she blurted out, "Magic."

Mr. Tinker gave a thoughtful. "Ahhhh." He laid a finger in front his nose. His spectacles reflected the finger, so it looked like he held up three fingers instead of just the one. "There are many types of magic. Your mother was a sorceress. Was her magic the same as the Witches in Oz?"

Glinda shook her head. "No. My mother did a lot of research. She was always working with experiments and trying to figure things out. She knew a lot of incantations—she taught me some."

Mr. Smith and Mr. Tinker exchanged a glance. An entire volume of information passed between them, but Glinda couldn't tell what it was they said.

"What?" she asked. "What was that look for?"

Mr. Tinker's eyes were twinkling. Mr. Smith was beaming in his dour sort of way. He folded his hands neatly on the table in front of him. "You, *missy*, know a secret. You are a *sorceress*, no doubt, and you have a bundle to teach those witches!"

Mr. Smith took over. "What incantations did she teach you?"

Glinda looked sheepish. "They aren't much. The last time Sonadia visited—it was a while ago, a long time ago, actually—my mother made sure that she taught us how to make clouds. That Sonadia taught me and my mother, not that my mother taught Sonadia. She already knew how…and then I can make hats change shape."

"Transformation magic." mumbled Mr. Smith.

"And then I can make an hourglass turn over. Whatever good that will do." Glinda lifted her eyebrows hopefully at the two inventors. "That's what I know. Doesn't make me much of a sorceress."

"Oh, I don't know…You might be surprised how much you actually do know."

"I know that my mother didn't care enough to let me do anything. I never saw her. She never saw me. All I got from her were books and gifts. All I wanted was time."

Wickrie-Kells reached out and touched her friend's arm consolingly.

"How many books have you read?" Mr. Smith asked, looking at Glinda.

She shrugged. "I don't know. Probably two hundred. Probably more. I've got a lot of bookshelves. Or I did before the tower fell down."

He turned to Wickrie-Kells. "And you, young lady from the Emerald Lands, at the center of Oz, how many books have you read?"

Wickrie-Kells looked startled at the question. She thought, and then counted on her fingers. "We have five books. I know friends that have one or two, and I have looked through those. But I like listening to stories more than I like reading books. They're more alive when I listen."

Mr. Smith accepted that answer. He turned back to Glinda, "More than two hundred books you have read and you keep on your bookshelves. I have been in the royal library in Central City. Do you know how many books they have there?"

"A thousand?"

"Two hundred and twelve."

Glinda sat back in her chair. Her puzzled look betrayed the struggle going on inside her mind. The inventors were clearly leading her someplace, but she didn't know where. And that feeling of uncertainty reflected both in her eyes and on her face.

"On your bookshelves alone, you have at least as many books as the central library of Oz. And you have read them all. How much knowledge do you have inside your head that you don't even know you have?"

Wickrie-Kells looked at her friend with a newfound respect.

Glinda's eyes brightened and she managed the start of a smile. Then she remembered the state of her tower back home. "Only…my tower is ruined. Kalinya destroyed the Ruby Palace. My tower was partly destroyed by the explosion."

"The Ruby Palace is gone?" Mr. Smith and Mr. Tinker said in unison. This was clearly new information to them.

Mr. Tinker hit Mr. Smith in the arm. "I told you we should not've left Gayelette with those witches." He turned to Glinda, "When did it happen?"

"The night of the bazaar."

"Oohhh. That explains it, then. The moon. We were…*elsewhere.*"

"But you couldn't have gotten far. The tremors. I felt the ground move when I was in the meadow of midnight orchids. That's got to be at least a day's walk." Glinda protested. "How could you not know? Didn't you go to the coronation?"

Both men pursed their lips and shook their heads. Mr. Tinker spoke for the duo, squinting his eyes seriously, "We make it a point not to travel often. We move quickly. Things to do. Things to create. Like the wheelers. Saw 'em first in Ev, but thought, we can do it *better.* Make 'em tame. Couldn't bother with the Coronation. King Oz is gone. Nitwit brother in his place. Don't bother us. Just leave us alone and we're pleased as peach plum cake."

"So you didn't know that my mother is gone?"

Again they exchanged a glance. This time, Mr. Smith spoke. "Aye. That one we knew. You see, we maintained a regular correspondence with Gayelette. A sorceress is a powerful ally to have, especially for practitioners of the technical arts. When she didn't send us the moon-message, we deducted something happened with her experiment. She was going to bridge dream and waking—"

"*Too much!*" Mr. Tinker interrupted, "Too much information for untrained ears. Maybe when she's older. Your mother was a trusted ally of Smith & Tinker. With her gone, we are *personas non grateful* with the other witches. So we are leaving. Bidding farewell to this guessing game. Heading back South to our laboratory. Incidentally, we found *something* that belongs to you, but you'll have to come south to see it."

"I will. But I have a question." Glinda said, her mind still spinning under the weight of new knowledge that she finally knew that she knew. Her head felt a little bit heavier on her shoulders, and she had to steady herself on the table. "How did you find us? I mean, how did the Wheeler know we would be on the brick road?"

Mr. Smith closed the conversation. "These brick roads have power. We just monitored the power, and measured the changes. We saw that it was two girls heading west. Well, not saw, exactly, we figured it from the movements."

"Then we sent the ornithopotamus. That, at least, could see."

"That's right. So it saw."

"Red hair."

"Red hair." Mr. Smith repeated. "Only one that has red hair. Two, well, *one*. So we sent IgNob. Fine lad he is. And here you are."

Mr. Tinker concluded the answer to Glinda's question. "The brick roads have power. If you stay on them, you will have a connection to that power, and where that power comes from. You," he pointed at Glinda, "Have much to learn about yourself."

Then he pointed at Wickrie-Kells, "And *you*, have a great responsibility to her as a friend. See that she does not forget who she is."

Mr. Smith nodded. "You are welcome to sleep here tonight. Here, meaning here, right here." He pointed at the floor. Morning comes and you'll be on your way then. Just remember, surprises waiting in the south, sure as righteous rain. Our laboratory is big—holds many answers. Probably all the available answers, now that the Ruby Palace is…not...*currently* available."

Wickrie-Kells interjected, "What do you mean, *currently*?"

Mr. Tinker repeated his earlier statement. "Just that, 'not currently available.' Too much for untrained ears. Good night, lassies. It's been a pleasure. We look forward to your *becoming*."

"Aye, 'night." Mr. Smith backed out of the tent, and they left the girls alone.

The girls had supper and talked into the night. Smith & Tinker provided comfortable beds for them from somewhere in their magic wagon. Above them, the half moon shone, signifying the ongoing cycle of passage. The girls slept—Wickrie-Kells slept silently and peacefully, but Glinda was tormented the entire night through with visions of strange things—things she did not understand.

She wondered in the early morning hours if these nighttime visions were the things that her mother called *dreams*.

11 THE BLOOD AND SAND AND MAGIC

Mombi walked through the night, alone with her ever-more-clarifying thoughts. She had put the sandy steed to rest inside its hourglasses, giving her time to be fully alone. She was in no hurry to get back to report to the other witches.

The grinning moon shone down on her as she made her way through the emerald grass. She did not have to join the other witches. There was another option. Her life held meaning. Even if there was no one else that valued her, she was a valuable person. After all, hadn't she placed one corner of the crown on the head of the new king of Oz? While he might not have full power throughout the entire land, in the Emerald Lands he was supreme. And she was one-fourth of the power that had crowned him! She stood in for the North and pronounced final blessings upon him.

If she was the power that made the crown, why could she not also be the power behind the crown? She had no desire to replace the king. Let him remain the figurehead. Mombi could remain in the peripheral shadows guiding the course of the kingdom. But what about the other witches? What would they think?

Not that it really mattered. After Kalinya nearly snuffed out Mombi's life in the Ruby Palace, she didn't trust that witch even one parsnip. There was no role-playing in *that* situation. While Mombi was playing a part, Kalinya was wicked to the core. There was no doubt that Kalinya would have killed her, just to make a point to Gayelette. It did not matter that Mombi was wearing someone else's face at the time. In fact, that seemed to make the brutality *easier* for Kalinya.

No, Mombi would not be partner to this war. War *was* coming to the land. She wanted no part of the terror or the destruction. The war was completely preventable, but the twin egos of the witches—Kalinya and Ondri-baba—would not let any gain go unpunished. Each would raze the land just to spite the other. With their one true rival from the North out of the way, and the witch of the South mysteriously slain, there was no one to stand in the way of their conquest. The impossibility of anyone standing in their way was enough to force a bitter laugh out of Mombi. "No one can stand."

"*Never again.*" She turned her face to the East and the setting moon.

The next morning, on the Emerald Plains, far away from intruding eyes, Ondri-baba proudly displayed the crates of glistening hourglasses. Kalinya forced a tight smile at her younger sister's achievement. "I have all but seven, and Mombi bought those."

"And you will need all of these servants to clean your crane-legged home?" Kalinya gestured to the stilt-legged contraption that Ondri-baba called her hut. "Just how many servants will you have?"

"Five hundred…minus the seven that Mombi had. And they are servants. They will do exactly as I order them to do. Watch." She poured the contents of one hourglass into the metal tiger mold and a sandy tiger arose and roared. "They can be whatever I shape them to be."

"Fascinating." Kalinya circled the sand tiger, running her hand along its back to feel the texture of the sand. "So you can create animals."

"I can create warriors!" The one-eyed witch proudly stuck out her chest. "They are mine. They do what I say. Nothing will stop me from getting exactly what I want. Not even you."

"Me? Why would I get in your way?"

"You always get in my way. Always proving that you are more powerful than I am. Always getting the upper hand. Always thinking…but you're not the only one who can think. I can think, too. And I have been thinking. We have an alliance. I am the leader because I have the army. You and your apprentice will be my generals. If Mombi comes back, she can be a general, too."

"What do you mean, *if* she comes back?"

"Mombi hates you. She said you tried to kill her."

Kalinya shrugged, dismissing the accusation. "It was a necessary ruse to distract the sorceress."

Ondri-baba warily watched Kalinya as she circled the table to look at the hourglasses. "She had to get a message to Smith & Tinker to stay out of the way. I still want them on my side when I conquer the Winkies. Have you seen their molds? They could make molds of whatever creature I wanted, then I could make sandy soldiers into anything."

She continued, excited by the sound of her own plan being spoken out loud. "I want you to take fifty soldiers. You get fifty and Locasta gets ten. You will be my generals. Once we move past the Emerald Lands, you will go in first and strike the Winkie army. Then I will come in and crush any resistance."

Kalinya glanced over at her apprentice, Locasta, who raised her own eyebrows in disbelief. "You don't trust us, but you're giving us some of your soldiers?"

"You bet your stripey socks. Keep your enemies close, and your rivals closer. With you right next to me, you can't do anything that I can't see. I have the invisibility factor, remember that."

"And what is to stop me from throwing you into the sky right now?" Kalinya raised her hand threateningly.

Immediately she was pushed down to the ground by an unseen force. Her breath exploded out of her lungs as the pressure on her back intensified. Her arms were pulled behind her back and pinned in place by rough hands.

Ondri-baba waved her hands and a large sandy soldier suddenly became visible. Ondri-baba smiled as the shock of sour recognition appeared on her sister's dirty face. "Go ahead. Throw me into the sky."

Ondri-baba led the way in her walking hut. Fully one-third of her army marched ahead of her. Every two hours they stopped. Ondri-baba had experimented enough to know that if she used half of the sand in the hourglass, it would still last for one hour. But if she added the remaining sand, the servant would last for an additional hour. It remained to be seen if additional layers would add additional life to the servant.

They marched toward the West, toward the Winkie Country. Ondri-baba had staked her claim. The mineral-rich lands of the Winkies guaranteed plenty of raw materials with which to build her kingdom, her armies and her power.

In the center of the sandy army were Kalinya and her apprentice witch, Locasta. They were exactly where Ondri-baba could keep an eye on them. Wisely, Kalinya did not attempt to deviate from the established course of this war. Her own plans would unfold in due time. Inside her mind, Kalinya burned. Glinda had disappeared, Quelala was gone without a trace, and the mysteries of the Ruby Palace were no closer to being solved. She longed to go back up to the lands of the North, where the Ruby Palace once cast its long shadow, and search and dig and find something, *anything* that she could use as a weapon.

Knowledge was weaponizable. If only she knew what Gayelette had known, it would be *her* leading these armies, not Ondri-baba.

The armies marched for the full day. Every moment, Kalinya watched for Ondri-baba to make a mistake, to leave an opening that reflected her poor judgment, but it never came. Ondri-baba was not clever, but she was brutal in her determination. And she was determined to rule the West.

The sun set and Mombi had not returned from her errand. Ondri-baba had sent Mombi as an ambassador to Smith & Tinker to warn them against getting involved. With war marching forward, the fewer weapons that were involved, the shorter the battles would be. Ondri-baba was not concerned for her own armies, or so she said. She was more worried about the armies that stood against her. If they had a continual supply of arcane items, such as those continually procured and peddled by Smith & Tinker, they would draw out the battle longer and longer, and more of them—the Winkies—would be hurt before they surrendered to Ondri-baba. With more injuries among the Winkies, there would be more time spent dealing with whining, and the longer it would take them to establish Ondri-baba as their queen.

Kalinya magically produced a large tent for herself and Locasta. As the sun dropped below the horizon, Kalinya closed the door on her tent. She did not want to deal with any of the nightly foolishness of her sister.

Outside, Ondri-baba stepped from her walking contraption and into a tent of her own. Her tent was ablaze with bright lights. Ondri-baba could not stand the darkness. She moved around her tent as a shadow puppet would, removing the collars and ruffles. Every exaggerated movement shown on the wall as a mocking pantomime of reality. Ondri-baba's silhouette was that of a storybook witch, right down to the bump on her nose.

Inside Kalinya's tent, the silver slippers glowed with a magic of their own. Kalinya whispered her plan to Locasta. They were careful, especially Kalinya, for neither of them could be sure that there were no invisible ears floating around, listening to their words. "I am going to the north to find answers. You, my apprentice, must watch through the night. Ensure that our fearless leader does not discover I am gone.

"I will return before the morning march. For tomorrow we battle the Winkies. And then we can be finished with this Oz-forsaken drudgery. She will have her land, and we can continue our own pursuit of justice and power. *Yes*, power. We will gain it, you and I. Much, much power."

Kalinya stuck her head outside the tent, sighted a spot on the horizon and took three steps, and she was gone.

Locasta saw the silver slippers glimmer once on the horizon as Kalinya headed north. And then she settled in to watch the strange shadow puppet show in the lighted tent across the camp.

Kalinya leaped from horizon to horizon on her travel northward. Always moving toward the red star, she raced over valleys and streams. At last she arrived at the site of the once-powerful Ruby Palace. She walked twice around the crater, but she found nothing in the silver moonlight. Even Glinda's tower was empty. Kalinya thought it was probably the scavenging villagers that Gayelette had kept in a constant state of repression. She was sure that they had taken all that had belonged to Glinda as their way of getting revenge on the red queen that had ruled them. Even though Kalinya explored the whole area she could find nothing that would help her.

When she got to the garden, she stopped cold. All of the damage she had done in her battle with Quelala was gone. It was not that the garden had overgrown in the intervening weeks, hiding the scars—the garden had been carefully replanted. It had been tended with care and repaired. Kalinya glanced suspiciously around, but she saw no one.

She followed the sandy path down to the dark corner where she had spent two terror-filled days. Even though it was not shaded by taller trees, this section was strangely shadowed in the moonlight. The twisted plants did not look diseased, but they did not look normal, either. They looked strange and otherworldly. These were not plants native to Oz. So where did they come from? The shadowed section was in the southwest corner, beyond the yellow section and the sandy path.

That was where Kalinya had been trapped by Quelala. Somehow he had overpowered the magic of the silver slippers, and made it so that she could not escape. And then he trapped her in the shadows of this strange corner. Trapped her like an animal. Trapped her like a common criminal. Her anger rose within her.

Kalinya's fist clenched as she remembered the vines circling around her, preventing her feet from touching, negating the power of the silver slippers. Her hand slipped into a pouch at her belt. She grasped one of the small hourglasses given to her by Ondri-baba. Kalinya's magic coursed through her. She could feel the sands vibrating inside the glass. She idly wondered what would happen if she exploded the hourglass. What would happen to the sand?

In that idle moment of lapsed control, the hourglass shattered. She felt the shards of glass cut into her fingers and hand. She pulled her hand quickly out and shook out the sand and blood from her lacerated hand. The shards of glass tinkled against the shadowed plants. The sand fused with the droplets of blood and rose up, taking on the humanoid form of Kalinya. The blood gave a more lasting and detailed shape. The golem quickly took female shape and even mimicked the look of Kalinya's large eyes and face.

"Interesting." the witch murmured.

The blood-sand figure looked unblinking at Kalinya. The witch circled the creation admiring its form—it looked like her before the years of magic had taken their toll. "What can you do, I wonder? How long do you live before you turn back into sand?"

Kalinya walked around the entire crater where the Ruby Palace had once stood. From a distance she saw villagers watching her curiously, but none of them approached close enough for her to see faces. Though she searched and magically threw up a small mountain of dirt, she found *nothing*. There was absolutely *nothing* left of the Ruby Palace.

It was the same for the nearby tower. There was nothing there. Things had changed in the last month. While she had been attending to her duties as a Witch and then scheming with her sister, all of the effort she put in to destroying her rival had been ruined. The ruins had been combed over neatly, leaving nothing behind. Kalinya screamed in frustration. Her golem behind her screamed also, a hoarse, inhuman cry. The creature was learning. But that didn't make things here better.

Kalinya searched the area thoroughly. There was nothing that she could scavenge. No clues left to what Gayelette had been researching. Not even any sign of Quelala.

Kalinya was more than two hours searching, and still the blood-sand golem followed after her. The sandy creature was much more active and attentive than the dumb sandy soldiers Ondri-baba was using. When she tried to reduce the golem to sand again, it didn't work smoothly. The blood had made the sand clumpy. The hourglass was broken. When she finally reduced the golem back to sand, Kalinya scooped up the clumpy red sand and placed it in her pouch.

Then she took three steps and she was gone. Kalinya headed south, back toward the sandy army.

From the shadows of the forest, Quelala watched and worried. He saw that where there was one witch appearing suddenly, then there were two, then there was one again. He certainly could have brought her back to him, using the power of the Golden Cap, but he was curious what the witch was about. So he decided to watch and wait before putting his plan into action.

In the south desert sands, a faint glow in the west signaled the coming dawn. At the Twisted Lighthouse on the south shore of Oz, the last remaining testament that the deadly desert was once an inland sea—a part of the Nonestic Ocean—the inventors, Smith & Tinker, entered into their Aeronautic Confabulator and lifted off the bridge, heading south over the desert. Behind them their vast laboratory-castle lay still. All of their creations were asleep, frozen, awaiting the kiss of the promised morn.

"Will she come, I wonder?" Mr. Tinker mused.

"Aye. But she must." Mr. Smith answered.

Back on the Winkie Plains, Locasta watched anxiously as the sun stretched higher above the horizon. Kalinya had still not returned. Ondri-baba was not yet awake, but all of the clanking of metal pots and pans from her tent would not let her sleep much longer—sandy servants did not make breakfast very quietly. Even though the sun was obviously up in the morning sky, a bright light still shone inside Ondri-baba's tent. This cast out all shadows, and it kept silhouettes even in the broad daylight. This allowed Locasta to monitor the witch's sleeping form. Still, the apprentice fidgeted nervously as she dreaded having to explain her master's absence.

Even more than trying to explain Kalinya's absence to Ondri-baba, Locasta worried about falling asleep and having Kalinya return to find her sleeping and unprepared.

Kalinya had a wicked temper. Locasta had bruises that had never healed because of Kalinya's constant temper. She had been thrown into the sky more than once. The terror that Kalinya exacted on her apprentice was a punishment that no one should ever have to face. But it was not a punishment for occasional misdeeds; it was simply a *normal* part of life. *Normal*—how twisted that word had become to Locasta. The life she imagined as a witch was intended to escape normal, but right now she would give anything to go back to the normal that she had once known as a Munchkin.

Mombi entered the gates of the Emerald Valley and walked past the Emerald Pillars which jutted out like misplaced fangs. Everything around her screamed in warning, but she was certain. If magic would not win the day, she would ensure her own safety through political power. She would become the true power behind the throne.

Mombi followed the river down to a circle of boulders inside the forest. She pulled out the silver mirror with the frozen picture of Kalinya and Gayelette. She also pulled out a standard mirror and looked at her face, once fresh and beautiful, now finely lined and aged by magic. With a soft brush and the Imaginary Paint, she painted her face, copying what she saw in the silver mirror. Within a few minutes, she had changed the appearance of her face completely. She didn't look exactly like Gayelette, but she didn't look like herself, either. There was only one thing left to do.

Mombi pulled out the strands of red hair and wrapped them around her fingers. Then she ran her fingers through her straight dark hair. As the red hair passed over the dark strands, it changed them to red.

When her new look was complete, she put away the tools of her disguise kit.

Thirty minutes later, with the sun peeking over the walls of the Royal Palace, Mombi folded a note into the shape of a bird and tossed it into the sky. It obeyed her transformation magic and flapped away. "Find Ondri-baba. Do not rest until she has you in her hands."

One hour later, with the full support and endorsement of the Butler, Mombi entered into the throne room and inclined her head toward Pastoria on his throne.

"King Pastoria, I am Mombi, witch of the North."

Pastoria narrowed his eyes and studied this red-haired witch in front of him. "You look different than you did at the Coronation."

"By design. I have enemies that I do not wish to awake." She stepped forward. "You have heard of the red-haired witch of the North?"

Pastoria studied the face and the bearing of this red-haired witch of the North. "Continue."

"I have come to ally myself with the King who will change Oz forever." Her voice dropped to a whisper. "There is war coming. You need allies. You need a witch next to you."

"I have the blessing of *four* witches. Why should I keep *one* at my side?"

Mombi scrambled, searching for something that Pastoria might find desirable. Then she noticed a book by the king's side. He was limited in the books that he could read, but she was not. "Magic. I can read magic. Can the king read magic? Magic holds many secrets."

"I would know more of these secrets." A sly smile played at the corners of Pastoria's mouth. "Return here tomorrow. Until then, I will enjoy having another beautiful face around the palace."

THE BOY

12 THE BATTLE OF WINKIE PLAINS

As Glinda awoke, the tent around her was gone. The bright morning sun streamed onto her face, pulling her out of the reach of dreams. Smith & Tinker were gone. The brick road was still there, but it was missing the wheeler loop. Everything that Smith & Tinker had laid out the night before was gone with the dews in the morning sun. Even the mattress upon which she slept melted away in the sunlight. Just another wonderful mystery to add to the intriguing secrets of Smith & Tinker.

Nearby, Wickrie-Kells was gathering jelly eggs to go with their breakfast biscuits. The eggs grew in the shadows of the widegrass. They were sweet, and served as a very good substitute for homemade jam. "Smith & Tinker certainly left quickly." Glinda said, shoveling a biscuit into her mouth.

"They were gone when I woke up. First light and my mattress started sinking." Wickrie-Kells pulled her hair to the sides and bound it in pigtails.

"Did you find any sort of message?" Glinda asked.

"Not that I could see. But they made it pretty clear last night that they wanted you to go down to visit them in the South."

"We will. We'll get down there. But first, we've got to get to the West."

The girls ate a quick breakfast and then headed west, into the rising sun. After more than an hour of walking, Glinda glanced behind them. A distant brown line, a different color than the rocky ground beneath their feet, undulated like a wave.

"What is that? A storm?" Wickrie-Kells asked.

Glinda shrugged. "It's moving. That's all I can tell."

"It's coming towards us, right?"

Out of caution, the girls picked up their pace. The morning sun was pleasant, but there was no shade in this part of the land. The afternoon looked to be very hot. Their water supply was getting low, and they worried about getting sun scorched. Also, with the strange brown wave behind them, they didn't want to get caught up in the inland tide.

The brick road wound to the south down through the foothills to disappear below. Ahead of them was a slope upward to the horizon. It was either go down or up, so they chose to go up.

The slope seemed to go on forever. The grade was not steep, but Glinda was getting tired. Wickrie-Kells urged her on. Wickrie was more active than Glinda was, and she was just hitting her stride as they came within sight of the crest of the hill. Once they could see the top, Glinda's heart took courage and they hurried forward. Though she was familiar now with the sights of the Ruby Palace and the Central City, nothing could prepare them for the wondrous sight they now beheld.

They stood at the top of a high ridge. Below them, to the south, there was the brick road winding through the foothills. It turned in a different direction, coming north, so there must be a crossroads somewhere down there among the foothills. The rocky valley beneath them held streams of traffic traveling both to and from the great Yellow Castle. It looked like a great stone flame of fire rising up out of the valley floor.

This was the capital of Winkie Country. The castle rose into the sky, but did not quite reach the height of the ridge on which they stood. The castle was a blend of yellow gold metalwork and a tan-colored granite. Jutting pinnacles of rock rose up behind the castle, creating a crown around the flame. This crown served to reflect the afternoon sun, making the castle even more brilliant.

Behind the girls, distant clouds were gathering and moving in on their location. Wickrie-Kells said, "There is a storm. And the brown…what is that? Those clouds look like rain. We'd better hurry."

Glinda pointed to a group carrying flags out in front of the castle down below. "*There.* That looks like somebody important. See? They're all around that fat person. He looks like he's dancing."

In the distance beyond them, Wickrie-Kells saw a green-haired young man running far ahead of the group. He was the scout for the king's procession. Wickrie-Kells explained that kings usually sent a single scout ahead of their honor guard to make sure everything was safe. It was mostly a ceremonial role, but in times past it had served to keep the king safe.

They found a trail down the ridge, and the girls picked their way down the slope toward the procession. It took them nearly an hour. But the moment they reached the bottom, they were apprehended by Winkie soldiers with long spears. Glinda looked sideways at Wickrie-Kells. "You know, we really should have seen this one coming."

The Winkie soldiers were not amused. "In the name of King Winko, you are under arrest for trespassing and approaching the king in the middle of his morning frolic."

The girls were brought into the exquisite throne room of King Winko, which was decorated with metal works of all shapes and varieties. There was engraved in the metalwork the story of a legendary hunt that went from the mines to the rivers and up to the clouds. The hunt was crafted in silver and gold and copper. The carved beast looked like a lizard, but made armies of metal men. The hunt ended in the clouds, and the beast was sent away on a special cloud. That was the story, coded into the architecture. The Winkies were known the land over for their skill in metalcraft, but they were not prone to underestimate strangers in their land. Even in a time of peace, under a king such as this one, they were wary.

King Winko danced a ceremonial kingly jig on the way up to his throne. He stood in front of his throne and continued his fancy dancing as he addressed the girls.

"I am King Winko, son of King Lanternhans, keeper of the rainbow mist. I have ruled this people for fifty years and there has been peace. To strangers in my kingdom, a very done deed has been closely watched. I, by rights, have the way open to me to hang you outside by your pigtails—"

Wickrie-Kells whispered to Glinda, "You don't wear your hair in pigtails."

"And I'm not going to start, either." Glinda whispered back.

King Winko continued, unfazed by the girls, "—until such time as the dinner bell rings, for your intrusion into my personal space as I pursued my daily frolic. How do you plead?"

"I don't plead very well." Glinda jutted out her jaw defiantly.

"Well enough, I should hope, to preserve a modicum of civility." The king retorted. "I suppose merriment must wait. So who are you?"

Wickrie-Kells stepped forward to answer, but Glinda stopped her. "I am Glinda. This is Wickrie-Kells. A powerful villain has emerged and destroyed the Ruby Palace. The King Oz of the Emerald Lands is dead. You might be next. We need your army to stop this destruction."

King Winko stopped cold in the middle of his jig. His belly jiggled once. Then he stared in disbelief. Then his belly jiggled again and he could not hold in the chuckle. "*You?* You want to *borrow* my army?" He roared with laughter. Everyone in the room around them clutched their sides they were laughing so hard.

"I don't see what is funny about that. My mother is gone. My father may be dead. Everything I have is gone. And now you are laughing."

King Winko wiped his eyes as he tried to stand up, but he couldn't. He put one hand out to the arm of the throne. "It's just that you are a little girl. Girls don't lead armies, and they never will." He slapped his knee, "*Girls* leading an *army!*"

"This is a bad idea." Glinda said to Wickrie-Kells. "We should go."

"We can't." Wickrie-Kells replied. "We're arrested."

The king composed himself and nodded solemnly at Glinda. "You are arrested. And that can be a very sad thing. Especially when you have such marvelous delusions of grandeur. You actually want my army, don't you? And you thought I would just give it to you?"

Wickrie-Kells stepped forward, "Your majesty, if you only knew—"

"Pish posh and summer squash." The king waved both hands to silence her, but Wickrie-Kells continued.

"—she is Glinda, daughter of Gayelette, Red Sorceress of the North, and Queen of the Ruby Palace."

All of the laughter stopped. They all stared at Glinda.

King Winko plopped right back in his throne. "That makes a difference." He said, nodding very solemnly.

A messenger arrived, breathless and frantic. "Majesty, A witch queen is approaching with an army of soldiers. She demands complete surrender of Winkie Country!"

King Winko rose up to his full height and puffed out his chest, but it didn't quite peek out over his round belly. "Never! Who is this impresario that demands such demands?"

"Ondri-baba, Queen of the West. She has two other witches with her."

"Prepare the army. We march immediately, if not sooner!"

The Winkie army was not a large one. At its greatest strength, there were nearly three hundred Winkies. Most of these were farmers and metal workers conscripted to serve as a means of ensuring adequate patrols for the land. Only fifty trained soldiers existed in all of Winkie Country, and more than half of those were gray-headed old men, given prime positions in the king's honor guard.

Many years had passed since war had come to Winkie Country, so the army was primarily used for parades. The army did not have much to offer the rising generation in a time of peace. Certainly there were great heroic stories of the past that left the young boys starry-eyed and yearning for glory, but the opportunities were few and far between. Mostly the opportunities for soldiers lay in patrols and training. For more than two generations there had been peace, so a sense of complacency sat heavily on the people. It was good, and it had been good for almost as long as anyone could remember, so why worry unnecessarily?

Still, there were a few young men who joined the army as soldiers. Some of these young men were exceptional warriors indeed. They exhibited skill and talent in the martial arts, and they learned from the decades of experience contained in the honor guard. Unfortunately, there were not enough young men who chose a life in the Winkie army to replace the older generation, which meant simply that the military capability of the Winkie army was in drastic decline.

All fifty of these warriors, along with whatever farmers or merchants that heard the call, quickly gathered in front of the Yellow Castle. The gray soldiers stood in the front, wielding their long spears. If this was truly to be war, then their spears would be the first to draw blood. The young men were at the back of the army, organized by rank. Behind them were the volunteer soldiers. There were less than one hundred soldiers in total.

Glinda and Wickric-Kells stood behind the king as he overlooked his army from the balcony. In the distant south they saw the brown wave from earlier in the day. It had followed the brick road, taking the easier route. The muddy wave consisted of hundreds of shifting figures, seemingly made of sand, marching toward the fields of battle. Behind them was a strange walking contraption, like a hut on legs. It walked stiffly behind the army. At a command from the hut, the sandy army stopped.

A black-and-blue-robed figure walked out in front of the ranks. Even from this far distance, Glinda saw the twinkling silver at her feet. "Kalinya." Glinda whispered. Wickrie-Kells cast a worried glance over to her friend. Then she took her hand and squeezed it to give her courage.

They watched as a Winkie runner ran out to confer with the witch. Glinda felt a dread anticipation in her heart as the runner came back to Yellow Castle.

"They are asking for the red-haired sorceress." The returned Winkie runner informed King Winko.

King Winko turned to Glinda, "You came to me asking for my army, and on your heels another army arrives. You, perhaps, would have doomed my entire people to destruction or even slavery. I bear you no ill will, but you are highly suspect, daughter of Gayelette. If you are as you say, your magic will protect you. If not, may the great faeries watch you and carry you to your reward. If you so desire, I will send my standard bearer with you."

Glinda thanked the king politely, but refused the offer. The runner, a green-haired young soldier watched as Glinda turned nervously and walked out the door. He caught the eye of Wickrie-Kells and gave her a hopeful smile, accompanied by a wink and a nod. Flattered, Wickrie-Kells smiled back, and then hurried after her friend.

Glinda walked out the front gate and through the ranks of the assembled army. It took every ounce of courage she had to keep moving forward. Step by step she marched out to the field. Even with Wickrie-Kells at her side, believing, she was trembling.

When they approached hailing distance, Kalinya called out, "Leave your friend. This is between you and me, Glinda."

Glinda turned to Wickrie-Kells and embraced her.

"I have a sword." Wickrie offered.

Glinda forced a smile through the clustered tears that were too frightened to fall. "No. She wouldn't do anything in the open like this."

"Are you sure?"

Glinda shook her head. "No. But that's what I'm telling myself." She blinked away the frightened mist in her eyes and took a deep breath. She walked toward the wicked witch, leaving her best friend and the proffered sword behind her. She stared straight ahead, trusting and hoping that her courage was leading her right.

Kalinya tried to smile warmly as Glinda approached, but it looked cold and menacing. "Glinda, child, what are you doing here? Ondri-baba saw you early this morning with her eye, but we could not catch you in time. We could have prevented this messiness."

"What messiness? The only mess I see is your dirty army. What are you doing? I thought you wanted nothing to do with your sister."

Kalinya stiffened in anger. Through clenched teeth, she forced out, "Ondri-baba has plans for this land. I have agreed to help her."

"There's plenty of dirt. Your army should be right at home."

"It's not my army, it's hers."

Glinda felt a strange shifting of emotion as she faced this wicked opponent. Kalinya seemed to shrink in Glinda's eyes. She dropped in size from the dark giant of a witch to a rat-sized squeaker trapped in a cage. With that image in her mind, Glinda fought the urge to giggle. "You're working for your sister?"

Rage flashed in Kalinya's eyes, and Glinda knew that she had struck a nerve.

Glinda clapped her hands over her own mouth to suppress the giggles trying to fight their way out.

Kalinya glared, and then forced the words out between clenched teeth, "I do not *work* for my sister. I came here to offer you a way out. This is not your war. The Winkies *will* be conquered. Ondri-baba will rule the West. You do not have to make their fate your own."

"You killed my mother."

"You hated your mother." and with that point, Kalinya swung the advantage back to her side, and Glinda was again on the defensive.

"That's not the point!"

"I offer you the chance to join me. Join me and we can rule all of Oz. I will be the mother you always wanted. You can be the daughter I need. We will free the Winkies from Ondri-baba. We will free all of the nations from the other witches. They will not be able to stand against our combined powers."

Glinda shook her head. "No." She continued shaking her head, as if the action would force her mind to believe what her mouth was saying.

"No?"

"I said no." But Glinda's voice was not firm. She was wavering. "I don't want to. I don't trust you. I don't trust that you won't do to me what you did to my mother."

Kalinya's rage was now white-hot. Her fists clenched and all of the ground around them began to shake. "If you will not join me, then you will be destroyed by me!"

Great mounds of dirt shook all around them. Kalinya pulled up loose dirt and whirled it around in a vortex.

Glinda's eyes grew wide as she saw her doom rising up in front of her, but she could not move. She noticed her red hair blowing in front of her face. Even though one hair blew into her eye, she could not move her hands to brush it away. The vortex surrounded Kalinya and expanded outwards toward Glinda. The wind howled, but Glinda only stared. In that moment, Glinda thought about the Toad Prince, one of her books, and how she would never get the chance to kiss a prince and turn him handsome. Instead, I have a wicked witch who has intentionally become ugly.

Just then a rock flew from behind Glinda and hit Kalinya in the head. The whirling vortex of dirt fell to the ground as Kalinya's concentration cracked. Wickrie-Kells grabbed Glinda by the hand and pulled her back toward the Yellow Castle.

At the sight of this attack on their general, the sandy armies moved forward.

On the other end of the field, the Winkies also moved forward into battle to meet their enemies.

It was late afternoon when the sandy army charged the Winkie Plains. Clouds darkened the sky, threatening rain. Distant thunder echoed the pounding of hundreds of feet. Glinda and Wickrie-Kells raced toward the charging Winkie army, seeking safety. A mound of earth crashed and exploded in front of them, hurling the two girls apart.

All around them was flying sand and exploding dirt and people screaming, but Glinda couldn't make sense of it. She looked back at the sandy army behind her, but she couldn't see past all of the yellow uniforms pushing forward. The Winkies were not taking the invasion of their country lightly. They battled valiantly against their inhuman adversaries. They battled out of fear, and anger, and insult. Nobody marches in and conquers the Winkies—it had never happened, and it would not happen today.

For a brief moment it appeared that the Winkies had the upper hand. Their initial charge plowed into the sandy army and decimated more than half of the soldiers. But the Winkies were few, and the sandy soldiers kept coming. After a soldier fell and the Winkies moved on, the witches came in and reformed the soldier into humanoid form. For all of the damage that the Winkies did, the numbers of sandy soldiers dropped by next to nothing.

Glinda looked around, but she could not see Wickrie-Kells anywhere. Then a great shadow rose over her. A giant sand warrior, at least ten feet tall towered up. It must have been made from the remnants of at least three fallen soldiers—that would explain the multiple arms. It raised a huge fist to crush down on Glinda, when it suddenly exploded!

Sand showered everywhere. Glinda looked up to see the wicked witch Kalinya standing over her. The wind whipped around and thunder boomed. A gust of wind swirled around them, bringing with it the smell of falling rain.

"You will find that I have a sliver of pity, Glinda. I could have let you die there. Or are you so much like your mother that you refuse to die?"

"I thought you said she begged for mercy?" Glinda questioned.

Thunder cracked the sky. The clouds rolled and boiled above the battlefield. The sound of rain pounding the ground grew nearer. A strange inhuman wailing went up. The rain pounded the sand creatures and they were screaming without lungs, a husky, nasally sound that set Glinda's nerves on edge.

"You have *ten seconds*, Glinda. *Ten seconds*, and then I will let the beasts destroy you. *Ten -*" Behind Kalinya, several sandy warriors were silhouetted against the cracking lightning. Glinda couldn't hear for several thudding heartbeats. "*—five, four -*"

Three bolts of lightning struck near them, and the smell of ozone drenched the air. Kalinya panicked, and in three steps she disappeared, leaving Glinda alone in the shadow of the sand giants.

A devastating thunderclap convulsed the ground, interrupting the entire field of battle. Everyone stopped and stared upward at the unnatural storm boiling lower and lower. Above Glinda, the dark clouds roiled and churned, dropping closer, brushing the ground with their wet fingertips.

Then the clouds parted above Glinda, opening the sky and bathing a patch of ground in pure sunlight. In the center of this grounded patch of sunlight, Glinda looked upward, shading her eyes with her hand. Time stopped completely as she stared into the otherworldly rift in the sky. It was as if two distinct and real worlds connected for the briefest of moments. Lightning flashed, and the clouds closed up again.

But the clouds had birthed a strange new thing. Suspended from a great floating sphere was a basket. Inside this basket was a young man with dark hair. His brown eyes were wide as he looked down at the scene below. Then his eyes locked with Glinda's. Time stretched out to infinity in each direction as their eyes joined and they saw each other.

"Watch out!" his voice cried out as the basket came closer. Glinda stared unblinking as the basket raced closer and closer.

The basket flew directly at Glinda's head. At the last instant, she recognized the danger, and she fell to the ground, narrowly dodging the impact. The large sandy warrior directly behind her, however, did not move, and the basket decimated that warrior in an explosion of sand. The basket caught and held fast in the sand, losing its forward momentum.

The basket slowly dragged on the ground for a few more feet, and the large sphere slowly lost its shape in the pouring rain and dropped to the ground. Looking up from the ground, Glinda noticed that the sphere had, in large letters, written on it, *"O"* and *"Z"*.

The sandy warriors continued to push forward. The sheets of rain sliced into them, starting in the east by the high ridge. Where the drops hit the sandy warriors, the sand darkened. In some cases, a little bit of sand came off them.

One of the warriors approached the basket. It was carrying a spear that it had taken from a fallen Winkie soldier. It raised the spear high into the air to stab the basket.

"YOU SHALL NOT!" boomed a voice from the basket, echoing across the battlefield.

The soldier froze. At that moment, lightning flashed out the sky, the forked bolt streaking toward the ground. It struck the highest metal point in the vicinity, which just happened to be the raised spear. The lightning struck with a *crackle-boom.* And the sandy soldier was immediately super-cooked, the tremendous heat turning the sand into glass.

Glinda looked at the basket. From the other side of the basket, just above the ground, peeked a male face, handsome in a slightly toadish way, just a little bit older than her. In this face were the same eyes she had seen just a few moments before, but now, at the foot of the glass statue, she saw that he was far more than he had at first appeared. Where he had been, just moments before, a mysterious person from the sky, there was no doubt now, that he was a wizard with great powers. After all, he had called down lightning, right?

"Hi there." He said.

"Hi." said Glinda.

He rolled out of the basket and crawled over to Glinda. He offered his hand and pulled Glinda to her feet. So intense were Glinda eyes focused on this mysterious stranger, that she did not even notice, as she took his hand, that there were now twelve of the sandy soldiers surrounding them.

The young man was just as intensely focused on Glinda. "I am Oscar Zoroaster Diggs, known through stages across the West as Oz the Great."

13 THE SOLDIER WITH GREEN HAIR

Glinda held the proffered hand and cocked her head slightly at Oscar. Then she realized she was staring, and she blushed, averting her eyes. She looked up under her lashes to see that the boy was still looking at her.

"Circumstances are not ideal for courting. We have a less-than-friendly jury." Oscar quipped, looking around at the twelve sand monsters around them.

"I'm Glinda."

The sand monsters pressed in closer to them. "Any thoughts?" Oscar asked. "Giant cats, litter boxes, hand puppets…no. Nothing that will work."

Just then a *clank-roar* sounded behind them, like a wheel of metal plates crashing against the pitter-patter of rain. A large caged wheel rolled right over the top of half of the monsters, shredding the sand and dissolving the magical bonds. A large contraption, composed of a large hollow wheel with running legs inside and large suspended baskets outside, skidded to a stop in front of Oscar and Glinda.

Wickrie-Kells leaped out and swung a spear at the nearest sand monster. Right behind her, the soldier with green hair pulled a golden sword and effortlessly took down three of the remaining sand monsters. Within a minute, the remaining sand monsters were scattered to the wind and rain.

Wickrie-Kells planted her spear in the ground. "And they say girls can't lead armies."

Glinda stared in surprise. The soldier with green hair sheathed his golden sword and nodded politely at Glinda.

"This is Omby-Amby." Wickrie-Kells smiled. "Isn't he great?"

"Ombrosius Ambrosius." He corrected, preferring the more formal name for first introductions. "We have a ride for you back to the castle. The storm is gathering strength. Good for us, but bad for our sandy scrappers." He gestured to the vehicle. "The *Hamstrambulator* will get us back in a swifty-jif."

Oscar cleared his throat. "I'm Oscar, known throughout—"

"Neat to meet you, Oscar. Come out of the sky to join her? Nice work. Hop on then."

"Won't the lightning strike the metal? That could cause some problems if we're riding, couldn't it?" Oscar asked warily. Though the sandy soldiers were stirring nearby, taking note of the strange vehicle, Oscar showed no inclination to climb aboard.

"Not a bit." Wickrie-Kells answered. "Omby-Amby has it grounded. The more lightning strikes, the faster the legs run." She patted the baskets to show how grounded it was.

"How fast can it run?" Oscar asked.

"Let's find out. Got a visitor." Omby-Amby gestured with his eyebrow behind Oscar, who ducked just in time to avoid a giant fist in the side of the head. Oscar reached out his hand from the ground and Omby-Amby grabbed him. He pulled him into the basket just as lightning struck the large flexible antenna of the Hamstrambulator. The wheel kicked up sand as it sped away from the monsters. Wickrie-Kells was right. The legs did run faster.

The Hamstrambulator had a pair of metal legs inside the large wheel that ran around—a hamster wheel, but on a much larger scale. As the legs ran, the wheel rolled. The baskets were suspended above the wheel on a frame for passengers to ride in. The Hamstrambulator wheel spun and kicked up dirt as it raced back to the Yellow Castle.

Behind them, the sandy armies were pelted with rain from above. The witches gathered the fallen sand and moved their armies away from the rain. Glinda pulled her wet hair out of her eyes and looked up at the clouds. They were gingerly poking at the shafts of light coming from two of the Yellow Castle towers, experimenting to test the power of the light.

The clouds acted as if they wanted to get beyond the light into the great sky beyond. They were actually stopped at an invisible line marked by the Yellow Castle. Glinda pointed this observation out to her friends, "The clouds aren't going beyond the castle. I wonder if we can push them back. That would push the armies back! *Hurry!* We've got to get up there!"

"We've got to get those towers lit! Drive the clouds back into the army!" Omby-Amby shouted orders as he ran up the stairs.

The Winkies raised a network of metal rods, attracting lightning strikes to the Yellow Castle and lighting up all of the towers. The entire castle lit up just like a lantern.

The clouds reared back, dismayed at the sudden change. Then, like animals stopped in a bright light, the clouds froze. Then they fled back in the direction they had come—inland. But they were so low to the ground that they could only go as far inland as the high ridge. The only other direction available was south. As the clouds retreated, so did the sandy army flee before them. The battle was won, but the cost was terrible. Nearly half of the Winkie army had fallen. It was unknown how many of the sandy soldiers were truly gone.

They watched the sandy army retreat in front of the dark clouds. For hours the rain fell, saturating the rocky soil and flooding the ground.

King Winko joined Glinda out on the south balcony. "It will be several days before the slopes will be firm enough to travel up. The witches control the road south. The floods here in the valley will keep the mud monsters away. We're safe until then." He paused and took a deep breath.

"I owe you an apology, Princess Glinda. These witches *are* what you said they were, and I did not believe you. However, I cannot cede control of my army to you. Not the least reason is because you are a *girl*. But also because they are needed here. We have been dealt heavy cards—our losses are great. It will require all the soldiers we have just to maintain the lands of our possession."

The air was cold in the aftermath of the storm. Fog appeared over the flooded fields. Glinda wrapped her arms around herself to try to keep out the chill of loneliness and isolation that she felt. "I want to go home. King Winko, will you at least grant me safe passage back to the North?"

The sun had set, and stars were twinkling above them. The moon had not yet risen, and a chill wind blew above the valley. Oscar shuffled his feet behind them, drawing attention to himself. "I'm a long way from home, myself. I'd like to go home, too. But I'd like even more to know where *here* is? This doesn't look much like Nebraska."

Glinda spent the first half of the night talking with Oscar on the balcony. Servants provided blankets for them, and brought them food, and then left them alone.

"So, *Nebraska*? Where is that?" Glinda asked.

"In the middle of everything. Well, it's in the middle of nothing, actually. No, that's not true. It's a territory of the United States; just this year, in fact. We may get to be an actual state someday."

Glinda smiled like she understood, but her eyes wandered in a way that implied that she did not.

"I've been a lot of places. Been in front of a great many audiences." Oscar said.

"Up on stage? Like at the Abracadabra Bazaar?"

"Um... yes?"

"I knew it. That's what wizards and witches do. You probably amazed them with your magic every single time."

Oscar's eyes shifted. "I do better when it's only my voice they see."

"What does that mean? You can be invisible?"

"No, not exactly like that. It's just—" Oscar tried a new tactic. He cleared his throat and then a bird whistled behind Glinda. She turned, but saw nothing. Oscar looked back at her, puzzled. Then it whistled off to the side of him.

"There's an invisible bird!" Glinda exclaimed.

"Maybe there is." smiled Oscar. "If you're really still, it might land on your shoulder."

Glinda held very still. Oscar reached out and brushed Glinda's hair off of her shoulder. A quiet whistle sounded near Glinda's ear. She grinned ear to ear.

Oscar whispered, "Can you feel it on your shoulder?"

Glinda closed her eyes and smiled. "I feel it" she breathed.

A twittering whistle sounded, and Glinda held her breath. Then a flapping sounded above them, and the whistle sputtered into a stifled shriek as Oscar leaped backwards. Glinda opened her eyes as King Klick dropped to the balcony in front of Oscar.

Oscar scrambled backwards until he crashed into the wall at the side of the door. His mouth gaped open like a fish and his eyes bulged. He had never seen such a creature as a Winged Monkey and it terrified him.

"King Klick!" Glinda embraced the Winged Monkey. "I am happy to see you. There has been so much that has happened."

King Klick smiled a mischievous smile at the trembling young man at the wall, and then turned to Glinda. "I have a message from your father. The man-Quelala desires to see you."

"Wha–what is that?" Oscar pointed at the Winged Monkey.

Glinda turned to Oscar, who was now pale as a ghost. King Klick screeched and jumped onto the wall right above Oscar and hopped around, hooting. Oscar scrambled around and might have jumped off the balcony had Glinda not grabbed on to him. "Your Majesty, please stop! You're tormenting him! Enough. Enough of your fun."

King Klick laughed to see Oscar trembling. Oscar would not even look at the monkey.

"King Klick, this is Oscar Diggs, a great wizard from a…country," she glanced at Oscar for confirmation.

"Territory." He corrected quietly, sitting down next to Glinda by the metal balcony railing. He could not make eye contact with the monkey.

"*Territory*, of Nebraska. Somewhere far from here. He came from the sky in a flying basket and called down lightning to save me from the sand monsters."

"I have seen these creatures." answered King Klick. "They are not *natural* magic. They are from some magic not native to this land. The Witches spread their wickedness."

He turned to Oscar, "Many apologies, great wizard. My purpose was mischief only. It is the nature of the Winged Monkeys to seek fun, even at the expense of others. I thank you for saving Princess Glinda. She is daughter of the man-Quelala, to whom I owe my life, and the life of my people."

Oscar struggled to his feet. He still couldn't look at the strange creature. Monkeys were not supposed to talk, and they were definitely not supposed to have wings or fly. Something was very different about this land, or maybe this was all normal, and Oscar was the one who was different.

When the morning sun rose on the yellow land, a stately procession entered the throne room of King Winko. King Klick was ushered in as representative of his people, to enter into an alliance with the Winkies. At his side were Brutus and Beriyel, to witness the binding of two peoples. King Winko and his advisors unrolled the parchment. Glinda stood by and watched as they formally made an alliance to fight against the wicked witches.

The Winged Monkeys promised to fly patrols over the Winkie Country and bring word to the Winkie generals. In return, the Winkies gave nets of fine metal mesh to the Winged Monkeys. These could be used against the sandy warriors to break the magical connection. Each monkey was given a net of the fine metal. The metalwork was so fine that the net could be folded up and tucked into a belt pouch.

King Winko solemnly pronounced a blessing on this alliance.

"With these links, forged by my people, and placed in your hands, we bind the fates of our people together."

14 THE ALLIANCE FOR FREEDOM

Glinda hurried about, making preparations for the journey north. King Winko had agreed to provide the resources to get Glinda and her friends back to Gillikin country.

King Klick was engaged in continual meetings with the Winkie generals, so he was not able to converse with Glinda any more. Oscar was just as happy not having the monkey around. The monkey delighted in tormenting him. Glinda seemed to find it funny, even though she tried hard not to. She tried to hide her smiles, but Oscar had been up on stage—he knew when something was funny by watching their eyes. And Glinda's eyes would glitter and shine whenever Oscar was around.

Oscar gladly helped Glinda with all of her travel preparations, and learned a lot about her in the process. He found ample opportunity to summon "invisible birds" for the entertainment of both Winkies and Glinda alike. He dared not tell them it was just a vocal trick called *ventriloquism*. They thought him a wizard, and so he was, at least in their minds. He could play the part for a while. It was just another part—one of many. They wanted a show, and that was something he knew how to do well.

Oscar was a showman. After he went west he shared his stories with people. They tossed him coins to take them away from their world, if only for a few moments. With the small treasure he was able to purchase passage to the West—far away from his history. He made a new life on the stage, dreaming out loud. It didn't take him long to develop quite a name for himself. One of the famous circuses even hired him on as an entertainer. They gave him his first top hat and coat. Both were emerald green. He wore the coat inside out most of the time when he traveled among the people. It was only in front of certain audiences at the circus that he wore the emerald green and called himself Oz.

Oscar had effectively changed his world. He was no longer just Oscar, who could not bear to see his mother cry. He was Oz, the Great, known on stages all across the West. Now he was here, in this much different place. He had worked as both a ventriloquist and a balloonist for a famous circus on the edge of the uncivilized territory, entertaining frontier towns and army forts. This was a castle, it was the middle of a war, and so it was not all that much different than the American frontier. The people wore different clothes, but an audience is an audience anywhere in the world. He loved the attention from the people—they listened to him.

Oscar especially liked the attention from Glinda. He noticed that she made the effort to eavesdrop whenever he started to tell a story. One interesting thing that Oscar noticed was that Glinda was the only one who had red hair. Where he had come from, red hair was not common, but it was not unheard of. Here, though, Glinda's red hair was completely unique. That made her special.

He looked into the kitchen and saw that Wickrie-Kells and Glinda were preparing food for the journey northward, so Oscar went down to the stables to talk with Omby-Amby. He wasn't mechanically handy, but he needed to feel useful as everyone else prepared for the trip. He wanted to see if he could help with the Hamstrambulator. The shiny vehicle fascinated him. It worked on different principles of locomotion than Oscar had ever seen in use before. He was familiar with the steam driven locomotive engines that were coming from the East to the West in America, but this was completely different. It was not powered by burning fuel of any sort.

"So, how does it work?" Oscar asked.

"Smith & Tinker gave it as a gift to King Winko on his day of coronation. It's got legs inside, it goes really fast and it's shiny. This lever raises the baskets. These tilt the main wheel side to side and this button makes the legs really run. I learned how to fix most of it when it broke. King Winko, bless his jolly feet, he drives just like he dances—like an old man."

"So why does he let you drive it?" Oscar ran his fingers over the smooth metal.

"Because only I can fix it."

"And I can only assume that you do not drive like an old man?"

"Life is too short to move slow." Omby-Amby handed Oscar a wrench, "Make sure the baskets are tight." And Oscar scrambled up into the front basket.

"Have you always lived here?" Oscar asked the green-haired young man. "I mean, what other places are there here? Is this Winkie country connected to California?"

"I don't know of any place called California," Omby-Amby said, tightening a bolt on the mechanical legs, "But I've been a few places in Oz. My mum is from the Emerald Lands."

The basket dropped almost to the floor. Oscar peeked out from the basket sheepishly.

Omby-Amby frowned, then laughed at Oscar's sheepish expression. He stood and pointed into the basket. "Not that one, *that* one."

Oscar tightened the correct bolt and lifted the driving basket back into position. "Thanks. Sorry about that. But you said *Oz*. That reminds me, why is this place called Oz?"

"Oz is a fairy word meaning *'great and good'*. It is the name of this whole land, surrounded by desert. There are five countries—one on each side, like a square, but more of a rectangle, and then the Emerald Lands, in the center. Greener than my hair, is what I hear. In history, there has usually been a king or queen named Oz or Ozma that ruled the Emerald Lands." He scratched at his green hair with a wrench. "Only now there's Pastoria. He was the Seventeenth King Oz's brother. Kings don't die unless they want to. People say that there was an accident." He dropped his head and went back to inspecting the right foot inside the bit wheel, "There have been a lot of accidents recently."

After a few moments of silence, it was Omby-Amby's turn to ask questions. "What about you? That thing you rode in with the basket said OZ on the side."

"Balloon. It was a balloon—my balloon. My name is Oscar Zoroaster Diggs. I was a balloonist sometimes; it got people to come and see." Oscar stared off into the past, "It was so quiet up there. Nobody to cry...but nobody to laugh, either. Dreams were just silent. But anyway, the balloon was filled with gas to float up in the air. When I would perform on stage, I took the name Oz because of my initials, O-Z.

"But I want to go back to that last thing you said. Recently there've been accidents. How recently?"

Omby-Amby slammed the metal foot down on the inner wheel. "The witches always generally kept to themselves. Not even my grandfather recalled a time when they were so angry as they are now. There have always been witches in all of the countries. Usually just one, but sometimes more. It started with Gayelette, that's Glinda's mum. She was a sorceress that refused to die. See, like I said, kings are the only ones who don't die—I mean the Emerald Kings, everyone else dies. Only Gayelette didn't. She lived in the Ruby Palace. People say that she did strange things in there."

Oscar listened intently. The wrench dropped from his fingers, but he didn't even notice. This was the inside scoop on Glinda's family. Newspapers would eat this stuff up, if they even had newspapers in this land. He knew that Glinda should be the one to tell him private family business, but he was insanely curious, and couldn't wait for the proper occasion to ask her. "Go on."

"There were things that happened at night. Things that she would see. Nobody I ever heard knew what they meant. I don't know what happened. I just heard that things did happen. And then Kalinya destroyed the Ruby Palace and likely killed Glinda's mum."

Oscar mused on this newfound knowledge. "But not her father?"

Omby-Amby shook his head. "Not a bit. That's why we're going north. I have leave of King Winko to drive Glinda back to her homeland. I assume since the monkey honors you, you're going as her protector. And," he smiled, "Wickrie-Kells is going, too."

Far out on the rocky plains, Ondri-baba watched with her magical eye as the Hamstrambulator drove northward. She raged and threw a colossal tantrum as she saw them escaping. Immediately she called her generals to her. "They are escaping!" She cried. "They are afraid, so they are running away! They cannot do that! It is not fair."

Kalinya's eyes hardened against her sister. "Perhaps you should chase them."

An idea popped into Ondri-baba's normal green eye. "Yes. You're right. You can certainly manage the siege of Winkie Country here. I will go after them. Besides, they have that shiny rolling machine. I want it. It certainly makes this walking house look stale, doesn't it?"

So Ondri-baba gathered her strongest sand warriors and galloped northward in her awkward stilt-legged hut. She did not even give a second thought to leaving her armies under the control of her generals—her enemies.

As Kalinya said of her sister as she galumphed away, "She expects loyalty, but she is easily distracted by bright, shiny objects."

Dozens of Winged Monkeys circled over Yellow Castle when the Hamstrambulator rolled out. The Winkie people were gathered to bid the four young people farewell. They were most distressed to see Omby-Amby—the greatest young warrior in their army—leaving them. King Klick assigned four of his monkeys to go with them on their journey, including Brutus.

Despite the fanfare and sad celebrations, the people were very aware of the sandy armies lying just beyond the drying mud flats. The only thing that kept their enemies away from them was the soggy terrain. Even that barrier would not last long against the heat of the day. The women sang songs and the men sharpened their swords.

Omby-Amby waved his farewell to his people. He and Oscar had polished the Hamstrambulator so that it gleamed in the morning sun. Omby-Amby spun the vehicle around in the courtyard and raced away, spitting up dirt.

Children and young monkeys ran after them as they raced across the muddy fields toward the north pass.

For the remainder of the day Omby-Amby drove the Hamstrambulator north. Above them flew their contingent of monkey guards. They group stopped for the night in the meadow of the night blossoms.

Glinda recognized the field. "This is where we came, where my father brought us that night. The flowers glowed."

"There are no petals on the flowers." Wickrie-Kells held up a withered stem. "They are dead."

"There are other green things growing here." Glinda responded.

"But the one thing that made this meadow special, different from all of the other meadows, is dead. Don't you realize what happened here, Glinda?"

Omby-Amby raised his eyebrows, and Oscar quickly turned to help him with the Hamstrambulator. They left the girls to figure this one out on their own.

"Honestly, I haven't given it much thought." Glinda shot back. "Why don't you tell me what happened here."

"War. This is what happens when war happens—things get killed."

"It's a flower. It's not a person."

"And what is the definition of a person? Does a thing have to look like you to be important?"

"It certainly helps."

"And does it have to be from here? What about Oscar? Is he a person? He's not from here. Or is he a person because you think he's cute?"

Oscar heard his name and perked up, but Omby-Amby shook his head, so Oscar went back to untying the tents.

"You're going too far. It's just a flower."

"But from the way you told me the story, it was the most beautiful thing you ever saw. And now it's withered and gone. Glinda, you don't seem to care."

"That's not fair. I'm almost home. King Klick said that he saw my father. I just want some answers."

"Well, I hope you find them. Then we can go back to the way it was before, again."

15 THE SECRET OF THE ELDERS

Late the next morning, they arrived at their destination—North Village. Glinda walked up the central street. She held her head up high, even though the people stopped and stared. Everyone looked at her strangely as the red-haired girl walked past with her three strangers. Things had been quiet in the village up until now. The older people frowned, and the younger people came to life as they saw adventure strolling up the central avenue.

A few of the young men gravitated toward the Hamstrambulator. They gathered around, one of them getting enough courage to reach out to touch the beautiful chrome. Omby-Amby was happy to show off his shiny vehicle to all of the admiring viewers, including a few Gillikin girls. Glinda saw Wickrie-Kells giving the evil eye to more than one of the smitten Gillikin girls. After the tense evening last night, Glinda was glad to get some space away from her best friend. Glinda saw more than one local girl that seemed to be more interested in the handsome driver than the exotic vehicle, so she turned Wickrie-Kells back to the young man with green hair. "Play nice with the local girls. We won't be long."

Wickrie-Kells happily turned back from the street to go back to Omby-Amby. She was nearly a head taller than most of the girls, and they stepped back to give her wide berth as she came to lean on the lowered basket. Her eyes shifted from Omby-Amby's face to the two girls that didn't step back. They got the message and smiled tightly, swishing their skirts as they turned and walked away. Wickrie-Kells allowed herself a smile and shifted her gaze back to Omby-Amby. He was watching them. Wickrie-Kells raised an eyebrow, and the soldier with green hair smiled bashfully.

Glinda and Oscar headed toward the fairgrounds. Only a few short weeks ago, Glinda had watched as Smith & Tinker sold the presumably innocent wares—the hourglasses— that were now the tools of war in Oz. More than a few of the townspeople glared at Glinda as she smiled cautiously at them. They recognized her and they were none too happy to have her back.

Oscar waved to a few of the onlookers, who just stared in return. He commented on their cold reception. "They don't like us very much, do they?"

"I thought they loved my mother. She ruled the people fairly. My father always said that the people wanted freedom and my mother gave them just enough."

"Freedom is an interesting thing." Oscar said. "Where I came from, freedom was an idea that caught fire in the hearts of many people. They fought wars to be free—lots of wars. *'No taxation without representation,'* they said. They formed the United States of America. Had a Constitution that laid out all of the things that government should do, and specified in no uncertain terms that whatever the government was not specifically authorized to do, it could not do."

"I've never heard of such a thing." Glinda remarked.

Oscar continued, "Each person has freedoms that they are born with. These are not given by another person, nor can they be taken away by another person, or even by a ruling government. Freedom of speech, freedom to print newspapers and books, freedom of religion, and freedom to peaceably assemble. They can also gather peacefully to petition for redress of grievances. Not riot and demand, but peaceably petition. They can ask that their leaders stop whatever it is they don't like. These are just the beginning of the rights that each person has."

Glinda thought deeply about this. Her brows furrowed as she digested these strange and wonderful new concepts. "There has been no ruler in any land that has addressed these ideas. They make sense. But who ensures that the people are taken care of?"

Oscar smiled broadly. He was finally able to talk about history—the backbone of the stories that he enjoyed the most. It took his mind off of the strange land that he had been brought to. "If the king, or ruler, or government just gets out of the way and lets people be the best they can be, then people will naturally do what they are good at doing. For some people that is being a farmer. For others it may be writing. For me, it was stories. I love history and stories. But I had to pay my way in the world. *Nobody gets something for nothing,* my father would say. He...he had some different plans for me." Oscar drifted off, remembering, and then quickly shook his head and smiled, moving on. "We saw the world through different spectacles. He was a man of war. I was not." Oscar forced a hard smile, and Glinda pretended not to notice. "So I worked up on the stage, or for the circus, whatever was the next audience. I went up in the balloon."

"Wait a minute, you said, *'nobody gets something for nothing,'* where did you come up with that? I've never heard that before."

"My father would always say it to me. He always found a way to put that into every conversation. It means that you have to work for what you get. I've been working since I was a young man, big enough to carry a satchel. Not all work involves blades or guns, though. Don't you have people that work here?"

"Of course people work. They are expected to work. And then the kings and queens give them carnivals and fairs to show how good they are. It's a reward for the people."

"But what about the people themselves? Do they work because they enjoy working? Or is it because they are expected to work, and they will be punished if they don't work?" Oscar asked.

Glinda stopped in her tracks. She cocked her head to one side and looked quizzically at Oscar. "I—I don't know."

"Something to think about. Give a man something to do that he loves doing, and he will do amazing things."

Glinda managed to obtain an audience with the town elder, Bombo, an old man who had been blind for years. They sat at a table in the council house and watched him eat mashed potatoes with pepper. When he finished and wiped his beard, Bombo cleared his throat and folded his gnarled hands in front of him on the table. "I am told that Glinda, the daughter of the late Queen Gayelette, the Red Sorceress and Queen of the Ruby Palace, is before me. To what do I owe the reasoning of this audience?"

Oscar moved to speak, but Glinda motioned him silent. She thought back over all of the stories and books she had read of etiquette before she answered. "I am glad to meet you today. I have returned to this, my home, after a long journey."

"But *this* is not your home."

"I was born here." Glinda protested.

"You were born in the Ruby Palace. And the Ruby Palace is no longer here. Where it is, nobody knows, but *here* no longer encompasses that place."

"I want to know about my mother."

"Your mother was a queen. She was a sorceress. What more is there to know?"

Glinda glared at the unseeing man. "What is that supposed to mean?"

"A child of privilege is not meant to see the underbelly of the kingdom. Your mother kept you far away from us. She kept us far away from you. Do you ever wonder why you never saw any of our people by your tower?" Bombo did not wait for her reply before he continued, "It was because you were meant to join your mother inside that cursed palace when you came of age. Then you two queens would rule as mother and daughter, over all of the land." He smiled tightly and angrily, forcing his unseeing eyes to look back in time. "Two immortal queens could rule the land forever."

"My mother was not immortal." Glinda protested.

"No? What did your mother look like?"

"She was beautiful. Always she was so beautiful."

"*Always*. There is the operative word. She was *always*."

Oscar nudged Glinda. "What does he mean by that?"

Bombo looked around with his sightless eyes. "Who spoke? Who is that with you, Glinda, daughter of the Red Sorceress?"

"This is Osc-"

"I am Oz." Oscar quickly jumped in. "I came from the sky to join Glinda in her quest."

"Only wizards come from the sky. Only they have power to do so." Bombo retorted. "Prove, then, your wizardry."

Oscar smiled and rubbed his hands together. He snapped his fingers, and then a bird whistled. Bombo looked around though he could not see the bird. "The bird! Where is it?" He demanded of his gathered council.

"We cannot see it." The council pronounced, startled.

"An invisible bird, summoned from magic. What else do you have, wizard?"

A mewing from beneath Bombo's chair made the old man jump in surprise. "Get it away, get it away!" Bombo clambered up onto the wooden table.

Glinda laughed and clapped her hands, breaking several rules of written etiquette, but she was lost in the moment.

Oscar clapped. "Kitty cat. Begone!" He snapped his fingers and pronounced calmly, "It is gone."

Bombo turned in the direction of Oscar's voice. He pushed his plate away and ensured that his toes no longer hung over the edge of the table. "There is no doubt you have abilities far beyond normal men. You truly are a wizard. Only a wizard would have known that my greatest fear is sitting on a cat."

"Naturally." said Oscar.

Glinda stared at Oscar with newfound respect.

"I believe we were talking about the princess' mother and the word *'always.'*"

Glinda smiled and squeezed Oscar's hand as he sat down next to her.

Bombo composed himself and sat down gingerly as the entire council moved forward to help him back into his chair. "Yes, yes, of course. Queen Gayelette was always beautiful. As the years went by and my grandfather's beard and then my father's beard grew down to their knees, still Gayelette was beautiful."

Glinda stormed out of the council house and slammed the door into Oscar, who was following closely behind. He rubbed his forehead and followed after her. They went back to the Hamstrambulator and climbed in.

"West." Glinda commanded Omby-Amby.

They drove across the fields toward the distant ruins of Glinda's tower. The monkeys appeared from their various hidden posts across the village and followed after them. In the side basket, across the large wheel, Wickrie-Kells reached out and touched Glinda's hand. "What's wrong?"

"They're wrong. They are *all* wrong. This place was *not* cursed."

Oscar stepped out of the side basket and climbed up next to Omby-Amby in the driver's seat.

"What happened?" Omby-Amby asked.

"She learned that they hated her mother and believed she was a curse on the land. They said that she drank the blood of the land to stay forever young."

"Blisteringly strange." was all Omby-Amby said.

The great crater still yawned wide where the Ruby Palace had stood. The Hamstrambulator skidded to a stop beside it. Glinda got out and stared at the gaping hole in the ground. With tears in her eyes she looked back at her friends. "It's gone."

She shrugged and laughed and cried. Oscar went and stood next to her as a show of support. Wickrie-Kells hugged the red-haired girl. Omby-Amby looked out over the cliff to the wild lands barely tamed beyond the reach of the local farmers.

Glinda went and sat in her ruined tower alone for many minutes.

Oscar joined her a few minutes later, taking a seat on the stairs. "This was yours?" he asked.

Glinda nodded. "I hated it here. I wanted to be out there, in the world, having great adventures. But now…adventure doesn't seem like everything I thought it was."

"Adventure is life." Oscar responded, smiling helpfully. "I worked for a man who could hold audiences enthralled, right in the palm of his hand—like they were sitting right there. Right there in his hand, he could have fed them dry bread crumbs and they would have licked his fingers. Simple little acts, he did. He sold an entire crowd on a *flea circus*. Can you believe that, a flea circus? Tiny little tent and acts—trapeze, high wire, rolling balance ball. They were little models. Nothing else, just the models. But oh, how he could make that story dance. Everyone would peer in to see the fleas performing. And you know what? Just about every one of them did. He was the prince of humbugs. He was wonderful. He gave the people what they wanted—a show, an *adventure*. The people didn't care that it was all in their head, inside their imagination. They would pay to see the fleas dance and perform…*even though they weren't really there.*

"You see, Glinda, the trick is recognizing that quite often what you want is already in front of you. Sometimes you just need to squint a little to see it."

Glinda squeezed Oscar's hand. "Wizards don't need tricks. They already have the power."

"It's like the flea circus. A wizard is what he needs to be to get the job done." Oscar stood and stretched his legs. "Are you going to be up here for a while?"

Glinda nodded, and Oscar left her to her imaginings.

Wickrie-Kells walked about the multi-colored plots of flowers as she studied the garden. Everything was beautiful again. Oscar walked up behind her. "So what is the pattern?"

"Isn't it obvious?"

Oscar shrugged. "I'm still the new guy here. I can see that there is a definite order and pattern to this garden. I just don't recognize the big picture."

"This is Oz." She said. When Oscar looked puzzled, she clarified. "The entire land is called Oz. Didn't Omby tell you that? That's kind of an important story point. You would think that the soldier would have laid the groundwork for this adventure. Oz is broken up into smaller countries. The blue is Munchkin Country. Yellow is Winkie Country, where we came from. Red is north, but it is changing to purple; interesting. Maybe something...never mind. South is...white changing into red...weird."

"And this is different from the way the land is laid out?"

"North is supposed to be red. South was white. Green in the center. North, Gillikins. West, Winkies. East, Munchkins. South, Quadlings."

Oscar noticed that East and West were reversed—but he would ask that question later. He gestured to an empty stone platform on the north side of the garden. "What is that?"

"It's in the North. Probably a representation of the garden here. I'm not really sure."

Glinda descended from her tower and walked toward them. She brushed her long red hair back behind her ear, watching the sky and the forest—everything except Oscar, who was very clearly watching her. Then a whistle drew Glinda's attention from her ruined tower to the forest. A familiar-sounding whistle. Then she remembered the message given to her by King Klick. *Her father was waiting in the forest.*

Glinda ran toward the forest. Omby-Amby stood as sentry, watching over everything. He followed a short distance behind, still on guard. He took note where the monkeys were, at least three of them. The large one with the eyepatch—Brutus—was nowhere to be seen. Nearby, Oscar and Wickrie-Kells ran from the garden to follow Glinda into the forest. The monkeys fanned out and followed through the tops of the trees.

Glinda ducked under branches and leaped over gnarled roots, heading toward the nearby sound of whistling. But it was moving away from her, deeper into the forest. At last she burst into a clearing.

In the center, standing straight and tall, with his arms wide open to her, was Glinda's father—Quelala.

16 THE GOLDEN CAP

"Father!" Glinda cried, running into his arms.

"Glinda! You got my message." He glanced up to see Brutus and two other Winged Monkeys drop into the trees. "I owe King Klick a great debt of gratitude." He held his daughter at arm's length and took a long look at her, seeing a change in her disposition. "You have grown up."

At the southwestern edge of the forest, Ondri-baba stopped her walking hut. She pulled out a carved metal frame that held the design of a Soliyak Lizard monster. She opened the tops of several hourglasses and poured in the sand. The sands took shape, forming a gargantuan six-legged monster that stood up on its rear legs, its head rising above the height of the treetops. She also poured out individual sand warriors and commanded them all to find the red-haired girl and the shiny roller.

Nearby, flapping above the trees, the fourth and final monkey that was sent with Glinda abandoned its scouting efforts and screeched through the forest, staying below the treetops. "Monster! Monster!" it screamed as it approached.

In forest near the clearing, Brutus and the other Winged Monkeys took to the air to see.

Brutus glanced down from above to see the man Quelala pull the Golden Cap out of his pocket and put it on Glinda's head. He dropped lower, back into the treetops, rustling the branches. Quelala flicked his eyes toward the source of the noise, but he didn't move his head. He focused on his daughter.

"Glinda, the Golden Cap is used as a focusing device for wishes and dreams." When Glinda's face registered confusion, he waved it away. "It's okay if you don't know exactly what that means right now. There is a great charm on this cap. You must discover it. Your mother sold half of her kingdom to secure the means to create this item. That is why Kalinya gained so much power—she was the purchaser." He glanced over his shoulder toward the approaching tumult. "Time is short. Be good to the Winged Monkeys. You have the Golden Cap now. Keep it." He adjusted the Golden Cap on Glinda's head and said, "I am proud of you. There is more that I wish I could teach you, but I can't. Not if I—" He sighed sadly. "I want you to live to discover all of the wonderful things this world can offer you. Your books only told you what other people saw and knew. I want you to know. And so I have to go. When I give you the signal, you *go*, anywhere but here."

"But I don't understand." Glinda cried.

Crashing sounded in the forest nearby. First it was cracking branches then falling trees then crackling flames. They were, after all, in the Sparkwood Forest. "*That*," said Quelala, "is all that you must understand right now. There are things coming for you. The witches want you; they want your mother's power. They want the secrets she put in your head."

"Was my mother old?"

"What?"

Glinda repeated, "How old was my mother when she—"

"At least one hundred and twenty, maybe older. I don't know exactly. She was a good woman, Glinda. Don't let anyone tell you different. She raised me from a boy and taught me to be her assistant. When the time came, we married. But she looked the same—just as beautiful, every day of her life. I cannot tell you more. We have no time. But, please, Glinda, find the Ruby Throne. It will give you power to outlive your enemies." Quelala pushed his daughter toward Oscar and backed away, toward the approaching din. "Now, go."

He stared deep into the young man who took Glinda's hands. To Oscar he said, "Take care of her. I see in your eyes that you can be trusted. *Don't lie to her.*"

Glinda pulled the Golden Cap tightly down on her head and took Oscar's hand. Crashing sounded all around them in the forest.

Then Quelala disappeared into the trees.

Omby-Amby shouted, "We can outrun them if we get back to the wheels!" He grabbed Wickrie-Kells by the hand and slung her forward as they raced out of the forest. They burst clear of the trees and saw the Hamstrambulator parked a hundred yards away. Less than ten yards behind them, the first of the sandy warriors cleared the trees. Omby-Amby pushed Wickrie-Kells further ahead of him. "Start the legs running, but don't let them touch the wheels yet!" He drew his sword and whirled backwards against the two sand warriors.

The sandy warriors were not mindless doppelgangers anymore. They were learning the martial arts. They did not fall quickly to his blade. He sliced the leg off of one, toppling it, and then he chopped the head off of the other.

Fourteen more emerged from the forest and moved quickly toward him. He stomped on the outstretched hand of the fallen one, shattering its fingers. The warrior swung its stump at his legs. But Omby-Amby was already sprinting back to the Hamstrambulator.

As he got one hand on the basket, he yelled, "GO!" and Wickrie-Kells dropped the feet onto the wheel. The wheels spat up dirt as they found traction and sped toward the forest. Omby-Amby pulled himself up and took the steering levers and steered the vehicle toward Glinda's tower. "Where are they?" He asked.

"I don't see them anywhere." Wickrie Kells stood up and shaded her eyes with her cupped hands. "Where could they be?"

"Which way were they running?"

"That way." Wickrie-Kells pointed, and the Hamstrambulator sped in that direction.

In the forest, Oscar pulled Glinda along as quickly as they could run. "Which way is out?" he gasped.

Glinda shot Oscar a panicked look.

"Didn't you grow up here? How can you not know the forest?"

"Trapped in a tower."

"Great." They ducked underneath a low branch and tumbled down an embankment into a creek bed. Now neither one of them knew exactly where they were going. All around them they heard the crashing and husky bellowing of the sand warriors, but they saw nothing. Oscar pulled Glinda up the far bank and pushed her ahead of him as he turned. The noises revealed that the sandy warriors were on the embankment behind them. A branch ripped off the tree and crashed to the ground, bursting into flame. The exploding flames licked up all around the invisible warrior. Oscar paled. Glinda grabbed his hand and pulled him back into terrified reality. They ran.

"They're invisible!" gasped Glinda. "Can't you summon your invisible animals to fight them?"

Oscar remembered Quelala's last admonition to him—don't lie to her—and he confessed, "No. I can't summon invisible animals."

"But I saw you…"

"You thought you saw. I made noises. I threw my voice. I'm a ventriloquist."

"A ventril-a-what?"

"A ventriloquist. I make noises to make—to entertain people. Like at the Yellow Castle." Oscar gasped, leaping over a log.

Glinda shook her hand loose from Oscar's. "You're not a wizard?" The hurt and betrayal clouded over her blue eyes.

"I am—I am what people think me—to be."

A great husky roaring ripped out a tree right behind them, sending Glinda flying. The sparkwood tree crashed to the ground, erupting in flames. Heedless of the flames, Oscar ran to her side and pulled Glinda to her feet.

Ahead of them a brassy clanking cut through the crashing, and flashes of metal glinted in the mixed shadows and flames of the erupting forest. Wickrie-Kells cried out, "Look out!" as another tree fell right behind them. The Hamstrambulator turned, and Oscar pulled Glinda onto a parallel path. The vehicle slowed down, and Wickrie-Kells reached for Glinda. Their fingers connected, and Wickrie-Kells caught Glinda's wrist. Oscar grabbed Glinda's waist and gave her a shove upward, thrusting her into the basket. Then Wickrie-Kells reached for Oscar's hand. Their fingers brushed and then Oscar tripped.

The Hamstrambulator roared away.

"He fell!" Wickrie-Kells cried to Omby-Amby, "He fell down!"

Omby-Amby said, *"Hold on!"* and he whipped the machine around, nearly throwing Glinda out. Wickrie-Kells reached out and snatched her friend from danger.

Omby-Amby sped the Hamstrambulator back toward Oscar, who was now running toward them. "Lower the side basket." He commanded Glinda. She pulled the lever that lowered one of the side baskets down. "Drive."

Wickrie-Kells slid into the driver's seat as Omby-Amby dropped down into the basket. "Arms up!" he ordered Oscar. Oscar jumped up just as Omby-Amby grabbed his wrists. Then the Hamstrambulator hit a large stone, launching the vehicle into the air, and threw Omby-Amby off balance.

Oscar grabbed onto the front edge of the basket just as Omby-Amby tumbled over the back edge. Both of them were now hanging onto the basket with their feet dragging on the ground. The vehicle sped forward as soon as Wickrie-Kells verified that neither one of the boys had been left behind.

"Thanks." said Oscar, dragging backwards.

"We're not sparkly-clean yet. Can you get your feet up here? Step on my shoulder and get in."

Oscar curled his legs around, holding them above the speeding ground and then putting his feet on Omby-Amby's muscled shoulder. "Sorry." he said, climbing up and leaving muddy footprints on the shirt.

"Please hurry." Omby-Amby grunted. "This is not as easy as I make it look."

Oscar pulled himself into the basket and reached down to help the green-haired warrior.

All around them, Ondri-baba's invisibility spell wore off, and suddenly more than a dozen of the sandy warriors appeared, charging at them.

"Basket *UP!*" Omby-Amby shouted, and Glinda pulled the lever. It went very slowly, lifting both Oscar and Omby-Amby. *"UP!"* he shouted again as the press of sandy warriors pushed in closer. He got his elbows up over the edge of the basket.

"I'm upping!" Glinda screamed back at him.

One of the sandy warriors lunged at Omby-Amby, and he pulled himself up on the bottom of the basket. The sandy warrior missed its mark and went into the large wheel. *"Feet UP!"* ordered Omby-Amby, and Wickrie-Kells pulled the lever to pull up the feet.

The wheel kept spinning, coasting, and the sandy warrior spun around and around. The centrifugal force broke the sand to pieces, and it dissolved. "Feet down!"

Omby-Amby pulled himself into the basket and climbed back into the driver's seat. "Nice driving." He complimented Wickrie-Kells and she smiled, blushing. The running feet dropped back down, and the Hamstrambulator sped through the trees.

Quelala ran through the trees toward the oncoming destruction. The only thought on his mind was giving enough time for Glinda to escape. His own safety was not important. Not anymore. The Golden Cap was safe. Glinda had enough of a clue, she was a smart girl, she could figure out the rest. Very soon he could be with Gayelette again.

Trees crashed all around him. Flames shot upward from the sparkwood branches. The great monster pushed through the smaller trees of the old forest. All escape was blocked by flames, so Quelala ran between the monster's front legs. He stopped short when he saw the witch's walking hut behind the beast. "Ondri-baba! Stop this now!"

He was immediately seized by invisible hands. The rough grit on his arms unsurprisingly revealed the identity of sandy warriors. Screeching echoed above and behind him as the Winged Monkeys dropped down from the sky to free him. They twisted arms off of the sandy warriors and pulled Quelala into the air.

"Come with us to safety." Brutus said.

"NO!" Quelala kicked and twisted. "Save *Glinda.* She has the Golden Cap." He locked eyes with Brutus. "She is your best chance for being free. On my honor I could not free you. *She can.*"

Brutus needed no convincing. He immediately slackened his grip, increasing dramatically the load for the other three smaller winged monkeys. Brutus pushed higher into the sky to gain a better vantage point to find Glinda.

Quelala looked at the others. "I can give you time. *Drop me.*" They descended and dropped the man the last few feet to the ground. He stood up right in the path of Ondri-baba's walking hut.

The hut stopped. Ondri-baba stepped out onto her porch as the legs bent and the hut crouched down.

Quelala stared down the one-eyed witch. "Stop this, now. Leave my daughter alone."

Ondri-baba cackled. "So you think this is *about the child*? Dear man, I am not my sister. I have something much *shinier* in mind."

Quelala went pale. Did she know the truth about the Golden Cap? If that was true, then she could use that power to rule Oz absolutely. If that was true than all of his best efforts were in vain. He turned to look, but the Winged Monkeys were already gone.

"Take him." she commanded her soldiers.

Quelala's heart dropped and he made only the barest of arguments as the sandy soldiers bound his hands and arms.

The Hamstrambulator sped through the forest. Every few seconds they caught glimpses of blue sky beyond the trees. The crashing had faded in the distance, and the smoke from the burning sections of the forest was far behind. A new sound approached from above—screeching and hooting. The Winged Monkeys had returned.

"How was that for some fancy driving?" asked Omby-Amby.

"Absolutely flawless." responded Wickrie-Kells, smiling at him and brushing loose wind-blown hair out of her face. Much of her usually-bound and braided hair had come loose in the excitement. In the rush of the moment, she brushed this back.

Omby-Amby turned to meet her smile. Just then, the Hamstrambulator burst free of the forest and whizzed down the shore to plow into the river.

The machine hit the water of the wide river and stopped its forward momentum completely. Now inertia being what it is—even in magical land—the four passengers continued their forward travel, launching out of their baskets and flying out over the river.

Brutus and the other Winged Monkeys swooped in and grabbed each of them by the hands, holding them aloft for a bare moment. Brutus grabbed Glinda and lifted her higher. He was the largest and strongest of the Winged Monkeys, and Glinda was the lightest of the four people.

Wickrie-Kells looked backward at the half-submerged Hamstrambulator, and then looked at Omby-Amby. They had the same idea. He nodded. She called out to the Winged Monkeys, "Take Glinda and Oscar. Get to safety. We will find you. Head south."

The monkeys looked at each other and chattered, laughing. They dropped Wickrie-Kells and Omby-Amby into the river below. With two additional sets of hands on Oscar, they gained altitude. With the two additional sets of monkey hands on him, Oscar screamed—all the more panicked.

"Let me go! Let me go!" echoed in the distance as the Winged Monkeys laughed and followed after Brutus and Glinda.

Ondri-baba marched her great monster toward the North Village. She followed in her hut alongside the great Soliyak Lizard. Inside the hut, Quelala was bound and lay hopeless and despondent on the floor.

The sandy soldiers had bound and gagged Quelala and placed him on a chair in the middle of the magic hut, so that he would not be in the way. His hands were bound so that he could not reach anything. When the hut stood up, Quelala had fallen over with the chair and did not move.

The hut was larger on the inside than it was on the outside. An elaborate system of gears and levers controlled the leg-works. Next to Quelala's fallen chair was a Sapphire Stove—a potbelly stove that was the heart of the hut. The stove clicked and whistled and hissed as the fuel burned inside. Ondri-baba turned and talked to the sapphire stove at regular intervals, warning it of rocks or large steps coming up. She was verbally controlling the direction of the contraption.

Meanwhile, just inside the Sparkwood Forest, Kalinya spied on Ondri-baba. She looked around, but did not see any sign of Glinda or her friends. She did not bother to look any further for additional prisoners, so she did not see Quelala. Glinda was the only one that she cared about. Three steps, and Kalinya was gone, heading back south to the battlefront.

In the North Village, the wise town elder, Bombo, was carried out on a chair to sit before Ondri-baba. He had been informed of the plumes of smoke rising from the distant forest. His eyes were closed, but he held his head up high. He had given counsel to this town for many, many years, but this was the first time that he had been called on to face an occupying enemy.

When it was explained that Ondri-baba had marched into town with a magical army, he turned to face toward the witch and said, "We have no quarrel with you, Queen Witch. But your place is not here. We have recently been freed from the rule of a Sorceress, and we have no desire to give place for another to rule over us."

Ondri-baba fumed. "You gave refuge to Glinda and her friends."

"We talked with them, but they have no place with us, either. They did not ask for food or shelter, only information."

"And what information did you give to them?" the witch demanded.

"Glinda's mother, Gayelette, was far older than she appeared. My grandfather remembers the red sorceress when she first came of age to marry. This was before the Red King and Queen left the land. She was approached by a very dark queen from across the desert. I have heard that you, yourself, have been gifted by this queen, Ondri-baba."

Ondri-baba touched her cursed magic eye, but remained silent.

"This queen wished to unite the two lands and proposed an alliance. For the promise of marriage into that family, the queen would share her secrets. And she did. Gayelette spent more than a hundred years working on those secrets. What they were, we do not know, and I will not say what little I believe. Such things should never be."

"And you told this to Glinda?"

"I did."

"Then you shall suffer for your misplaced confidence!" To her soldiers, she commanded, "Burn the town! Not one structure shall stand. Let the lands of the north know the power of the one true Witch Queen in Oz!"

The village burned for a night and a day. It was long into the night before the screams of the terrified Gillikins stopped.

THE WITCHES

17 THE SILVER SLIPPERS

Back on the Winkie Plains, Kalinya burst into the tent, startling Locasta, who was trying to catch a few minutes of much-needed sleep. *"Get up, you lazy girl!"* she shrieked.

Locasta jumped out of the cot and fell to the ground, completely disoriented. She quickly got up to her feet, straightening her pointed hat.

"Ondri-baba has failed to catch Glinda. She failed, she failed, she failed." Kalinya cackled gleefully. "That means you," she pointed to Locasta, "have the opportunity for glorious success."

"Me?"

"You are my apprentice. You won't be missed in battle. Besides, it might take a few days to find the girl. I have to stay here, to keep up appearances for when Ondri-baba returns."

"But how will I get there? It is so far."

"I will take you. Come."

They stepped outside the tent. "Hold tightly to my hand. Step as I step. And do not let go. I don't want to have to backtrack over half of Oz to find you again."

Locasta did as she was commanded. She stepped, *one, two, three.* The shock of speed took her breath away. After five line-of-sight hops, Kalinya stopped on the top of a hill to get her bearings and let Locasta catch her breath.

"What was that?" Locasta gasped for air.

"The sliver slippers allow me to travel anywhere I can see in just three steps. Come, we have eighteen more hops to make before we reach the forest in Gillikin Country."

Locasta took several deep breaths, then locked hands with Kalinya and stepped *one, two, three.*

The Winged Monkeys carried Glinda and Oscar for fifteen minutes before they landed. That got them far enough away that any pursuers would not see them beyond the horizon. They went to a nearby copse of trees, where the river bowed. Here they sat and waited. Finally tired of pacing back and forth, Brutus gave in to his impatience and flew away, back in the direction they had come.

The sky was blackened by dark smoke when the two traveling witches arrived near the edge of the forest. The stink of burning sickened the apprentice. Kalinya let Locasta fall to the ground to catch her breath. They had pushed hard to get here, and there was little time that Kalinya could spend coddling her weak girl.

In the skies nearby, Brutus saw the magical glimmer of the silver slippers and glided in close to take a look. He dropped into the trees and leaped from tree to tree until he came within hearing distance.

"Enough rest. Get up."

Locasta wearily climbed to her feet. Her balance was off from traveling such a great distance in such a little time, and she felt very sick and disoriented. Kalinya took her apprentice by the elbow and marched.

Kalinya stopped inside the forest, out of sight of the horizon, and then let go of Locasta. It was late in the day, and the sun was dropping lower in the sky toward the eastern horizon.

Brutus followed the two witches through the trees.

"My apprentice, you must find Glinda. She is the key to securing power. We may not have the Ruby Palace, but we have the daughter of the sorceress, and that will unlock the secrets of the Queen of Dreams."

"Where shall I look?" Locasta asked, weakened and still puzzled by her role in all of this. They had left the armies back on the Winkie Plains doing drills and exercises. That should keep the Winkies occupied, wondering what the army was up to. The plan was to let the longbeard Winkie generals overthink their enemy.

"You have your tricks. I have seen your oracle. It may not be specific, but it is accurate." Kalinya pulled the bag of blood-sand from her pouch. "I will offer some assistance." She pulled out a folded piece of paper—a page ripped out of a book—and placed it on the ground. It was a picture of a fierce tiger.

"There is more to this sand than you can know." Kalinya whispered mysteriously. She pulled a small blade from her pouch and cut across her finger. She dripped the blood onto the tiger, then dumped the small bag of sand onto the picture. For good measure she squeezed more blood on top of the sand.

The pile of sand whirled, taking on the attributes of both the blood and the sand. It grew into the form of a dark red tiger. Kalinya bound her finger in cloth then stroked the tiger's face. "Find Glinda. Locasta will be your guide. Obey her when I am not around." Kalinya shot a warning glance at Locasta. "If she does not obey my orders, treat her as you would Glinda."

That was enough for Locasta. She paled even more at the threat. The display of blood magic was more than a threat—it was a descent into darker magic. That was dangerous for everyone. The tiger growled its understanding in its husky voice.

"We are understood then. Good." And Kalinya walked back out of the forest.

Above her, Brutus followed her through the trees. As she stepped out into the open air, Brutus dropped down in front of her.

Kalinya screeched in surprise and flung out her hand, launching Brutus into the air. He quickly regained his equilibrium and landed a safe distance from the witch.

"I mean no harm to you, witch. I bring a message."

"You are allied with the Winkies. Enmity is between us."

"I bring a message of the sorceress daughter."

Kalinya's eyes brightened. "Ah. Perhaps *enmity* was too strong a word. You know where she is."

"I know it. And I am bound by the power of the Golden Cap."

A sardonic smile crossed Kalinya's face. This Winged Monkey had just let his strongest secret slip. "Bound? Nonsense. You were assured of freedom when Quelala held the cap."

"Yes. But we were not free. Now he no longer—" Brutus clapped his hands over his mouth.

"Glinda has the Golden Cap." Kalinya deduced, formulating a plan.

Panic shone in Brutus' good eye. "The Cap is hers." he admitted, losing his composure. He pounded on the ground and roared, but Kalinya was unfazed. She sauntered around the fuming monkey, circling her aged fingers merrily in the air.

"Will you get it for me? I will give you whatever you desire." Kalinya purred.

"You are the enemy of Glinda."

"What is it you want? Gold? Silver? Perhaps a *throne*?"

The hunger in his eye at the mention of a throne easily gave away his desire. "So you want to rule? That can be done. As you are bound to the Golden Cap, if you get it for me, *and* prove your loyalty to me, I swear you will rule the Winged Monkeys."

Brutus grinned an awful grin. "I so swear."

As the sun touched the distant horizon, one of the monkeys cried out happily, "Friends! Friends!" Indeed it was. Walking along the riverbank, Omby-Amby and Wickrie-Kells came into view.

They all laughed and hugged at the happy meeting. Omby-Amby built a fire, protected from view by the trees. Wickrie-Kells produced some nut rolls from her loaded backpack, full of things she salvaged from the sunken Hamstrambulator. The nut rolls were supplemented by some nuts they found on a tree in the copse. The food was a welcome sight after a very eventful day. The fire warmed them as they ate their simple supper.

"Oscar was telling me about the kings where he comes from." Glinda filled in the other two on their conversation. "They actually let the people rule themselves."

"That is strange. I never heard of such a thing." Wickrie-Kells exclaimed.

Oscar gestured to get their attention. "No, no, no. That isn't exactly what I said. There are no kings where I come from, at least not in my land. The people vote to choose their leaders. The leaders are bound by the laws so that the people can stay free."

"You mean the laws they make up." Omby-Amby pointed out.

"No. The laws that written are on the books. There are three branches of government outlined in the Constitution. Each has powers and each has balances by the other two branches. It is set up specifically so that there cannot be a king."

Hopeful curiosity sparked in Omby-Amby's eyes. He listened, spellbound, as Oscar talked about the history of the Constitution, how his land went to war to fight for the right to govern itself. Then how other countries also came to war, but normal people—farmers and bakers and shoemakers—fought to maintain their right to live a life of liberty.

They talked late into the evening. Oscar yawned first, and pulled off his shoes. "Sleep sweet. Dream well." He wished everybody.

"What do you mean, *'dream well?'*" Glinda asked.

Oscar struggled to keep his eyes open. "It just means have good dreams."

Glinda exchanged glances with the other two. Their puzzled faces revealed to Glinda what she had suspected. "People in Oz don't dream."

Oscar shrugged sleepily. "Then just sleep sweet."

"Do you dream?" Glinda asked Oscar.

He nodded. "Every night."

"May I watch you dream?" Glinda asked, but Oscar was already asleep.

18 THE DREAMS THAT CHANGE

The three flying monkeys took their places above the group. One of them sat in the top of the trees, watching, or flew patrol while the other two slept. Brutus was still nowhere to be found.

Wickrie-Kells and Omby-Amby had fallen asleep. Only Glinda sat awake. She kept her curious vigil, excited and more than a little nervous about what she might see.

She watched Oscar closely, to see how he dreamed. She wondered what would happen when the dreams started. Would strange things come to life? Would transparent images dance above his head? Would she even know what she was looking for when she saw it? All of her life, her mother had researched dreams. Somehow her father had helped with the research. But if no one in Oz dreamed, then how could they even understand what a dream was? She would have to ask Oscar in the morning.

Glinda looked around at their secluded campsite. The small fire at her back was nearly down to coals. Fallen logs served as their backstops, and everyone was curled up on the ground. There were no blanket-branch trees nearby, so each person was curled in on themselves. The small trees in the copse were only about fifteen feet tall. The river murmured nearby, rounding around the northern corner of their camp. A nice, gentle slope led down to the river.

Glinda nodded once, sleepily. The trees seemed to shimmer and grow. She watched, as the world seemed to get hazy and unreal. The bark on the trees grew rougher and their limbs spread out further. The creaking and growing of the trees sent all of the Winged Monkeys aloft, hooting in surprise.

A husky roar in the night brought Glinda back to full wakefulness. The monkeys screamed as something large moved out in the grass beyond the trees.

Glinda jumped to her feet as the ground shook, rousing Omby-Amby and Wickrie-Kells. "What's going on?" the soldier with green hair demanded. His sword was already in his hand.

"Something is out there." Glinda pointed. The coals cast a dim red light over them.

Omby-Amby listened. "That something is in *here*, with us. Wickrie, take left. I'll go right. Glinda, you stay down. Keep your head."

Glinda pulled the Golden Cap tighter on her head. At her feet, Oscar snored.

The blood tiger padded forward into the forest. The ground shook, but the quarry was near. Locasta had said so. There was a strange feeling, like the land was rising, but the predator kept moving forward. *There.* There was a red light ahead. The blood tiger moved faster. *There she was.* There could be no doubt. The red hair was a dead giveaway. The blood tiger raced to the edge of the campsite and attacked.

Glinda heard the heavy footfalls nearby. They came from something *other* than a person. She climbed over one of the logs and crouched down. Across the campsite, Oscar was still snoring. She peeked above the log, keeping her eyes locked on the approaching sound. It was getting louder and louder. Then it was upon her. Crashing through the trees, a great cat—a *tiger*!

Glinda turned and ran.

She crashed through the underbrush, running toward the river. A husky roar echoed behind her. Then she was at the edge of the thicket … *and the edge of the land!* Glinda leaped out into space. Her arms and legs flailed as she dropped toward the river. Right behind her the blood tiger leaped out into the air, swiping its claws at the girl.

"NO!" a voice cried out behind the tiger. But it was too late.

Glinda plunged into the water, and the abrupt change in temperature forced all of the air from her lungs. So cold. Above her the blood-sand tiger hit the water and dissolved as it splashed and struggled. It did not even surface before all of the blood-sand connection was gone.

Glinda gasped as she broke the surface and swam to the bank. She lay gasping on the bank, clutching a smooth boulder. She looked up at the embankment she had leaped from. It was fully twenty feet above the surface of the river. When they had found the copse of trees, the land was level—there was no embankment. The landscape had changed.

A scream of female terror sounded from the direction of the campsite. Glinda pulled herself out of the water and made her way back up into the thicket.

"Wickrie?" Glinda called.

"Glinda! We're over here."

"Keep talking. I'll follow your voice."

"We thought you were dead. That tiger…"

Glinda came back into the camp soaking wet. Oscar sat up, rubbed at the sleep in his eyes, and looked around in bewilderment. "Why is everyone yelling?"

Omby-Amby held a young woman's arms pinned behind her back and Wickrie-Kells held a knife to the woman's chest.

"Who is this?" Glinda demanded, and then she gasped when she saw the woman's face. *"Locasta."*

Locasta's eyes fixed on Glinda's face. "I—I didn't mean to—I didn't want to hurt you."

"The tiger was hers." Omby-Amby said.

"*NO!* No. Not mine. It wasn't mine." Locasta protested. "It was Kalinya. She made it. I could never—"

"It's dead." Glinda stated with frustrated finality.

Locasta's jaw dropped in shock. *"Dead?"*

"I am guessing that it was sent for me, by Kalinya." Glinda's nerves were cooling down and she realized that she was right now rather cranky and soaking wet. "How would you feel if a great beast came to kill you? Well?" Glinda yelled in Locasta's face. "I'm tired of it! I am tired of running. I'm tired of being scared. I'm tired of being alone. I'm tired of things changing all around me without anything making any sense."

Glinda walked up to Oscar, pointing her finger at his face. "*You!* What is this? Did you do this? Did you dream this?"

Oscar shrugged and shook his head, clearly not understanding. "Why are you yelling at me?" but Glinda pulled him to his feet anyway.

She marched him through the dark trees to the embankment. She pointed down to the river. "*That.* Did you do that?"

Oscar rubbed his eyes and stared in wonder as he recognized the landscape. "I've been here before. As a boy. The Platte River. We went swimming here." He turned in surprise to Glinda. "I just dreamed about this place. Pinch me. Am I still dreaming?"

Glinda laughed. The release of all of the emotion and anger and frustration all melted away in that instant. It bubbled up inside and spilled out. She laughed and the ludicrous wonder of it all. "You *dreamed* this? And it happened?" She hugged Oscar. "And you say you're not a wizard."

Locasta sat in front of the fire, her hands bound behind her back, when Glinda and Oscar came back to the campsite. Omby-Amby tossed sticks into the coals to build up the flames. Wickrie-Kells arose as Glinda approached. "She has a message for you."

Glinda pulled the pointed hat from Locasta's head and threw it on the ground. "How did you find me? Were you with her? Were you with those monsters chasing us?"

Locasta shook her head no. Her gaze was locked on Glinda's stormy blue eyes.

"What do you want with me? What does your master want? Why does she want me? *I am not my mother!* I don't know her secrets! The Ruby Palace is gone." Glinda stopped and picked up the pointed hat. She murmured some words under her breath and twisted the hat in her hands. It changed shape into a rope. She draped the rope around Locasta's neck twice. "Your master killed my mother. Why should I do any different with you?"

Locasta gulped nervously as she witnessed Glinda's display of magic. *"The Queen of Dreams!"* She hoarsely confessed.

Glinda blinked in surprise.

Locasta pressed her small and unexpected advantage. "Kalinya wants your mother's secrets so that she can contact the Queen of Dreams."

"I don't know her secrets."

"Kalinya says you do. And she wants you to join her. I was sent to bring you back."

The rope slithered down off of Locasta's neck and down to the ground. It wriggled and writhed, changing and twining. Locasta caught Glinda's look and quickly absolved herself of any sort of intentional control, "It's not *me*."

The rope twined into a word. Then another. Then another. The message read, *"Meet Kalinya in Boneyard of the Clouds."*

Glinda turned to all of her friends, "What is the *Boneyard of the Clouds?*"

None of them knew.

The rope twisted into, *"Smith and Tinker."*

"Smith and Tinker are gone. They left Oz, is what they said." Wickrie-Kells said.

"Maybe their castle has something." Glinda snapped her fingers. "Didn't they say that they had something for me and that I could visit whenever I wanted to?"

"That's right, they did." Wickrie-Kells nodded.

Glinda picked up the rope and wound it. She turned to Locasta and held up the rope. "We are going to find the Boneyard of the Clouds. This rope seems to know something. It was made from your hat. Where did you get it?"

"It found me. It is an *oracle*. How did you change its shape?"

Then Glinda remembered that her mother could travel anywhere with the Silver Slippers, even through closed doors. The same might hold true for Kalinya, but she did not want the witch to know that. To have Kalinya always able to travel to her location at any moment would be for Glinda to live in fear. And if she lived in fear always, Glinda would end up like the apprentice,

Locasta. She quickly resolved on a plan to limit the witch's understanding of the Silver Slippers' true power.

"That is one of the things I *do* know. When the time is right, ask your rope where I am. I will be in the Boneyard of the Clouds. Do not tell Kalinya where I am, only tell her that I cast a spell that will allow the silver slippers to bring her to my location and then allow her to return to her location. This won't be until at least another day and night passes. Maybe longer. If your rope is truly an oracle, it will know."

Glinda dropped the rope at Locasta's feet. "I won't threaten you again. That is not my way. I am *not* a wicked witch."

She continued, "We will find the Boneyard of the Clouds. I will meet Kalinya there alone. I see in your eyes that you are not like her. Locasta, you have a choice. You can either remain a slave to Kalinya—and live in fear of her anger—or you can live free from fear and choose your own way. Both ways hold great risks, and neither is a guarantee of safety. The choice is yours."

Glinda walked away from Locasta. "Take her away from here. Free her hands. The choice she makes is hers alone."

Wickrie-Kells sliced through Locasta's bonds, freeing her hands. The witch called after Glinda, "How do you know I won't kill you myself?"

"Because you didn't." Glinda answered. "Now go."

Omby-Amby escorted Locasta down from the thicket into the grassland.

Glinda sighed deeply, "I'm soaking wet. Please, give me a few minutes. I need to dry off. I need time to think." Glinda walked back into the woods, waving away Wickrie-Kells' offer of assistance.

Up in the trees, Brutus watched Glinda walk away from the group. He followed her silently in the branches above, waiting for his moment to strike.

19 THE TRAITOR IS REVEALED

Glinda marched, soaking wet, deeper into the thicket. When she was out of sight of the campfire, she sighed deeply and pulled the Golden Cap from her head. She gathered up a handful of her red hair and squeezed the water from it. In the darkness, the Golden Cap gave off a soft glow.

She laid the Golden Cap on a shrubbery beside her as she started wringing out sections of her dress.

Something dropped from the top of the tree right next to Glinda. A dark hand reached out for the Golden Cap. Glinda saw the hand and grabbed one side of the Golden Cap just as the dark hand grabbed the other side. Glinda screamed.

Oscar heard Glinda's scream and charged into the darkness. He had no weapon, but he barreled in anyway, heedless of the danger.

Wickrie-Kells pulled her knife and charged after Oscar. She came upon Glinda clutching desperately to the Golden Cap as Brutus, the Winged Monkey pulled at her.

He turned to face this new attacker and bared his teeth, flapping his wings and beating on Glinda.

"Let GO!" Glinda snarled. She heaved and pulled, twisting her body around the monkey's arm.

Oscar braved the large beating wings to grab Brutus in an armlock. Brutus swung his arm and hit Oscar, knocking him silly. Brutus tried to leap into the air, but Oscar's hands clenched around his wings, ripping deep gashes in the connective tissues.

Above them, crashing through the trees, the other three Winged Monkeys screamed and dropped to the ground.

"Look out!" cried Wickrie-Kells. But before Glinda could react to the new threat, the other three jumped on top of Brutus, beating at him and pummeling him with their fists.

Glinda pulled the Golden Cap free from the monkey's grip. She lost her balance and fell backwards to the ground. Brutus lunged for the cap. A flash of silver, and Wickrie-Kells' knife got there first, severing three fingers from the traitor monkey's hand. He howled in pain, spinning around. But the other monkeys would not be thrown off. They ripped fists' full of feathers and sinews from his wings. They battered him and beat him, screaming and hooting. Finally Brutus was driven away—far away into the grassland.

Omby-Amby returned, rushing in with his sword in hand. "What happened?"

Wickrie-Kells patted him on the arm. Glinda picked up the Golden Cap, pulling it out from beneath the three long, dark fingers.

Glinda sat down on the ground. She shook her head. "Betrayed. How could he? I mean, King Klick—"

Omby-Amby answered, directing the group. "We should move from this place. We've made a lot of noise. Everyone in five miles knows we're here now." He pointed them back to the campsite. He went first, back to the fire, followed by Wickrie-Kells.

Oscar slowly rose to his feet. He reached out to steady himself against a tree. He smiled goofy as his head swam circles around him. He staggered forward and held out a hand to Glinda. He pulled Glinda to her feet. "Are you all right?" he asked.

Glinda shrugged, shaking her head in denial. She still clutched the Golden Cap in her hand. "How could he?" Then she broke down and cried.

Oscar did his best to console her, but there was only so much that made sense to him, especially after getting pounded by a monkey fist, and that little bit that made sense was not very much at all. She accepted his open arms and allowed him to hold her for a couple of minutes while she sobbed. Then, just as quickly, she was finished. She lifted her head and smiled at Oscar, "Thank you," and squeezed his hand. Then she went back to the fire.

Oscar shook his head and followed after Glinda. Now *nothing* made sense.

"There's dry clothing in here." Wickrie-Kells offered her backpack to Glinda, who gratefully took it. "Boys, you go down to the river. Give us girls some privacy."

Omby-Amby and Oscar walked down to the river. Omby-Amby picked up a few stones and tossed them in the river. Oscar found a nice flat stone and skipped it across the water.

"Omby, do girls make any sense in this land?"

"Do they in yours?"

"Hmm. Good point."

Glinda quickly changed into dry clothing. She handed the Golden Cap to Wickrie-Kells. The unspoken command was, *protect this.*

"Are you all right, Glinda?"

Glinda nodded. "I had a good cry. Oscar held me." Glinda smiled. "I like him."

Wickrie-Kells nodded in understanding. "He ran right at Brutus. He didn't even have a knife. I think he may like you, too."

Glinda smiled broadly at her friend. There was really nothing more that needed to be said on that.

"We've got a long way to go." Wickrie-Kells changed the subject. "I wish there were a way that we could get there quickly. Smith & Tinker's castle is all the way down south." In her hands, the Golden Cap glowed softly, working its magic.

Out at the river, Oscar's skipped stone stopped cold in between skips. "*Five, six, seven—hey!*"

Something huge emerged up out of the water, stopping Oscar's stone. The watery thing turned and headed directly toward Oscar. Twin waves trailed behind it as the unseen leviathan raced toward the shore. The monstrous bulk heaved up out of the water. Oscar scrambled backwards and Omby-Amby drew his sword.

The huge fish was at least twenty feet long, with fins that extended out at least that far on either side. It gaped open its mouth and blinked at the two young men. Then it smiled.

"Glinda!" Oscar called. "I think we have a visitor."

Glinda and Wickrie-Kells hurried down to the river shore. They skidded on the rocks as they stopped short.

"Oh, wow." Glinda said.

"That is one big fish." Wickrie-Kells pointed out, rather obviously.

The fish turned to look at each in turn. Then its eyes settled on Wickrie-Kells. It spoke with big, rubbery lips, "I am here at your call. Where do you wish to go?"

"How did she call you?" Glinda asked.

"I was summoned to carry you wherever you wish to go." The fish smiled again. Its long moustache-like whiskers twitched happily.

Glinda took back the Golden Cap from her friend and put it on her head. Her hair was mostly dry now. She didn't want to lose the cap again, not after her father's admonition. "But we want to go south, great fish. How can you help us beyond the river?"

"Apparently, this doesn't seem strange to anyone else but me." Oscar commented to no one in particular.

"The great rivers of Oz do not connect the north and the south countries. We are traveling to the edge of a desert. That is no place for a fish." Glinda said.

The fish propped itself up on its fins, lifting its head into the air. It thrust itself upward, pumping its fins up and down and lifted off the ground into the air. Great rubbery lips gulped in great amounts of air, filling its internal bladders. The fish rose off of the ground. Its fins flapped gently, keeping it in position over the beach. Then it laughed, "I am a flying fish. Where would you like to go?"

Flapping from the south sky drew Omby-Amby's attention. The three Winged Monkeys dropped down into the trees and ran down to the beach. They bowed continually to Glinda. "Apologies, apologies. Forgive, forgive."

"Rise, noble warriors. Report your doings." Glinda commanded, taking a royal tone that Oscar had not heard before.

"Brutus gone. Exile. He fly no more. Broken. Come back not." Then the spokesman turned to the other three. It was clear that they were all hurt. "No fly. Rest. Not carry Glinda."

Glinda reached out her hand and stroked the monkey's head. "You have done well. You have my thanks. When you have rested, return to your king and report all that you have seen. I will send summons to King Klick when it is time."

The monkeys bowed and reached out and touched Glinda's feet. Then they backed away into the thicket of trees and they were gone.

Then Glinda turned back to the flying fish. "We are ready. Take us to the castle of Smith & Tinker!"

20 THE FLYING FISH

Upon the back of the Flying Fish, Glinda and her friends rode through the cool night sky. The twinkling stars were close enough to touch, and Glinda trailed her fingers through their soft light, smearing it across the inky darkness.

"Tell me, noble fish, why you have never been seen before in Oz?" Glinda asked.

The fish responded, "I am the last of my kind in Oz. Before the great inland sea was destroyed, there were many more of my kind to be found in the rivers and lakes of this beautiful land. My tale is long, but I am happy to share it."

Glinda and the others agreed, and the fish began its tale.

When Oz was still a young land, it was a continent of itself surrounded by an inland sea on the greater continent of Nonestica. Beyond that was the Nonestic Ocean, and islands and lands of wonder. There was free commerce between all of the lands. With Oz at the center, it became a vital destination for all traders and adventure seekers. There were important ports on all four sides of the land. The central lands were primarily farmlands and ranching. This land was the envy of all the others. It was protected by the waters on all sides. It was a precious land. Many people from all of the lands came to see the beauties and wonders of Oz.

Across the sea were many kingdoms that brought their goods and their arts to Oz. The Kingdoms of Ix, Boboland and Ev were friends to this land. The Nome Kingdom was always envious of the surface dwellers in Oz, and they were always seeking ways to take the treasures of Oz for themselves. This led to several wars, in which the great Kings Oz, along with Ozma the Third, conquered the invading Nomes and sent them back to their subterranean dominions. They let the Nomes depart and keep their own lands. The great kings had no need for more lands. The treasures of Oz were enough to satisfy all.

The threat to the land came not from outside of Oz, but from within. There were witches that had visited some of these other lands, and they saw how power could be used to get great gain and to exact control over others. These witches saw that the rule of King Oz was limited severely by the goodness of the king. Thus began the first Witch Wars.

The Witch Wars nearly destroyed the land. Before that time, Winkie Country was a lush forested country. Now it is rocks and grassland. Great changes came upon the land. The cities that once housed generations of Ozzians were destroyed. Some were rebuilt. Others are still buried, awaiting the day that their bones will again see the sun.

King Oz led all the armies of Oz against the Witches and their magical machines. He very nearly defeated them, but they sent an envoy across the damaged sea to the Kingdom of Dreams, where they appealed to the Dark Queen of Dreams. They swore to her that if she would aid them, they would grant her whatever she wanted. The Queen of Dreams agreed, though she did not specify her conditions. She went with the Witches to Oz, and while they traveled, she slept.

While she slept, the Witches discovered great power. They conversed and acted before they made landfall. Drawing on the power of dreams, the witches lashed out in their anger, and the great inland sea was destroyed.

The Witches crossed over the disappearing sea and made landfall. When they tried to transport the sleeping body of the Queen of Dreams onto the Land of Oz, her body disappeared. They gave it little thought, for they had achieved their objective of isolating King Oz and his land-bound armies. Ships full of soldiers were stranded out in the toxic desert, where once there had been beautiful sea. They were stranded and left to die slowly. Their bones are unremembered now, known only by those who have seen them.

The Witches marched to the Emerald Plains to defeat King Oz, but he had a weapon unknown to the Witches. King Oz invoked the power of the blood of the land.

The war raged day and night for more than a week. Despite all of their magic, the Witches could not kill a single soldier in the army of Oz. They retreated to regroup and re-think their strategy.

As their forces regrouped, the Witches were faced with an additional complication—the Queen of Dreams reappeared, demanding payment for the use of her powers. The time she could walk the Land of Oz was extremely limited. Only when the Blood of Oz was stopped could she enter. And so it came time to exact the payment of the Witches. The Queen spoke, and it chilled all of them who heard.

She said, "The child of my flesh shall wed of your flesh. Be ready, for you know not when the groom comes."

And then the Queen of Dreams returned to her kingdom across the desert.

The Witches were left wondering when the price would come due of their flesh. Would it be them? Would it be from their children? Either way, they could not continue the path they were on. None of the witches were married, so there was no possibility of having children in the immediate future. They determined that in order to satisfy the power that they had used, they would need to disband and prepare for the fulfillment of their price.

Without another sword raised, or another fire started, the witch army disappeared. The individual witches, each not wanting to be the one to betray their oath, settled down and started families. They dispersed to the four corners of Oz, leaving the Emerald Lands for the people of King Oz.

When King Oz went looking for the Witches, he could not find them. They were identified primarily by their magic, and they had stopped using magic openly. They were gone. The people went back to enjoying peace.

The Witch Wars were over, but the land paid a terrible price.

In process of time, the witches died, and their children after them. Then the oath was forgotten. The demanded payment had not been extracted. The Queen of Dreams had not returned to the land to seek out their flesh, and so the need to remember passed away. The rising witches and sorcerers were much more interested in obtaining power than in looking to the past.

So it was that the Red Sorcerer, King of all the lands of the North, built a magnificent palace of Rubies, said to be supplied eternally by a spring beneath. It was this Red Sorcerer that became an unwavering ally of Queen Ozma, the Fifth. During the next fifteen years. Queen Ozma and the Red King stood together and repelled the Second Witch Wars as they attempted to conquer the lands of the North.

The Red King had a daughter, more beautiful and more intelligent than any other in all the land. The time came that the Queen of Dreams came forth to claim her price. But the King, being wise, and understanding the limitations of the Queen of Dreams, sent his daughter away, on a month-long tour of the kingdom. He entertained the Queen of Dreams for two weeks, after which she left. The following week, the King's daughter returned home.

Twice more the Queen of Dreams came to claim her price, but each time was disappointed. The fourth time that she came, the King's daughter was already married.

It is said that the Queen of Dreams sleeps in her kingdom, plotting her revenge on the land that would not pay in flesh what it owed in power.

Glinda stared down at the fish's head, shell-shocked. It was clear from Glinda's face that she heard something more in that story than they had.

Then the Flying Fish asked, "To which castle are we flying? Smith & Tinker keep several castles, all in different lands."

Wickrie-Kells answered for her silent friend, "To the one in Oz."

"To the South Tower it is." And the Fish winged ever southward.

21 THE ARRIVAL AT SOUTH CASTLE

Glinda and her friends arrived at the South Laboratory of Smith & Tinker before daybreak. The Flying Fish hovered just above the ground as they disembarked. Glinda turned and placed her hand on the fish's head, looking down at one of its large eyes. "Thank you."

The fish bowed its head in acceptance. "I go now to the ocean, to find my lost brothers."

Glinda watched as the fish turned and headed to the east, and disappeared into the darkness before the rising tide of the coming dawn.

"I'm hungry." said Glinda. "Let's find something to eat."

They passed through the front gate into the castle, and it was like stepping into another world. Experiments of all kinds were in progress. In one room, trees grew out of the ceiling, dropping polished steel apples on the floor. There were tracks on which rolling heads pursued their course. Propellers and wings and strange glowing engines met their gaze as the group pushed further into the weird and wonderful world of Smith & Tinker.

On the wall, Glinda saw a poster that read, *"The Hidden History is Here"* and another one read *"The Clockwork Cycle is Coming."*

They found the kitchen and discovered enough food to satisfy them comfortably for quite a while. They ate a fine breakfast of fruit, nuts and biscuits.

Glinda and Oscar walked outside to explore the grounds, leaving the other two to explore the building. In the distance they saw a sandy blur where the green grass dropped deep down into the Great Sandy Waste. Beyond that edge was a lighthouse, twisted and multi-towered. A stone bridge connected the lighthouse to the land. They found a brick path that led to a closer building and so they followed that, saving the Twisted Lighthouse for later.

Inside the building were constructs very strange to Oscar, but Glinda recognized them from a previous meeting. The constructs had a vaguely human body with limbs ending in wheels. They appeared to be sleeping.

"Wheelers." Glinda whispered excitedly. "They're wheelers." She closed the door to let them sleep.

"What are wheelers?" asked Oscar.

"Smith & Tinker made them. They are powered by the brick road. It's some connection to energy that they have. They can go really fast. One of them pulled both me and Wickrie when we left the Central City."

"*Gadzukes*. Is there anything you haven't done?" Oscar asked.

Glinda blushed and looked down. "*Maybe.*"

Then Oscar got embarrassed, and stammered, "I just meant that you've done a lot of things. It seems to me like you've done just about everything."

Glinda smiled. "You're nice."

Oscar started to feel all warm and toasty inside. He saw the faint blush on Glinda's cheeks and could see that she felt the same. He watched her face.

The rising sun peeked above the horizon. A glint of deep red in the stretching morning rays caught Glinda's eye. "Hey, I know that." She ran to the courtyard, and Oscar was left alone with his toasty feeling, slowly going cold.

Nice? She thinks I'm nice? Oscar mouthed silently, "Come on, Oscar, you've got to get better than that." He turned around to follow after Glinda.

Half buried in the ground after falling from a great height was *the Ruby Throne!* Glinda ran her hands over it.

"It's the Ruby Throne. I used to sit here. Not here, *exactly*. The Ruby Throne was in my father's garden."

"Ah, that's what was on the stone pedestal in the garden. It was empty, like something had just been plucked right off it."

"Kalinya threw the throne into the sky. I had no idea it came this far."

"She is powerful."

Glinda nodded slowly. "I know. But I have to face her. We have to find the Boneyard of the Clouds. Oscar, I believe what the Oracle said. It wouldn't lead us wrong. We're at Smith & Tinker. So the Boneyard has to be here, or we have to find something here that will lead us there."

"What do you want me to do?" Oscar asked.

"Find something useful. I'm going to keep looking." Glinda flitted away.

Oscar kicked at the dirt around the fallen throne. It was loose. In the distance, the stable door opened, and the first of the wheelers peered out. Oscar looked at the brick pathways crossing the courtyard and got an idea.

Glinda walked among great piles of junk, stacked from years of failed experiments and spare parts. These piles reached far over her head. Some of the many failed experiments included self-heating wash tubs, cooking trays, broken window frames that opened into different places, lifeless automatons, and winged bicycles. They were a testament to the continually inventive natures of Smith & Tinker. They truly were inventors extraordinaire. If it didn't work it was put aside until a need came for it. With the phenomenal rate of invention, the items set aside quickly piled up to be forgotten in the excitement of creation. Smith & Tinker were stackers. If there was any level of organization, it was only that the things on top were the most recently touched. Other than that, the experiments were haphazardly scattered.

Glinda peered through window frame into a dark cave. She pulled the frame down off the pile; a pair of broken mechanical wings crumpled and lost some brass feathers. There was no cave in the pile, but the window frame clearly opened into a cave. Looking at it from the back side, there was no cave—it was strictly one way. Glinda turned the blue frame cave-side against the pile and pushed a washbasin against it, to make sure that nothing came through.

Glinda came to a gap in the piles. An arch of rusted metal spanned the space. It was adorned with bits of tile and marble. This was a gate. Glinda entered and saw a row of trees. Strange. In the middle of a junkyard, they would plant trees? All around the trees were piles of junk, shielding this place from view. Glinda walked around the trees and saw that the trees followed a specific rectangular perimeter. Inside this perimeter was another perimeter of trees. A solemn, quiet feeling entered Glinda as she stepped into this place of sanctuary.

Before her eyes, the air shimmered, and Glinda thought she saw strange ephemeral ribs sticking up from the ground. They appeared to be made of mist, but when she blinked, they were gone. All around her she could feel a heaviness, like the feel of dew on a damp morning.

So this was the Boneyard of the Clouds. When clouds had finished their usefulness, they came here to expire. There were, doubtless, thousands of lost clouds all over the land, but this was a place specially set aside for these wondrous creations to expire in peace. A place where they could forget and be forgotten; a place for the passing storms to pass on.

Glinda walked to the center where she found a marble pedestal at the head of a pure spring of luminous water. She dipped her finger in the pool. It was cool and refreshing to the touch. She brought her finger up to her lips, but then stopped. A thought gave her pause. It was as if a voice on the wind, faintly heard, said to her, *"That water is not yours to have."*

Untouched she let the droplet fall from her finger back into the spring.

Unbidden, the words to the spell taught by Sonadia, the former Witch of the South, Mistress of Weather, came to her mind—the spell for how to create clouds. Upon Glinda's spoken words, the misty ribs sticking up from the ground solidified. Mist rose up from the pure spring and filled the ribs with cloud meat. Up from the ground rose a fully-formed cloud.

Glinda reached out and touched the cloud. It was firm to the touch. Curiously, she stroked what she believed to be its face as she would a horse or a new pet. She smiled and pushed the cloud upward and watched as it floated into the sky.

As Glinda walked back to the castle, she heard strange creaking and rapid thudding. She picked up her skirts and ran back through the maze of junk piles, fearing the worst. Had the witches found them? Had Locasta betrayed her trust? Would they have time to run?

Time played a part, but not how Glinda thought. The moments stretched out as she ran toward the sound. Then she pulled up short. What she saw was a wheeled race of magnificent proportions. Crouched behind speeding wheelers, Oscar, Omby-Amby and Wickrie-Kells raced around the brick pathways in the courtyard.

Oscar looked up to see Glinda. He rose halfway from his crouch, waving, and Omby-Amby used the opening to elbow him, throwing Oscar off balance. He tried to correct his momentum, then overcorrected, and then he went flying off of his skates. His wheeler stayed on the path and continued the lap, but Oscar did not. He flew off the curve and hit the ground at Glinda's feet.

"Glinda! Hi. We were, um, racing."

"If that's what you call racing, *twinkletoes*."

"I got the Ruby Throne out, and it's inside now. But you were gone, and we just thought that since we already had the wheelers harnessed—I was going to build a chariot, but then Wickrie found some skates. She said that you and her did that." He paused in his explanation. "How are you? You look different."

"I found the Boneyard of the Clouds." Glinda said.

"Good. So, what next?"

"I really don't know." Glinda took a deep breath and shook her head. "I don't know."

Oscar got a twinkle in his eye and held up the skates to Glinda. "Game?"

Glinda won the next two races handily.

The Twisted Lighthouse stood atop a jagged promontory surrounded by deadly sand. In centuries past, this would have been an island, but now it was sided by cliffs leading down to certain doom. It was a lonely bastion, waiting forever to be needed once again.

At the top of the lighthouse, there was a great magnifying crystal to project beams of light to approaching ships. But there had been no ships to approach this lighthouse for countless decades. When the inland sea was destroyed, the need for the lighthouse faded.

The original light source in the giant lantern had long since crumbled to powder, leaving the large crystal endlessly waiting. Glinda noticed a window in the top of the cabin. "Could the crystals catch the sun?"

"Sure." Oscar said, "But why? We're not going to see any ships out there. If there ever was an ocean, its ghosts are probably dead, too."

On the top rail of the lighthouse there was also a large voice magnifier. This megaphone had a twisted mouthpiece receiver, like an overzealous French horn, and a large bell to project the user's voice. It was fixed on a rolling stand, but connected to the top rail so that it could slide all the way around the cabin. Glinda recognized it from the description she had overheard at the Abracadabra Bazaar. This was the *mega-trump-o-phone.*

There was also a spyglass connected to the railing. This large spyglass magnified through a large crystal on the end. The jointed body allowed for multiple levels of magnification. There was an arc apparatus connected to the stand that allowed it to roll around the entire railing. When it encountered the mega-trump-o-phone on its slide around the rail, the apparatus reached around the mega-trump-o-phone with the arc, creating a temporary rail that the spyglass rolled across. This allowed both of the devices to be on the same part of the railing but switch places when necessary without having to slide the long way around the cabin.

The lighthouse had internal staircases going halfway up. These led to the various storage rooms, laboratories and sleeping quarters that made up the base. Once the twist in the construction started, the staircase only went up the outside of the lighthouse. There were three levels, each with their own railing on the outside. In the middle of the lighthouse, there was notably only one window, and it was pointed to the West, probably to harness the light of the rising sun.

Glinda and Oscar climbed to the top and experimented with the mega-trump-o-phone. Oscar did some bird calls. Then they saw Omby-Amby put his arms around Wickrie-Kells. Perhaps he was just teaching her some hand to hand combat or grappling, or perhaps not. This opportunity was too good to pass up. As Omby-Amby put his arms around Wickrie-Kells, Oscar made a loud *"ppbbbphhhrrrttttt!"* into the mega-trump-o-phone, sending the noise echoing over the entire estate.

The unfortunate bodily noise startled them both, but Wickrie-Kells took advantage of the momentary distraction and flipped Omby-Amby over her shoulder, throwing him flat onto his back, and knocking the wind out of him. When he rose, gasping, to his feet, Oscar and Glinda watched through the spyglass as Omby-Amby yelled and gestured very angrily at them—far away in the lighthouse. They couldn't hear his words, but his gestures indicated without question that he was very angry. They laughed and laughed until the tears were running down their faces.

Two days passed. Glinda and Oscar were reading in the castle library when Wickrie-Kells came to get them. She was breathless from running all the way from the lighthouse to the castle to find them. "Lighthouse. Quick."

They jumped up out of their seats and followed after Wickrie-Kells.

Halfway up the lighthouse, where the internal staircase ended, there was a hallway. In this hallway Wickrie-Kells opened a room door. This was the one room with the window to the outside.

"I think there is something in here that you should see." Wickrie-Kells said to Glinda. Her glance to Oscar removed him from the equation. This was for Glinda's eyes alone.

Glinda pushed past her to enter into the room. Oscar stayed outside the door. The room was, without a doubt, a laboratory. Strange implements and beakers and tubes of all shapes and sizes lined the work benches. Mirrors lined the walls, with several mirrors on wheels that could be moved around. Glinda recognized this place. Her mind immediately flashed back to a memory from more than ten years previous, from when she was a young girl, when she had been inside the Ruby Palace.

Young Glinda watched her mother array mirrors very precisely in the fading light. Gayelette blew some powder in between two mirrors, revealing a beam reflecting between them and creating a ring of light around all of the mirrors.

Glinda reached up to touch the beam of light, but Gayelette stopped her reaching fingers. *"Not now, Glinda. We are going to capture some dreams."*

Glinda blinked rapidly. "I know this place. My mother had a laboratory set up like this in the Ruby Palace."

"There's more." Wickrie-Kells pointed Glinda to a mirror, half-obscured by a dropcloth. There was movement in the mirror as Glinda walked toward it, but the movement was not from Glinda. It was something in the mirror. Glinda pulled off the dropcloth to view a window into the past.

In the mirror, Gayelette moved back and forth arranging mirrors. She blew dust into the path, making the beam visible. She looked back toward the mirror, as if she was looking at Glinda, and smiled. Then she continued her work. She looked back and scolded, *"Not now, Quelala. We are going to capture some dreams."* This continued until a bright flash of light obscured everything. Then the action began again. It played on a ten second loop.

Glinda stared as this scene played out three more times. Then she turned back to her friends. "It's my mother."

Wickrie-Kells nodded. "I thought that you should know." She excused herself and closed the door behind her. Outside the door, she stopped Oscar from entering. "She needs some time."

Omby-Amby hit Oscar in the arm and said, "Hey, gives us some time. Tell me about this Republic idea. How do the people keep it?"

Oscar looked long at the closed door before he replied, "It takes work. A lot of work. People are alone in what they know. They have to watch and make sure that they are always ready. You never know when the time will come."

Omby-Amby waved his hands to get Oscar's attention. "Brud, I'm over here."

Oscar shook his head to clear it. "Sorry. I was saying, because there are no kings, the people are responsible for guarding their own freedoms. They watch their leaders closely and hold them accountable. The people elect representatives to make laws. These representatives are elected every two years."

"So they are not appointed at the will of the king?"

"No. No, you're not understanding. There *is no king.* There is the people—*'We the People'*. The people vote for men that will vote for them and make laws. If the representatives don't do what the people want, they don't get re-elected. So the government is always changing. But it is built on a structure that will last. It's amazing."

Omby-Amby led them down the internal staircase. "Could it be built here?"

Oscar thought for a moment as they emerged at the base of the lighthouse. "I would imagine so. Yes, it probably could work. We would need our own country, or city, at least, to experiment. Everyone would be accountable for their own actions. Everyone would work. Nobody would get something for nothing." Oscar glanced back up at the door in the middle of the lighthouse. "It would require that people be honest with each other."

"We have a place *here.* Could we not draw up a Constitution, as you say, and establish a law in this land?"

The two young men walked outside into the bright sunshine of the day and crossed the bridge back to the castle, great and world-changing hopeful thoughts on their minds.

Two more days passed at the South Castle. Glinda immersed herself in the great treasures of knowledge found in the library. She found references to the inland sea, and old maps that showed a much different land in previous centuries. She read about the First Witch Wars, finding no additional information than what the flying fish had told her. But it was a big book she was reading, there were bound to be more details. She vowed to research it more fully at a later time. While she was gaining a better idea of what motivated the witches in previous times, she still didn't know what she was going to do with Kalinya in the here-and-now. But the time was drawing very close—she could feel it. Even if she wasn't ready, it was nearly time, and she would act, just like she had said. She had given her word to the apprentice witch, Locasta, and she would be there, as she said, when the time was right.

Oscar and Omby-Amby discussed their ideas for a constitutional city. It would be a large city, surrounded by a wall. The wall would be both symbolic and functional. It would signify the departure from the old world and the entrance into a new world. It would be tall and strong to stand through the wars that would inevitably come. The city would be full of people that would work, but also people that would beautify their surroundings. The ideal city would not just be stone and cement, but also art and music and stained glass. It would be forever a work in progress. When people stopped dreaming, then the city would stop changing. Even though Omby-Amby didn't dream, he recognized that Oscar did, and he saw the power in dreams. Their city would reflect the power that individuals have to create the world they want.

Wickrie-Kells explored the lands all about the South Castle. She rode behind the wheeler, IgNob, as he learned and explored along with her. She discovered the hidden brick roads that led toward different parts of the land. She found a map in the stable that showed the brick roads of Oz that linked all major areas in the land together. A dashed line linked the roads to a place in the North Mountains. That was a place they would have to investigate someday. If the brick roads were truly magic, then that magic had to be generated in some way, and that was a mystery that even Glinda would approve of—when she was finished with her current gloom and doom.

Far away from the South Castle, the exiled Winged Monkey, Brutus, crept into a shallow cave to nurse his wounds. He had wandered for days and finally he succumbed to exhaustion. Deep within his heart a hatred grew. A cold and gnawing sense of injustice welled up inside him. He stretched the stubs of his formerly magnificent wings and grunted in pain as the lacerated skin broke open again. His eyes burned with hatred for Glinda, for King Klick and for all of the people in Oz. He would have his revenge. He would have…sleep.

22 THE WITCH'S OATH

Locasta waited until the oracular rope urged her to leave in the morning. She walked west for four days. She took her time, knowing that Kalinya would be far more than angry when she arrived empty-handed. Even the word *furious* was not a strong enough description for Kalinya's rage. Locasta walked alone, and for the first time in her life, she liked the silence. There was no screaming, no insults, and no bruises to nurse back to health in frightened solitude. She resolved to be strong and stand her ground against Kalinya.

The morning of the fourth day the young witch marched over the last hill. She heard the sandy army before she saw it. At the crest of the hill she looked down to see giant sand warriors hurling great rocks at the small Winkie army. It was only a matter of time before the Winkies surrendered. The surrender would come when the price of fighting for their life became too expensive. They were being systematically worn down. When they were tired of resisting, they would surrender, just so that they could survive.

In the distance she saw the acting general over the armies—Kalinya—turn in her direction. But it was too late, Kalinya saw her, too. In a heartbeat Kalinya was beside her.

"You have returned, my apprentice. I thought...you might have been destroyed." She looked around. "Where is my tiger?" She grabbed Locasta's arm tightly, "And where is Glinda?" Three steps, and they were in front of Kalinya's tent.

Kalinya shoved Locasta into the tent.

The sand warriors neither heard nor cared about the muffled crashing in the tent, nor the sobbing screams afterwards.

Kalinya studied the words of the oracle as they appeared. Locasta had practiced all the way back, trying to figure out the murmured words that Glinda had used. Finally she had cracked the syllables, so now she had a spell to change the shape of her hat. In this case, she changed it into a slate. Writing mystically appeared, giving instruction.

Locasta nursed a bruised cheek as she warily watched Kalinya.

"You have learned something. Your hat used to speak. Now it changes shape. How?"

Locasta looked away, avoiding Kalinya's gaze. "I figured out a spell."

"Interesting. How do I meet Glinda?"

"She cast a spell. It allows the Silver Slippers to target her location. You can go there."

Greedy fires gleamed in Kalinya's eyes. "I'll teach that little brat. Just like you. A few lessons and she'll break, just like you." Then Kalinya turned to leave.

Locasta dropped her gaze, humiliated. But something had awakened inside her—a small whisper, like a tiny candle in the darkness. She could not see the future, but she could see the next step. Without lifting her head, Locasta glanced over to the oracular slate. The words on it verified the decision she had already made. *"Blood binds sisters."*

The tent flap swished once, signifying Kalinya's departure.

Locasta counted to twenty; to be sure that Kalinya was truly gone. Then she exited the tent herself, and went to find Ondri-baba.

Glinda watched as Kalinya appeared in a flash of silver. Her quick appearance punched a hole through the surrounding clouds. The mist quickly filled in the witch-shaped hole.

Kalinya looked around at her surroundings. The light was dim. There was no clue of where they were, as the clouds completely surrounded the boneyard. Dim trees could be seen through the mist lining the entire perimeter.

"What is this place?" Kalinya demanded.

"The oracle should have told you. This is the Boneyard of the Clouds." Glinda stood on a marble slab surrounded by the clear spring. Her hands were behind her back holding a handkerchief to keep them still. She didn't want anything to betray to the witch how nervous she really was.

Kalinya faced her at a distance of twenty feet. The Witch stood among ghostly remnants of clouds. Bits of mist floated all around her as if they were creatures sniffing a new visitor.

"Are we in Oz?"

"Perhaps." Glinda was intentionally evasive. "Perhaps not. Perhaps we're inside a dream."

In this dim region, the two primary sources of light were the Silver Slippers and the Golden Cap. Both drew attention to themselves in the very neutral atmosphere.

"Why have you summoned me here?"

Glinda waited before responding. She met Kalinya's stern gaze coolly.

"Why have you called me?" Kalinya repeated impatiently.

"You and your sister are destroying Oz. I will not permit another Witch War."

"You will not *permit*—?" Kalinya cackled. "How could *you* stop it? If we want to march from one end of Oz to the other, nothing will stop us. And when Ondri-baba has completed her conquest, I will assume my rightful place as elder Queen. There is nothing that you can do to stop me." Kalinya sneered.

"Smith and Tinker are gone. There are no more weapons. What is *here* is here. There will be no more. When your sandy armies are gone, there are no more to replace them."

That was not something that Kalinya anticipated. "So they really left? Ondri-baba warned them not to interfere." She harrumphed, "*Cowards*. Can't face the truth."

"It is you who does not face the truth, Kalinya. You are a murderer."

Kalinya swirled her hand, causing ripples in the pool at Glinda's feet. "Murder is a term that only applies to persons subject to the law. *I AM THE LAW!*"

Glinda braced herself, but her resolve cracked a little bit with that scream.

Kalinya chuckled. "If you were my daughter-"

"But I am not."

"No matter. If you were my daughter, you would respect the power I wield."

"And what power is that?" Glinda prodded.

Kalinya stood up straight and glared at the red-haired girl, "I destroyed the Ruby Palace. I took the Silver Slippers by force. I conquered all of the secrets of the Red Sorceress."

"Yet you are here, at my feet." Glinda declared. "Your conquests are not power. They are indecipherable marks—scribbles—on crumbling wall. True power eludes you."

Kalinya's eyes blazed. "What power eludes me?" She gestured, "I *have* everything! I have power to fling you into the sky and let you fall to your death. I control an army. I march and nations tremble."

Glinda clenched her jaw. Behind her back, her hands nervously twisted the handkerchief.

A rumble of thunder shook the clouds. Glinda allowed herself a smile. Good for Oscar. The Wizard was with her, showing solidarity. She took courage from her friends standing by her, even in the face of evil.

"Then fling me into the sky!" Glinda shouted. "I control the sky! At my word, the thunder roars!" On command, the thunder echoed, and Kalinya fell to her knees in astonishment.

"That's impossible. Sonadia is dead. You cannot know—"

"Oh?"

Kalinya rose and looked on Glinda with a new wariness. "It will be war."

"It will be on my terms." Glinda demanded.

Kalinya scoffed, but her careful pause showed that she was listening to Glinda and starting to take her seriously. "Name them."

"The Emerald Plains. Two weeks' hence. I will face you on the field of battle. The winner will take all."

"You have no army. You have nothing. Before the two weeks pass, all of Oz will fall to me."

Thunder rumbled again, and Glinda took greater courage. "Then consider this a challenge. After you conquer your sister, then only I will stand in your way. And I *will* stand in your way."

"What proof do I have that you will surrender?"

Glinda touched the Golden Cap on her head. "*This*. I wager my Golden Cap against your Silver Slippers."

The Witch laughed, but there was a hint of nervousness that escaped. "You'll have to pry these slippers off my dead feet."

Glinda's eyes hardened. That was how Kalinya got the slippers from her mother, by killing her. Glinda forced the rage deep inside and took a calming breath. "You want the Golden Cap. Meet me on the field of battle. If death is the end, then the survivor gleans the reward."

Kalinya frowned and glared at Glinda. "You have two weeks."

"*You* have two weeks." The girl waved her hands and gestured with her fingers. "I release you. Focus on the oracle and return there now."

Three steps and Kalinya was gone.

Glinda exhaled and slumped to the ground. The clouds lifted from around the trees and drifted lazily up into the sky. The Boneyard once again felt the sun of the morning. Behind the trees, Oscar shook his flat sheet of metal, creating the thunderous noise. Glinda smiled at him, exhausted.

"Thank you. That is another time you saved me."

Oscar beamed. "People hear what they want to hear."

But Wickrie-Kells was not happy. She exploded at Glinda, "*The Golden Cap!* How could you? The monkey almost killed you for that. And now you're just going to give it away? Just wager off the most precious gift your father had?"

Glinda looked around at her friends. Oscar shrugged, but his eyes said that he would support Glinda. Omby-Amby maintained a stern silence, which probably meant that he agreed with Wickrie-Kells.

"I meant what I said. I am not going to give away the Golden Cap, and I'm not going to surrender. The only way that she will get this cap is if she pulls it off my lifeless head herself."

That mollified Wickrie-Kells somewhat, but she was still irritated. "What about our army? Oh, that's right, *we don't have one!*"

Oscar helped Glinda to her feet. The red-haired girl smiled impishly and said, "Then it's time we get one."

23 THE DECLARATION OF LIBERTY

On the Winkie Plains, Ondri-baba rolled back into camp in the Hamstrambulator, returning from a review of the front lines. Her stilt-legged hut followed her loyally and then took its place and sat silently next to the tent that served as central command. She looked out with pride at the giant warriors hurling boulders at the Winkies. Now and then a giant would fall, but she would pick them up later. The skies were clear, so there was no chance that rain would spoil her day. Everything looked excellent. Nothing could ruin her imminent victory. She stepped down from the Hamstrambulator onto a half-sized kneeling sand warrior that she kept handy as a stepstool, and then stepped onto the ground.

Waiting for her was Locasta, the apprentice, who said, "Queen Ondri-baba, you have been betrayed."

In the Central City, each day arose with Mombi sitting beside the throne. At Pastoria's request, she had returned at the same time to the king's throne. She whispered secrets into the king's ears. Each day her visits grew longer and longer. Yesterday, Mombi was not asked to leave at all. She had become the shadow behind the throne. It was beside the throne that she stood today. She did not have to sit. She held a book open and showed Pastoria. "The History of Oz."

"It is blank." Pastoria said.

"Perhaps it is only a part of the hidden history that you do not see. Perhaps the history is still being scribed. Perhaps it is a mask to guard its secrets. My king, to those who have eyes to see, it contains many secrets. If you continue to listen, I will continue to speak."

Pastoria smiled as he steepled his fingers in front of his face. "I am listening, and you are speaking. It appears I have a new advisor."

Glinda and Oscar restlessly wandered over all levels of the Twisted Lighthouse. Sometimes Glinda sat in front of the magic mirror, watching her mother. Sometimes she would talk to the mirror, but there was never any response.

It was up to Glinda and Oscar to plan the message that they would use to build an army. Oscar kept talking about establishing laws and self-governance. Glinda proposed rebellion against tyranny.

Omby-Amby and Wickrie-Kells studied books of maps, planning the war strategy. They scavenged every level of the Twisted Lighthouse and the South Castle for weapons or strategic tools they could use to turn the battle in their favor.

Each day, Oscar slept. He snored. He dreamed.

And each day, new things appeared around the South Castle. Walls appeared with turrets, new wings appeared in the South Castle, and books appeared in the library.

Oscar's dreams were shaping the reality in this place.

Curious visitors appeared, first by ones and twos, and then by tens and by scores. They had heard that the Great Wizard was building in preparation for a war. These visitors saw the wonders for themselves and then they went home and spread the message across the land. At one gathering, Oscar and Glinda jointly addressed the group from the north balcony of the South Castle.

Oscar said, "There is a choice that lies before you. Some say that I am a Wizard. What say you?" At which the crowd cheered, for they had heard of his great and wonderful works. "There are Witches that seek to rule over you. Why do they seek for this power? Why do they wish to crush you beneath their heel? Is it for gain? Is it for wealth? Or is it for the wicked need to feel self-important?

"Answer for yourself, who knows best how to rule you? You? Or someone else?

"Who has your interests in mind? You? Or someone else? If it is someone else, then by all means, go, and live your life under the heel of oppression.

"In my land, my fathers bled and died so that they could live a life free from oppression. Did that mean the life was easy? No. Crops died. Disease destroyed families. There was sorrow. Sometimes bad things happen. But my forebears knew that if they, and people like them, could decide how they wanted to live, and lived peaceably with their neighbors, then there would be no oppression. They enacted laws that protected the people from their rulers, and gave the rulers limits on power.

"Are there such laws in Oz?"

The people shouted, "NO!"

"And why are there no laws like that? It is because you are ruled by kings and witches and power that is beyond you, because it says it is so. Oz has many lands. Each may be ruled by itself. There is no central ruler that unites the land. Not any more. Take this opportunity, my friends, to raise your voices and be heard. Let those in power know that you will not be silenced any longer."

The cheering lasted for several minutes. These were words that none of them could have imagined. Such things had never been spoken before in Oz. It took a stranger—a messenger from the sky—to help them see what they could become.

Then Glinda arose to speak.

"There comes a time when you must realize who you are and in what you believe. Every one of us was born to do something, to be something. But just because we were born to a certain position, whether it be a princess or a pauper, a knight or a night watchman, we do not need to limit ourselves to that alone. We can be what we determine. We choose how we make our way in the world. I was born to be my mother's daughter. For fifteen years I hated her for it. But that does not mean that it was wrong. I can take that calling and make it more than it was.

"There is a place where people dream. You see that place here. You see what the great Wizard is dreaming into reality. He is making this a place where imaginings can become reality. If you can dream it, you can become it."

Later, inside the library of the South Castle, Omby-Amby laid out his list of required weapons for the upcoming battle. "The sand warriors are not like people. We've tried swords. We've run them over with the Hamstrambulator, but we lost that. We can't cut the sand like we would a flesh and bone person. So we found more appropriate tools for battling sand—shovels, picks, rakes and other gardening tools."

"We could use the magnifier from the lighthouse." Oscar suggested. "With enough sunlight we could turn the sand to glass."

"Brilliant." said Wickrie-Kells. "We'll prepare that, too."

"Those are all of our weapons." said Omby-Amby.

"With Oscar's rallying cry of freedom to the people, we will have our army." Glinda said.

"It's not just a promise of freedom. It's the responsibility to rule themselves." Oscar clarified. "It means that each person is responsible for themselves. But they are also responsible for seeing that things are done correctly under the law."

"Still," Glinda said, "your message is resonating with people. They like what they hear. Even if it is an experiment, it is something that they want."

Omby-Amby proclaimed, "They want to know that the rules are not going to change just because the king says so. They need that. We all need that."

Glinda agreed. "Then we shall have that."

They gathered in the throne room, where Glinda sat in the Ruby Throne. Oscar provided the pen, and Wickrie-Kells unfurled the parchment. Omby-Amby laid his sword on the table as Glinda wrote the *Declaration of Liberty*.

"I will send a messenger to Ondri-baba. She will know of the terms we established with Kalinya. It will be war. Not because we want power, but because we want to rule ourselves. The war will be because they want power. It is not theirs to take." Glinda wrote the declaration and assigned the mission.

Wickrie-Kells suggested the perfect agent for the mission. "I know just who you can send. He's smart, he's fast, and he believes in you."

The Wheeler, IgNob, carried the parchment with him as he sped northward to find Ondri-baba.

At that moment, on the fields of battle, near Winkie Fields, Ondri-baba stormed into her tent, followed closely by Locasta. Right behind Locasta, following them into the tent, a paper bird fluttered. The bird went directly into Ondri-baba's hands. She read the note and looked up sharply at Locasta. "What do you know of this?" She demanded.

Locasta pleaded innocence. "I know nothing. That is not mine."

"Then how do you know I am betrayed?"

"Kalinya."

Ondri-baba squinted her good eye at the younger witch and studied her closely. "Not Mombi?"

"No. Only Kalinya. Isn't that enough?"

"We have lost Mombi. She is no longer one of us." Ondri-baba crumpled the paper and held its edge in the flame of a burning candle on the table. She held on to the paper until it was completely engulfed in flames and then dropped it down to the ground, turning the flame invisible before stamping it out. "Invisible flames cast no shadows." She said, and then she turned to Locasta, "Now tell me, what would be so dire that an apprentice would turn on her master with accusations of betrayal?"

Locasta wrapped her sliced finger in a bandage as the blood-sand creature rose to its full size. "They last much longer than an hour. I had Kalinya's blood-tiger with me for at least ten hours. Then Glinda destroyed it."

This blood-sand warrior was bound to Locasta by her blood. She tried but could not make it disintegrate and go back into its vial. "Maybe the blood makes them more alive." It took the form and likeness of Locasta, and even studied the apprentice witch, tilting her head sideways, just like Locasta. It was learning her behaviors through imitation.

"This is an interesting turn of events. You were right to bring this to my attention. Forthwith, I shall deal with my sister."

24 THE BRAVE LITTLE WHEELER

In the Witches' camp, Kalinya returned to see the battle proceeding, but Ondri-baba was nowhere to be seen. She went to her own tent, but she did not find her apprentice, either. Suspicion drove her to the command tent in the center of the camp.

Kalinya froze when she opened the command tent door and saw her apprentice standing behind Ondri-baba.

"Enter, Kalinya." Ondri-baba commanded.

Kalinya's gaze jumped between her two accusers, for that is what they were. "I appear to have interrupted something." She feigned ambivalence and raised her hands nonchalantly. "Locasta, you naughty girl, what stories have you been telling?"

Locasta stepped to one side, revealing what she had been hiding—her blood-sand warrior.

It was defined from its generic sandy siblings by its deep crimson color. The form mimicked Locasta's, for it was her blood that created it. Locasta stared calmly at her master.

A kaleidoscope of emotions crashed like waves across Kalinya's face. Fear, anger, pain, betrayal, success, exultation, reluctance and determination all mixed to a scrambled whirlwind, rising to a silently smug crescendo.

"What is your explanation for this?" Ondri-baba demanded. The tent door swished. "My guards are in here with us. Any attempt to throw me into the sky will result in your arms being ripped out and sand being poured into your mouth. Am I understood?"

Kalinya stared down her sister, then relented. "An *experiment.* A way to improve on the magic. They can still be destroyed." Kalinya shot a deadly glare at Locasta, who looked away guiltily. "But they are stronger and smarter and last longer than the regular sand. These ones don't get defiled with dirt. But they don't fit back in the hourglass. They require a larger container."

Ondri-baba's eyes were alight with a cruel fire, illuminating the new possibilities opening up before her. "How large can they get? I created a beast fifty feet tall with eight vials."

"Don't do this." whispered Locasta.

Kalinya smiled wickedly, "My tiger was twice as big as me. That was on the second blooding. Perhaps the more blood used, the larger it gets."

"Please don't do this." Locasta begged.

"Begone, little one." Ondri-baba flicked dismissively at the apprentice witch. "The Witches are talking."

Locasta stepped back and shoved her blood-sand doppelganger toward Kalinya. In that moment of physical contact, silent instructions were passed from flesh to blood-sand and memories imparted. The doppelganger knew what it had to do and why. The blood-sand girl charged, flailing its arms as clubs. But it was stopped in mid-leap by an invisible force. The invisible guards ripped the arms off the blood-sand warrior and pinned it in position. Ondri-baba removed the spell of invisibility, revealing the large sandy-warriors as they pounded the blood-sand warrior to pieces with its own arms. Then they stomped the remaining pieces until nothing was left joined.

"Foolish." Ondri-baba said to Locasta. Then she turned to her guards. "Remove the little witch and guard her. She will have penance in the very near future."

The sandy warrior reached out for Locasta, but she pulled her arm away. "I'll go." And she marched out in front of the warrior, leaving the command tent.

Kalinya and Ondri-baba schemed late into the night. Finally Kalinya revealed her upcoming battle to the death with Glinda. "The armies must move to the Emerald Lands. We have the chance to crush Glinda and her rebellion once and for all." Kalinya demanded.

"It was you who swore a Witch's Oath, not I." said Ondri-baba. "This army is mine to command."

"We can defeat her and Oz will be ours!"

Ondri-baba cocked her head to one side. "What is it about that girl that irks you so much? Why have you spent time and blood to turn her? Why not kill her, as you did her mother? That is how you got the Silver Slippers."

"Yes. Of course." Kalinya repeated the conceit, insulating herself with another telling of the lie. "Of course that is how I got the Silver Slippers. And how the Ruby Palace was destroyed."

"Yet you cannot destroy the girl. She is not even a shadow of her mother, and you cannot even bring her to her knees and beg for mercy."

Kalinya stopped, speechless. Her sister had never spoken to her like this before. White-hot anger started deep within her and crinkled the corners of her mouth until they dropped nearly down to her chin.

"Take your armies to the Emerald Plains. Fulfill your Witch Oath. Fight the enemy on the field of battle."

"You do not forbid it?"

"The less I need to clean up after you, the more I will rule when this war is complete. The Winkies are defeated; they just have not accepted that fact yet. Their yellow army is a fraction of what it was. My army is nearly full strength. And you have given me a weapon of blood that can defeat every army that Oz can bring to bear against me."

"You are delivering me into destruction!" Kalinya accused, not understanding Ondri-baba's swift agreement.

"No. I am delivering you into *humiliation.* You have given your enemy every advantage because of your blind ambition." Ondri-baba stood up from the table and lit every candle in the room, banishing all shadows from her presence. "What you refuse to see will be your undoing."

She stood in the center of the lighted tent, far away from the shadows. "Your enemy is young. She will follow the rules of engagement. She will meet you on the field of battle. If she is an idealist, she will send a messenger with a challenge to me also. When she has betrayed her position, I will bring the battle to her. I will destroy whatever army she has created, and you will be helpless because of the oath. You will march out at the head of your armies on the Emerald Plains, and you will have no enemy…and no power. Your humiliation will be gorgeous." That was that. Ondri-baba finished her plan and prepared for sleep.

Kalinya watched as Ondri-baba gathered blankets around her and settled down into the middle of the floor. Even after she had fallen asleep, her magic eye stayed open. It kept moving around, *seeing.* At the moment of greatest eye movement, Ondri-baba would always start screaming about the shadows and the darkness.

The moon was high in the sky before Kalinya retired to her own tent. To her surprise, Locasta was not inside. Her bed was removed. Another tent was set up at the base of a nearby hill. A large sand warrior stood guard at its front.

Locasta had moved her meager belongings and her cot out of Kalinya's tent to put in her own small tent. If Locasta was not permitted to leave, she would not be a party to those actions taken without her approval. She would not stand silently by and let the others decide for her. Moving out was her first action against her master. She was pulling away, attempting to remove herself as far as possible from the influence of the Wicked Witches.

IgNob raced through the night. The Wheeler was tired, but his mission gave him purpose and strength. He was serving the measure of his creation by obeying this order. Once it was fulfilled, he could rest.

The brick road wound westward, toward the Yellow Castle. As the sun peeked above the western horizon, IgNob screeched to a halt. In the distance stood the base camp of the Witch Army. But IgNob could not leave the brick road. He experimented by reaching one rear foot off of the brick road, and then quickly pulled it back. It was cold, lifeless. He shook his entire leg, trying to get feeling back into the numbed part. He had no way to get to the camp. But he had to deliver the message—it was his duty. He was the messenger. And so he cried out.

Locasta entered into Ondri-baba's tent. The recently-awakened witch looked up, fatigue lining her face, as the apprentice entered. "What is it?" she demanded.

"A messenger has arrived for you. It requested that you come to the brick road that it might deliver its message."

"What do you mean, *'it'?*"

Ondri-baba ceremoniously drove the Hamstrambulator out to the brick road where the lone wheeler waited. "What is this? A wheeler? Smith & Tinker were warned to stay out of this war."

IgNob rolled back and forth, more to stay awake than out of nervousness. "Not Masters Smith & Tinker, Witch. *Mistress Glinda* sent me." IgNob held his head high.

Ondri-baba stepped out of the vehicle, down the pint-sized sandman's back, and walked to the brick road. She put her hands on her hips and stared down her girth to face the wheeled messenger. "*Mistress Glinda* sent you? So she has taken up residence in the South Castle."

"She is our master. We serve her with honor." IgNob proclaimed. He extended the rolled parchment to Ondri-baba. She read it, mumbling.

Ondri-baba gestured and sandy warriors surrounded the wheeler on the brick road. "I do not accept the terms of this declaration. Let my silence by my answer."

IgNob bristled as he felt the press of the guards. There was no retreat. IgNob felt within his chest a pang that he recognized from a story that Master Smith had once told the wheelers, shortly after their creation. It was a story of noble sacrifice. The hero died, but he saved the land. That pang IgNob now felt was a mixture of sadness at his impending destruction, but also the indomitable anthem of courage. He would not cower in the face of a tyrant. He would stand, even as it destroyed him.

"Destroy him." Ondri-baba ordered.

From her position on the hill, Locasta watched as the wheeler charged at the witch. It leaped, and was struck down by a guard. The wheeler was batted and shoved back and forth between the guards. She heard the cackling of

Ondri-baba as the wheeler was flung high into the air, landing with one arm touching the brick road. It lay still, only the arm twitching on the road.

Ondri-baba called for the guards to stop. She studied the wheeler and then ordered the guards to put it back on the road. The wheeler came back to life and charged at Ondri-baba again. Again it was swatted down, and then thrown into the air. Then the scenario replayed *again.*

Then Ondri-baba tired of the game. The wheeler was flung far away from the road. The sandy soldiers commenced the destruction of the magic by tearing apart the brick road. One of them even threw loose bricks at the fallen wheeler, denting its head.

The Hamstrambulator rolled back to Ondri-baba's tent. She spent the next hour gathering sand into containers from the battlefield.

In the distant sky, the Winged Monkeys circled, flying patrols—the ever-present eye in the sky. But they did nothing more than patrol, so they were not considered a threat to the Witches.

The Hamstrambulator stopped in front of Locasta. Ondri-baba looked down at the apprentice contemptuously, "Tell your master she is free to continue against the Winkies. Or she can wait for her humiliation on the Emerald Plains." Then she drove away, the Hamstrambulator loaded down with all of her supplies of war. Behind her, the stilt-legged hut trundled awkwardly after.

Out of one of the windows, Locasta saw a bearded face look out—Quelala. His haunted eyes met hers, but there was no hope left in them. For the briefest of moments, Locasta saw what it meant to be dead inside. The horror of it all wrapped around her like a familiar blanket.

She felt sick. But what sickened her most of all was the closeness and familiarity of the feeling—it was not foreign. That *dead inside* feeling was very, very *familiar.*

25 THE WORDS OF A FATHER ENDURE

In the library of the South Castle, Oscar and Glinda conversed.

"What was your father like?" Oscar asked.

"He was always seeing more in me than I could see." Glinda answered.

"Oh. That's not exactly what I was expecting."

"What were you expecting me to say, hmm? What was your father like?"

"He was...a good man." Oscar shrugged. It was clear that he had more to answer than that, but those were the only words that came out.

Glinda laughed. "*You*, who carry an entire land's history inside your head, along with systems of government for two other lands—"

"Basic principles." Oscar corrected.

"—that can change the course of not just one kingdom, but all of them, and you sum up your father as *'a fine man'*?"

"I said *good*."

"But there is a great deal that you didn't say. Nobody pauses like that to think and describes their father as *a good man* if they don't have a lot more to say. So what is it? What don't you want to tell me about him?"

Oscar reddened in the face and chewed on his words before he spoke them. "It's not about him, it's more about me." He took a deep breath and straightened his backbone. "My father was a warrior—he was a soldier in the Mexican-American War. My grandfather served in the Continental Army. Every man in my family as far back as I can find has been a soldier. I'm not." Oscar's eyes got hard, then they got soft, then they hardened again. "I'm not. I left. Went west." He forced a smile, leaving many, many things unsaid. "I joined the circus. I entertained people, soldiers. I gave them rest from war. I am not like my father. He was...*a good man*. That's what my mother always said. And she wasn't wrong."

Glinda reached out to take Oscar's hand. Her heart hurt for him—not for the things that he said, but for all of the things that she could see that held inside. "You have a lot going on inside you, Oscar, more than anyone else has any idea of. So maybe you weren't born to be a soldier. You *dream*. How many people can say that? Nobody *here*." Shyly, Glinda admitted, "I don't know if I've told you, but you fascinate me." she blushed. "I know you *think* more than anyone else I know. So I don't expect you to jump through the hoops of small talk to get to what I really think. That's why I said that my father was always seeing more in me than I could see. I see more in you, too."

"That is...*respect*." Oscar nodded slowly, tasting his words. "I didn't know you thought that way."

"You charged a really big Winged Monkey for me. You hate the Winged Monkeys. King Klick saw it, which is why he taunted you so. But you charged at that monster for me."

Now it was Oscar's turn to blush again. "You were in trouble."

"Nobody else was there ahead of you. You came running."

Oscar laughed a little. "I did, didn't I? That was really dumb of me." He thought back on that moment, "I don't know what I thought I could do. It just needed to be done."

"Maybe it's the doing that makes the thing happen." Glinda whispered, as if it was a big secret.

Oscar leaned in toward her and blinked. Glinda thought back on what she had just said. They both burst out laughing. "That's a little bit obvious, isn't it?" she admitted.

"Yeah." Oscar picked up a knife and absently whittled on a scrap of wood he had brought in from the workshop. "Just a little. So about your father. You said that he saw more in you than you did. What do you mean by that?"

"I hated my mother. She was always too busy with her experiments for me. I had a temper—"

"Red hair, temper? Nooo." Oscar remarked facetiously.

Glinda nodded sarcastically right back at him. "A temper, but it stayed bottled up inside of me. Sometimes my eyes would get pretty dark and stormy. When my dad saw that happening, he would always do something that would take me away from the situation. Something to take my mind off of my troubles, even just for a few minutes." Glinda's eyes glistened as she recounted a memory.

"I was eight, I think. Mother was supposed to bake a cake with me. But she was in the Ruby Palace again. Something important, my father said, but I was so angry. I wanted a cake. I wanted something that would make the day into mine and mine alone.

"My father tried to help me bake a cake, but he was *not* a baker. We got flour everywhere—in the room and all over us. We looked like ghosts. We were going to go down to the stream to wash it off. I guess he thought that I needed to get out of that room before I exploded. So we were going to catch frogs or something and wash off the mess. He looked back at the Ruby Palace and waved. I couldn't see what he saw, but then suddenly there were clouds that came over us.

"It started raining. I know there weren't many clouds before, if there were any, and now it was raining on us. But I wasn't a bit upset by that. Sure it would ruin my nice dress, but I was eight. I was covered in flour, anyway. What more was a little rain going to do?"

Oscar raised a finger. "Water and flour make paste."

The smile rose up into Glinda's eyes. "Yes, they do. But at that time, it was just me and my dad, dancing in the rain. Running, jumping, screaming. We never made it to the stream. Never went to catch frogs. Never made the cake, either." Glinda smiled at the memory. "The next day I went out with my mother and Sonadia, from here in the South. That's where I learned how to make clouds."

"I wish I could have met your father." Oscar said, "I mean, for real. What he said to me, in that moment. I think you're right. He did see something in me."

Glinda rested her elbows on the table and her chin in her hands, looking at Oscar. "Remind me what he said to you. I didn't hear it."

"He said, *'Don't lie to her.'*"

"And you haven't."

Oscar shook his head, agreeing with her. "I have told you the truth. I certainly don't feel like a wizard." He continued when he saw Glinda starting to protest, "But other people think that I am. I mean, who else is going to do it, right?"

"So maybe it just needs to be done. *And it's the doing, which makes the thing happen.*" Glinda repeated. She smiled genuinely at Oscar. He was definitely more than what he appeared.

Oscar smiled hopefully back. He was not a wizard in his own mind, but Glinda believed in him, and that belief might just break through that wall of doubt that he carefully hid behind his garden of optimism.

The next day, when the sun neared its zenith, Ondri-baba stopped the Hamstrambulator. She stopped before she came within sight of the South Castle. Her magic eye could see over great distances—far greater distances than a normal person. So she could see the South Castle, but they could not see her—yet. Her shiny new vehicle, *the Hamstrambulator*, was loaded for war. Behind Ondri-baba, her walking hut trundled quickly to a stop with its captive cargo inside.

With her magic eye, she could see that Glinda and her friends were there at the South Castle. They had built up greater fortifications. They were preparing for war. And there were people around. These worthless common people were actually coming to see Glinda. They were bringing things—weapons, and building materials, and food. They were actually building *an army*.

Ondri-baba took great pride in dragging out her humiliated captive. Quelala blinked in the bright southern daylight as the ceremonial blinding bag with one drawn ink-eye was removed from his head.

When he regained his sight and looked around, he recognized the distant South Castle. "Why are we here? The South has nothing to do with your war."

"Smith & Tinker are gone. But their little trinkets have decidedly changed the course of this war. I would not have thought to look here for Glinda. After burning the North Village, I thought that I had made my point. I thought that I made it very clear that anyone who opposed me would be destroyed. But it appears that the spawn of the Red Sorceress inherited her mother's knack for making enemies."

Ondri-baba made a deliberate show of pouring out and creating her sandy warriors. She created her guards first, then waved them invisible, and waved her previously invisible guards visible again. The first guards she allowed to return to their vials to recharge. "You didn't really think that I would travel alone, did you?"

She looked southwest toward the South Castle. "Ah, there she is. There is our little princess. Now she's climbing up the outer staircase to the top of the lighthouse. Perfect. Then she will be able to watch your execution."

"Leave her alone, Ondri-baba. You have me. I have secrets. I can tell you what you need to know."

The witch scoffed. "You mistake me for my sister. I have no need to know what esoteric imaginings the sorceress did in the Ruby Palace. I could not, frankly, care less. I have not lost sight of my goal, like my sister has. Your secrets will die with you. Then shortly thereafter your daughter will surely die."

"You are doing this just to spite me?" Quelala spat, incredulous.

"*No.* No. Yes—*in part.* You are a noble man, undeserving of the fate you have chosen. But that is not enough to even give me even a moment's stay in your execution. You are an unwelcome thorn in my side. I will remove you, and then I will yank out that *weed* that is your daughter and prove that I am the true Witch Queen in Oz."

"This is only about your power?"

"Yes."

"Then leave Glinda out of it. She doesn't know anything."

"For a child who knows nothing, she certainly has evaded capture and caused a great deal of damage to my army. I am going to eliminate Glinda because I *want* to. And then my sister will have no choice but to bow down to me." Ondri-baba looked out at the distant lighthouse. "Ah, she's up top now. There's the spyglass. And she sees us. Wave, Daddy. Wave to daughter dearest."

Quelala turned away. "You don't know the power you are facing."

"And you don't know the power I have. Or have you not noticed my lovely, shiny trinket?" The Witch gestured to the Hamstrambulator. "It's shiny, and it's mine. There is nothing else like it in all of Oz."

"Shiny…" Quelala whispered. "So that is what you were after when you captured me?"

"Of course it is. What did you think I was after? Certainly not that atrocious headwear Glinda has on. That unfashionable monstrosity gives poor taste a bad name."

So the secret was safe. He lifted his head. His eyes had a new light in them. "Keep your shiny toy. Play your little games, Witch. You will lose."

At the observation deck of the Twisted Lighthouse, Glinda looked through the telescope and saw Ondri-baba. "What is she doing down here? She's supposed to be fighting the Winkies."

Oscar panted behind her. "Maybe she came to surrender."

"No. She's got someone with her. *Father!*"

Oscar reached around Glinda to take a look. It certainly looked like him. But Oscar had only seen him for a few seconds. This man was hunched and nearly lifeless. Then Oscar stood and took Glinda by the shoulders. "It looks like him, but we don't know for certain."

"It is him. Look again."

Oscar looked through the telescope again. Something had changed. The man had straightened and was standing tall. He held his head up and his eyes…there was a light in them. "Okay. It is him. What are we going to do?"

"We have to go to him. Fight her for him, I don't know. But we have to get him back."

Oscar grabbed Glinda before she could run down the stairs. "Think for a second. Glinda, if your father was right here, what would he tell you to do? Would he say run off and rescue him? No…because he'd be right here. Okay, bad example. But just think, we can't go there. She's got the Hamstrambulator. She could outrun you "

Fretting and wringing her hands, Glinda went back to the telescope. She watched.

On the cliff edge, Quelala knew that Glinda still had the Golden Cap, and that she was still standing. His heart took courage. He turned back to Ondri-baba and stared clearly into her eyes. "What you see now will not be made known for a long time. You will not hereafter see me with eyes natural, but you will see me. I will haunt you."

Ondri-baba paled, and her magic eye blinked uncontrollably as strange things appeared in her visions. Visceral half-screams bubbled up in her throat and she clawed at the air fruitlessly.

Quelala turned to look up to the glint of red at the top of the distant tower. "I am sorry Glinda. I cannot keep my promise to you. You have the cap now, and I belong with your mother." He pulled the words from memory that he had learned from Gayelette. Behind him, Ondri-baba swiped helplessly at unseen strangeness all around her. Quelala pulled the ruby from his pocket and said the words, "*Let this ruby blood this flesh regress, and the cause of life forgotten bless. Out of time once, twice, thrice and ageless. Let the land be locked in blind duress. So to stay 'till the truth enkeyed through silent world, three-worlds' daughter dreams unfurled.*"

Without another word, Quelala stepped off the cliff and plummeted toward the desert below.

Far away, Glinda screamed as she saw her father falling toward the Deadly Desert sands. Her scream cut short as she gasped and fell backwards. *Quelala was gone!* He disappeared!

The fist-sized ruby—all that remained of the fabled Ruby Palace—dropped far below to the desert floor and lay there silently.

Through the mega-trump-o-phone on top of the Twisted Lighthouse, Glinda's scream echoed across the cliffside.

Ondri-baba composed herself and looked over the edge at the sand below. Even with her magic eye, there was no sign of Quelala. "Good riddance." she spat, then shivered uncontrollably as an icy chill passed through her. The strange things had gone, for now.

"One thorn removed. One screaming princess to go."

From the Hamstrambulator, Ondri-baba pulled a great metal artwork of another Giant Soliyak Lizard. She added bits of glass and metal to make the lizard more spiky and fearsome. This customization was an experiment, but she needed something even more formidable than the lizard she had used in the sparkwood forest. When the template was sufficiently wicked-looking, Ondri-baba sliced open her hand and dripped the blood over the metal. She emptied ten of the hourglass vials into the metal frame and stepped back to watch the magic.

The bloody sand stretched and twisted, forming into bizarre new combinations as the wicked blood bent the magic sand to its will. The sand fought, but the blood roared as the giant monster grew from the spiky template. It grew and grew, towering over Ondri-baba. She cackled in glee and danced as the monster seemed to know her thoughts exactly. It stared at the girl and the spyglass, knowing its duty and purpose. Then it turned its massive body toward the Twisted Lighthouse and roared, shattering the air.

The witch cried, "*Go! Ravage the land!*"

THE WAR

26 THE TWISTED LIGHTHOUSE

In the South Castle courtyard, Omby-Amby whirled around as the roar sounded. He was training the volunteer army, going through attack drills. "Warriors, to your positions!" he called. Quickly every one of them ran with their weapons to the wall.

Wickrie-Kells was working with the cavalry soldiers. These were the girls like her that were not quite as strong as the young men, but they were handy and willing to fight. These girls became the cavalry. They put on skates and strapped themselves behind the wheelers. In their free hand they were armed with a large, flat blade on the end of a long pole. It was essentially a garden trowel with a very long handle. They called it a trowel-lance. The wheelers were creatures of metal, but they were augmented with spikes and junk armor, fashioned from pieces scavenged in the scrapyards. Each one was anxious to do their part to help. However, the wheeler cavalry was only useful on the brick roads, so it was lucky that the region of the South Castle was criss-crossed by brick paths.

Wickrie-Kells had discovered through her explorations, and also through studying the maps, that the brick paths were arranged in specific configurations all over the South Castle estate. She had looked at the pattern from atop the Twisted Lighthouse and saw that the symbols matched the symbols that lined the outer edges of some of the blank scrolls that Glinda would not let her look at. She knew that the patterns and symbols in the brick paths made the South Castle a very powerfully-charged magical region.

Wickrie-Kells strapped on her own skates and took the reins of her stand-in wheeler in her left hand and the trowel-lance in her right. Unfortunately, IgNob had not yet returned from his mission. She would have liked to have him here with her. IgNob had become a trusted friend in these past two weeks. When she saw the sandy warriors charging into the brickwork she shouted and all of her girl warriors shouted with her. The wheelers screeched their eagerness to enter the fray. At the head of her contingent of fighting girls, Wickrie-Kells charged into battle.

A small army of sandy warriors charged at the South Castle. Their continued life had given them some memories of battle. They were not the ignorant clods that their first generation had been. These recognized combat and they had developed some fighting skills.

As soon as the warriors stepped within the grid of brick pathways, the battle began in earnest. They were attacked on all sides by screeching wheelers and flashing trowel-lances. The wheeler cavalry leaped and bounded across adjoining pathways. Unlike the Winkies, there was not a pattern to the cavalry attack. The Winkies may not have been an overwhelming adversary, but they were consistent and regimented in their attacks. Here, the sandy warriors were at a great disadvantage, for the randomness of the wheeler cavalry attacks made it impossible for the sandy warriors to implement any sort of strategy against them. These new running attacks crippled half of the warriors before the first five minutes had passed.

From the castle walls, rocks and other projectiles kept the sandy warriors from getting too close. An arm was knocked off or a head was fractured among the sandy ranks. These injuries were from Omby-Amby's warriors. Though they itched to get into the battle, Omby-Amby held them back as a second wave of infantry. He wanted to see how well the cavalry would do against this unliving foe.

Within another five minutes, all of the sandy warriors had been cut down. Not only had they been cut down, but they had been sufficiently stomped to prevent any more rising.

Wickrie-Kells' fighting girls stopped and raised a cheer. Their hoorays were met and echoed from the walls of the castle. Then the cheers died immediately in their throats, leaving a gaping void in the air.

"Look lively, lassies!"

On the hill, marching at double-time, dark red sandy warriors came, rank upon rank—far more than had been in the first wave.

Wickrie-Kells felt cold sweat break out on the back of her neck. Nevertheless, she screamed her battle cry and charged her fighting girls forward into battle.

Oscar and Glinda watched in morbid fascination as the horrendous beast thundered toward their position. The creature had six clawed legs and it was covered with horns. The mouth seemed far too large for the beast, yet the jaws were not nearly large enough for the multiple rows of jagged teeth. One large eye in the middle of the forehead was surrounded by a ring of smaller eyes, like a giant spider's head. The sound of its roaring was like the shredding of metal mixed with the sound of gravel falling.

There was no doubt the beast was coming for them. The sandy warriors were heading toward South Castle. The dragon was coming for them.

"She killed my father. Now she is going to kill me." Glinda intoned lifelessly.

Oscar shook the girl. "*NO! Not while I'm here.* We are not going down without a fight. We'll give them a story to light the campfires by. They will tell this story for generations!"

Oscar ran inside the cabin and pulled down all of the curtains, creating a full 360-degree view. He pulled the focusing solar crystal from its resting place. Then he loaded the large crystal into its socket and slid the customized lenses into position. He rotated the great lamp toward the roaring beast. Then he pulled the lamp cover off, opening the crystal bell to the midday sun. The sun gathered in the bell, focused through the crystals, then sent a superheated blast of energy out, shattering the windows. Oscar burned a long scorch mark in the distant green grass before sighting the monster. The beam burned across its back, instantly melting the blood-sand into red glass. The beast roared in pain, and Oscar slid the top lamp door back in place to allow the superheated crystal to cool down while he whipped the light around for another pass.

"Firing!" Oscar shouted as he opened the cover again.

Glinda ducked to the floor on the outer railing, barely avoiding the superheated ray. She flinched as the melted railing splashed down next to her, burning a hole in her dress. "Oscar! Be careful with that thing!"

Oscar burned a large swath in front of the monster, stopping it in its path. *"Ha HA!"* he shouted in exultation. *"You shall not pass!"* The flames rose up in front of the giant beast, and it rose up on its hind legs standing nearly half the height of the Twisted Lighthouse. "I've got you now!" Oscar growled. This would effectively cut the beast right in half.

Oscar whipped the beam back for another pass, and then saw Glinda standing up right in the path of the death beam.

At the last instant, Oscar cranked the beam back the other way, singeing Glinda's dress as she lurched backwards away from the heat. The beam shot out toward the South Castle, melting two blood-sand warriors, turning them to glass, and then striking part of the castle wall as it rotated, blasting a hole in the wall.

The monster dropped down to all six feet, its body halfway over the line of flame, and it moved forward. The heat from the flames polished the outside sand, but it was nowhere near as hot as the death beam from above. It thundered to the stone bridge connecting the land and the Twisted Lighthouse.

"Are you okay? I am so sorry!" Oscar shouted.

"You could have killed me with that thing!" Glinda screamed back.

"Then get in here with me!"

Glinda climbed through the broken window frame and crouched behind Oscar. "It's on the bridge."

"Just where I wanted him." Oscar adjusted the lenses and fired down, striking the beam on the monster's tail, crystallizing it. He pushed the lenses further to continue his way up the beast's back, and the beam blasted through the window pane, outer balcony then floor of the cabin.

"What are you doing? *STOP!*" Glinda screamed. She threw the cover over the lamp bell, stopping the sunlight from focusing and forming the beam. *"You can't shoot straight down!"*

"Oh, yeah." Oscar looked out past the window to the blasted hole in the tower. The beast's tail was just snaking out of view. He turned sheepishly up to look at Glinda. She was scared, and she was angry at him. But he looked past her to see the mega-trump-o-phone. "Clouds! You can make clouds!"

"But I'm not in the boneyard." Glinda protested as Oscar dragged her out to the voice amplifier.

"There's a hundred foot sand dragon out there. It will be up here in about one minute. If we don't try, we are dead!"

The entire lighthouse shook as the beast raised itself up and pounded the base with its front legs.

"Do it!" Oscar commanded.

Glinda took the mega-trump-o-phone and pointed it toward the distant junk piles that hid the Boneyard of the Clouds. She shouted as loud as she could the spell to create clouds into the amplifier.

Far beyond the reaches of the South Castle, the clouds in the sky heard her cry. They heard the spell of making, and they assembled to join their fallen brethren in helping the maker of new clouds. Wispy clouds dropped down from their lofty perches and took on angry strength, becoming storm clouds. These storm clouds gathered, darkening the sky. From the Boneyard, a vortex of cloud matter rose up, whipping up a furious whirlwind. Winds howled across the entire region as every cloud within the sound of Glinda's amplified voice answered the call to battle.

The vicious winds whipped the fallen sand around, nearly blinding the wheelers and completely blinding the fighting girls. It blasted their skin raw. Still they kept fighting. Several of the fighting girls had fallen along with their wheelers.

The blood of the fallen mixed with the half-destroyed blood-sand warriors. The wind whipped the bloody sand around, pummeling the fallen wheelers. The bloodsand mixed with the leaking fluids from the fallen wheelers and gave them new life. This blood was a mixture of wicked witch, magic sand, and good soldier. The fresh blood gave life, but it was not able to overcome the wicked purpose of the bloodsand warriors. The broken bloodsand warriors still able to move used this new blood to pack their limbs back on them. They were awkward and lurching, but they had new life.

Two new types of creatures arose—the Zombie Bloodsand Warriors and the Bloodsand Wheelers. Neither type of creature maintained a clear vision of what it was supposed to do. The wheelers knew that they were supposed to fight, but so did the bloodsand. The confusion wrought among both the reanimated wheelers and the bloodsand warriors drove them into madness and they became berserkers, attacking everything.

The old bloodsand warriors had the blood memory of dealing with the good wheelers before, so they quickly recognized that removing them from the brick roads terminated their usefulness. Wheeler after good wheeler was knocked off the brick pathways.

Then it was just Wickrie-Kells and her wheeler left. They were all that remained of her cavalry. That made her a target.

The Bloodsand Wheelers screeched and attacked the nearest blood-sand warrior. It threw a wheeler off the brick road, but the wheeler picked itself up and came back at him. The bloodsand magic had given the wheeler a greater life than the good wheelers. The pack of Bloodsand Wheelers quickly overwhelmed the warrior and crushed it to powder.

The sand blinded Wickrie-Kells and her wheeler, and it skidded to a stop. Just at that moment a large bloodsand warrior swung at them, sending the wheeler flying off the brick path. Wickrie-Kells still had the reins wrapped tightly around her hand, and she was pulled along with the flung wheeler. Her trowel-lance went flying from her hand when she hit the ground. A sharp pain seized her arm. The wheeler had fallen on top of her clenched hand, which still held the reins. She was trapped.

From atop the walls, the trumpet sounded to retreat. Wickrie-Kells twisted her head to see the remnants of her fighting girls running back toward the wall. Then a monstrous shadow blocked her view. A blood-sand warrior stepped up to her and raised its spear high into the air for the killing blow.

A *crraaaacccck-thoomm* sizzled the air as lightning slapped down at the upraised spear, instantly melting the blood-sand warrior into glass. Behind and through this glass body, Wickrie-Kells saw in a split-second a green-haired warrior swinging his sword. Then the frozen glass warrior shattered!

Omby-Amby heaved the remains of the shattered statue out of the way and extended his hand to Wickrie-Kells. She gestured to the wheeler on her arm. Omby-Amby lifted the wheeler with one hand and pulled Wickrie-Kells easily to her feet.

"I had him." The soldier declared.

"I saw." Wickrie-Kells agreed, leaning heavily on him.

Then the rain started. But it was no ordinary rain. This was vengeance from the clouds—unmitigated fury from the sky. Each drop was large enough to sting painfully when it hit. Wickrie-Kells and Omby-Amby headed for the smoking hole in the castle wall as the torrents sliced through the blood-sand warriors.

Despite the slashing rain destroying them, the bloodsand zombies and the berserker Bloodsand Wheelers lashed out at everything they could reach. They even attacked each other. The zombie warriors fought the Wheelers even as the rain tore them to pieces. The pounding rain flooded through all of the open joints of the Bloodsand Wheelers, washing out the contaminants. The bloody-sand battle raged, but it was clear that the rain would be the only winner.

"Glinda, get in here!" Oscar called, working through the collection of lenses, trying to determine the best configuration for close combat. He glanced up to see panic and memories flood into Glinda's eyes.

"My father wanted to be with Mother. He loved her more than me. I—my mother!" Glinda cried as she ran down the external staircase.

"NO!" Oscar cried, reaching after her, but it was too late.

Glinda raced down the outer winding staircase. Below her the great monster gouged deep furrows in the lower levels of the lighthouse. Glinda only needed to make it to the middle floors to get to the laboratory with the mirrors. Then she would be safe from the dragon.

The beast pounded its body against the lower lighthouse wall, shaking the entire foundation. Cracks appeared in the base level. The entire tower groaned on its base. Far above the desert floor, the Twisted Lighthouse was perched precariously on the island pinnacle. If it fell, only death would follow.

Glinda rounded the twisted corner and met the bloodsand beast's alien gaze. It roared its metal-gravel shriek and convulsed upwards after her. Great rows of teeth opened wide only thirty feet below. The open door in the middle of the lighthouse slammed open between Glinda and the beast.

It was a race—Glinda leaped down the steps, four at a time as the beast lurched upward. She dove beneath the huge snapping jaws into the open doorway, sliding hard into the wall. She scrambled to her feet as the dragon's head reared back and its massive jaws splintered the doorway behind her. She lurched side to side crashing into both sides of the hall as the tower shook.

Above Glinda, at the top of the lighthouse, Oscar finally figured out the correct lens configuration for maximum close range damage. He peeked over the edge to survey the situation. The beast's rear legs were scrabbling for purchase on the tower. With the cracks in the foundation, the churning rear legs damaged the bridge. The near side of the stone bridge crumbled. The broken bridge severed their escape route to the mainland.

Oscar's heart sank. They had no path to flee. There was no escape.

In addition to that, now Glinda was beyond his protection. Though he couldn't blame her, really. She wanted so desperately to cling to something that made sense in her life; even if that thing was her mother who she hated. She was willing to risk her life and limb and everything just to retain that reminder of normalcy.

You know, on second thought, Oscar *did* blame her. It was stupid and foolish and crazy to go after a mirror when she had a flesh and blood Oscar right here. That blame led to anger, and that anger led to a foolhardy plan.

"No escape. Big monster. Bigger death ray. *Big, shiny blaze of glory.*" He stubbornly set his jaw.

Thunder crashed all around them, shaking the lighthouse tower even further. The clouds expanded out to the lighthouse and they pounded torrents of rain down, but the blood-dragon was monstrously huge. It did not damage and melt as easily as the smaller blood-sand warriors had done. The fused glass on its back did not melt at all. The slicing rain bounced off the glass and fell the interminable distance to the deadly sand far below. Lightning jabbed all around, shaking the island even more and sending explosions of rock and mortar into the howling wind. The beast roared as the thousands of heavy raindrops pelted its exposed sandy skin.

The clouds brought the weaponized rain, but they also blocked the sunlight. As long as the clouds were blocking the sun, Oscar had no sunlight to focus in the beam. He roared in frustration as the clouds prevented even a single beam of sunlight from passing through. He slammed open the crystal door and then pried it loose, opening the aperture up even further.

Oscar watched for a break in the clouds for just a slatchy hint of sunlight, but none came. He ran out onto the platform outside the cabin and screamed at the clouds, *"Hey clouds! Give me some sun!"*

The clouds obliged, and created a hole through which a beam of sunlight streamed directly onto the lighthouse cabin. "There's the slatch." Oscar ran inside and pulled the cover off the lamp bell. The crystal reactor blazed to life and the death beam sliced through the wall. Oscar pushed his end up further and further, tilting it so that the beam pointed more and more downward.

The floor burst into flames as the death ray exploded through wood and stone and mortar. It blasted through the wall and hit the monster square in the upper jaw, crystallizing the blood-sand. The beast screamed and reared back, pounding its head against the wall, cracking the wall through completely. The dragon roared wider than it ever had, fracturing its glass jaw. It clambered up the weakened tower, blood-glass claws gouging deep paths in the stone.

Another blast froze the beast's right shoulder, but it was already nearing the top. Oscar wiped the sweat and tears from his face. Smoke and flames choked the air all around him. The blood-sand dragon raised its head above the balcony. Behind the death ray, Oscar grinned and narrowed his eyes as he turned the weapon toward the monster. He screamed the one name that inspired him to fight and to die.

In the laboratory below, Glinda staggered as more lightning hit the tower. The mirrors were falling over, and in this reflecting maze, she could not find the magic mirror. Finally, she could bear it no more.

"Mother!" she cried. At that precise instant, her gaze settled on the reflection of Gayelette looking at her. She lunged forward, but the mirror slipped from her grasp and fell to the floor, shattering.

"*No!* No, no, no, no, *nooo!* Don't do this to me, Mother. Don't leave me." A great groaning in the tower froze Glinda in place, and she felt the floor start to tilt. She turned her head upward toward the ceiling, as if she could see through to the cabin high above. "Oscar." she gasped, and she remembered her dear friend that she had left all alone up above.

Time moved in slow motion as she pushed out into the hallway and back toward the outside door. She could see individual particles of rock and mortar exploding as lightning struck. She could feel the building shudder as the winds buffeted and the giant sand monster thrashed and clawed.

The floor tilted up even further—the tower was falling over.

Glinda pulled her head out the door and looked upward. She grasped the railing and screamed silently at what she saw.

With the winds howling and the torrents slashing down, the blood-sand dragon was wrapped around the top one-third of the tower. It was roaring in pain. Oscar's beam of death seared the dragon's eyes then mouth, and then pushed even further down into the neck and chest, crystallizing and superheating the glass. Even above the wind and monster, she could hear Oscar screaming, *"Gliiiiiiinnnnnddddaaaaaa!"*

The superheated glass beast shattered, exploding into shards large and small. The lighthouse fragmented into four parts, the upper three them falling in slow motion into the Deadly Desert far below. Glinda screamed as her world turned sideways, but then she saw Oscar flung backwards out of the cabin by the force of the explosion. His arms and legs flailed helplessly as the wind sliced around him.

Glinda reached out for him. Her words were lost in the howl of the storm, but the Golden Cap heard her desire, and it glowed as its power was made manifest.

The fallen Twisted Lighthouse fractured into three separate parts and collapsed into the Deadly Desert, raising a huge cloud of dust. Then everything was still, save for the pounding of the insensate rain.

27 THE GIRL WITH RED HAIR

In the Deadly Desert below, the Twisted Lighthouse was broken into pieces. Even the closest section would be far beyond the reach of anyone on the mainland. Omby-Amby and Wickrie-Kells watched the lighthouse fall in slow-motion from their refuge in the South Castle.

The storm raged for hours longer. The blood-sand warriors and the zombie sand berserkers were finished. Their connecting magic was washed away in the pounding rain. The Bloodsand Wheelers were the only bodies left on the field of battle. They were damaged beyond any sort of repair that even Smith & Tinker might have attempted. They were all dead.

The blood-sand dragon drained off into the Deadly Desert. The only pieces left to remind anyone of its existence were the crystallized portions. Those stuck out of the sand like frozen drops of blood. These were a grim reminder of the damage done in this battle. Much blood had been spilled, and these tokens bore solemn testimony in their grisly, crystalline memorial.

Ondri-baba was gone. She left when she saw that her warriors were beyond rescue, and when she saw that the lighthouse had fallen with Glinda inside. Her work was done, so she left, heading north.

Through the entire night, the storm raged on, pounding the South Castle. The huddled survivors of the battle crouched and worried through the darkness. They had survived the sandy warriors, but now they had the raging elements to contend with. The elements did not distinguish between friend and foe—they were angry and exacted their vengeance on everything, especially the South Castle. The storm bruised the South Castle, collapsing sections of the roof and completely demolishing other outlying buildings. The monstrous ammonite water wheel fell over, toppling four of the five flagpoles and burying their standards in the mud.

The sun dawned cold. A thin mist hung over the ground. The storm had subsided, but the damage was done. Physical structures had been destroyed, but the greater damage was done in the hearts of the survivors.

Omby-Amby and Wickrie-Kells emerged from their hiding places, followed by the other shaken warriors. The devastation they witnessed was only matched by the despair they felt in their hearts. The castle was in ruins. The brick roads were destroyed. Even after they found a section of road that seemed to be connected, the wheeler they carried there did not respond. So none of the wheelers were left alive.

They saw that the lighthouse was fallen. They could not bring themselves to say what each one of them was thinking, so they forced themselves forward into the new day and busied their hands so that their minds would not have to think.

Omby-Amby put the people to work cleaning up. He later followed Wickrie-Kells out to the remains of the stone bridge. She stood on the edge staring out at the absolute devastation. The Twisted Lighthouse was broken into three massive pieces, but even the nearest one was far away from the island. The island was separated by thirty feet from the stone bridge. Given their very limited resources at the moment, the gap might as well have been three thousand feet.

They called out to Oscar and Glinda for the better part of an hour, but they were answered with only silence. Finally Wickrie-Kells left Omby-Amby standing there in the cold desert wind. His warrior eyes searched, but there was no movement in the desert-trapped ruins. He stared and stared into the blowing wind until the tears streamed down his cheeks. Still there was only silence.

Glinda and Oscar were gone.

Omby-Amby later searched the palace grounds but could not find Wickrie-Kells. It was mid-afternoon before he found her in the kitchen. She had her head leaned over a basin, and was pouring liquid from a glazed earthen jug over her hair.

"What are you doing?"

Wickrie-Kells wrapped a towel around her wet hair. "They're gone. Glinda's gone. Oscar's gone. They were *our* friends. But those people *out there*, the ones who bled with us yesterday—who are still with us—I have to ask you, who are Oscar and Glinda *to them*?"

"I know." murmured Omby-Amby.

"Do you?" snapped Wickrie-Kells. "To them, Glinda is a sorceress. Oscar is a great wizard. We know them as people. They know them as symbols." Tears flooded her eyes. "The *people* are dead." It took several seconds for her to control her sobs.

Omby-Amby stood rigid. He felt the same emotions, but he drew his strength from controlling emotions, not letting emotions control him. He waited for Wickrie-Kells to compose herself. He would wait as long as necessary. He would always wait for her.

"The *people* are dead. Not the soldiers we fought with. The people—Oscar and Glinda. The *people* are dead." Wickrie-Kells repeated. "But the *symbols* live on." She unwrapped the towel from her hair, revealing the change. Her hair was now dyed red.

Omby-Amby immediately recognized the ruse. Wickrie-Kells was going to pretend to be Glinda. "*That* is crazy." he said.

"Glinda *was* a little crazy. I doubted her severely when she made the oath with Kalinya. I thought that we would all be going up there together to fight. Instead," she sighed deeply, "the fight came to us. Now Glinda..." She stopped, and lowered her voice to a whisper, "Glinda *is dead.* That doesn't change Kalinya's oath. That doesn't change what they stood for. Oscar's ideas will change this land forever. They just need people to believe in them. You and I, we're nobody. We supported them. You can't be Oscar. People know your green hair. I'm a little taller than Glinda was, but most people in Oz wouldn't know my face. Our soldiers here know our faces, so they will need to be in on the secret. Glinda is a symbol. People know of her red hair. Nobody else in Oz had red hair except Glinda and her mother. That is a symbol we can raise up. We can raise Glinda's standard for the people—her red hair."

"You are looking at suicide if you go up to the Emerald Prairie."

"And if we stay here, it's a slow death. Omby, I am not Glinda. I don't have what she had. But I believed her when she said that we don't have to limit ourselves to being what others expect us to be. We are not rebelling; we are doing what is right to help others. I've watched you when Oscar speaks. You want it, too. You want to know that you will be free. That your family can live under the law, and that the law won't change just because a king gets greedy."

Omby-Amby nodded his approval of Wickrie's crazy plan. "Your hair is longer than hers. You'll have to let it blow in the wind. Glinda didn't wear her hair in ponytails or braids."

"I know. It's going to drive me crazy."

"So what is the plan, O Red One?"

"We keep moving forward. We made plans with Oscar and Glinda. We have weapons. We have a message, a story. We send runners in every direction. We stop in every village and hamlet between here and the Emerald Prairie. We raise our army. We build our army and face Kalinya as Glinda promised."

"And then what?" Omby-Amby asked.

"Then we do what it turns out we're good at doing—we fight for what is right. Let the consequences come as they may."

"Where will the wizard be?" he asked, running a hand over his green hair.

Wickrie-Kells thought for a moment. "Gone back to his brother wizards in the sky, I suppose. He's watching over us. With any luck, we might get some rain to help us out."

"That was Glinda yesterday."

"I know." Wickrie-Kells reached out, and Omby-Amby took her hand. "Omby, promise me something."

"*Anything.*"

"Promise that no matter what, you'll stand by me."

Omby-Amby pulled his sword from its sheath and knelt before Wickrie-Kells. "I swear it."

In the morning, the fighting girls gathered at Wickrie-Kells' request. These were joined by the warriors, led by Omby-Amby. The soldier with green hair addressed them first from the top of the wall.

"I see before me heroes—my countrymen. Men and women who love freedom and hate tyranny. We will be ruled by laws, not by tyrants. Our friend, the wizard, has journeyed to meet with his brother wizards in the sky. He watches us, and he expects us to do what we have promised to do. Our sorceress," Omby-Amby gestured, and Wickrie-Kells, with resplendent red hair, stepped forward into view, "is with us, and she will lead us."

The fighting girls recognized her face and immediately whispered in confusion to each other.

Wickrie-Kells understood the murmuring in the small army. She put up a hand to silence them, and they obeyed. "You all saw what happened to the lighthouse yesterday. What is fallen cannot be restored to its proper place. We can be true to the ideals we embraced yesterday, by marching today to defend our freedoms. I am no better than any of you.

"I wear this symbol," she held up her long red hair, "because *I believe.* I ask you to believe *with* me. Our cause is the cause of all people. I beg you to carry this secret with you. I will be your Red Sorceress, but you must be the People's Army. We fight not for our own power, but for all of the people of Oz.

"*Please,*" she begged, "please be true. We march to battle on the Emerald Prairie. We will build our army on the march. Omby-Amby has selected runners to go in every direction. I will march at the head, and I will lead you into battle. I ask only two things—stand with me, and tell the story of Glinda. Will you do that?"

The army shouted their approval and pledged their lives to uphold freedom.

They marched northward two hours later. By that time, their army had already doubled in size.

28 THE ENSLAVEMENT BEGINS

When the rain hit the Twisted Lighthouse, Ondri-baba retreated northward in the Hamstrambulator. She only stopped when she was safely outside the reach of the storm. Behind her, to the south, the black sky rained down lightning on the remains of her emblooded army. It was an excellent experiment in longevity. She learned what she needed to know by watching how they fought and how they survived. In heavy rain and wind, the smaller soldiers were the quickest to fall. The larger soldiers lost their sharp features and their honed skills, but they still kept brute strength and determination.

Then she turned her face northward. She saw a pack of wolves running in the distance, and she steered the vehicle toward them. Seeing their strength and power, she let a wicked idea slip into her mind.

Ondri-baba gestured with her hand and the invisible warrior bent the King Wolf's head backwards even further. The wolf yelped in pain. It contorted unnaturally as the invisible force bent the animal's joints nearly to the breaking point. Finally it howled out, "*Mercy!* Mercy, great witch."

Ondri-baba approached, focusing on the wolf king's eyes. "You have something I want, King Wolf. I want your loyalty. I am going to rule this land. You can join me, or you can be destroyed. What you choose will also affect your people. You have discovered that you cannot harm my warriors, but they most certainly can harm you.

"What do you require of my people?" the king wolf yelped.

"I demand your obedience when I call."

Ondri-baba was flanked by the King Wolf as the invisible warrior ripped a handful of feathers from King Crow's wings. "I can rip the feathers from your body and feed you to the wolves. I can do the same for your people. You see that you cannot peck out the eyes of my warriors."

The King Crow squawked, "Mercy! Have mercy on me, powerful witch! I will agree to whatever demands you set."

"I demand your obedience when I call."

Ondri-baba was surrounded by invisible warriors. Her crows circled overhead. Black bees angrily buzzed around, diving in to sting Ondri-baba, but they were frustrated. Their stings continued to strike at the invisible warriors, but they had no effect. Then the crows dove down and struck at the beehive. The black bees were frustrated in their attacks, and their home was under siege.

The Queen Bee flew out to negotiate with Ondri-baba. "What is it you demand, great witch? I would see my people preserved."

"I demand your obedience when I call."

Ondri-baba returned to the battleground to find the siege abandoned. Kalinya and Locasta had packed up their sandy warriors and moved to the next battle.

The one-eyed witch found them on the Emerald Plains. "Your wait will be a long one." mocked Ondri-baba. "Your adversary is dead."

Kalinya glowered but said nothing.

Locasta squirmed uncomfortably. She kept looking for a way out.

"Your day will come. Your oath will be kept. And then you will bow to me as your queen. I demand your obedience." commanded Ondri-baba. That was the final straw.

"I will not bow to you! You are my sister—my younger sister. It is my right to rule, not yours! I will not bow."

Locasta looked for an escape. Ondri-baba saw this, and nipped that thought in the bud. "Oh, no, Apprentice. I have made you a general. You are here until this war is done. And be assured, it will find its finish very soon."

That threat was no consolation for the young witch.

Wickrie-Kells watched the sun set in the east. She stood outside the camp where her followers; *No*, she corrected herself, *make that Glinda's followers*, had set up camp for the night. Omby-Amby was running drills with the soldiers. He had even taken over temporary command of the Fighting Girls. Wickrie-Kells needed to keep her distance so that she could maintain her role as the

Red Sorceress. After nightfall she would put more dye in her hair to maintain the illusion.

The flapping of wings drew her attention. A Winged Monkey dropped lightly to the ground. "Good evening to you, sir monkey." She said.

Then five more monkeys dropped down around her, including King Klick. The silver monkey sniffed, and then looked more closely at the young woman. "What is this? Where is she?"

Wickrie-Kells gestured for the monkey to be quiet. "Please, your Highness, I can explain. But not here."

King Klick fur bristled. He bared his teeth, but kept his silence. He motioned for two of his monkeys to carry the girl. They winged for ten minutes, far beyond the reach of the army camp.

"Where is the girl, Glinda?" King Klick gnashed his teeth and growled at Wickrie-Kells, the imposter.

"Glinda is dead. The Witches attacked the South Castle. They created a giant monster. Glinda was in the tower when everything fell. We could not get to her."

"I will go and find her."

"No, good King, please. These people, they need to believe. Right now, my red hair is the symbol they believe in. I know I'm not Glinda. What I have done is a lie, but it is for the freedom of the people."

"You people all lie. You humans lie for good, for bad, for nothing, you lie." King Klick ripped up grass and shrubs in his anger. He pounded the ground. The other monkeys were also agitated, bobbing up and down all around Wickrie-Kells.

"I am keeping Glinda's oath!" the girl shouted. "Glinda swore to battle Kalinya to the death. The winner would get the Golden Cap or the Silver Slippers."

King Klick stopped and stared. His lip twitched. "It was Glinda's oath, not yours. Where is the Golden Cap?"

"Glinda had it. She was wearing it when the lighthouse fell—with her inside. She is dead. I am all that she has left."

"You are not fit to wear her hair. You lie."

Wickrie-Kells fired back, "So you've never told a lie? A mistruth?"

"No."

Wickrie-Kells shifted uncomfortably. "I am sorry. I mean to honor Glinda's memory and what she stood for. If you will not help me, then I will go." She walked back in the direction they had flown.

"The Witches assemble their armies not far distant. They mean to give you battle."

"I know. We swore, I mean, Glinda swore an oath. We will conquer or perish."

"That was her oath. You are not bound to it." King Klick called after her. "A wise leader knows when it is time to retreat. Heed my words, friend of Glinda. I, too, believe in Glinda's cause. It was the cause of her father, who was a great friend to the Winged Monkeys. My loyalty, and the loyalty of my people, cannot be yours, as your hair is but a counterfeit."

"Then look on my heart. Stop looking at my hair. Judge me by my actions. War does not make honest girls."

"War makes monsters of men and burns the rest." King Klick looked southward. "You are unproven to me. But know this, if the battle goes badly, an escape will be opened for as many as we can save. The choice is yours as a leader. Sleep on this and choose wisely. If you meet in battle tomorrow, I wish you favor. If it is the next day, I will send word to you." He motioned to the strong monkeys again, and they carried Wickrie-Kells back to the camp. King Klick launched himself southward, winging into the night.

Omby-Amby met her at the outskirts of the camp as the Winged Monkeys slowed then dropped her to the ground. His soldier eyes held grave concern as he saw the questions in her eyes.

"Are they against us?" Omby-Amby asked.

Wickrie-Kells shook her head no. "He's going to look for Glinda."

Omby-Amby swallowed hard. "So? What's the problem with that?"

Wickrie-Kells looked up, her eyes full of frightened tears. "If he finds Glinda and brings her here, what will the Army think of me, a liar?"

29 THE DREAM OF FREEDOM

Meanwhile, as the People's Army marched northward, far away to the south, Oscar dreamed.

All around Oscar, mirrors reflected parts of his life, from balloons, to wagon trains, to rainy nights spent alone in a tent, to angrily sold pistols, to war stories hung like tarnished tinsel, to a mother's tears that would not be comforted—no part was left out. A great thunderous bellow echoed through the darkness outside the mirrors. Lightning flashed.

Quelala called from the darkness, "Come to me."

Oscar stepped through a mirror into a brighter world. Shards of crystal hung in the air all around, reflecting not only the room, but memories of things they had seen. Glinda was curled around a sealed book on the floor. She was shaking silently, as if she were sobbing. Oscar reached out to touch her, but the distance was infinitely far. No matter how far he reached, she was always just out of touch.

"She has never had a book she could not read." Quelala's voice sounded behind Oscar.

Oscar turned to see Quelala as a giant floating head in the air beside him. "I want to help her."

"You will." Quelala promised. "But first there are things you must show me."

The floating head of Quelala led Oscar from the hall of floating shards out onto the upturned belly of a sinking ship. Oscar looked to see ruby icebergs floating nearby. "How many ships are nearby?" asked the head.

"I see two." answered Oscar. "But they have no crew."

"Can you call them closer?"

"The iceberg is floating between them. I may be able to get over."

"There are oars on your ship. What use are those?" the voice asked.

Oscar pulled the oars from the belly and laid them between the ship and the iceberg. "They are locked together. They can be a bridge to the iceberg. They should reach the other ship."

They stood in the hull of the second ship. "How far is land?" asked the voice.

"I cannot see it from here, but the third ship has a map." Oscar studied the distant third ship, turned belly-up in the endless ocean. He turned his head to look at the giant head, and when he turned back, he was on the third ship, in the Captain's Quarters. "The map has a compass rose; I've never seen one like this. It's a face inside a crystal. There are vines and flowers all around the map. I see a clock..."

"If the map grows, which direction will the clock fall?"

"Up." Oscar said. "It's spelled..."

"Where is the mountain dock? Will the basket fall?"

"There is a plank. I think that can reach the dock."

Then Oscar stared at the book on the table in the captain's quarters. He traced the letters *"O—Z"* with his finger on the cover. The letters turned into glittering emeralds. As he turned the pages, he saw elements of his life written on the page in red ink. But those words were a small portion of the words on the page. When he reached the halfway point of the book, there were more red words, but there was still much black mixed in.

Oscar read one line on the last page that had writing on it, *"This is the account of the dreamer who became a humbug."*

"The red is dreams and memories—what *you are* and what *you desire.* The black is stories that surround the blood that you hold, the lies you tell. The book is yours. Who are you?" the voice asked.

Oscar turned, but the giant floating head of Quelala was nowhere to be seen. Then Oscar was standing by himself on the seashore, holding the book. He locked the clasp on the front of the book and swallowed the key.

A whisper floated on the misty breeze behind him, *"Awaken."*

Oscar awakened to a strange sensation. He felt a pressure on his chest. All around him were dancing points of light. He groaned and lifted his head. Draped all over his chest and dropping down into his mouth was long, red hair. He blew the hair out of his mouth, and licked his dry lips, but the hair kept finding its way back into his mouth. He breathed in deeply, and the pressure on his chest subsided.

Glinda looked up, lifting her head from Oscar's chest. Her pale, tear-stained face was worn with exhaustion. "Oscar?" she whispered.

"I'm here."

A smile spread on Glinda's face as she studied his face and touched his cheek. Then she wrapped his head in a hug. "You're alive!" She laughed hoarsely, an exhausted, relieved sound. Oscar heard it first-hand as his ear was pressed against her chest. He could feel her tension ease as she laughed.

Then he couldn't breathe. He tapped her arm. "I can't—can't breathe." he croaked.

"Sorry." Glinda let go, and Oscar's head dropped to the floor with a clunk.

"Ouch."

"I'm sorry." Glinda laughed again, but this time her eyes were shining with happy tears.

"Where are we?" Oscar asked.

"In the laboratory. With the mirrors. Most of them are shattered now. I don't know what time it is."

Oscar sat up, carefully placing his hands away from the broken glass. "I was going to ask how long I was asleep."

"I thought you were dead. I couldn't get any response from you."

Oscar ran his hands through his hair. He looked at Glinda's tear-stained face and felt great regret in his heart. "I saw you crying."

"How could you? You were not responding to anything. It felt like your heart was slowing down."

"I was standing right there. You were there…but you were holding a book. *Oh.*" The pieces of the dream snapped together in his mind like a puzzle.

Glinda shook her head. "I was holding you. I fell asleep after a while. Then I woke up. Then I fell asleep after a long time of crying. Then you woke up."

"I must have been dreaming. Your father was there. At least his giant floating head was. And he was asking me questions. I said I wanted to help you, but he took me to a sinking ship." Oscar got to his feet and pulled Glinda up.

He looked around. Everything was sideways. The floor was the wall. The wall was the floor. "What happened?"

"The lighthouse fell. Don't you remember?"

Oscar scratched his head and stared blankly, trying to return to the reality of his situation. "That seems like another lifetime ago. The dragon came up and I shot at it with the beam. And then there was an explosion. Everything was frozen in the air. I was floating. The lighthouse was right in front of me, but so far away. I saw that the sand was below. There was lightning. I saw two flashes. And then…I guess I was dreaming."

Glinda shook her head. "I don't know how much of a dream it was. Only when the tower started to fall, I remembered you. I made it to the door and saw you. There was the explosion, but I only saw you against the sky. I reached out and screamed for you."

"What did you say?"

Glinda's face reddened, giving bright color to her pale cheeks. *"Come be with me."* She forced an embarrassed smile and wiped away a hanging tear, "And then you were there. The tower crashed to the ground. We fell in here. And this is where we've been."

"Magic. What did your father say when he gave you the Cap?"

Glinda thought back, "That it's a focusing device for wishes and dreams. So maybe that's why—because you can dream, so it brought you back to it."

"Or because you wished it."

Their eyes met and connected. Glinda stepped into Oscar and kissed him. Surprised, pleasantly so; Oscar kissed her back. Warmth and life flooded through them both. In that instant, everything was acceptable and the world was filled with magic.

They parted. And Glinda looked away, bashful. "I shouldn't have done that."

"It had to be done. You were just the first one to get there." Oscar smiled.

"We can't tell anyone else right now."

"I don't see anyone. Your secret is safe with me, Princess."

"And your secrets are ever safe with me, Wizard."

30 THE FALLEN TOWER

Oscar poked his head out the outside entrance to the fallen tower. The tower was broken into three pieces at the base of the island. They were currently on the middle section of the three pieces. Each of them was far away from the others—too far too jump. He turned his head to look up. The round side of the fallen tower looked like the belly of a ship. He stepped out and climbed up onto the stonework. The base of the tower was far above them on the top of the island. If they could get to the rock, they could work their way up. There. A staircase, carved into the rock of the island, leading into and upward. That would get them back up to the top.

Glinda was late in coming out the door. She wrapped a cloth around a shard of glass as she stepped out. Oscar lifted a questioning eyebrow.

"*My mother.*" She explained.

Oscar offered his hand to help Glinda step up. "Let me help you with that. It's got some sharp edges, so we need to make sure that it is wrapped tightly. We should be able to wrap this and put it on your back and wrap these sides and tie these ends around the front of you." Oscar tied the final knot—it was good. "That won't go anywhere. Just don't lean backwards too hard."

Glinda embraced Oscar and squeezed him tightly. "I'm glad you're with me."

Oscar treasured the warmth between them, but the time came to separate. They looked around at their situation. "We're together. That's going to keep us safe. You've got the Golden Cap. Maybe you could wish for a way to get us back across."

"I don't know if it works like that." Glinda looked skeptical.

"Doesn't hurt to try."

"Okay, fine. I wish that there was a way we could get across." She shrugged. "Well?"

"The best magic takes time. It takes a little bit more belief than that." Oscar looked at their bleak surroundings. It was a mess.

Even up on the cliff top to the east, the South Castle showed extensive damage. They could see that even from a distance. The Twisted Lighthouse was broken and the three pieces bent like a bony finger in the deadly sand. They were on the middle section of the three. The stone bridge above them was fractured. The island on which the lighthouse stood was beyond reach of any of the pieces. Great red pieces of glass from the shattered blood-sand dragon poked up out of the sand.

"First course of action—we need to get back onto the mainland. How deadly is this desert supposed to be?" Oscar asked.

"Are there *degrees* of deadly?" Glinda answered, rhetorically. "It's a deadly desert. That is how deadly it is."

Oscar walked the length of the tower section. At the north end, there was a large red chunk of glass, like an island, between this tower section and the next. But it was a very dangerous jump. Even if they made the first jump, it was too far to jump to get to the next section.

"If this was a boat, where would the oars be?" Oscar asked. Then he found the answer. The exterior staircase stuck out from the building. They were almost completely disconnected from the stone of the wall. If they could just disconnect the near end, they might have a bridge.

Oscar worked at loosening the railing while Glinda rummaged around the laboratory and the storage rooms for tools to use. She found a crowbar and a hammer and a few unbroken flasks, but nothing presented itself as the absolute answer that would solve all of their problems.

Glinda found a pretty sash that she wanted to keep, so she tied it around her waist with a nice bow at the back. Oscar complimented her on it when she joined him back outside.

They succeeded in removing the stairs and the railing. They carefully maneuvered the portable bridge into position, dropping the far end on the red glass island.

"I'll secure this end. You'll have to be careful and climb on the outside at that part *there*, but you can do this." Oscar directed.

Glinda scampered across, losing her footing once, but she had a tight grip and she was able to pull herself back on to the railing without her feet touching the deadly sand. Then she turned back to smile at Oscar. "Easy as splatberry pie. Now you do it."

Oscar went much slower than Glinda, but he was able to cross the perilous distance with a minimum of shaking. When he had joined Glinda on the red glass, he wiped the sweat from his forehead. "No problem." he joked.

"Now we just need to get to the next one."

Glinda removed the sash around her waist and re-tied it, removing the bow and making the knot more functional. Then she reached down between her knees and grabbed the bottom skirts at the back of her dress and pulled it forward to tuck it into the front part of the sash. "There. That should do. Keep me modest."

"Where did you learn to do that? You're a princess."

"It's called *'girding your loins'*. I learned it in a book, silly. Doesn't anybody wear skirts where you're from?"

"Yes, but not me. Never felt the need. I'm Irish, not Scottish."

"See, you create a kind of breeches by pulling the back skirts through and tuck into your front belt. This just means that you're ready to work. Keeps the skirts from getting in the way. In the book it was robes, but it works just as well with a dress."

"So how are we going to get the stairs from there to there?" Oscar mused. "They look long enough."

"Couldn't we just swing them around from here?"

"That's a lot of weight to control if we pivot it. And I don't think there's room to slide them across. That would put us pretty close to the sand. Too close for me to be comfortable."

"What if we had stepping stones?"

"Dangerous. But less dangerous than trying to move the stairs. I don't know if I can make it back across the stairs." Oscar looked at the twisted staircase nervously.

"It's no problem, I can do it." Glinda said, scrambling onto the framework.

Oscar lurched out and secured the bottom portion as Glinda wiggled up the rest of the distance. The stairs slid, but they didn't fall.

"See? No problem." Glinda looked back and smiled. I'll find something we can walk on."

They discovered that the Deadly Desert was, in fact, very deadly. This shouldn't have been a surprise, given the name, but the toxic sand was afflicted with the curse from the First Witch Wars. Glinda found some wood and tossed it down on the sand. It quickly dissolved into sand.

"Maybe things that are living turn into sand." Glinda suggested.

"Or things that *were* once alive."

Glinda went back and rummaged through the rooms again. It took almost an hour, but they created a footpath across the deadly gap with mirrors from the laboratory. They were the only things large and flat enough that Glinda could manage that would serve their purpose.

Glinda cracked every mirror as she created the path. But she managed to step on only one edge of the mirrors, leaving the majority of the pieces unbroken for Oscar. Oscar insisted that Glinda be the one to lay the path, *so that she would definitely be safe.* He was larger and heavier, so he would cause more damage to the mirrors. At least with Glinda, the mirrors did not crack completely in half.

Now it was Oscar's turn. He was sweating again.

"You can do this, Oscar. It's just seven steps."

Oscar steeled himself to take the first step, when Glinda spoke again. "You can take more steps if you need to."

"What?"

"I made it in seven steps, but you don't have to. If you need to take smaller steps, you can."

"Just let me do this."

"You don't have to impress me."

Oscar steeled himself and jumped out on the first mirror, sliding a little on the landing. Then two, three four, five, six—*cracked completely in half*, throwing him off balance. He lurched forward, barely getting his front foot on number seven. His foot slipped and his arms flailed out. His rear foot swung forward and hit on his front heel, sending him falling forward.

Glinda reached out and caught Oscar's arm, yanking him forward into the tower. Oscar fell on top of Glinda, gasping.

"Just seven steps?" Oscar panted.

"You don't have to impress me." Glinda smiled and tapped her finger on Oscar's nose. "I like you anyhow."

Inside the bottom section of the tower there were storage rooms and crates. When Oscar told Glinda about the dream he had, she asked about the Captain's Quarters.

"I was standing there in my dream, but I don't see one in here."

"Could you dream have been wrong? No, wait, never mind. You create in your dreams, so whatever you dream becomes the reality. If you dreamed of a Captain's room, then it's got to be here."

The tower was fallen, so the wall became the floor. Glinda noticed an unfinished mural on the wall, or rather, on the floor. The mural was a work in progress. It showed several castles and brick roads. All around the edge were pinned paper pages of twining ivy and vines. Debris from the collapse covered most of the mural. Glinda uncovered it.

"Here's your map."

But there were no clear answers how to get to the island from this tower section. It was another long distance—too far to jump. They no longer had the staircase. They found nothing long enough that they could use for a bridge.

"What else was in your dream?" Glinda asked, sitting down right in the middle of the mural.

"Just a map. No. There was a map, and the voice—*your father's voice*—asked me which way the clock would fall, and I said up. Then a book." Oscar trailed off, wanting to be honest, but not wanting to talk about the book in his dream.

"A clock? Hmm. I don't see any clocks in here."

"The map was supposed to show the way out."

"That's *me*." Glinda said. "*I'm* supposed to show the way out. And you, you're the book that you mentioned. If you read the book, then it's definitely you. I mean, I can't read you, but you can. So you don't have to talk about that if you don't want to."

Oscar's mouth dropped open in surprise.

"Don't look so surprised. I'll find a way out. You came back from the dead for me, so it's the least I can do, right?"

Glinda crossed her legs and rested her chin on her hands. Then something sparkled over in the corner. She cocked her head sideways, squinting. There was definitely something sparkling there.

She kept her head cocked sideways and gestured to Oscar. "There's light that's shining back over there. Where is it coming from?"

Oscar found the point of light and followed it in a straight line back to the top of the tower section, or rather, the south opening, where they had come in.

"It's from the sun. It's shining on the mirror—the one that I cracked and slipped on. One part went into the sand, tilting it up at an angle. That's what's shining the light in there."

When he went back, Glinda was already digging out a large hourglass from behind some crates. Only a very small part of the glass was visible, and the light hit that part perfectly.

"Sunlight only visible at this time of day, from a broken mirror tilted at the perfect angle—and you think you're not a *wizard*?"

"That's just a *coinciden*—never mind." He waved his hands. "Abracadabra. *Ta-daa!*"

"There's your clock. Now how do we make it fall up?"

Oscar was stumped. He shrugged.

"Come on. You've dreamed us this far. It must be something we're missing. What else did you see on the map?"

"There was a compass rose. A crystal. It had a face in it."

"Crystal? Crystal is like glass." Glinda pulled out the shard of the magic mirror with her mother's face in it. "I've got a face in a crystal." She put it down in the corner of the map. "So there is the center of the compass rose. Now we just need the four directions."

Oscar gathered broken pieces of wood and glass to use for the cardinal points. "If this is a map, then North is up. East is right. South is down. West is left." He placed everything in position and then stood back very proud of himself. He glanced over to Glinda for approval, and his self-admiration collapsed.

Glinda was laughing at him.

"Wha-?"

"No, silly goose." She shook her head. "East is left. West is right. Haven't you watched the sun rise and set? What land are you from, anyway?" She giggled.

Oscar's puzzled and confused look sent Glinda into another fit of giggles. "No. It's cute. I'm sure you didn't mean it."

"Where I'm from, my directions were right."

Glinda put her hands on her hips. "Well, you're not where you're from now, are you *Mr. Smarty-Pants*?" Then she giggled again.

It was several more minutes before Glinda composed herself well enough to talk with Oscar about the map. She had to walk up to the map and then walk away several times when the giggles started before she could talk normally.

"Are you all right now?" Oscar asked, still flummoxed by Glinda's fits of giggles.

"Yes. I'm fine." But it was clear that she was not. Her eyes were still dancing, but she forced a very neutral face.

"Good. So we've got the *cardinal directions*," Oscar forced himself to keep his gaze on the map, and not look at Glinda. He could see out of the corner of his eye that she was shaking with barely contained laughter. "We've got the compass rose. What are they pointing at?"

Glinda shrugged. Oscar shrugged back.

"I'm not from here, *Miss Smarty-Pants*, so you're going to have to help me out. What are the cardinal directions—" Oscar cast a pointed glare at Glinda, but she managed to mostly keep from smiling, "—pointing to?"

"The vines. The borders."

"Yes, of course they're pointing to the borders..."

The realization hit them at the same time. They both turned to look at the large hourglass full of sand.

"Smith & Tinker must have filled the smaller hourglasses from something, right? So this might be the same magic sand." Oscar began.

Glinda continued his thought, "And Ondri-baba poured the sand out onto pictures and metal molds. I saw her do it from the spyglass. So if we have a big hourglass full of magic sand—"

"And drawings of vines—"

"We have our way across the gap." Glinda jumped up and down in excitement. "Have I told you how wonderful you are?"

"Wonderful Wizard..."

"Yes. *The Wonderful Wizard of Oz*, that's what you are."

"So we just need to get this over to the gap."

They had to break through the floor, or rather, the wooden wall at the north end, in order to get the large hourglass in position. Glinda gathered up all of the drawings of vines. Luckily they were drawn on long rolls of paper that she could just roll up. She found some scroll rods that she put in the center of the rolls of paper to give them some weight.

Then she bundled up the shard of mirror in the cloth and put it around her back, securing it with the sash. This let her skirt fall back down, from its previous breeches position.

"Ready?" Oscar asked.

"Just about." Glinda said. "I liked that map. I think I'll make one. On the floor of the throne room. Have the entire Land of Oz. Maybe the adjoining lands, too. Desert, definitely. Need to have some good boundaries. I like the vines. I'll put some of those in, too.

"My father had his map in the garden. He liked that garden. I want my map. I want it to be *me*."

"That sounds like a good plan."

"Here goes." Glinda looked at Oscar expectantly.

"Wait. If these scrolls are paper, won't they turn to sand like the wood did?"

"No." Glinda shook her head. "That's just silly."

"But paper is made of trees—ground up trees."

Glinda shook her head. "You worry too much. This is Oz. This is good paper. Everyone knows that good paper is made from marble."

Oscar didn't have anything to say to that. He crossed his fingers for luck.

Glinda unfurled the scrolls by holding on to the loose end and sending the furled paper unrolling across the toxic sand. She managed to get all four of the scrolls side-by-side, with very little space between them.

"Very nicely done." Oscar complimented. "And they didn't turn to sand."

"Thank you. And of course they didn't turn to sand. I told you. Now for the magic."

"If you'll give me a hand lifting this." Oscar began.

"Step aside, Wonderful Wizard. As I said, time for the magic." Glinda unscrewed the top base of the hourglass and stepped back. She raised her hands into the air. "This is one thing that my mother taught me. I never thought it would be useful at all—*how to turn over an hourglass.*"

Glinda said the words to the incantation, and the hourglass rose and followed her fingers, rising up to hover over the top of the drawn vines. Then she completed the hand motions and turned her hands to dump the hourglass.

The magic sand dumped all over the four scrolls of drawings. Instantly the magic recognized the pattern and sandy vines grew up from the papers. The sandy vines grew from all across the paper, so the network of growth was strong and sturdy. They grew up and out, bending toward the island. Growing and growing and…there. The vines bridged the gap to the island, providing part one of their escape.

Glinda reached out and grasped the vines. She shook them, and they held strong. She reached up and hung on the vines, swinging out over the deadly sand. She laughed as Oscar lunged after her and pulled her back. The sand vines were flexible enough to bend but rigid enough to hold weight. "Not bad, eh?"

"Don't *do* that." Oscar demanded. "What if—"

"But I didn't." Glinda smiled and her eyes twinkled with mischief. "Well?"

Oscar waited. "Aren't you going to *gird up your loins* again?"

"Nope. But you go first this time. See, I want *you* to definitely be safe."

"But you should go first. You're the girl."

"How about this, Oscar? You can be the big, strong, mighty man and go up first to check for danger. If there is anything dangerous up there, you fight it, then I'll come up, then you can climb back down here and then climb back up again."

Oscar narrowed his eyes and glared at Glinda sarcastically. She stuck her tongue out at him, but she smiled as he climbed up the sandy vines. Glinda didn't wait for Oscar to get all the way up, but followed right behind him. The afternoon shadows were starting to lengthen. It would be a hard climb to get to the top of the island by sundown.

Glinda looked down at the toxic sand beneath them and mused, "I wonder if this sand is deadly only here in the desert, or if it would be deadly if we carried some with us?"

"Why are you thinking that? We're twenty feet above certain death, hanging by our fingertips."

Glinda smiled. "I'm just thinking. That's all."

31 THE NECESSITY OF INVENTION

King Klick flew all evening towards South Castle. As he had told the girl, his people were directed to watch the battle, but not to interfere. If the battle began, and the human army was in trouble, the monkeys could create a diversion to allow an escape, but they were not to change the tide of the battle. King Klick had a duty to preserve and protect his people. He would not have them throw in their lot who could offer nothing in return for their lives. The only hope for the freedom of the Winged Monkeys lay with Glinda. So King Klick flew south to find her. And if Glinda truly was dead, as her friend had said, then he would search for the Golden Cap.

After a hard climb up the stairs both outside and inside the island, Oscar and Glinda arrived at the top. They looked back and watched the sandy vines dropping little by little. Glinda sat on the edge of the lighthouse foundation, kicking her feet out over the edge. They watched the sun touch the eastern horizon. Oscar found some food in the cellar and brought a biscuit to Glinda. "Vines are about to go." She said. Oscar sat down next to her, looking over the edge.

The sandy vines had lasted close to four hours. Coming out of the master hourglass, the amount of sand was calculated to last longer than a single hour. When the sandy vines first grew, they grew up around the large, master hourglass, entangling it in their growth. The weight of the large hourglass on the weakening vines bowed them downward. "Almost ready to fall."

The master hourglass slipped halfway, catching a vine at the last instant. Then the vines turned back to sand. The master hourglass hung suspended in the air for a brief moment as the entangling magic all around it dissolved. The fading sunlight shimmered on the cloud of magic sand. The master hourglass fell.

Oscar counted, "Three, two, one." He held up his finger and the sound of shattering glass reached up to their perch. "It's gone. Out of our reach. Even if we could bring it up, there's not enough sand left in there to bridge the last gap."

They settled down to sleep on the stone island that night. The cellar was open to the sky, now that the lighthouse had collapsed. The moon smiled down on them in the cool, dry air. There was food and blankets here in the cellar, so they were comfortable…mostly.

What frustrated them most was the broken bridge. Scarcely spitting distance away from their resting spot, the short gap separating them from the mainland was maddening—a mere thirty-foot span kept them from freedom.

Oscar fell asleep quickly. His snores were the only sound on the island. Some breezes whispered by below, but they were no match for the noises Oscar was making.

Glinda stared up at the moon and the stars. Though she had flown on the back of the flying fish just a few days earlier, she was not used to seeing the night sky. Always her tower had been locked and shuttered when the night fell. Now she saw everything blazing in the darkness, staring down at her. What eyes looked down as she looked up? Why did they not answer her questions spoken up into the night? What secrets did the stars hold? The open sky was so big and unknown.

After an hour of restless tossing and turning, Glinda quietly got up and climbed the stone stairs. She took a seat up at the top of the broken inner staircase, watching the crescent moon swim across the sky. Below, Oscar snored like a foghorn as he slept in the exposed storage room. If the lighthouse was still functioning, Oscar could have guided the ships into the harbor.

She heard the familiar wingbeats long before she saw their source. She stood up and waved her arms, hoping that she was silhouetted enough in the night sky for the monkey to see her. She was, and King Klick arrived a minute later. He wheezed as he dropped down on the stone stairs next to Glinda. "I am no longer young. My flight has been long."

Glinda embraced him. "I am happy to see you again."

"And I, you, Princess. I was told you were dead."

"I thought we were dead, too. It was magic that saved us. We made it this far from the second tower piece down there, but we can't go any further—at least not at night."

King Klick explained the situation and the strategy introduced by Wickrie-Kells. He ended with, "My loyalty is to your father, and thereby, you. She has proven to be a friend to you, but I cannot pledge my people for an unproven ally."

"Wickrie-Kells is good."

"That may be, but she lied. I am a king, and I must think of my people. This war is not just for power or for lands. This war will change the Land of Oz forever. My duty is to my people. As much as I care for your welfare, Princess, you are *not* my people."

Glinda wept silently as she thought of Wickrie-Kells leading the army. "I understand, Majesty. You have a duty to your people. When do they fight?"

"Perhaps tomorrow. Perhaps the next day. It is in the hands of the Witches."

"Could you get me there?"

"As a younger monkey, I might have, but I cannot carry you alone for that distance. And I cannot fly it tonight. Before I fly again, I must rest."

"Then go down below and take your rest." Glinda ordered, assuming her regal composure. "We will talk more in the light of morning."

King Klick dropped down off the stairs and swung through the half-destroyed ceiling in the storeroom to find a place to go to sleep.

Glinda stared up into the sky, searching for answers, and hoping that Wickrie-Kells would not do anything foolish. Then she clarified for herself, that she hoped Wickrie-Kells would not do anything out-of-her-ordinary foolish.

Oscar slowly woke up to feel a hand on top of his head. With his eyes still closed, he pulled the hand next to his cheek. He wrapped the hand around his and squeezed it. "I like waking up next to you." He reached out to stroke what he thought was Glinda's arm. Only it was very, very hairy, which made him pause.

"You are very gracious." King Klick said in his gravelly voice.

Oscar's eyes flashed open. He saw King Klick's silver face grinning broadly two inches away from him.

Oscar screamed.

Oscar sullenly emerged from the storage room with a biscuit in his hand. He wouldn't meet Glinda's amused gaze. She did her best trying to control her expression, but the laughter danced in her eyes.

"Sleep well?" She raised an eyebrow at Oscar and did a marvelous job in refraining from laughing.

Oscar paced back and forth on the island until he couldn't stand it anymore. "No. *No*, I didn't sleep well. I thought you—and then—that is not the least bit funny!"

Glinda couldn't hold it in any longer. Her laughter pealed across the desert. "It is very much the least bit funny."

"Social grooming is a sign of high affection." King Klick said. "For your affection, it appears the Princess now has some competition." He smoothed his hair back, shaking with laughter.

Oscar stopped and pointed a finger at King Klick. "No. That is not even funny."

"Perhaps I should grow hair on my arms." Glinda suggested. "That might draw your eye back to me."

Flustered, Oscar sat down. "Can we just not talk about this?" He pulled off a piece of biscuit and put it in his mouth, chewing it and grumping.

Glinda and King Klick kept laughing. Finally Oscar could stand it no more. "Okay. I understand. You're both laughing at me. For the record, *you*," he pointed at Glinda, "I really like you. And *you*," he pointed at King Klick, "you creep me out. I don't know how you can even *be*. Monkeys aren't supposed to talk or have wings or fly. You scare me. Now can we drop this?"

"I am sorry." said King Klick, but Oscar saw there was more in his eyes."

"Really?"

"Sorry that I am not twenty years younger, and have red hair."

"I'm sorry, too." said Glinda.

But Oscar would not be tricked again. "I don't think you are."

"I am. Truly."

"Okay. You're really sorry?"

"Sorry that I don't have silver hair and monkey breath."

"Ha ha. Now can we please figure out a way to get across? I would very much like to forget all of this." Oscar walked out to the edge of the island, where the bridge had crumbled, and did his best to ignore the string of jokes hurled his direction.

"But this time has been so special. You really want to throw that away?" Glinda said.

A light went on in Oscar's eyes. "Throw that away." He whispered. "That might just work."

Later, after Oscar studied out the problem and formulated a solution, he asked, "So you can fly Glinda over to the other side? That takes care of half of our problem."

King Klick studied Oscar. "You are heavy. I am only one. I can glide, but not fly. I glide from here with you and you land in the sand."

"So if Glinda goes across first, we know that she will be safe. Then it's just me. How do I know that you'll help me once Glinda is safe?"

"Oscar! Don't ask that. Of course he'll help you."

"He isn't offering any suggestions."

"Perhaps the boy is right. Perhaps he should go across first." King Klick stroked his chin and flew away to the top of the stairs.

"What?"

Glinda pulled Oscar to the edge of the island. "He's testing you. Don't you want to know if you can do this? Don't you want to know if you're clever enough to solve this riddle?"

"So he thinks I can't do it. He thinks that I need saving. Well," Oscar searched around to get an idea of their assets. "He can fly you, but he'd have to glide me, but gliding from the island ends up in the sand. We need to get more altitude to glide. That means up. We don't have materials to build a tower. Hourglass is gone. But we have planks, and we add a fulcrum…and we can make a catapult."

"A catapult."

"Yes."

"That's crazy."

"I know."

Long planks of wood stuck out of the side of the foundation like broken ribs. These ribs were the inner framework of Oscar's building materials. King Klick watched as Oscar pulled together the materials for his launcher. For most of the morning Oscar placed long planks and targets. Glinda watched most of the time with a puzzled, doubtful expression. "It'll work." Oscar kept saying.

And then he finally said, "It's done."

Oscar presented his handiwork. A catapult with a basket to sit in, and a large target for the weight to fall on. "See, the weight goes down on that end. I go up and out, and King Klick, with his Majesty's permission, of course, then glides me over to the other side."

Glinda smiled dubiously.

"And the young wizard knows this will work?" King Klick scratched at the wood.

"It will work."

King Klick raised an eyebrow, and a tiny doubt wormed its way into Oscar's mind.

"Okay. We'll try a barrel first."

They loaded the barrel into the basket and weighted it down with bricks.

"Now, King Klick, if you will, fly up and drop down onto this target. That will launch the barrel. And if my calculations are correct, it will go up and then onto the bridge."

King Klick jumped into the air. "I am not going to try to catch this barrel."

"No. No. I know. This is just a demonstration."

King Klick flew up to about twenty five feet, and then curled into a full tuck position to drop down on the catapult target. As predicted, the barrel flew up in the air in a perfect trajectory to reach the bridge. It landed right in the center of the broken edge of the bridge, and the barrel shattered.

"Ha HA!" Oscar shouted triumphantly.

The bridge groaned. Then a ten foot section of the bridge collapsed, leaving the gap ten feet wider than before.

Oscar froze in mid-celebration. Glinda burst into giggles. King Klick turned slowly to Oscar and pointed. A smile spread over his face. "It worked?"

"Yeah. It worked." Oscar said shakily.

He climbed up and sat in the basket. "You won't drop me?"

King Klick circled above. "Hold up your hands. I will jump after I drop and I will hold your hand. After all, you held my hand."

"Can we please not talk about that right now?"

"On your word."

"Okay. One." A blur shot downward, "Wait! -TwoOOO!" Oscar screamed as he launched into the air.

King Klick chuckled as he leaped into the air and flew up to the flailing young man. As Oscar reached the apex of his trajectory, King Klick grabbed his hands. It was at that very pinnacle of his flight that Oscar was at zero motion, so it required the least amount of energy change his direction and motion. King Klick spread his wings wide to gather the greatest amount of air to slow their descent. He grunted. "You are heavier than I thought you would be. Or, I'm getting older."

Oscar held on for his life as they quickly glided over the deadly chasm and onto the bridge. His feet hit and he flopped down onto his belly, skidding. Oscar didn't trust trying to roll on the bridge, so he accepted the pain of having the wind knocked out of him.

"It worked." This time, Oscar laughed.

King Klick caught his breath after a minute and then flew back over the gap to get Glinda.

She said, "I can see that you are tired from your long flight. Would it be easier for you if I got in the catapult and you glided me over?"

Glinda set down her cloth-wrapped mirror safely on the stairs. "Will you bring this over for me when we are safely on land?"

King Klick agreed and leaped into the air. Glinda reset the catapult basket and got into position. She raised her hands. "Ready."

The Winged Monkey dropped down onto the target and Glinda launched into the air. But she was much lighter, and so she went higher than Oscar. Her trajectory actually put her on a path to overshoot the bridge. At the apex of Glinda's trajectory, King Klick grabbed her wrists and actually had to circle out over the yawning desert in order to wheel around and get her to the bridge. He pumped his wings once, but lost altitude.

"Get her over here!" Oscar cried.

The edge of the bridge was at the level of Glinda's knees, and they were still not there. Glinda braced for the impact. Oscar leaped forward onto his belly, reaching out for their hands. Glinda hit the face of the broken bridge at chest level, knocking the wind out of her. Her hands scrabbled out for a grip on anything. The shock of hitting the bridge knocked King Klick off-balance.

Next to Oscar, a sliver-furred shape rolled onto the bridge and then fell off. Only a silver hand was hanging on next to Glinda. Oscar reached out his hands to both of them. Glinda grabbed on to him, her eyes wide with terror. King Klick looked up calmly into Oscar's eyes.

"I can't pull both of you up!" Oscar gritted his teeth, but he could not pull them up. He needed both hands to pull even one of them up. He looked between Glinda and King Klick. But it was clear that his decision was already made. "I'm sorry." King Klick nodded slightly and smiled sadly. He let go of Oscar's wrist and twisted his hand from Oscar's grasp. Oscar's hand snapped closed, but missed the falling monkey. *"NO!"*

Glinda screamed at the same time. But her scream was cut short as Oscar got a firm grip on her and pulled her up and onto the bridge. "You dropped him! You let him go!" She swung her fists half-heartedly at Oscar as the sobs came. She peered over the edge, but there was no sign of the silver monkey. Perhaps he had been turned into sand.

"I couldn't hold…I couldn't save both of you. I chose you. I made a decision. Right or wrong, I made a decision."

Behind them, a gravelly voice agreed. "He made a decision. The right decision."

"You're alive!" Glinda ran to King Klick and embraced him.

"Of course I'm alive. I may be old, but I am still a monkey."

"Then that was…?"

"A test. You are called a wizard. It is said that you have great powers. I had to see for myself if these powers extended into wisdom. I see that they do—*a little bit.* You need a great deal of work. You are young yet, but you are finding wisdom."

It was now Glinda's turn to hit King Klick. "You forced him to choose!"

"No. I forced him to recognize that he had already chosen." His eyes grew hard as he met Glinda's gaze, "Look at me, Princess. Look at you. Look at him. Who is different? I hold no loyalty to him, nor him to me. *You* are his light. He will choose *you.*"

Oscar tried to justify his decision, "It's just that you…monkeys shouldn't have wings."

King Klick brushed away Oscar's explanation. "My loyalty is to the Golden Cap, and to *your father*, Princess."

"My father is dead. I saw him fall off a cliff. That cliff over there. Ondribaba killed him."

"I am sorry." King Klick looked up at the sun. "It is nearly midday. I will search the cliff soon. First I will recover your treasure." He easily flew the distance to the island and dropped onto the stairs. He hefted the wrapped cloth, judging its weight. He peeked in and saw that it was glass. "What is your greater treasure, Princess? Is it this wrapped item? Or is it the Golden Cap?" King Klick raised the cloth to shatter the mirror inside on the stone stairs. "I offer a trade."

"You agreed to bring it over."

"I will, when you decide. Your decision."

Glinda reached out. "It's mine. I want it. Give it to me." The Golden Cap glowed magically.

King Klick felt the weight leave the cloth and he angrily thrust the cloth down on the stone stairs.

Now the magic mirror was in Glinda's hands. Gone was King Klick's bargaining chip. He growled gutturally and glared at them. Then he flapped off toward the cliff.

"Did I choose wrong?" Glinda asked Oscar sadly. "Was that a test?"

"You made a decision." said Oscar. "Your father gave you the Golden Cap, but he also said to be good the monkeys. If it was just about giving the cap to the monkeys, I'm sure your father would have done it."

They walked hand-in-hand across the old stone bridge to the grassy mainland of Oz. When they finally reached the other side and stood on the mainland again, Oscar looked back at their path. "We did it."

"We made it." Glinda said bittersweetly. She took his hand and swung it. "We made it together. And we always will."

Oscar made no reply. He looked out at the distant speck that was King Klick. If a lesson here had been taught, Oscar had missed the last part.

It couldn't be as easy as a right or wrong answer. There was too much power at stake for a simple solution. All of the destinies involved and wound together made it necessarily complicated. But were they making it too complicated?

Did it really boil down to which decision was it the lesser of two evils? Or was it the greater of two goods?

32 THE BATTLE OF EMERALD PRAIRIE

Wickrie-Kells marched at the head of the People's Army of Oz. It had been two days, and their numbers had grown to nearly three hundred. This was ten times the number they had departed with. Each new addition brought strength and courage to the army.

In their ranks they found singers who crafted songs and taught the others. When they crossed the boundary into the Emerald Lands, they were singing swelling anthems that set their hearts firmly upon the battle for freedom that lay ahead.

The day came, like every day had come before—only today promised to render judgment and provide a final answer whether the blood spilled here would be remembered, or whether it would be buried in the sand.

All of the armies took their designated places—arrayed on the Emerald Plains like game pieces. The People's Army was composed of soldiers from all over the land—clothed in yellow, red, blue, purple and green—people who had heard Glinda's message of freedom and flocked to her cause. These were farmers and bakers and shoemakers, all people who paid taxes to kings and rulers. These were people who believed that they had a voice that had gone unheard for too long.

The sandy army commanded by the Witch Queens was a brown scabrous stain on the verdant prairie. Three distinct sandy armies were united against the humans, each led by a witch.

Kalinya's soldiers were half blood-sand creatures—tigers and bears—and half were regular sand.

Ondri-baba had many regular sand-soldiers also, but she added blood-sand giants. She still had many hourglasses left in the Hamstrambulator, which sat parked on the far side of the field of battle.

Locasta had a small army composed entirely of sand soldiers—she adamantly refused to pour her own blood into this battle.

Locasta was not here for power. If the story were told truly she would not be here if she were anything other than a coward. She felt distinctly disconnected from her current reality. Her bruises ached, but her mind was floating. None of this was real—it couldn't be. She was standing here at the head of her tiny sandy army only because she was too weak inside to fight anymore. She was following brutal orders out of fear, not out of any kind of loyalty. She was outside herself—an innocent bystander watching her iniquitous body follow shouted commands.

Innocent. She laughed bitterly at that irony. Though if she truly were innocent she would not feel this guilty, sinking dread inside her heart. That pervasive guilt only sunk deeper as the morning progressed.

Wickrie-Kells addressed her army. They were armed with shovels and trowel-lances and pitchforks. She tossed her hair so that it flowed in the wind. She wanted to ensure that both her army and the enemy army saw that symbol of red. "You see the enemy there. We are facing an enemy that is not like us. They have no faces. They have no hearts. They seek only for power. What do we seek for?"

"Freedom!" came the resounding cheer.

Omby-Amby gave strategy orders. "They are sand. It is unlikely that we will have any rain with us today, so the full responsibility for defeating these sandy armies is ours. Remember that these creatures are made of sand. The red ones are stronger. Be careful, but be bold. If you can, remove their arms—that will decrease their effectiveness in battle.

"They will still fight without their heads. To ensure that they do not come back up or keep moving, stomp the limbs flat. Crush the magic. And, if you can help it, please don't bleed on 'em. Makes 'em go crazy."

In the nearby Central City, atop the Grand Tower, King Pastoria watched the events unfolding. At his side was his new Royal Advisor, Mombi. She leaned in over Pastoria's shoulder and whispered in his ear, "Who is your real enemy, Highness? Is it she who laid the crown on your head? Or is it she who wanted your army as her own?"

Pastoria looked in the spyglass again. "So you are saying that this girl is come to the Emerald Lands under false pretenses."

Because Pastoria was not looking at her face, Mombi allowed a small smile to dance across her lips. "Look at what she is doing, my King. She has raised an army, and she has come to the Emerald Plains. Her voice is drawing warriors and farmers alike to battle for her. She cries freedom, but she rallies against the witches who crowned you as king. Who then is the enemy?"

"Her army is formidable. Still, the Witches will crush her."

"Oh? Will they? I have intelligence that proves that they have been trying to destroy that girl since your coronation. They have been unsuccessful. She has powerful magic assisting her."

"So she will win?"

"She must not win." Mombi advised.

Pastoria turned to his butler. "Call my general."

When the General came, Pastoria ordered, "Deploy the Royal Army. March against the girl Glinda and her so-called People's Army of Oz."

Trumpets sounded from the direction of the Emerald Valley. It was a false call to battle, but it was enough to set off the tense and anxious armies. At the sound of trumpets, the armies charged into battle. Melee erupted all across the field of war.

The chaos of battle required complete attention from the witch-generals. The sand giants swatted away the human warriors. But for every warrior swatted, three more dug chunks out of the giants.

The battle raged, but Omby-Amby had prepared his novice soldiers well. Many of them were farmers. They were unaccustomed to swinging swords, but using a pitchfork was their livelihood. They knew shovels and trowels. Omby-Amby had taught them to do what they had always done—to dig.

And dig they did. The battle roared for more than an hour. The People's Army had decimated their foes by nearly half. Despite being outnumbered, this ragtag army of farmers knew how to till the earth, even if the earth was up and walking on two legs.

Then the trumpets sounded again, this time much closer. A green-uniformed army marched into the fray. A cheer went up from the fighting girls as the initial emerald soldiers cut down sandy soldiers. But it quickly turned to confusion as the Emerald Army engaged the People's Army.

The People's Army was well-suited to battling a soulless earthen enemy, but they were ill-prepared for facing flesh and blood opponents trained in the arts of war. They were quickly separated from each other. Omby-Amby shouted orders, but the press of the sandy army continued, and the Emerald Soldiers seemed less interested in stopping the confusion than in incapacitating the ragtag army.

"Capture the red-haired one!" came the shouts from the Royal Army of Oz.

Omby-Amby saw Wickrie-Kells across the field, desperately trying to lead her fighting girls to a stronger position. He leaped on the back of a fallen blood-sand tiger, smashing its head, and jumped up the back of a giant. With a vigorous shout, he jammed a shovel into the giant's neck, loosening its head. The giant twisted and flailed its arms, knocking the green-haired warrior loose. Omby-Amby fell to the ground. Wickrie-Kells disappeared from his sight.

The Witches were among their sandy armies, shouting commands and pushing and pointing. Ondri-baba was caught off-guard when the red-haired girl led the army onto the field of battle. She made it a specific purpose to destroy the girl before Kalinya got to her. Then the Emerald Army showed up. They seemed determined to get the red-haired girl also. So Ondri-baba sent blood-giants over to crush the girl.

Kalinya saw the disproportionately large force directed toward the fighting girls, and she sent the blood-tigers.

The apprentice witch, Locasta, saw the dire tribulation that the People's Army faced. With an epiphany born of disgust and self-loathing she realized that she was part of the problem. The dead feeling sucked at her soul, urging her to fight the searing light of truth and just to go along with the wickedness. Then she remembered what Glinda had done for her. Glinda had bound her and sent her away, but she had not harmed Locasta in any way. She had showed mercy when none had been deserved. Glinda had done the hard thing, trusting in Locasta's ability to choose for herself. She had let Locasta go free, knowing where her loyalties lay. Knowing that Locasta could very well turn around and become a thorn in her side—if not a knife in her back—Glinda had done the hard thing, without regard to any benefit or convenience to her. She did it because it was the right thing to do.

In that moment, Locasta determined her course of action. She pushed the dead feeling down and commanded her sandy soldiers to attack any and all blood-sand creatures.

Locasta's sand warriors plowed into the maelstrom with a ferocity unseen in this battle. They tore into the blood-sand warriors like a sandstorm. They ripped off arms and pounded and crushed.

In the mayhem, Wickrie-Kells had fallen. Omby-Amby disappeared from her view. Wickrie-Kells noticed absently, as she looked up to the sky, that the Winged Monkeys were circling like vultures over the field of battle. Then she heard very human shouts of *"Get the red-haired one!"* bringing her back to the present. And then she realized with horror that this new enemy was after *her*.

Then she was surrounded by sandy warriors, but they were facing away from her, battling the red sand soldiers. She scrambled to her feet and pulled the two fighting girls next to her underneath and through the legs of a giant and into the center of the field.

Ondri-baba saw the sandy soldiers attacking her giants and realized that she had been betrayed. There was only one witch who would benefit by betraying her—Ondri-baba. In her anger, Kalinya ordered her blood-giants to attack the blood-tigers. The carnage was indescribable as the blood-sand constructs viciously mauled each other.

Omby-Amby spotted the Hamstrambulator shining across the battlefield. Then he spotted Wickrie-Kells halfway between his position and the vehicle. He rallied his soldiers and cut through the sand warriors. A path opened up for him and he raced to Wickrie-Kells.

"You have to get out of here!"

"I can't leave you here alone."

"I'm not alone. I have people who believe. But those green soldiers are after you. That means Pastoria is siding with the witches. We can fight sand, but we can't fight trained soldiers. Our people are willing, but I don't want unnecessary blood on my hands."

Wickrie-Kells looked back at the chaotic battlefield. The Emerald Army spotted her red hair and pushed toward them. "I can't leave these people. They believe in me."

Omby-Amby grabbed Wickrie-Kells by the arms and shook her until she looked him in the eyes and focused on him. "Listen to me. *You are not Glinda!* To save the army, you have to leave, *now!*"

Wickrie-Kells locked eyes with Omby-Amby and kissed him fiercely. Then she pulled away. "Take care of them."

Omby-Amby boosted her into the Hamstrambulator. It was still loaded with vials of sand. "Go. I'll find you when this is done."

The Hamstrambulator spit up dirt as the large wheel spun. Wickrie-Kells' shout of, *"Independence!"* was lost in the wind as she sped away.

Omby-Amby charged at the emerald soldiers coming toward him. It had been a long time since he had fought a flesh-and-blood adversary, and he savored the opportunity. He attacked with such savage brutality that they turned tail and ran. They ran as if a demon from the underworld itself chased them.

Nearby, Kalinya saw the Hamstrambulator speeding away. She looked back at her blood-sand creatures being attacked and destroyed on the field. She had been betrayed fully, she realized. Cold hatred burned in her breast. She resolved to end the war once and for all. Three steps and she was gone.

Ondri-baba saw the Hamstrambulator going west; and with it, the reserves of her sand army. She had been betrayed. She ordered the destruction of Kalinya's blood sand creatures.

The remainder of the day was spent decimating those traitor creatures and then gathering the fallen sand for her army.

Unseen by any of the other witches, Locasta turned and walked away. She crushed the empty hourglasses, ensuring that her soldiers could not be re-used. Then she turned her face toward the south and did not look back.

33 THE ESCAPE TO THE EAST

Wickrie-Kells drove the Hamstrambulator east. Suddenly Kalinya appeared in the path of the vehicle. The Witch raised her hand and lifted the vehicle off the ground—with the wheel still spinning. She saw Wickrie-Kells underneath the tousled mess of red hair and squinted her eyes. "You are not Glinda." She observed.

"No. *I'm not!* Now put me down."

"Interesting. Where are you traveling to, friend of Glinda?"

"Anywhere but here."

"Is it true what Ondri-baba said, that Glinda is dead?"

"I don't know." Wickrie-Kells answered, but her averted gaze betrayed her real answer.

"I see." said Kalinya. "Perhaps we strike a deal, you and me. You take me to the East; to Munchkin Country. I take these vials of sand and I give Ondri-baba the battle she wants. I will destroy her—she betrayed our Alliance. Traitors deserve no less than absolute destruction."

Wickrie-Kells hesitated. "You will not try to destroy me, or throw me into the sky?" She kept the wheel spinning and reached a hand down to her sword.

"I have no need for you other than your driving skills. You are not Glinda. I have no quarrel with you, but I also have no *interest* in you. You are not my immediate enemy. My strength must be to destroy that Witch who was born as my sister."

Still Wickrie-Kells was skeptical. "What do you get out of this?"

"Only a ride east and cargo delivered. Nothing more."

Wickrie-Kells agreed to the terms and Kalinya dropped the metal vehicle to the ground and climbed in. They sped toward the East and the setting sun.

Omby-Amby regrouped his forces. The Emerald Army was forming up their ranks and retreating. Rumors flew about the green-haired demon leading the People's Army. It was clear from the looks given by the Royal Army that they wanted nothing to do with the ragtag band led by Omby-Amby.

The sandy armies were fighting amongst themselves. It was chaos everywhere. And above, as before, the Winged Monkeys still circled, not getting involved. They flew like vultures, just watching and waiting for scraps.

For the humans, it appeared the battle was over. The focus of all their attention had been the red-haired leader of the People's Army of Oz. And now that she was gone, there was little purpose to continue.

The Witches were fighting among themselves. Omby-Amby kept a one eye on that, in the event that they would gather their forces and again come after the small group of common soldiers. His mind was eased considerably when Ondri-baba marched with her sandy giants down toward the retreating Emerald Army and the distant Central Valley.

Ondri-baba marched her blood-sand army down into the Central Valley. The Royal Army stood between the Witch Army and the Family Palace. "Send out your king." the Witch demanded.

Inside the Family Palace, Mombi advised King Pastoria as he walked to the door. "They must not know that I am here. Such a revelation would jeopardize the King. I advise to give her what she demands, but just get rid of her. Let her take the war elsewhere. But if it is to be war, let us roll out the scroll of diplomacy first."

King Pastoria rode in his chariot out to the head of his Emerald Army. He was resplendent in his finest Robes of State. "You have my attention, Witch. What is it you want?"

"The King has witnessed the treachery on the field of battle. Kalinya, the Witch of the East, has betrayed the Land of Oz. She has betrayed the King, and she has betrayed the other witches." Ondri-baba laid out her case against her sister.

"You may not have my army. Others have asked and have been rejected. Those others will be swiftly brought to justice if they ever come into the Emerald Lands again."

Ondri-baba cackled politely. "I do not wish armies. I have my own. But I need to build my strength as I march against Kalinya. I require sustenance."

"So it is food you request?"

"Yes. Pie. *Specifically*, pie. Lots and lots of pie."

The royal bakers worked all afternoon and evening to create scores of pies for the Witch. As quickly as the pies came out and cooled, they were passed to Ondri-baba. When she had eaten her fill, the pies were loaded onto a wagon to travel with her.

The horizon was slowly swallowing the sun when Wickrie-Kells pulled into Munchkin Village. This was the primary city in Munchkin Country in the East. All around, blue-clad men and women turned to look at them. One of them recognized Kalinya and said, "The Witch has returned."

Everyone stopped to stare at Kalinya. She descended from the Hamstrambulator and walked through the assembled crowd. "Where is your king?"

A gruff voice sounded from the upper window of one of the round, blue houses. "What do you want, Witch? We have left your Tall House in peace. We gave you our daughter to enable peace between us."

"I bear ill news, King Widdershins. A powerful army is marching here to conquer your land." Kalinya made her case to the people, not only to the king.

"If it comes, *you* brought it. This is your battle, not ours. King Widdershins turned his great bulk around and reached to close the window.

"Wait!" Kalinya cried out, "This army is filled with magical giants, unstoppable by mere hands. Here, I will show you. Fetch your best warrior and have him fight." She pulled a sand vial from the Hamstrambulator and poured the sand through her fingers onto the ground. The sandy warrior arose.

Gasps of astonishment pushed the crowd backwards. Up from the back, sliding easily through the crowd was a brawny Munchkin lad, Tabulo. He sized up the sandy warrior and then pulled out his club and swung mightily, knocking the warrior to the ground. Tabulo snickered and looked back at the crowd.

Then the sand warrior got up. Again and again Tabulo pounded on the warrior until its head cracked and fell off. Tabulo raised his arms in triumph and turned to the cheering Munchkin crowd. The sandy warrior clubbed its arms and attacked the Munchkin relentlessly. Tabulo fought back, shattering both of its arms. Still the creature came on. It would not be stopped.

The horror grew in the crowd, and several Munchkin ladies fainted in fear.

Kalinya commanded the sandy soldier back into its vial. "That," she declared "is what is coming. An army—more than one hundred, some of them giants, others strange creatures from across the desert, still others faceless men who look like people you once knew."

King Widdershins watched his people through all of this, aghast. His pipe fell from his open mouth to shatter on the cobblestones below. The people were terrified. "Can this be true?" He asked. "*You*, with the witch," He said, calling to Wickrie-Kells, "Is it true what she says? Is there an army coming?"

"Answer the king's question." Kalinya grinned at Wickrie-Kells. Kalinya was like a fox moving toward an open chicken coop. And Wickrie-Kells was drawn fully into the trap and the betrayal of an entire people. These were not strangers that Wickrie-Kells was betraying, but relations—relatives—on her mother's side. By even coming here and aiding Kalinya, she may as well have shackled the people in chains herself.

"*Yes*. They *are* coming." Wickrie-Kells spat the words, disgusted with herself.

The crowd erupted in hysteria. "What can we do?", "Who will save us?", and "We're going to die!" were among the many cries heard.

"Your warning is for naught if we perish!" Exclaimed King Widdershins.

Kalinya smiled and slammed the trap closed. "I can save you. My army is here. I will fight for this land. I will protect you as my solemn duty."

Tabulo stood forward and said, "But it is the solemn duty of the King to protect us."

King Widdershins' face went pale. He stammered, but somehow he could not find his voice. The years of peace had made the king soft and lazy. He was a leader that enjoyed the good things of his people, but was unwilling to do the hard work. King Widdershins was pale and weak.

Kalinya watched both King Widdershins and the panicked people and waited for the right moment to pluck again at the strings of fear. "The boy warrior is right. *I* cannot protect you. Only the ruler of Munchkin Country may protect you."

A light flickered on in King Widdershins eyes. "Perhaps you could protect us. Be our queen." He suggested to Kalinya.

Kalinya smiled, "I came to warn you. It was not my stated intention to rule you. But what do the people say?"

The people were panicked, and they looked to a strong person to rule them. They unanimously cheered Kalinya.

"It will be as you wish. My army is powerful. I shall be your Queen. I will protect this land from invaders. You may declare the coronation after supper."

Wickrie-Kells went cold. Her heart sunk in her chest. *This is how freedom dies,* she thought. *With applause and fine speeches.* She refused to help Kalinya unload the vials of magic sand, but there were plenty of hands willing to help in her place.

"You lied to them."

"Foolish child. There was not one lie that passed my lips."

"You said that you weren't coming to rule them."

"No. I said that it was not my *stated intention* to rule them."

"Ondri-baba is coming. *You* know that. *I* know that. She is coming for you, not for them." Wickrie-Kells accused.

Kalinya smiled calmly, as if addressing a foolish little child's question. "Then you would condemn this people to destruction? You would see them all crushed under the coming army? I thought better of you. You are nothing but a *charlatan*. That red hair is a poor mask for your coward's heart."

"I brought you here. My agreement is done. I have nothing more to do with you."

"Such was our bargain. Begone, *little one*."

Wickrie-Kells sped away in the Hamstrambulator, leaving Kalinya to her supper and coronation as Queen of the Munchkin Country.

The coronation crowned Kalinya as Queen of Munchkin Country, from the desert of Shifting Sands in the East to the rugged forest in the West. The Munchkins cheered their hero as she piled the food on her plate and stuffed it into her mouth as fast as her hands could manage.

For the next two days, the Munchkins built fortifications and digged ditches and diverted waterways to create moats. In every fence, stakes were angled outward as spikes. The Yellow Brick Road was blockaded.

Kalinya spent all of her time building the blood-sand army. She gorged herself on Munchkin food to keep her strength up, and she fed her blood to the magic sand. For two days and nights she fed her blood until she passed out. When she woke up she ate more and did it again.

With one vial of magic sand left, Kalinya ran out of blood. No matter how she cut or jabbed or pinched, she was fully out of blood. She managed to get a few grains of sand out of her fingertip, but no blood.

Her blood-sand army awaited her command. It was a mighty army. It would have to be, because there was no possible way to create more. For this battle would determine supremely who would live and who would be utterly destroyed.

In the Emerald Valley, night fell, the moon rose, and Ondri-baba readied her stilt-legged hut. The pie wagon was hitched up and prepared to travel beside the hut. She ate another large meal of splatberry, apple and twisted chocolate pies.

At her departure, the King's Butler was the only one who was there to bid the Witch farewell; however, he was only there to fulfill his official duty as a representative of the King.

All of the blood-sand warriors were still intact, even after the battle earlier in the day. She pointed her army to the East and began marching. They saw fires to the distant south—most likely the remnants of the People's Army of Oz. They were no longer a threat.

The only thing that mattered now was vengeance on the traitor, Kalinya. And so the army pushed forward, passing by the small encampment. Along the way, she created more blood-sand warriors. Ondri-baba continued to eat the pies to keep up her strength. The cycle continued of sleeping, eating pie, creating the blood-sand warriors, and moving ever Eastward.

From atop the Grand Tower in Central City, Mombi looked out toward the setting sun. That was where the armies would meet—at the place where the sun set. Ondri-baba's army had been gone more than a day. If she marched through the night, the armies would meet the following evening.

She released from her hands two folded paper birds—one for Kalinya and one for Ondri-baba. These birds were folded messages that promised no interference from Central City if the Witches kept their wars among themselves. If they needed a mediator, Central City was willing to provide a mediator to arbitrate a truce between them. But under no circumstances were they to march their armies to Central City again. Such an action would constitute a declaration of war and would invalidate all previous treaties and former agreements.

Mombi sped the paper birds on their way and watched her long painted red hair blowing in the evening wind. A tear streaked through the magic paint, exposing her true skin beneath. She would have to fix that before she went in to see the king. The mortar of her lies was hardening around her, encasing Mombi completely within the hollow life that had become her prison.

34 THE FOUNDATIONS OF EMERALD CITY

Wickrie-Kells drove the Hamstrambulator through the night, bitterly angry with herself for allowing Kalinya to manipulate her. She had betrayed her proclaimed principles by consorting with the enemy—even if only for a short time. She was sick, and angry, and wept bitterly. She drove until she could not keep her eyes open any longer. Then she stopped to sleep.

The morning dawned bright, proclaiming a happier day. With the rising sun came a happy reunion. As Wickrie-Kells crested a hill in the Hamstrambulator, she saw in the distance two people walking toward her—one of them with *red hair!*

"Glinda!" she cried.

The Hamstrambulator pulled to a stop in front of the pair. Glinda and Wickrie-Kells ran and embraced, both of them crying.

"You're alive! I thought you were dead. We called, but you didn't answer. We had to go fight, Glinda. I am so sorry. I didn't mean to help her."

"Slow down, Wickrie. We're both okay. But we woke up and you were gone. Everything was destroyed. We thought you were dead. But there were no bodies."

Glinda took a look at her friend and finally noticed. "Your hair is red."

Wickrie-Kells explained everything—how she thought Glinda was dead, but that the oath was still in force and it must be honored; that people only knew Glinda because of her red hair, and if they were going to go down fighting, they could at least be fighting for something, and someone, that they believed in.

"You risked everything. How can you believe so much?"

Tears flowing down her cheeks, Wickrie-Kells nodded. "I just do." But there was something more behind her tears.

Glinda looked at Oscar, who gave a concerned half-smile.

"Freedom rings like a bell. When you hear it you can't get the ringing out of your head." Oscar said.

"I do believe. But I ruined everything. I didn't mean to help her, Glinda. I really didn't. I was just afraid." Wickrie-Kells explained the situation with Kalinya and her manipulation of the Munchkins and becoming their queen. "Have I spoiled everything?"

"No, dear friend, you have not. The Witches want power. They will destroy themselves in their hunger."

Oscar asked. "Where is Omby-Amby?"

Omby-Amby led the remnants of his army toward the south. They lost many on the battlefield, and they took time to bury their dead. Each group had its own section of the graves—Munchkin, Winkie, Gillikin and Quadling. There were none of the Ozzites that had fallen in that battle. Few Ozzites had actually joined the People's Army of Oz. Those that knew how to fight were already conscripted into the Royal Army.

When all were buried and names written both to memorialize them and to pass on to their families, Omby-Amby led his army back toward the South. Ondri-baba had ignored them as she marched eastward with her sandy army. They were no longer her opponents.

Dejected and exhausted, Omby-Amby wondered if Wickrie-Kells had survived, and where she would end up. *Where would he find her? Would she be the same person? Would he be the same person? Would she hate him for making her leave instead of fighting?*

They stopped for the night at the intersection of three brick roads—one led northwest, passing by the Central City and then on toward Winkie Country; another led east, toward Munchkin Country; and the other led south, toward the South Castle. Here they made their camp and rested.

Painting a distinct silhouette against the rising moon with her peaked hat, Locasta approached the weary army encampment.

Immediate shouts of *"Attack!"* and *"Witch!"* roused everyone.

Omby-Amby strode forward and questioned the Witch. In the firelight, he glared at Locasta. Then he noticed the bruises covering her face and arms. By the way that she walked, there were many more bruises that he couldn't see. His tone was stern, but softened somewhat. "I know your face. You were sent away when we were up north. Why are you here now?"

"I am tired of this war. You saw Ondri-baba leave. Kalinya is gone. They will fight until one of them wins, and for what? Both of them are hungry for power. But whatever they get will never be enough. I got tired of the bruises.

I am tired of falling off the ladder of so-called success." Locasta let an exhausted tear fall down her face.

"Why were you with them? You are a witch, right?"

"I was the apprentice of Kalinya. She chose me from the Munchkins when I was a young girl. I had some natural affinity for magic, and she thought she could shape me into her."

"Where is your army? I saw you commanding soldiers."

Locasta held out her hands. "I have no sand. I do not want any. I have seen enough spilled blood to sicken me. My magic is oracular—you saw it in my hat before. I cannot harm you."

Omby-Amby still hesitated. "We have lost many brave warriors today."

"I do not ask for your confidence." Locasta admitted. "I only ask that I may spend the night in your camp, among people. You don't have to talk to me. Just let me be here and listen. Let me feel like a person instead of this dead *nothing*."

Omby-Amby nodded his permission and stepped aside. "Give her a seat by the fire." He ordered. Then he directed Locasta privily, "You'll need to remove the hat. Wearing it is a bad reminder of this day."

"Of course." Locasta removed her hat and mumbled a few words, and it changed shape into a slate.

Locasta took a seat by the fire and just listened. She watched the crackling flames and heard the murmur of conversation. She felt the heat of the fire on her face and hands and it warmed her. But she felt even more the nearness of belief and faith and courage from very human souls all around her, and that cast off the chill on her bones far more than a roaring fire ever could. She closed her eyes and felt the dead rags of her life stirring in the winds of change. It was painful, but it was *real*. And *real* would help her maintain her sanity in the face of all of the horror she had permitted in these last two months of war.

The oracular slate wrote a new message. Locasta felt the fingers of fate nudging her mind, forcing new thoughts in. She opened her eyes and looked at the slate. *"Become what Glinda cannot be."*

Shouts from the sentries gave warning as the Hamstrambulator pulled into the encampment. Warm greetings were passed all around. Omby-Amby wrapped Oscar in a great bear hug and lifted him off of the ground. Then he embraced Glinda, much more gently. When Wickrie-Kells stepped down, he saved his best hug for her. Wickrie-Kells had her hair wrapped in a cloth, hiding all of the red. "There is only one girl with red hair." She whispered to Omby-Amby.

Glinda and Oscar walked into the encampment. Many fine words and thanks were given them as they passed through the soldiers. They shook everyone's hand and received many pats on their backs. Then a path opened to the fire and Glinda saw Locasta.

Glinda stopped and narrowed her eyes defensively. "What is *she* doing here?"

Omby-Amby stepped forward. "She is here with my permission. She wants to sit and listen—to be with people. That's all. I didn't see any harm."

Glinda took a seat facing Locasta. Oscar and Wickrie-Kells stood behind Glinda. "Your master has conquered the Munchkins." Glinda said.

"She did that years ago." Locasta answered her face blank of any expression. Her voice was more weary than worried. "They lived with it so long that they forgot that they allowed her that privilege in the first place. I was part of the price paid for Kalinya retreating to the Tall House."

"Why are the Witches fighting?"

"You have seen them. They are sisters that cannot live with the blood they share. They fight over who is stronger; who has more power; which one can control more—they are horrible." Locasta smiled sadly. "Your fighting girl is a brave one. She would have died today. I don't know what you told these people, Glinda, but they believe in you."

"It's actually Oscar that promises a new way of life, not me. But I believe in him, too." Glinda reached back and squeezed Oscar's hand.

Locasta repeated, "I don't know what they are believing, but I just have to trust that it's better than what the Witches are promising. If the Witches win, then the best we can hope for is that nothing changes. But we both know that isn't true at all. They will reign with blood and horror. That's all they know inside. That is what manifests in their magic. So when I saw that your fighting girl was going to die, I *changed* the course of the battle, and the course of the *war.*"

"What do you mean?" Glinda was now very puzzled. She turned to Wickrie-Kells for clarification.

"The sandy things just started fighting each other. I told you that already."

Locasta nodded in agreement to the fighting girl's story. "As she said, the sandy warriors started fighting each other. Both Kalinya and Ondri-baba wanted her—the one with red hair, *you*—dead, or captured. King Pastoria also sent out an army to capture you. That is a lot for one red-haired girl to deal with, don't you think? So I created confusion."

"You sent your warriors to fight with the red sand warriors that were after Wickrie-Kells." Oscar said.

"They are *blood-sand warriors.* Both Witches mixed their blood with the magic sand from Smith & Tinker. The creatures they made are stronger and smarter. They last longer than an hour, too. So Kalinya thought that Ondri-baba was attacking her army, and Ondri-baba thought that Kalinya was attacking her. In the confusion, your girl escaped."

Omby-Amby joined them at the fire. "Kalinya disappeared right after I got Wickrie-Kells to the Hamstrambulator. "Ondri-baba picked up all of the sand and then marched into the Emerald Valley, probably to Pastoria. Marched out when night fell. Went right by us. Heading east. That was a couple of hours ago."

Glinda finished the story. "So she is going to give battle to Kalinya. It will determine who becomes the Witch Queen. I am not going to let that happen."

Oscar recognized the look on Glinda's face—determined anger and righteous indignation. "You have a plan." He said.

"I have an idea. But first we sleep. In the morning I will share with you." Glinda dismissed the group. She touched Locasta's sleeve as she turned to go, saying to the young witch, "I believe you, but I still don't fully trust you. You'll have to prove yourself."

Locasta nodded. "I understand." And then Glinda left the fire to go find Oscar.

Locasta closed her eyes and looked at the rags of her life. For all that she had done, Locasta believed that she was just like the sand from the hourglasses—only fit to live for a short time, commit acts of atrocity, and then be dissolved and unremembered. She felt unworthy of anyone's confidence—especially her own. So it was a sobering surprise that Glinda allowed her to stay by the fire. She let out a ragged sigh. Glinda's words echoed through her soul as she drifted off to a remarkably untroubled sleep, *"I believe you."*

By the time that Glinda had settled down enough to find a place to sleep, Oscar was snoring. So she sat down, and Glinda watched Oscar dream. As he dreamed, great misty green walls arose, with citadels reaching toward the sky. The city stretched translucent all around them. Glinda watched as the towers increased in height, becoming beacons to all the land.

At last she fell asleep, the visions of Oscar's green city going through her head.

Morning rose, but Glinda was already awake and planning. Oscar awoke to smell breakfast cooking. He meandered over to where Glinda and Locasta were discussing the strategic features of Munchkin Country. "The Tall House controls the clouds from that border. It's like Yellow Castle. The clouds aren't going to push past the Tall House to go into the desert, so they can be directed there to prevent retreat."

"How do we secure this Tall House?' Glinda asked.

"That is Kalinya's place of solitude. She keeps her magic there, or she did before the war. It will be protected by charms and powerful magicks."

"Can you navigate them?"

Locasta shook her head. "I *will not.* I have had enough of this war. I support your goal of ending this, but I cannot be a part of this any longer. Once I finish here, today, I will leave."

Oscar chimed in, "Where will you go?"

"I'm not sure yet. The oracle doesn't make sense. How can I be what Glinda is not?"

Glinda paused, searching for the right words. "There are a lot of things that I am not. For example: *I'm not my mother—*"

"That's it!" Locasta exclaimed. "Never mind. I will go north. Find me when you are ready. Sorceress, a word, if you will."

Glinda followed Locasta outside the borders of the camp. Oscar watched them talk for several minutes. First Locasta would speak, then she would make motions with her hands, then Glinda would mimic her. When the information was imparted to Locasta's satisfaction, she took Glinda's hand and squeezed it. And that was all. Glinda turned and walked back into the camp. Locasta turned northward. She walked away and did not look back.

"That was unexpected." said Oscar, when Glinda joined him again.

"You get that with Witches. But we have what we need now, and we have an ally up north." answered Glinda. Then she changed the subject and gestured to the camp around them. "Notice anything different here? You certainly had some big ideas last night."

Oscar looked around and shrugged. We got here after sunset. I didn't get a good look at the place. What am I looking for?"

"Walls. Towers. Buildings. Don't you remember? You dreamed a city here last night. I watched as everything changed. Tall towers to reach the sky. Thick walls all around."

Remembrance flickered in Oscar's eyes. "It was a city. There was a city right here. People came from all over to build and work and trade and live in the city. It was beautiful."

"That sounds like the beginning of a wonderful plan to me." Glinda said. "You and Omby-Amby can build the city you talked about. Guide it according to your ideas. Make it an experiment."

"An experiment in *Ozzian Exceptionalism.*" Oscar finished.

Glinda called to Wickrie-Kells. She still kept her dyed hair covered. "I have one last duty for you, my dear friend."

Wickrie-Kells tossed the headscarf into the wind as she drove the Hamstrambulator southward. They drove back in the direction they had come the previous evening. Oscar and Glinda rode in the baskets. The single duty assigned to Wickrie-Kells was to let her hair blow free. She volunteered for the rest.

Oscar had left Omby-Amby with the basic outlines for a city, just like the one they had talked about. This city would be built in the Emerald Prairies, at the intersection of the three brick roads.

It would stand as a beacon of freedom, and a remembrance of those who gave their lives for freedom. When he heard of those who had fallen in battle, Oscar immediately decreed that their city would create a monument to them—with catacombs that would give these volunteer soldiers the honor and respect they deserved. Omby-Amby sent runners to his home city in Winkie Country to bring architects to begin designing the city. Construction would begin immediately.

Glinda, Oscar and Wickrie-Kells raced south, knowing that this coming battle held even greater dangers for them than the previous battles. This was not a matter of helping one side to win and making the other lose. If either side crushed the other and kept a large portion of their armies, the entire land would remain at risk.

The only way to obtain a victory for their cause here was to ensure that both Witches lost completely and lost equally. How could they possibly ensure that? Glinda and Oscar were only two people.

Yes, they were only two people, Glinda smiled grimly, but those two people were a *sorceress* and a *wizard.*

35 THE STORM THAT RAGED

Glinda stood in the Boneyard of the Clouds, explaining her situation to the spectral remnants of the clouds. She detailed the wicked exploits of the Witches and asked for the help of the clouds to end this war.

Whispers in the rising wind signaled the acceptance of both physical and spectral clouds to join in this war. Glinda murmured softly the words to the spell. Then she repeated it louder. Then she shouted it from the top of her lungs. Geysers of pure water spouted skywards to fill the spectral frames of ghost clouds, giving them corporeal mass. Great billowing clouds soon surrounded the Boneyard and all of the South Castle grounds.

Oscar emerged from his expedition into the workshop with his arms full of creative materials. Following behind him was a large wire mesh ball. This was tied to a string on his leg. With each step he pulled it along.

Glinda lowered her cloud to the ground and extended her hand to Oscar. "You found enough building blocks for your part?"

Oscar grinned and passed his armload up to Glinda. Then he lifted the large ball up. "I found them. Plenty to create a legend. This is going to be unforgettable."

The clouds lifted from the ground and headed northeast. Thunder rumbled, raising other clouds from their slumber in valleys and along rivers. Their thunderous call to action added legions to their cloud army.

"I brought you something." Glinda said, as Oscar tinkered with his materials. He looked up, surprised. Glinda pulled out from beside her the mega-trump-o-phone and held it out to him. "You said you could throw your voice, Wizard. Now you can throw it farther."

Glinda held up a glass flask and shook around sand inside it. "I've got a toy, too. *Sand from the Deadly Desert.*" Her eyes twinkled in curious excitement.

The great cloud army thundered its way across the land, raising a storm, the likes of which had never before seen in all of the history of Oz.

The great storm attracted the attention of all of the races of Oz, including the Swift Horses. They galloped upward in the rising tempest. As the lightning flashed, Glinda and Oscar saw the outlines of horses racing on the wind. Glinda waved and called to Zephyr. The great midnight-blue stallion galloped over.

"You have a mighty army of cloud-friends here, Princess Glinda."

"You told me that clouds were good friends to have."

"What are you doing with them? This is not just a run for joy?" King Zephyr questioned.

"No. There is a war. I am going to rain on it."

"I shall be watching." Zephyr said. "Your warning to my people saved them. When the witch, Ondri-baba, came through our valley, she burned it. If we had not known of the danger, we would have been destroyed. I owe the safety of my people to you. I shall watch for a moment to repay you, Princess."

"Thank you, noble horse."

Later, King Klick flew at the head of a great flock of Winged Monkeys. He was followed by all of his people, save Brutus, who had disappeared into exile. King Klick flew up above the clouds to converse with Glinda. Oscar felt apprehension as he saw the determined expression on the silver monkey's face.

"Be careful." Oscar said to Glinda.

"You have a mighty army, Princess Glinda." King Klick said. "Are you going to fight a war?"

"I am going to *end* a war." Glinda declared.

Oscar stayed silent. He still did not trust the monkey king's motivations. With the great flapping cacophony of Winged Monkeys behind him, he felt very uneasy.

"When you flew off to find my father, you did not come back." Glinda said.

"I did not find him. Then my people required my attention. With Brutus gone, the rabble he led has been disorganized and unruly. They required a firm hand to settle their rebellions."

"Why did you try to get the Golden Cap from me?"

"My people are bound to serve the possessor of the Golden Cap. That is not a simple oath. As I told you before, to save the lives of my people, your father intervened. He prevented your mother from making the Winged

Monkeys extinct. For that, we owed him our lives. But to retain our lives, we agreed to bind ourselves and our children to the Golden Cap. This is a magically enforced oath. When the wearer of the Golden Cap calls, we must come. Three times we are bound to obey.

"Your father was also bound by oath. He would have freed us, but your mother required his oath also. He swore that he would retain the charm of the Golden Cap. He maintained his oath. So we are bound.

"Your father gave you the Golden Cap in the hope that your soul was made of better stuff than his—he knew the weakness and the darkness that he came from. He could not tell you this while your mother was alive. The Witches came too soon for him to train you in the proper use of its magic. I have endeavored to watch you and protect you. So long as you live, there is hope for the freedom of my people."

Glinda thought on these words for a few seconds. "I will free you and your people from the oath of the Golden Cap."

"You can liberate us from our captivity right now." King Klick suggested. "Destroy the spell that binds us."

"Help me *win* this war and destroy the Witch armies, and you shall be free." Glinda's eyes were hard—she was determined to obtain the victory and end this war.

"Swear to me that it will be so." King Klick demanded in return.

"I so swear." said Glinda.

What Glinda did not realize in her youthful naiveté and her determination to win, was that if she had freed the Winged Monkeys at that moment they would have helped her and carried her to the ends of the earth, if needed. For when one has lived a life of slavery, freedom becomes his only goal. When he is liberated from those binding shackles, the gratitude he feels for this newfound freedom and liberty motivates action. And for the ones that they love, those actions can be amazing. It might have been very different, had Glinda listened more closely.

King Klick jumped off their cloud and dropped backwards to join his tribe. Glinda heard chattering, but she could not make out any words.

"Do you trust him?" Oscar asked.

"I believe that he will lead his people in helping us." Glinda responded.

"Is there any doubt in your mind of his loyalty? You heard what he said about the Golden Cap."

"I believe him. He wants to free his people. I can help him."

"Then why didn't you?"

"We have a war to win." Glinda declared.

"That's not what you said earlier, to him. You told the monkey, *END* this war, not *WIN* this war." Oscar clarified.

"Is there a difference?" Glinda growled defensively.

"Yes. There is a big difference. If you want to end this war, you fight alongside your allies. If you want to win the war, you keep servants and slaves—whatever resources you need. They become tools and numbers, not intelligent beings...not *people.*"

Glinda was left to ponder those words as Oscar went back to building his weapon. The clouds roared and thundered their way across the landscape moving ever closer to the final confrontation in Munchkin Country.

Ondri-baba's army crossed the boundary into Munchkin Country as the sun dropped down to touch the horizon. In the distance, silhouetted against the setting orb, was the tallest structure in the land, the Tall House. That was Kalinya's place of solitude, where she looked out over all of the land and schemed her devious schemes. That was their target. That was the home of her enemy, her rival, her sister witch, Kalinya.

Booming footfalls nearby revealed the presence of her invisible giants. These were her secret weapon in this war. She would need them. The Witch Ondri-baba was haggard and pale. Her cheeks were sunken and her skin was dry and flaking. Hate glittered in her eyes like the metal necklaces she wore. The metal plates on her clothing hid her sagging and worn body. Empty holes cratered her fingertips where no more blood would come out. She had exhausted every last drop of her blood in creating her army. Only magic and hate kept her alive.

On the southern horizon, a storm raged. Lightning flashed in the dimming twilight. Thunder echoed across the land. It was of no concern to Ondri-baba, for she predicted that this war would be over before the storm arrived.

In that prediction she was sorely disappointed, for as her army crossed the threshold of the Munchkin fields, the wrath of Kalinya's army was awakened. In the deep shadows of the evening, Kalinya's beasts emerged. These monsters were of the sort that Ondri-baba had only seen in her sleeping hours through her magic eye. These were the horrid creatures that The Queen of Dreams had warned her would come, and Ondri-baba feared.

Strange, tentacled lions and hulking crab-headed bears attacked the first line of invading soldiers, tearing them to pieces. These nightmarish things were quickly overcome by Ondri-baba's giants as the invading army pushed further into Munchkin fields.

Darkness fell as the armies clashed in full. The lightning from the approaching storm dimmed the starlight as flashes revealed monstrous beasts locked in unmortal combat. Blood-colored sand stained the fields and roads. And still the monsters fought for their wicked masters.

36 THE BATTLE OF MUNCHKIN FIELDS

Lightning rained down like drops from the storm clouds, starkly illuminating an invisible giant moving in strobe-motion in the center of the field. Kalinya magically lifted a small mountain of earth and hurled it at the giant, coating it with slick mud and knocking it backwards. A blood-sand tiger eagerly pounced on the fallen giant and viciously raked its claws across the giant's face. The blood-sand titans tore up the field as they thrashed in the slicing rain. All around them lightning cracked, creating reflected fires in the flooded fields.

Every place that lightning pierced the fences and the isolated hillocks of trees, the wood burst into frenzied flame, lighting the insatiable fires of war. The sinister flames sharply illuminated the inhuman armies clashing in the darkness.

Kalinya's hands twisted and writhed as she lifted one of Ondri-baba's blood-sand warriors, plucking him mid-charge from the ground. She hoisted it into the air, then thrust it downward and dashed it against the ground again, and again, and again, until it broke into screaming pieces. Then a wave of fatigue engulfed the witch, and she gasped in horribly empty pain. She staggered and reached out to the foundation beam of the Tall House to keep her feet. Kalinya was haggard, jaundiced and pale. The deep magical lines in her face had glacially carved themselves even further. Her golden eyes sunk deep in their sockets. They glared out from the shadows like sickly yellow harvest moons. The twin pinpoints of her eyes now reflected the outer fires, but these reflections paled in comparison to the inward fires roaring within Kalinya. She had spent every last drop of her blood to create this nightmare army, and she was determined to conquer.

Up above the thundering battle, on the rapidly traveling cloud, Glinda furiously pulled out the first row of stitching inside the Golden Cap. She removed completely the first line of her father's bequeathed incantation. It was far more than merely a summoning spell for the Winged Monkeys. The incantation began with the runes known only to magical eyes. This was hand-embroidered by Gayelette, intended only for the eyes of her husband or child. This was the incantation for which she had sold half of her vast kingdom. These were the words that gave the Golden Cap its summoning and embodying power. Whoever held these words had power to bring all things to them in dream or reality. It was too much power to enshrine in one item, yet Gayelette had done it. Now it was up to her heir to undo all that she had done.

Glinda had already memorized the words and instructions. But she was rapidly running out of time. Inside her mind, Oscar's words to her burned in great searing accusations. He said that she could have freed the monkeys at that moment. And then he asked the burning question, *"Why didn't you?"*

Why? Glinda asked herself over and over as she pulled and pulled at the embroidered glyphs. She was trying to do at the last second what she should have done hours earlier, or even days earlier. She was trying to fix a critical mistake caused by her own inaction. Her father couldn't free the Winged Monkeys, and he had risked everything to ensure Glinda could make it right.

Was she making this war about her? She looked at the flask of toxic sand sitting on the cloud next to her. What was she going to do with sand from the Deadly Desert? *Sand from the Great Sandy Waste* was more accurate, but it was all deadly desert—all around Oz. She vowed then and there to put her own self-serving need for revenge aside. She tossed the bottle of deadly sand off the side of the cloud and into the thick forest below.

Ahead of the glowing ribbons of lightning slashing down from the clouds, King Klick and his tribe of Winged Monkeys dove at the battling blood-sand armies. Armed with their metal nets, they dove down at the clashing behemoths. King Klick swooped out of the sky with a large mesh net strung between himself and another large monkey. They swung the net around the head of a sandy giant and pulled it tightly, dissolving the sand through the mesh. But that did not stop the behemoth. Still the lumbering giant moved forward swinging its arms. It became instantly clear to the monkeys that the sandy soldiers would need to be completely dissolved for them to stop. King Klick hooted orders to his people and coordinated the aerial attack.

Glinda's cloud rolled in over the battlefield. Oscar excitedly lowered his mysterious project through the cloud. He had fixed flammable materials all throughout the mesh sphere and poured accelerant all over it. He lowered the sphere on a chain and asked the cloud very politely for a spark.

Lightning sizzled, and the sphere burst into glorious flame. Suspended below the cloud, surrounded by flashing lightning, the ball of fire roared in the darkness. Through the mega-trump-o-phone, Oscar shouted, and his voice was heard above the echoes of thunder. His voice was heard by all who were in the land. They heard the voice of the Wizard, and they remembered forevermore. The story was thereafter told of the Wizard's first words in the land of the Munchkins, *"I am OZ, THE GREAT AND TERRIBLE!!!"*

Then the rain hit. Like every storm before, the rain sliced into the sand armies. But unlike all the times before, these clouds had an intelligent pilot controlling them, and they had a specific mission to perform. The clouds dropped swirling funnels of wind, spawning tornadoes and dust devils. These whirlwinds tore into the sand giants, ripping away their bodies and disincorporating them.

The pounding rain sizzled as it hit Kalinya's exposed skin. It burned like acid every place that it struck her. She quickly sought shelter underneath the awning of the rapidly-constructed command center. Her skin was blistering and angry red where the rain burned her parched and flaking flesh. The droplets were melting her skin away from the bone. Without blood flowing through her veins to nourish her skin, she was a husk, vulnerable to the rain.

She looked in panic back toward the beckoning cover of the Munchkin Village. It was at least safe from the rain in there. In her moment of panicked weakness she saw what could be her salvation. On the dock next to the river there was a wooden chest. She twisted her hands out, magically lifting the chest, and she drew it in toward her. She cackled as she anticipated the glorious treasures inside the box. She was not disappointed. Off she ripped off the lid, and she laughed in ghoulish glee. Her gnarled fingers pulled out an oilskin coat and a large floppy rain hat. She could now cover every exposed part of her skin. Duly armored against the weaponized rain, Kalinya turned her glowing back to the battle. Now she was protected and she could focus on conquering and destroying and grinding into bloody powder her sister's armies.

In the fields beyond the command post, both sandy armies were melting in great smearing globules of mud and blood under the brutal and unending assault from the skies.

Ondri-baba's army was composed of two types of creatures—original blood-sand warriors and re-formulated creatures. The blood-sand warriors that were hers in the last battle fought truly for her. The pure-blooded sand creatures were loyal; that could not be questioned. They knew her mind and they fought as she would fight. Her blood animated them. However, those creatures and warriors that were formed from the fallen sand gathered after the last battle were less true—much less true. They were formed of magic and the wicked blood of both Ondri-baba and Kalinya. The blood-memories that animated these creatures conflicted with Ondri-baba's current strategies. So these mix-bloods fought, but they did not fight cleanly.

When the rain sliced into them, the mix-bloods roared in pain. The pain of storming destruction from the skies undercut and undermined the blood-memories, effectively wiping them out. Without the blood-memories, these mix-bloods were only left with the wickedness of the blood and confusion and pain. The pain drove them berserk. These mix-blood berserkers attacked everything they could reach, even each other. The awful spectacle unfolded as part of Ondri-baba's army turned on itself. In the frenzy of melting limbs and roaring splashes, one of the nightmares broke ranks.

One of the berserkers broke through Kalinya's defensive line, ripping a crab-bear in half. It pounded through the line of spikes and stepped onto the bridge into the Munchkin Village. Kalinya saw the charging Berserker and went into the rain after it. No creation of her sister would lay a foot on her land! Such a thing as this berserker deserved no less than being crushed into bloody mud. She vowed to stop the creature before it dirtied Munchkin village with its muddy prints.

Ahead of them both, in the center of the bridge, one obstacle stood between the raging sand-beast and the Munchkin Village—a brave Munchkin warrior named Tabulo. He stood with his grandfather's drawn sword. His head was lowered against the pounding rain, but his eyes were clear and sure. He clenched his fingers again on the sword hilt, ensuring his grip, and stared down the frenetic brute.

"You shall not go forth. You will not hurt my people. Even if no one else will stand, *I will.*"

Bravely heedless of the danger to himself, Tabulo burst into song as he charged at the berserker beast. Tabulo swung his sword and severed the hand from the arm. With the roaring thunder he raised his voice to the sky, shouting the hymn to the Mighty Munchkin. He stomped the severed hand flat, crushing it into mud. Then he whirled and leaped, thrusting his sword deep into the creature's chest. His song died in his throat as he realized too late that his thrust through the chest was useless against a creature with no heart. The berserker clubbed its arms together and smashed Tabulo. Then it turned, flinging the Munchkin warrior's limp body across the street and into a brick wall.

A door opened and a little Munchkin boy, Boq, peeked out. He saw Tabulo fallen to the ground, with his face down in a puddle. The young boy ran to him, crying. *"Brother, brother!"*

Boq pulled Tabulo's face out of the water and pulled open one of his eyes. Tabulo's eyelids fluttered as he forced a breath into his shattered chest. He coughed and forced a weak smile at his little brother. "Boq, my brother, be brave. Go inside now. Go where…safe."

The constant lightning illuminated the beast from behind. The vile shadow fell over the two Munchkin boys Tabulo saw it and his eyes opened wide. It was the last thing he saw. Boq's eyes didn't leave his fallen brother's face. Only when the blanketing shadow jerked spasmodically and suddenly disappeared into the sky did Boq look up into the rain.

There stood Kalinya in the center of the street, her eyes glowing orbs above a wickedly smug smile. Her face was lost in shadow under a monstrously large and ill-fitting hat. The rain pounded down on the hat and poured down in waterfalls all around her. The witch was covered from head to foot in shiny oilcloth. She cackled at the child and then turned back to the battle. As she crossed the bridge, the berserker howled far above as it hurtled toward the roaring fireball that was cursing the enemies of the land.

The child, Boq, patted Tabulo's waxy cheeks. The warrior's lifeless eyes stared unblinking as the raindrops fell. The water pooled in his eyes and poured down, lifeless tears for a life spent too quickly. Boq pulled on his brother's shoulder, but Tabulo would not move. Then Boq realized in innocent horror that death had claimed his brother as a victim. Fear crushed itself onto his face as he looked around as if he was going to be blamed. He tried to wipe away the pouring tears from Tabulo's eyes, but the water kept coming. "Wake up." He begged. Then his parents rushed out and pulled him protesting and screaming back inside, only to leave his brave brother's body alone to weep in the night.

"Oz, the Great and Terrible, brings vengeance on those who rule with blood and horror!" the giant fireball roared. The charging cloud approached the Tall House. Oscar was controlling the fireball with puppet chains. The construct had a rudimentary face connected to the chains, so it had the appearance of life, like a marionette. To any who looked up to the skies, they would see the giant flaming head of Oz roaring and proclaiming curses upon his enemies.

Glinda's head was down and she was thoroughly occupied, trying to pull the stitching from the Golden Cap. The clouds no longer needed her direction to hurl lightning bolts down onto the armies below. The clouds were their own masters now in this battle. Glinda was so completely occupied that she did not notice how close they were to the Tall House.

Suddenly a howling berserker sand-warrior came hurtling up from the ground toward them. It came from the direction of the village, but it clearly did not come of its own choice. It was thrust up at them by Kalinya; only she could manage such a thing. Glinda noticed in that moment that the creature was missing one hand. Then the berserker hit the suspended flaming head and both disintegrated in a massive explosion. The explosion sent a shock wave through the cloud, shattering it and flinging Oscar and Glinda into the air.

Nearby Winged Monkeys saw their plight and came to their rescue, reaching out to grab the falling humans. The exploded cloudstuff dissipated before them, and Glinda realized exactly where they were. Clutching the Golden Cap tightly in her hand, she pointed to the Tall House. "*There.*" She cried. "*Take us there!*"

The Winged Monkeys flapped hard against the wind and rain. Other monkeys flew to their aid to push them further upwards. At last they gained the necessary altitude to reach the high platform. It was a short glide away, but that path was pierced from every direction by lightning from the clouds and hurled bits of blood-sand from below. Two were hit by lightning and spiraled down into the darkness below. The other Winged Monkeys skillfully dodged the debris. They flew fast and hard and safely delivered Glinda and Oscar to the platform of the Tall House. Notably, King Klick was not among these Winged Monkeys.

"How do we get in?" Oscar shouted to be heard above the howling wind.

As he touched the door of the Tall House, it blazed with magical fire.

Glinda traced a symbol in the air and said the word Locasta had taught her, "*Múch tinte ealaíne*" and the flames went out.

"What was that?" Oscar asked, surprised.

"I'm a sorceress, remember? I told it to *extinguish fireworks*." She smiled impishly, holding the secrets on the tip of her tongue. "To get this door open—the fire was the first key. The second key is the name of the house. She traced another symbol in the air and pronounced the words, "*Grianán ard.*"

The magical locks fell away, echoing like falling chains. The door unlocked before them. Glinda smiled at Oscar and pushed it open.

Far below them on the Munchkin Fields, both of the sandy armies were pummeled by the rain. The remnants of the flaming head of the Great and Terrible Oz head, streaked through the sky like falling stars and finally crashed into the base of the Tall House, exploding in a brilliant shower of flame. The fuel added to the violence of the explosion, splashing accelerant over all of the foundations. The foundation was weakened by the force of the explosion, and the flames licked their way inside the damaged wooden framework. But the flames down below were only part of the fire that plagued the Tall House.

Kalinya saw the magical fire flashing high above her at the entrance to her private sanctuary. *"Traitor!"* She hissed. Only one person knew the way to turn off the firelock, and that was Locasta. Now she had been betrayed by both Ondri-baba and Locasta.

Rather than allow her house and all of her beautiful wickedness to fall into the hands of intruders, Kalinya focused all of her throwing magic on the Tall House. She ripped the house off of its foundation and lifted it, holding it at cloud level. She screamed her laughter as the rain pounded uselessly all around her. Then she thrust the Tall House into the sky—further than she had thrown anything before.

The Tall House disappeared into the far sky, beyond anybody's sight.

The house jolted sharply as it ripped from its foundations and flew into the sky. In a moment it was far higher than any birds had ever flown. The platform lurched, throwing Glinda off balance. She staggered backwards out the open door and tumbled off the edge of the flying house. Oscar lunged after her, grabbing her hand, but he was also pulled off the edge of the tumbling Tall House. They plunged toward the open ground below.

With the Tall House gone, the limiting boundary for the clouds was eliminated. There was no tall building to frighten them back inland. One cloud first pushed through the imaginary boundary. When nothing happened, the cloud dumped its rain and hurried forward. All of the other clouds looked out to the broad expanse of distant desert with room to drift freely. They stampeded in one thundering body toward that open expanse of freedom.

The piling clouds stormed unknowingly beneath the tiny humans falling far above them. Oscar plunged into a thick tuft, sending up a splash of cloudstuff. Glinda hit a bouncier cloud. Oscar scrambled after her, but it was too late.

The Golden Cap ripped from Glinda's head in the howling wind when she fell, and the cap blew in a different direction than the flashing red hair.

King Klick saw Kalinya's vicious uprooting and forced upward disappearance of the Tall House. He watched the migratory movement of the clouds and heard the inevitable scream on the wind. He watched the sky and saw Glinda bounce off the cloud. He also saw the sparkle of the Golden Cap as it fell separately from the red-haired girl.

Glinda screamed as she hurtled toward the ground. She saw a flash of winged silver in the lightning—King Klick! But then the Winged Monkey was gone, passing her by in the blink of an eye.

The Lord of the Winged Monkeys, King Klick, soared through the wind and lightning with his eye focused on one thing only—the Golden Cap. He dove past Glinda, abandoning her to fate, just as that girl had abandoned his people.

Near the jagged and broken foundation of the Tall House, Kalinya looked up at the boiling clouds overhead. Lightning jabbed out and struck near her location. She jumped away in fright. The entire storm system had changed course and shifted in her direction. That was too much rain for her to risk wading through. She used the power of the Silver Slippers to retreat. The Tall House was gone, and with it the painful reminder of Kalinya's betrayal and defeat. She had thrown the traitor into the sky. Where that traitor girl Locasta fell, it mattered not. She would be dead. Nobody could survive a fall from that height.

Kalinya turned her back on the melting armies. The battle was over. Both sides had suffered great defeat. It only remained for the blood-sand giants to melt. The torrential rain had quickly overwhelmed the fields, and the blood and mud and water flowed down into the river, turning the idyllic stream into a churning current of death.

Great hills of red sand in the pounding rain shrank as the sky-spawned rivulets sliced deep lacerations in their sides. Nothing remained of Kalinya's army. She retreated to a hiding place—a wooded hilltop in the center of the Munchkin Fields, far away from the battle. It was quiet, and it was sheltered from the rain, giving her protection. From this vantage point Kalinya watched the inevitable destruction of all of her beautiful wickedness.

Glinda screamed in anger as the ground loomed larger and larger before her. She had been abandoned by King Klick. She didn't know where the Winged Monkey was going, nor why she had been forsaken. Considering their last conversations, Glinda recognized that she, from a certain monkey's point of view, maybe deserved her fate. Instead of doing what was right, she did what was convenient. Only now, in the leering face of her own demise, did she question her own motivations.

Oscar had been right. She had wanted to win this war. Her clear objective was to end this war, but it was not about liberty—that was Oscar's promise. Glinda was totally focused on ending tyranny. By letting the ends justify the means, she had become exactly what she despised—a tyrant.

She couldn't tell if the wetness on her face was from her own tears splashing upwards, or if it was the raindrops that she was catching in her fall. Then she heard hoofbeats in the air all around her.

Ondri-baba saw Kalinya disappear from the blazing ruins of the Tall House. Then she saw a flash of gold fall from the sky into the flames. She maneuvered her hut across the muddy battlefield and through the obstacles to get over there. Then she saw silver wings flashing in the lightning. The

Winged Monkey king was there, going to the ruins of the Tall House. He was actually approaching the flames. Ondri-baba waved her hands and cast a spell of invisibility over the flaming ruins.

King Klick saw the Golden Cap fall into the flaming ruins. But it fell in a spot that he could reach it—almost—without getting too close to the licking orange flames. Suddenly, everything disappeared!

He could still feel the heat and hear the crackling of the burning wood, but everything—the flames included—had turned invisible. He knew where the Golden Cap was, and he pushed deeper into the stifling waves of unseen heat to get at it.

Recovering the Golden Cap meant freedom for his people. Many years ago he had willingly exchanged freedom for shackles. The choice to survive, for his people to survive, was one that burned him now. It was his decision that doomed his people. Now was the opportunity to fix that wrong decision and make it right. Nothing could stop him. He felt the unseen flames licking at his hair all around.

He jumped up into the air and saw the Golden Cap—the invisibility did not extend to that magical item. The heat stifled his breath and parched his throat. All around he felt the waves of heat as they kissed his fur. Biting his blistered tongue in pain, King Klick stretched his arm through the heat and pushed closer until it was just beyond his blackening fingertips. The invisible flames ignited the fur on his arms, charring his flesh. He screamed and stomped his feet as he struggled further into the heat. His fingers brushed the cool cloth and touched the jeweled edge. The flames now kissed his face fully. His eyes watered and flooded, but the tears immediately evaporated. If he had to give his own life on this pyre, he would free his people!

Outside the ruins, Ondri-baba in her hut watched the silver-haired monkey king as he screamed over and over. He was engulfed in unseen flames, burning himself alive, but still, he was pushing deeper. Curiosity drove the stooped witch forward, wondering what it was that would drive a monkey to risk the flames. Drawing closer, Ondri-baba waved her hands again, banishing the invisibility. All the flames became visible.

King Klick screamed in mortal terror as the flames appeared, engulfing his body. The white hot heat grew a face and became visible fire. He was surrounded by the hungry flames, and his body burned! The unseen enemy that he willingly braved when it was invisible became now a horror he could not bear. The mindless terror shattered his hold on courage. The melting pain and animal panic drove him away. He leaped upward, a burning silver streak into the sky. He flapped his melting wings as fast as he could. Feathers fell as burning embers as he plunged toward the small river.

Ondri-baba pulled out an umbrella and opened it against the rain. She stepped down into the smoldering ruins. "What was it you wanted so badly?" She picked her way around the flames and saw the Golden Cap. "Ah. Now the golden object my sister sought so desperately falls into my hands. *Come here, my little pretty.*"

Ondri-baba carefully collected the Golden Cap. She felt the burn of the raindrops on her dusty arm as she reached out to gather in the golden treasure. Then she retreated to the safety of her hut.

Glinda galloped to safety on the back of King Zephyr at the head of his herd of Swift Horses. They rode on the wind, above the field of battle. Glinda gasped in horror as she saw King Klick, his body blazing with white and orange flame, launch out of the burning ruins and dive into the river.

"Save Oscar." Glinda cried. "He's up there. *Please, take me to the river!*"

The midnight-blue stallion whinnied, and three horses sped upward toward the fleeing clouds to rescue Oscar.

Glinda threw herself off the slowing stallion. She was airborne even before his hoofs touched the surface of the water, diving awkwardly into the river after King Klick. The charred silver monkey was below the surface, drifting helplessly downstream. Glinda tumbled through the churning water after him. King Klick thrashed weakly, but he could not break the surface—his waterlogged wings pulled him deeper. Glinda reached down, grabbed one of the wings and pulled. But her fist only pulled out a handful of burned feather quills. She kicked again, diving deeper. Her panicked lungs felt like they were going to burst. Stars appeared at the corners of her vision as she reached down one last time. She caught the monkey's hand. Tightening her grip, she pulled his arm and kicked toward the surface.

They broke the surface and both of them gasped for air. King Kick reached up and grabbed an overhanging branch, momentarily halting their drift downstream. Glinda turned her head to see the churning red froth all around them. The thunderous roar could only be a waterfall. This close to the desert, it was a safe bet that the waterfall ended in the deadly desert—certain death for both of them.

King Klick's weakening grip on the branch was all that kept them above the surface. If he let go, Glinda would probably survive the river, but the monkey would not—not with his injuries. Neither of them would survive the falls.

All around them the water flowed sticky red with blood-sand runoff. Glinda clung to King Klick. His bloodshot eyes closed in pain and exhaustion. One finger slipped off the branch.

"Don't go to sleep!" Glinda screamed.

"I failed." King Klick whispered.

"It doesn't matter. *Stay awake!*"

Whinnies and hoofbeats sounded nearby against the pounding water.

"Stay awake!" She shook at him, but the cold water was relentless, pounding on his injuries. The monkey's grip on the branch slipped.

Glinda and King Klick plunged under the water again, pulled in the wounded current toward their doom. Then they abruptly stopped. The bloody water flowed over them, but instead of tumbling downstream with the current, they stayed where they were, and, amazingly, they moved against the current. Glinda choked as she tried to breathe, but the spray filled her lungs. A powerful force pulled them in toward the shore. When Glinda was able to keep her head above water, she saw Oscar waist-deep in the churning mix, pulling a fishing net and dragging them in. Behind him, Zephyr was pulling the net's rope, adding his great strength to their rescue.

They pulled the silver-haired monkey out onto the riverbank, away from the water. In the distance, the flames licked at the sky where the Tall House had stood. The storm moved away toward the eastern horizon.

The Winged Monkeys circled over their location. As soon as they saw their king, they quickly gathered, sending the cry out to all their people. They swooped down and encircled him.

Glinda's eyes burned with tears as turned her attention to the wounded monkey. From the muddy red water staining his body, she could not see clearly what blood was his, and what came from the river. His arms were smoking and charred from the deep burns. His great wings were tattered and many of the feathers melted. He was mortally wounded and in extreme pain. He forced opened his blackened eyes and studied the girl's tears.

"Why?" he asked, "Why do you weep?"

"I am so sorry." Glinda cried. Tears flowed down her cheeks. The teardrops were instantly lost amid the heavy raindrops that pelted down on the group. She could not catch her breath for all of the sobs racking her chest. "I am so sorry."

Oscar noticed that Glinda was not wearing the Golden Cap. He reached out to touch her hair. As his hand touched the top of her head, she felt the difference and she felt that her head was bare.

"The Golden Cap is lost. The invisible Witch has it." King Klick wheezed.

"Ondri-baba." said Oscar.

"Oh nooo!" Glinda wailed in despair. She ripped hair from her head and beat on her breast as she screamed in the deepest agony of her soul. She would not be consoled. This was her doing. She even pushed Oscar away when he tried to gather her to him.

King Klick looked up from the ground at the midnight-blue stallion. The encircled monkeys parted and allowed Zephyr to approach. King Klick gasped in pain as his seared lungs choked out the words. "Our time is very short. Take them from my sight." He closed his eyes then forced them open again. "Far away. Do not tell me where they are."

King Klick gestured to Glinda, and Oscar directed the distraught young sorceress back to the side of the Winged King. She knelt in the mud and forced her fists to unclench. She saw in her hands the strands of red hair that she had ripped from her head. But she did not yet feel that pain. The only hurt was inside her heart.

King Klick reached up with his unwithered hand and touched Glinda's red hair. "You are fierce like your mother." He lowered his hand into hers. He could still move the fingers on this hand. The other hand was burned and curled in on itself. Glinda bowed herself down and wept on the monkey's hand. "I will protect you where I can, Princess, but I am a *slave*, bound by oath and magic to obey the possessor of the Golden Cap."

He closed his eyes and breathed deeply, gathering strength for his final pronouncement, "Glinda, daughter of my friend and my enemy, for your failure you have my *everlasting hatred.* You also have my *trust* that you will honor your oath."

Glinda nodded mutely. Words were insufficient to describe neither the agony she felt nor the desperation that drove her to seek forgiveness and reconciliation. King Klick pulled his hand back and rolled over onto his side, turning away from Glinda. Oscar pulled Glinda to her feet and lifted her onto the back of the midnight blue stallion.

The Winged Monkeys turned their backs on Glinda and kicked mud backwards at her, a grievous insult. The younger ones scooped up handfuls of mud to throw.

With stooped shoulders and heaving sobs, Glinda buried her face in the stallion's mane. Oscar mounted another horse and they galloped into the wind.

What Glinda did not hear was the great anguished cry from the monkey king. If Glinda could not be consoled, King Klick was doubly so. It was he who led his people into slavery. It was he who could not free them because of his own weakness. The Winged Monkeys gathered around their fallen leader and sheltered him from the last remnants of the storm with their wings.

There was nothing more to be said. The Swift Horses lifted Glinda and Oscar and carried them away, back toward the central lands of Oz.

37 THE CONQUERING OF THE WINKIES

Ondri-baba waited out the storm inside her hut. She clutched the Golden Cap tightly, caressing it and holding it to her cheek as one would a beloved pet. It was now her precious treasure, hers and hers alone. No one else had this power, whatever the power might be.

With the dawn came the sun again. All of the clouds had disappeared out over the desert. Slowly the Munchkins emerged from their homes to see the damage in the morning light. But none of them dared cross the bridge into the bloody fields. And when they saw the distant hut on the far sides of the fields, they quickly disappeared from view. They did not know where their queen protector, Kalinya, had hidden herself, but they knew that their enemy, the other Witch Queen was not yet gone. So long as she stayed, the Munchkins were in danger. The less they aroused attention, the greater would be their degree of safety.

Ondri-baba studied the Golden Cap. It was jeweled and of unique workmanship. The entire surface glistened like a pearl. Her opinion of its looks had changed now that she had it in her possession. While it would never be pleasing to her eyes as a fashion accessory, it was a symbol now of her power over her sister. She was the one true Witch Queen in Oz. Inside the Golden Cap, long embroidery threads hung out of the inner band. These threads bore witness that some information had been removed recently. The needle holes were not enough of a clue to determine what those instructions were, or what shapes may have been embroidered. Not even Ondri-baba's magic eye offered any conclusions to the mysterious missing magic line of the Golden Cap.

Still, the summoning spell was mostly complete, and it was easy to read. Ondri-baba stepped outside her hut and followed the instructions. She placed the Golden Cap on her head.

Standing on her left foot, she said slowly, "Ep-pe, pep-pe, kak-ke!"

Then she stood on her right foot and said, "Hil-lo, hol-lo, hel-lo!"

Then she stood on both feet and cried in a loud voice, "Ziz-zy, zuz-zy, zik!"

And she went back inside her hut waited for the charm to work.

Ondri-baba did not have to wait very long. The morning sky darkened, and the echoes of many wings flapping drowned out all other sounds. She arose from her seat and walked outside the hut. On the field in front of her were the Winged Monkeys, led at the front by King Klick, burned and brutally disfigured from the flames the previous night.

King Klick's eyes burned with many things, but anger and hatred was the simplest to recognize. "This is the first of three times that you may call us. What is your command?"

Ondri-baba wickedly smiled. The magic of the last week had changed her. While her magic eye glowed with its own power, her other—her natural—eye had turned a deathly black. Her skin had taken a sickly shade of green. With no blood left in her body, she was, like her sister, a husk full of magic and hate. While she smiled, her thin skin pulled tightly around her mouth, giving her face the appearance of a leering skull. "The battle here is finished. I return to the land of the West. Conquer the Winkies and bring them into submission to await the return of their Witch Queen!"

"It shall be as you command." King Klick painfully launched into the air and led his people west. They obeyed, as they were bound by flesh and by magic to do, their first enslaved command—the gruesome betrayal and subjugation of their former friends.

The sentries on the Winkie towers saw the approaching Winged Monkeys and raised a happy cry. *Their allies were returning in victory.*

The Winged Monkeys pulled out their metal nets, forged by the Winkies, and turned the tools of enslavement on their creators. The happy shouts from the Winkies quickly turned to screams of terror as the Winged Monkeys fulfilled their grim duty.

Eight days later, Ondri-baba stepped from her hut into the shadow of the Yellow Castle. Gathered together to meet the Witch were King Klick and all his people. King Winko and his advisors stood in shackles before them, a token presented to Ondri-baba as proof that the subjugation of an entire people was complete. King Winko fell to his knees before the Witch and begged for release for his people.

"Will you accept me as undisputed ruler and Queen of the lands of the West?" Ondri-baba asked.

"Yes, yes, assuredly, yes. Please free us from this captivity—from these traitorous Winged Monkeys. We had a signed alliance with them, but they..."

At this, the disfigured King Klick roared in anger, sending King Winko scrambling backwards in fear.

"The Winkies are now under my protection. You are dismissed." Ondri-baba released the Winged Monkeys, and they flapped away.

King Winko dropped his head in shame. The Winkies were now beholden to a new Queen, and he had gladly sold them into slavery, eagerly exchanging one conqueror for another.

Later that day, Ondri-baba and King Winko walked through the Winkie throne room. She noticed all of the history coded into the architecture. "We'll have to do something about all of this history you have." She waved her hands and the carvings became invisible. However, they were carved into the walls, and so the invisibility only made them indistinct and blurry. They faded from vision. No one would know what was up there. In due time, the history of the Winkies would be forgotten, and the coded images would be cobwebs.

Ondri-baba pointed up to the walls, where the carvings were now indistinguishable from the lengthening shadows. "Tell me, fat, conquered, King Winko, what do you see up there?"

"I see nothing."

"Exactly right. Nothing. And neither will anybody else that comes in here. Your history dies with you. I will be the only history that matters to the Winkies. I am your queen. I delivered your people from slavery, and you love me as your deliverer. Tell it to your people. Tell it until they cannot remember anything else."

On the Emerald Plains, the excavation was well underway for the new city. The Winkie Architects and builders had come immediately upon receiving the call from Omby-Amby. They had left with the good grace of King Winko. Because of their timely departure, and the large numbers of strong workers that left, they were out of the land completely when the Winged Monkeys came. The smaller numbers of Winkies in the land had made for easy conquering.

As the builders dug, they discovered the ruins of a labyrinthine city beneath the ground. This would provide a strong foundation for their new city. While the buildings were in ruins, the solid foundations and the network of subterranean tunnels were still intact. Among the antiquities they unearthed were large pillars of solid emerald. These were taller, wider, and more ornately carved and emblazoned than the crude emerald fence around the distant valley. The architects raised these pillars as the beginnings of the outer walls of the Emerald City.

When Oscar Diggs returned to the construction site, he saw the great jeweled pillars. He said proudly to Omby-Amby, "The Emerald City. This will stand for centuries. People will know of this city the world over, and they will tell it to their children."

"They will know of the Wizard of Oz that rules wisely and fairly." Omby-Amby responded.

"The people will rule themselves."

Omby-Amby told Oscar of their excavation and discovery beneath the ground. "The builders found the ruins of another great city underneath." Omby-Amby said.

Oscar grinned. "Better and better. Up for a little exploring, my friend? Who knows what adventures we might find?"

Omby-Amby held out a top hat to Oscar. "With the compliments of King Winko."

"My hat." Oscar exclaimed. "I thought I lost it when I got here. Then we got busy. Wow. Thanks."

"King Winko also sent a book containing the history of the Winkie people. He intended for it to be the first addition to your royal library. You came to the Winkies first, so the Winkies will be first in your mind."

"It will have a prominent place in the library. I will personally read it starting tonight. History is meant to be shared. If we don't understand how history always circles around, we are destined to keep going around in circles. I plan on learning from history. I'm not going to live long enough to make all the mistakes myself."

In the camp, Glinda prepared to head south with her fighting girls. The Emerald City would be wonderful, but her place was in the South. The South Castle held the Ruby Throne. There were many mysteries in the former residence of Smith & Tinker that she had to unravel. Glinda was, after all, the Sorceress, and she had a duty to *learn.* She vowed to be ready when the Wicked Witches again set their hearts on power. And assuredly they would. Wickedness always craved power. So long as they did not rule the entire land, it would be a tempting, scintillating jewel, whether emerald or ruby, that would draw them forth from their lands to conquer. And Glinda would always be there to stop them. Wickrie-Kells had pledged to help Glinda evermore.

Nearby, in the deep grasslands, Wickrie-Kells walked close to Omby-Amby. The pillars of the Emerald City rose up far behind them. Wickrie-

Kells—the girl who made her hair red, the girl who had led an army—now wanted privacy to say her farewells.

"Glinda asked me to go with her to the South Castle."

"Oscar asked me to stay here with him. I wish there were a way that all four of us could stay together always."

"No you don't. That's silly. You'd get tired of me pretty quick. I'm always getting into trouble."

Omby-Amby reached out to touch Wickrie-Kells' hair. The dye was coming out, leaving streaks of red in her dark hair. "No. You're always *following* trouble. *Glinda* is the one that gets into trouble." Omby-Amby took the girl's hand and squeezed it possessively. "I don't want you to go."

"Then come with me." Wickrie-Kells pulled the young man's hand closer to her.

Now it was Omby's turn to pull away. "I can't. Oscar is building a city here. It's our city. It's what we talked about. It's what I have thought about my whole life. It will be a place where a man can be who he was born to be."

Wickrie-Kells smiled sadly. "And what of the women? What if they haven't lived up to those high standards? See, Omby, I helped the Wicked Witch—I helped Kalinya conquer the Munchkins. That's not going to be an easy forget."

"I don't think forgetting is the goal." Omby-Amby said. "Forgiving is. It's a learning process. Trust people in what they say, but verify for yourself. You got burned. Now you'll think twice before reaching into the flame." When the girl frowned, Omby clarified, "I'm not saying that reaching into the flame is the wrong thing to do, but you need to know exactly what you're doing when you do it."

"Would you ever reach into the flame? Or are you too noble to do that?"

Omby-Amby was silent for several moments. His eyes brightly shone his answer. "The Emerald City is a place where virtue and freedom go hand in hand. The people watch their leaders to make sure that freedom continues. I believe, so I will keep watch."

"Will I see you again?"

"Aye. Of course. I'll be here. I'll always be here. But maybe next time I'll have some whiskers on my chin."

"You'll be my soldier with green whiskers." She smiled as her eyes glistened with proud tears for her friend. "Good-bye, Omby." Wickrie-Kells kissed him on the cheek and walked away.

"Good-bye, Wickrie." Omby-Amby whispered, squared his broad shoulders, and turned back toward the Emerald City.

Two weeks passed before King Pastoria sent a delegation out to meet with Oscar and negotiate a truce. All of Central City had heard the amazing doings of Oz, the Great and Terrible, the man who could dream entire cities into existence. Pastoria may have been a pompous peacock of a man, but he certainly did not want to become an enemy to the Wizard. At least he did not wish to become an enemy in the same way that the Witches were enemies. He wanted to keep the Wizard close, to make him think that he was in control. The Wizard was not—could not—be all that he said he was. Everyone keeps their lies very closely guarded. Pastoria knew with his peacocks when one was faltering. Even if their plumage was brilliant, there was something in the presentation that betrayed the inner frailty. He saw something of that sort in the Wizard. So he planned the treaty in such a way that it would be rewritten. By allowing the Wizard to modify the treaty, he would be honor-bound to uphold his own writings.

Pastoria had learned well from the peacocks—it was not about what was said, but how you postured. He engineered the treaty presentation to open a doorway into the inner circle of emerald power. The winds were changing in Oz, and Pastoria intended to be on the right side of history.

Oscar spent an additional two weeks working out the details of the treaty. The Emerald City would be a sovereign city-state, and it would not answer to anyone. It would maintain its own army and conduct its affairs as it saw fit. It would require no taxes of any in the land except those doing business in the city. All were welcome to live and work there. The Emerald City was an experiment to see if man could rule himself. Pastoria scoffed at that, but he watched as homes in his own ancient city emptied and moved out onto the Emerald Plains.

In the eastern lands, in the Munchkin Village, Kalinya returned to receive her adulation as their queen. The sky was mostly clear, but even the sight of a cloud worried Kalinya. She wore the same oilskin coat and hat to protect her from any rogue cloudbursts. It had been several days since the great battle, and stories arose.

The parents of the child, Boq, had spread the tale of how Kalinya saved their home from the raging monster by flinging it into the sky. From that tale, other tales grew about how Kalinya had gone house to house, protecting each one. Each Munchkin household added their story to the now-epic saga of Queen Kalinya, Protector of Munchkin Fields. The stories got bigger with each telling. Songs were sung of her bravery and her selflessness in single-handedly fighting the blood-sand beasts.

She accepted these adulations at the feast given in her honor. She picked at the food placed in front of her. Though she felt it in her mouth, the food no longer gave her any pleasure, or even any taste. It was like sand on her tongue.

The great feast lasted several hours. Munchkin children sang, poets recited feats of bravery, and each family cooked their specialty for their queen. At length Kalinya tired of the songs and the praise. She called for silence, and the assembly grew quiet. "You have done well as my subjects. The threat is gone. The rebuilding of our land must proceed. The other lands shall know that the Munchkins cannot be conquered. We will rebuild from the ashes. Now," she said, "About my new home."

King Widdershins protested, "But you had a home—you had the Tall House."

"It was destroyed in the battle. I require a new home."

"We do not have the resources to build you a new house in the sky."

"Then build one on the *ground!*"

Grateful that they didn't have to create another eminent monument like the Tall House, the Munchkins began construction on Kalinya's new home. She chose a secluded spot on a hilltop in the middle of a field—the place where she had hidden for the remainder of that stormy night and the following days, nursing her wounds.

The walls were built quickly. It was a domed building, built after the pattern of the Munchkin Village. But there were strange changes that the Queen required. She demanded rooms added in peculiar shapes. The Queen had become a recluse after the banquet. She sat and watched every move that the builders made. While publicly songs were sung, in private the lyrics took on a different flavor.

Whispers went around the village about Kalinya. Some didn't even call her "Queen" anymore. From the village they spread to the land, among the more bold of the Munchkins. These were shocking to the average Munchkin, who refused to listen to such irreverent blather. But the whispers didn't go away. Even if no one claimed the whispers, the voices continued. They whispered about how Kalinya had thrown her own house into the sky. What goes up must surely come down. And wouldn't it be funny if the house fell down one day and *squashed her flat?*

38 THE RISE OF GLINDA THE GOOD

Down in the land of the South, the long-awaited day at last had come—it was Glinda's sixteenth birthday. The last several weeks had gone by quickly. The South Castle had been decorated by all of Glinda's girls for the big celebration. There were still areas under construction—the waterwheel was being rebuilt, along with the complex system of gears that powered the eastern wing of the castle—but by and large the entire estate was amazingly transformed from the recent devastation at the hands of Ondri-baba's hordes.

The land had its ups and downs in the recent past. Just a few weeks earlier the South Castle had been abandoned by Smith & Tinker and put to sleep. Then it was nearly destroyed by Ondri-baba's blood-sand warriors. Now it was a thriving center of information, learning and commerce. The Quadlings were productive farmers. Their crops of fruit, rice and wheat were in season, and it looked to be a bountiful harvest. The South Castle was also a place of remembrance. Nearby, the broken fragments of the twisted lighthouse still lay silently below in the deadly sand as a reminder of the scars of war.

Great decorative walls rose around the palace and parts of the castle grounds. The scrap piles of Smith & Tinker were walled off. In those walled areas there were fantastical experiments that could be used to make war. Glinda wanted no more war. Specifically, she did not wish to give up any strategic advantage to her enemies. So she walled off the genius-inspired scraps to dissuade any would-be warmongers from seeking out machines to make war.

There was a special memorial made among the scrap piles for the brave Wheelers that had battled alongside the fighting girls. The memorial was crafted from brick and inscribed with the names of the one Wheeler that was known—IgNob—and carved with the symbols of the other Wheelers. This was done at the insistence of Wickrie-Kells. She was adamant that they receive a memorial. The Emerald City was creating a memorial for fallen soldiers. How could another battle in this Witch War be any less important? She insisted that the Wheelers were just as surely soldiers as those who had fallen on the Emerald Prairie.

The South Castle had been renovated completely. Glinda had made the estate her own. With Smith & Tinker gone, the South Castle was in need of a caretaker. The young sorceress was more than willing to be the steward. There was a mystery with the Ruby Palace—in the words of Mr. Smith—*not currently accessible*, which puzzled Glinda. The Ruby Palace had been her mother's—it was in every way a symbol of Gayelette—timeless, ageless and beautiful, and in every way untouchable. That was not Glinda; she had made her new home in the south. She planted gardens of red blooms, turning the land around from white to red. Sonadia's color had been white—the traditional color of a sorceress. But Glinda was not the traditional sorceress. She had a very powerful pedigree running through her veins. Some of her transitional changes were because she wanted to maintain a connection to the place of her birth. The rest of it was simply a desire to be something else entirely.

Inside the South Castle, she had moved the Ruby Throne into the central chamber, which became her throne room. Builders from the Emerald Lands shuttled between Glinda's castle and Oscar's construction project. This ensured that the best builders in all the land were busy developing lasting monuments to freedom. They were sculpting lasting messages of liberty, hard-coded into the architecture—messages for future generations to look upon and remember what price was paid for freedom.

The time for the celebration came. Trumpets sounded outside, signaling the approach of guests. Sitting straight on her Ruby Throne, Glinda felt the great power built into it. She felt a strong connection to the land, and it energized her. She felt all at once what was happening in other places. The land was waiting. Some parts were sad. Some parts were at rest. The magic was flowing. She felt who her next announced guest would be. The power of that dreamer could not be hidden. Glinda waited with great anticipation for the official announcement. She quickly made sure that her long hair was perfect on her shoulders. She wore her red hair straight, pinned to one side with a jeweled comb. As befitted her rank of Sorceress, Glinda was draped in a lovely white gown.

Her herald, a Winkie girl named Ola Griffin, smiled as she cried out, "*The Wizard of Oz!*"

Oscar entered to thunderous applause. The entire room turned at his entrance. Oscar had expected a party of a few people, not the entire land. Oscar had left the multitude back at the Emerald City, but somehow Glinda had managed to get everyone here before him. Omby-Amby smiled from the side as Oscar noticed him standing next to Wickrie-Kells. This was Glinda's birthday, but they were certainly enjoying the time to mingle.

Oscar approached the throne. He dropped to one knee as he had seen once in a stage play. The visitor was always supposed to bow to the queen. He dropped his head and noticed that the tiles beneath his knees were inlaid with gems. They were specifically emerald vines that twined around the entire map of Oz—just like Glinda had wanted. Now she had her map.

Glinda rose from her throne and stepped down onto the map floor. Oscar kept his head down. A smile tugged at the corners of his mouth as Glinda stopped right in front of him. She touched his shoulder. Unfamiliar with Ozzian customs, Oscar stayed exactly where he was. He noticed Glinda's foot tapping on the floor right in front of him. He didn't want to make a scene, and neither did Glinda.

"You may arise, great Wizard."

Oscar tried unsuccessfully to keep the smile from his face. "If her sorceriousness please, I should like to remain below and dream a moment more."

Oscar waited the requisite moment more then arose. Glinda hardened her eyes at him, and he forced a smile at her unspoken frown.

"I'm not a dream." She said.

"No. You're not a dream. And this is really happening. We're standing here in front of all of these people."

"All of our friends." Glinda corrected.

"I must be dreaming."

"How could a dream be as wonderful as this?" Glinda pulled Oscar close and hugged him. "I'm so glad you came."

Oscar held her for several moments. He buried his face in her hair. He started to say something quietly to her, then her red hair got into his mouth and he sputtered. Glinda broke the embrace and pushed him back to arm's length. "What was that?"

"Sorry. Your hair...looks very, very wonderful. And this floor—" Oscar quickly shifted subjects. "Wow." He motioned to the inlaid tiles in the floor. "You made the map."

"Yes I did. My father had one. Now I have one. But the Ruby Throne isn't up north anymore. It's down south," Glinda stepped close to Oscar again, "here, where we are. See how the vines go around all the central lands? Those are emeralds. I hear you've done a lot of wonderful work up there with the Emerald City you're building."

"The floor looks really, really...*beautiful.* It really does. It's *perfect.*"

Glinda blushed and looked down at the floor, ostensibly admiring the work, but everyone watching them knew that these two were destined for each other. They watched Glinda as she watched the Wizard.

Oscar gestured to the yellow lands in the west on the map. "You've heard about the Winkies?" Oscar asked. "They were conquered by the Winged Monkeys. Ondri-baba *freed* the Winkies, in a manner of speaking. They became her slaves just to be rid of the Winged Monkeys."

Glinda's eyes took on a stormy color. She knew that she was the one responsible for that betrayal. "I heard." She said quietly.

"Something for you to consider: Is a benevolent slave owner better than a wicked one? Yes. But unless a soul is free to live for themselves, the chains of slavery will always be a burden." But that was not all. The Wizard had one last thing to say on the matter. He kept his voice low so that his words were heard by Glinda alone, "You swore an oath to free the Winged Monkeys. I will help you."

Then the moment passed. Oscar changed the subject. "I come bearing birthday wishes. Happy birthday to you, Sorceress. You are looking lovely."

Glinda smiled at both Oscar's promise and his well-wishes. The angry clouds left her eyes. Then she took Oscar's hand and walked him up next to her throne. *One day*, she thought, *he will also sit in this throne.* Turning to her assembled guests, she said, "Behold and listen. Here is Oz, the Great and Powerful. He is a wizard, indeed, and the protector of the Emerald City."

Suddenly the east-facing doors exploded inward, knocking one of Glinda's guards backwards onto the floor.

The Wicked Witch, Kalinya, appeared in the center of the throne room, standing above the embossed emerald vines on the floor. In the midday light, an hourglass sparkled at her waist, hanging from her belt. "*YOU!*" Kalinya sneered, "You think you're so great and imperious! You think that you can be one of us witches! Well, you can't!"

Oscar stepped in front of Glinda to protect her. Glinda put her hand on his shoulder and stepped around him. "Thank you." she whispered to him. "But this battle is mine alone."

"Kalinya, you were not invited into my land, or into my home. Trespassing. Also, you were not invited to my birthday party. That's right, *birthday*. Did you forget? I was supposed to join you before my sixteenth birthday. Here it is, and here I stand opposing you. Are you going to destroy me? That is what you promised."

Kalinya's eye twitched nervously. She looked around uneasily at the assembled crowd. There were more people than she thought there would be. None of them were Munchkins that she could see. This was not the way she had envisioned this final encounter. Still, she would humiliate Glinda in front of all of her people. "*Yes. Of course.* That's why I'm here. I came make good on my threat, and spoil your party." She pointed a knobby finger at Glinda. "You have one last chance to join me, or be destroyed. I'll....I'll throw you into the sky."

"You threw me into the sky once." Glinda said. At Kalinya's shocked expression, she explained, "I was on top of the Tall House. You threw it into the sky. Yet here I am. Your threats—just like your beady yellow eyes—are hollow."

Laughter. At her. Kalinya's sunken yellow eyes burned. She was the most powerful witch in the land, yet they mocked her. She was physically a shell of the witch she had been just weeks earlier, but the power was closer to the surface. All she was now was power—hate and power. The cost for her power was paid in beauty and physical strength—paid in blood. She was now a creature of magic and wickedness. Her hatred toward Glinda kept her doggedly pursuing her vendetta.

She stammered and pointed to Glinda's head and her red hair. "You broke your word. Give me the Golden Cap. You were defeated."

"You were defeated also. Give *me* the Silver Slippers." Glinda replied calmly.

Now Kalinya was rankled and vexed. "What have you done with the Golden Cap?"

"The Golden Cap is lost to me. It is now in the possession of your sister. She has proclaimed herself ruler of the West. The Winkies are her slaves, as she foretold. You have the East—no more and no less than that which you started with. I give you now one last opportunity to leave. Know this, Kalinya, Wicked Witch of the East; I will oppose you in every step you take."

Kalinya's hands twitched as she prepared to throw Glinda with her magic, but Glinda was a step ahead of her. Glinda had noticed *the last hourglass,* filled with magic sand, in Kalinya's belt.

Glinda gestured with her fingers and whispered through the incantation—one of the three that she knew—and the hourglass turned over, tumbling out of Kalinya's belt and onto the floor. The glass shattered, spilling magic sand all over the emerald vines in the map. Immediately the sand took the shape of the vines and twined upward around Kalinya, starting at her ankles and completely enveloping her. In a moment the wicked witch was bound by sandy vines and lifted off the ground. For the second time in her life, Kalinya was imprisoned by vines and held helpless before her enemy.

"You have no power here, Kalinya. You are old and withered. Your wickedness has destroyed your health, your power, and whatever beauty you may have had—if any." She raised her voice to all in the court, "Let it be known that the Wicked Witch of the East, Kalinya, was defeated by *Glinda the Good* on this day!"

Far away, at the western edge of Winkie Country a worthless creature pondered his demise.

Bruised and broken, the once-Winged Monkey, Brutus, limped toward the end of the land. At the hanging edge of the land, where the magic of Oz ended, and the strange sands of the desert began, Brutus stared out and pondered his fate. Ragged scraps of wings were all that he held of his once proud strength. He was outcast, exiled and shamed. There was no going back. All that remained was to end his miserable existence.

At the edge of the Deadly Desert, Brutus spread the stumps of his wings for one last flight. His muscles tensed and then he sprang out over the toxic sands. For an infinite moment he hung suspended, and everything he had ever done passed before him. He had been *counsel, confidante, strong right arm* and *traitor*. Each of those roles he had treasured in their time, even the last. He would have ruled the tribe with power and strength. He would have guided the tribe to a new era of glory, governing without the interference or oversight of Man.

Behind him, a sudden whirring sounded, and then his forward momentum was halted, and then Brutus was jerked violently backwards and upwards. Before he lost consciousness, Brutus heard voices above him from some sort of machine. "Oh, *aye*, he'll make a right fine project. D'ye think her majesty will approve?"

And so Brutus faded into darkness, wishing for two things. The first, *he wished that he could have wings again.* And the second, *he wished that he could return to the tribe to claim his right as ruler.*

Back in the South Castle, Glinda instructed her guards to follow her with Kalinya. "To the fountain." Glinda ordered.

The fighting girls closed in and hoisted the vine-bound witch. They followed after Glinda through the courtyard with their screaming and struggling prisoner. Glinda led them to the new walls surrounding the piles of scrap. Two fighting girls ran ahead and opened the large gates. Glinda led the procession into the Boneyard of the Clouds.

Kalinya panicked when she saw the pool of water. She struggled and writhed, but the vines held her fast. Then recognition flashed in her eyes as she saw Glinda on the pedestal. She had been here before! This was where that insolent prig tricked her.

Glinda knelt and scooped up a handful of water from the spring. She cupped it in her hands and blew the words over the water. The mist rose from her hands and fleshed out a nearly invisible cloud skeleton, giving life and breadth to the cloud. The mist grew and grew, taking on greater and greater size. It thundered happily as it again stretched its billows in life.

Glinda stepped in and caressed part of the cloud as she would a lamb and whispered to it. "Go north and east as fast as you can, toward the setting sun.

If the Wicked Witch *falls*, that is her doing. You have been given a new life. Go, and enjoy. *Be free.*"

Then Glinda turned to Kalinya and pronounced her judgment upon the Wicked Witch. "Your Tall House is gone. The clouds no longer have a shepherd, or a fence—they stray into the desert. If you can get off before the cloud dries out over the desert, you may live." Glinda motioned to her guards, and the fighting girls tossed the tied-up Kalinya onto the cloud. "Were your Tall House still built and in its place, you would have a far better chance of surviving. Know this—what goes up *will* come down."

"You won't even kill me? You are a shame to the memory of your mother! She would have destroyed me in a heartbeat! You sniveling little brat. You coward!" She laughed mockingly, but her yellow eyes shifted back between the cloud and the fountain. Certain death versus probable death. If she could roll into the fountain, it would all be over. She would have the last laugh and be the master of her own fate.

But then the moment of decision was past and gone. The cloud lifted off the ground. Kalinya's laugh died in her throat. Her voice rose higher and trembled in fear. "You don't frighten me. You don't have the nerve...Glinda! *Glinda, don't do this!*"

"Your fate is now your own, Witch. I give you your life back. If you come back again, I make no such promise."

The cloud rose higher and higher. Kalinya's screams grew more distant. Glinda watched the sparkle of the Silver Slippers until she could no longer see them.

As the day drew to its natural end, Glinda retired to her private bedroom. The moon was rising. Glinda stood in the window for a moment, but the night sky was still too large for her. She closed the shutters and went to her mirror.

She brushed through her straightened red hair as she sat down in front of her mirror. When the pang of loneliness pricked her heart, she opened the drawer and pulled out the shard of the magic mirror. She stood the shard on the vanity in just to the side of her mirror. Moving in the magic mirror shard was the red-haired sorceress—her mother—Gayelette. As Glinda looked at her own reflection in the larger mirror, she could pretend that her mother was standing right behind her. She straightened her shoulder and smiled at her reflection. It was different this time—Glinda's hair was straight, and she did not refuse to wear the white gown.

It seemed a lifetime ago, before all of the adventures had begun, when Glinda's mother, Gayelette, was beside her in the mirror, telling her exactly how to do her hair and what to wear. For a moment, it appeared to be that way again, with the shard showing Gayelette and the reflection of Glinda next to it.

But this time, when Glinda turned around to look at her mother, she was alone.

Glinda smiled solemnly. There was a part of her that missed the innocence of how things used to be—how things were when all she had were books and dreams. *Dreams*. She could say that word without distaste now—now that she had met Oscar and learned the power of dreams. The occasional visions in the night did not frighten her. She realized that dreams made change. Those dreams were now *one* part of her.

The other part of her treasured the knowledge, the freedom, and the experiences that she had gained with her friends. She had acted, and she had been acted upon. She liked the former better, even though her mistakes brought her heart bitterness. She resolved in that moment, that where she was given power to act, she *would* act, and let the consequences come as they may. She would not let others control her future. She was the queen of her own soul.

Then she turned back to the mirror. If only her mother could see her now, what would she think? Would she be proud of her obedient little girl? Would she see how she had grown?

Glinda smiled sweetly and defiantly into the mirror—smiling as only a teenage daughter can—and she twisted a curl into her red hair.

END OF THE WITCH QUEENS

APPENDIX

THE PLAYERS

A listing of the characters included in The Witch Queens of Oz

Note: Most characters are known by their first names only in this story. Full names are given for reference purposes.

Glinda Mahalia Kookaburr—Daughter of Gayelette and Quelala. Budding sorceress and adventure-seeking princess

Oscar Zoroaster Diggs—Ventriloquist from Nebraska Territory. Called the Wizard.

Gayelette Kronkob—Sorceress of the North. Powers: Time magic, dream research

Quelala Kookaburr—Regent of the Ruby Palace in the North. Father of Glinda

Kalinya Thistleswitch—Witch of the East. Powers: throwing magic

Ondri-baba Thistleswitch—Witch of the West. Powers: cast invisibility

Locasta Donovia Brenfire—Apprentice to Kalinya. Powers: Oracular hat

Mombi—Witch of many faces. Powers: transformation magic, disguise. Mombi is known to people of power by this name. Her birth name is Ozmombina Decheryon Lodoveen Carcose.

Wickrie-Kells Dunkle—Friend of Glinda; leader of Glinda's fighting girls

"Omby-Amby" Ombrosius Ambrosius Cake—Winkie soldier with green hair

King Klick—King of the Winged Monkeys; has silver fur

Brutus—A Winged Monkey, rival to King Klick

King Pastoria Mackoo Luneska Tonnason—King of the Emerald Lands

King Winko Dullimite Cake—King of the Winkies

King Lukasio Markell Widdershins—King of the Munchkins

Bombo MacElle—Elder of the Gillikin North Village

Beriyel—A female Winged Monkey

Tabulo Liyonechka—A Munchkin Warrior

"Boq" Lilboq Malarl Liyonechka—a Munchkin child, brother of Tabulo

Ola Serapenth Griffin—Glinda's herald at the South Castle

IgNob—a Wheeler

Mr. Smith—painter and inventor; real name Warcan Mosko Smith

Mr. Tinker—inventor; real name Alamus Tinker

Flying Fish, Beeberblubb

Zephyr—King of the Swift Horses, a midnight-blue stallion

King Oz, the Seventeenth—King of the Emerald Lands; His birth name is Aurelian Gyre Cornn-Luneska

Tjorn Kells Dunkle—Father of Wickrie-Kells

Persons mentioned by name in the story:

Sonadia Discontentia—Witch of the South. Powers: weather magic
Queen of Dreams, real name Ereline
Red Sorcerer, born as Garren Kronkob
Queen Ozma, the Third, born as Tyne Glendina Cornn
King Lanternhans, of the Winkies, born as Lanternhans Poe Cake

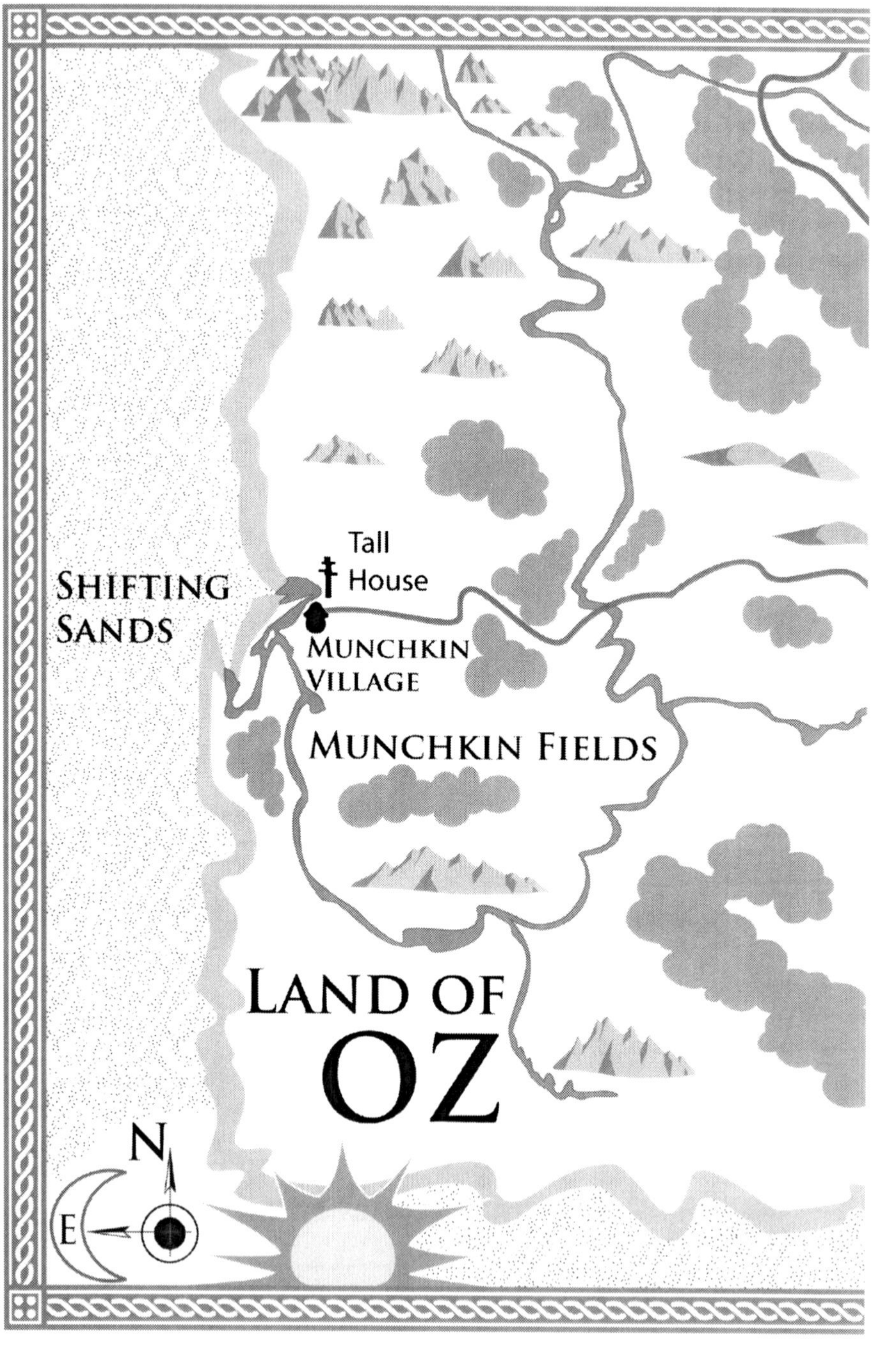
Tall
House
SHIFTING
SANDS
MUNCHKIN
VILLAGE
MUNCHKIN FIELDS
LAND OF
OZ
N
E

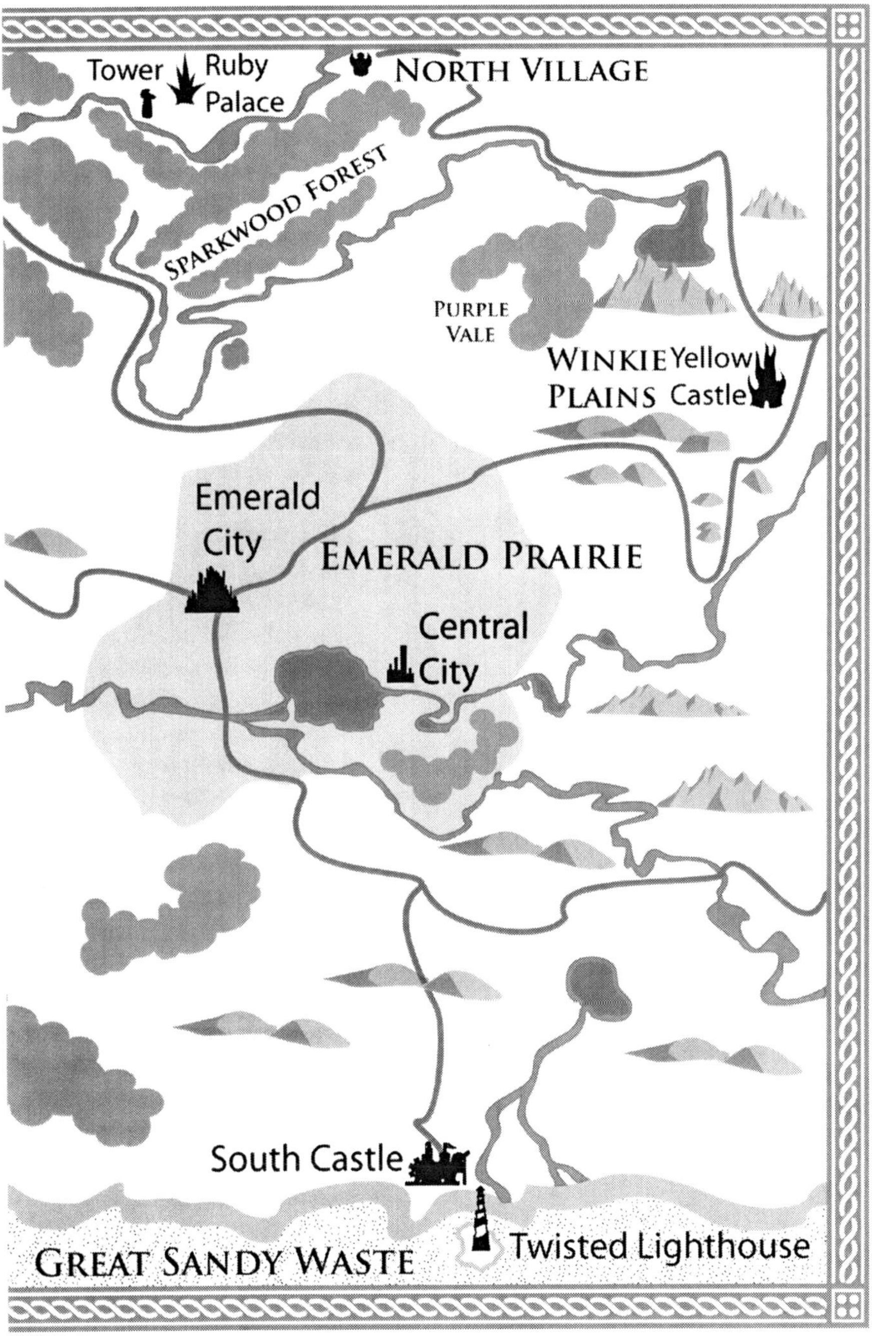
Tower
Ruby Palace
NORTH VILLAGE
SPARKWOOD FOREST
PURPLE VALE
WINKIE PLAINS
Yellow Castle
Emerald City
EMERALD PRAIRIE
Central City
South Castle
GREAT SANDY WASTE
Twisted Lighthouse

SNEAK PREVIEW

The following is a preview from **The Hidden History of Oz, Book Two: Crown of the Dreamer**, available on Amazon, or wherever eBooks are sold.

CHAPTER 1 SCHEMES AND THINGS

"If you all control yourselves, we will have the Wizard exactly where we want him." Glinda said. She addressed her Fighting Girls and all the maidens of her court. "The Sky Wizard's Ball is two days away. Everything will be perfect."

Glinda's definition of perfect didn't match exactly what the other girls thought, but Glinda was in charge. It was her castle, her sorcery, and her party. She controlled what happened in the South country in the Land of Oz. She had been here nearly two years, and the land had blossomed under her watchful eye. She felt confident sharing her scheme with the girls—they could be trusted.

Glinda's right-hand girl, Wickrie-Kells, the captain of the Fighting Girls, listened half-intently to Glinda's speech. Mostly she was focused on the carrot in her hand. She heard only about every third word from Glinda's mouth.

'Control...will...Wizard...exactly...Ball...days...perfect.' Exactly. That was all she needed to know. If there was anything else, Glinda would tell her.

"Wickrie, any thoughts you wish to share around that carrot?" Glinda asked. She tossed her red hair over her shoulder and raised an eyebrow.

"Truth? Good carrot. Good plan. I'll follow your lead." Wickrie-Kells smiled at Glinda's acceptance. That's what best friends were for. Wickrie already had her hands full with all of the new girls that had come to South Castle.

Glinda prided herself on attracting the best and brightest girls in all the Land of Oz to her court. Some of them were fine warriors, and they composed the Fighting Girls—Glinda's elite fighting force, led by Glinda's best friend, Wickrie-Kells. Some of them were singers, like Ola Griffin, who also served as Glinda's herald. Others served in research and experimentation. There were still others that stayed behind the scenes, maintaining the wondrous palace and tending the exotic gardens all around the castle. Glinda addressed them all today. Everyone was a part of this plan.

Ola Griffin closed her eyes and wrote with her bare fingers on the table. In her mind she divided her attention between Glinda's speech and the song she was composing.

Lost in the absence of doubt,

I know there's no easy way out.
Outside of this life,
Romance like a knife...

"Ola Griffin, paying attention, are we?" Glinda said. "Your lips are moving, but your eyes are not paying attention. Please share with us, if you will, what I just said?" Glinda folded her arms and narrowed her eyes at the blonde girl.

Ola Griffin ran her fingers through her hair and smiled. This was the easy part, quoting Glinda, "*We all know that Oscar Diggs, the Wonderful Wizard of Oz, arrived in our land two years ago this week. The Sky Wizard's Ball is to honor him, but more importantly, it is to bring him to me. You all have your assignments. There are those of you who are assigned to accompany the Wizard at various points during the Ball.*"

It was exactly as Glinda had said it. The girls applauded.

Glinda narrowed her gaze, but then the smile drove the stubborn glare out of her eyes. It was quite a display of memory and elocution. She even paused correctly saying Oscar's name. That drew some giggles from the younger girls.

Ola Griffin had the best memory of any of them. Her talents were very nearly a match for Glinda's keen mind.

The red-haired sorceress continued, "You know your roles and I expect that you will be suitably beautiful for the occasion. The rest of you—I am warning you now—the Wizard does not like to see anyone disappointed or let down. He will do whatever it takes to make you happy and smiling. On top of that, he likes pretty faces. Do not encourage him. Be polite and smile when he tells a joke or tells a story, but do not do anything—and I mean anything—that might interfere with our little scheme.

"Some of you will be leaving right after the ball for a joint training exercise with the Emerald Guardsmen. Let me express my gratitude right now for your exemplary efforts. You make me proud to call you friends."

Near the back of the hall a young teenage girl hung on Glinda's every word. She wasn't even supposed to be in here. Her parents were most recently from Munchkin Country, having left quickly after the harsh new laws were implemented. Eyve was too young to join the Fighting Girls, but she wanted to so badly. That desire drove her to break the rules and just follow the group into the hall. There was Wickrie-Kells, the Captain of the Fighting Girls—she was even taller in person. And there was Rala, and Corabinth, and Elka and Decla—she knew them from back home; both sisters wore their hair in side braids. These were names she had only heard of before, now she was right here, breathing the same air as they were. It was good air. It was good to be here. And Glinda had a good plan. The Wizard was important—too important to not let him know how wonderful he was. It was very absolutely clear that Glinda loved the Wizard. They were meant to be together.

When Glinda spoke, it was as if she was speaking directly to Eyve. The young girl's wide brown eyes took in every detail of the hall. This moment would be sealed into her mind and heart forever.

"There will be no additional smiling at the Wizard, batting of eyes, blowing kisses, or flirting in any way. The Wizard—Oscar—is mine, and I want him to realize in no uncertain terms, just how lucky he is to have me."

Far to the east and north of Glinda's palace, Kalinya, the Wicked Witch of the East, knocked on a door on the back side of Mount Munch. For nearly two years she had been waiting for this moment. If such a creature as she could drool in anticipation, she would, but she was very sensitive to water of any type. In addition to her water aversion, every last bit of blood and spit within her dried up two years ago, during the creation of her blood-sand armies in the Battle of Munchkin Fields.

Kalinya looked down on those faraway fields from her vantage point atop the mountain. These intervening months and years had been hard. Though she was the Wicked Witch of the East, and ruled over the Munchkins completely, she was a ghastly spectre of her former self. Where she had once been beautiful, the years of magic had taken their toll. The magic lines she had drawn on her skin to remember the spells marked her as a powerful witch once. Now, after the draining loss of all her blood, her face was sunken and aged. The magic lines crossed each other now, rendering their magic useless. What she lacked, though, in magic, she made up for in power.

Just this month she had enacted a law that forbade any Munchkin in the land from being taller than she was. It was a flattering rule, but a necessary one. It kept the Munchkins in line and fearful. So long as they feared her power, they were easy to control.

Two years—the endless months did not seem so awful now, here at the threshold of success. The terrible price she paid to create her blood-sand armies two years ago had aged her. Beauty was a thing of the past. She was a hideous shadow that ruled the Munchkins with flashing golden eyes. All of that would change today.

She knocked on the door of the small house on Mount Munch. This round dwelling served as the laboratory for the alchemist, Pipton Nikidik. Few knew of him. In fact, Kalinya had only met him two years ago, when she was on her way to an appointment with death. Glinda had created a cloud and bound Kalinya with sandy vines so she could not escape. Kalinya was unceremoniously tossed on top of the cloud and sent northeast into the sky. After almost a full day, the cloud had thinned out as it approached Mount Munch. Her terrified screams had drawn the attention of a singular Munchkin high up on the mountain.

He stood up a ladder against the cloud and retrieved her from her floating prison, thereby earning the witch's gratitude. After learning her story, the Munchkin shared his. He was working on a concept that would peel back the years of time—it was one of his many projects under development. For such a promise of youth, Kalinya swore she would pay any price.

That price now rested in her pocket. Today marked the end of her journey. For two days she had traveled slowly through the forest to arrive at this point. The line-of-sight was not clear enough through the forest, so the magic of the Silver Slippers, as far as Kalinya knew, was useless.

Pipton Nikidik, the alchemist, answered the door. He stared at the Witch for several moments.

Kalinya could not be bothered with formalities. "Two years I have been waiting for this. You have finished?"

"I have finished the ointment. Remember, Witch, when you came down from the cloud, you promised to pay any price? Have you the pearl?"

Kalinya narrowed her amber eyes at the alchemist. "I have it. But I require proof before payment."

"Fair enough." He said. He opened the door and Kalinya followed him into a small laboratory.

The alchemist pulled the cloak up over his head and covered his face with a protective mask. "Stand back, please." He measured the volatile ingredients into a small vial.

"I hear you have taken the title of Professor." Kalinya forced the pleasantries as she waited.

Professor Nikidik carefully measured the liquid into a small dish. "Beware of the burning. Keep it out of your blood."

"What are you adding to the potion?"

"Ointment. It is a topical cream. You want to look younger to catch a man—a specific man, I assume, based on the price. Keep it out of your blood."

"I have no blood." Kalinya confessed.

The man paused and glanced up. His dark eyes studied the twisted magic lines etched deeply into the Witch's face. "Interesting. And yet you live. Where did it spill?"

"I spent it battling my sis—my enemies."

Professor Nikidik held out a small dish containing the ointment. "Your sample as proof."

Kalinya rubbed the ointment into her gnarled hands and gasped in pain as the magic infused her parchment skin and peeled back the years. Her claw-like hands unclenched to become young again. The skin filled out to become smooth and unwrinkled. She laughed in astonishment.

She stepped behind a privacy screen and applied the ointment to her neck and shoulders. She gasped and laughed in pain as the magic in the ointment burned back the years.

She held out the pearl over the top of the screen, and Professor Nikidik snatched it from her fingers. He passed in the vial of ointment. Kalinya applied the ointment liberally and screamed and laughed in pain as the beauty of her youth returned to her.

She pulled on her robes and shook out her dark hair. She cinched her belt around her narrow waist and laughed in glee. She stepped out, younger than she had been in half a lifetime.

Kalinya put her hands on her hips. She laughed and swiveled her hips back and forth in front of Professor Nikidik. "What would your wife say if she could see you now?"

Professor Nikidik held the pearl up to the light, examining it. He gestured back over his shoulder and turned the light on a statue behind him. It was a round-featured woman, pleasantly plump with a pretty face. The statue was carved exquisitely in marble. The likeness in stone was uncanny. Upon closer inspection, Kalinya recognized the fear in the statue's eyes. That could not be carved, no matter how skilled the artisan.

"Ask her." Nikidik said.

Kalinya stopped in shock. She gulped. Then she smiled and shook her finger at Nikidik. "You almost had me. I believed for a minute that she was real."

"Margolotte, this lovely young lady does not believe that you are real." He reached back and stroked the statue's cheek. "For a witch, you lack a great deal of understanding. How old did you say you were?"

"I'm…older than I look."

Nikidik frowned. "You look young now, but your voice sounds raspy. Do you sing?"

"I haven't in years."

"Start. It will clear your voice and help you sound young again. A spoonful of honey twice a day will help."

"How did Margolotte…?"

"She interrupted me while I was working. I am working on an Unguent of Animation. It will bring the inanimate to life. Things that are of a form, but have no life, can be brought into activity and being. I tire of cooking dinner for one."

"How much of this Unguent of Animation are you mixing?"

"I have sufficient ingredients to make a full flask."

"How much will it take to bring Margolotte back?"

"Only a single drop."

"I wish to purchase this unguent from you. I'm looking for an army."

Nikidik stuck the pearl in his pocket, and rubbed his hands together. "An army. Hmm. That is a large request, but I believe I can help you. It will cost you five pearls."

Kalinya smiled tightly. That was her last pearl that she had paid. "It will take some time."

"Fine. Margolotte isn't going anywhere. I will be here when you call again."

Kalinya turned to leave. As her young hand wrapped around the door handle, she stopped and looked back over her shoulder. Nikidik was watching her.

She tossed her hair and flashed her amber eyes at him. "Professor Nikidik, you rogue. What would your wife think?"

"Ask her."

"Next time. I am certain I will see her face-to-face. But now, I have some diabolical schemes to unleash upon an unsuspecting populace." She flashed a dazzling smile. "Wish me luck."

Professor Nikidik pulled out the pearl again and examined it. He looked over the top of the pearl at the beautiful young witch. "Tell me—this man you are spending a fortune to entice—is he worth it?"

"I have been told that he likes pretty faces. As it was long ago, so it is again today, there are none prettier than mine. I have a stop or two to make to visit my rivals in this burgeoning love triangle, and then…I'm off to see the Wizard."

Order your copy of **The Hidden History of Oz, Book Two: Crown of the Dreamer**, on Amazon, or wherever eBooks are sold.

GUIDE FOR PARENTS

Overview

This review is based on the format used by Common Sense Media (http://www.commonsensemedia.org). This is not an official Common Sense Media review. The author created this review to give parents an idea of what the book contained, to determine whether or not it would be appropriate for their children to read, and to provide questions for discussion.

What Parents Need to Know

Parents need to know that this book is a prequel to L. Frank Baum's novel, *The Wonderful Wizard of Oz*. The character names are familiar, but the characters themselves are youthful and inexperienced. They make mistakes, get angry, and do things normal to young people, but very different from their older selves encountered in Baum's books. The story takes place in the year 1852 A.D., forty-eight years before Dorothy enters the Emerald City. The character of Oscar is from the western frontier of America before the Nebraska Territory was made a state. His ideas and stories of independence and revolution are much closer to the founding of America than we are now. The ideas presented may come across as old-fashioned and America-centric, but they are intended to be accurate to the time period in which this story takes place.

There is some violence, as soldiers made of magic sand fight against human soldiers, and against other sandy soldiers. Witches use their own blood to mix with the sand to make stronger soldiers. A character is physically and verbally abused.

There is material that may be ideologically sensitive. Slavery, freedom, liberty, and responsibility are dealt with in various situations in the story. Slavery is dealt with in both broad and personal terms. This is not intended to downplay the seriousness of slavery. To demonstrate the generational effects of slavery a tribe of Winged Monkeys is magically enslaved to the possessor of a certain magical item. The king of the tribe is willing to do anything except lie to win freedom for his people.

Liberty and freedom are discussed at length, and demonstrated in examples both good and bad to show the differences between freedom and tyranny (rule by fear and terror). With freedom comes responsibility to act and to protect that freedom, for the individual and for others. A character has the chance to free the Winged Monkeys from slavery, but misses the opportunity. Multiple perspectives are offered on liberty, freedom, slavery, tyranny, and responsibility. This story is not intended to preach one specific course of action, though it is clear which course the main characters believe. These multiple perspectives are intended to allow the reader to explore and see how different ages, cultures, and classes of people view these concepts.

The main character, Glinda, is inexperienced, rash, and impulsive. She makes promises, but then she does not act on them. This character flaw is intended by the author to demonstrate the effect that one person can have on another, and on an entire land, today, and through the generations. These unfulfilled promises are intended to make the reader think about the proper course of action.
This book is the first of many planned stories in The Hidden History of Oz series. The main series is intended for readers age 10 and older.

Educational Value
This story is written at a fifth-grade reading level. For unfamiliar words, readers may want to use a dictionary, or figure the meaning out themselves through context.
Readers may be interested in learning about principles of history and freedom from the early United States, prior to 1852 A.D. (when this story takes place).
Readers may be interested in comparing some parts of the story to L. Frank Baum's original novel, *The Wonderful Wizard of Oz*, to see how everything fits together.
This story is a prequel, or a story that comes before another already-told story. Comparing *The Wonderful Wizard of Oz* to this story gives many answers to questions that L. Frank Baum did not answer in his book. Consider this question: Why would the author, Tarl Telford, write this story?

Positive Messages
Much of this story deals with freedom in all of its forms. Glinda wanted freedom from her sheltered, protected life, and she became an orphan on the run from the Wicked Witches. She wanted help from others to accomplish impossible goals. In the end, she learns that she has to make the decision to act, and then do whatever is required, to accomplish her goals.
Glinda makes some promises that she can't keep. She recognizes the consequences of her actions, and she works to fix what her actions ruined.
Locasta has been verbally and physically abused for years. After talking with Glinda, and seeing the actions that Glinda takes, Locasta finds her way to freedom from the abuse. She leaves a bad situation to find a better life.

Positive Role Models
Glinda gets herself and others into trouble by refusing to conform to others' expectations of her. By the end of the story, she has learned that every action has a consequence, for good or bad. She takes responsibility for her actions, and she works to make the Land of Oz a place of freedom, where everyone can choose for themselves to live free.
Omby-Amby believes in liberty and freedom. He protects those who need help. He is a loyal and good friend.

Oscar hides his true feelings behind tricks. It is only in his dreams that he is honest with himself. His dreams literally change the land around him. Everyone believes that he is a wizard, but he does not think he is anything special. He learns to trust others and works to build a city where people can live free from fear and slavery.

Violence

Magic hourglasses create sandy soldiers, which make up the Sandy Armies. Characters discover that blood mixed with the sand makes more powerful sandy soldiers. Sand and blood-sand soldiers fight human soldiers and each other. A character uses a large solar ray to turn a sand dragon into glass. Buildings are destroyed. Forest fire. A character with telekinetic magic throws things into the air, including fallen trees, rocks, and a house.
A character talks about being abused and thrown into the sky. The character has bruises from the abuse.
A non-human character is critically burned by fire.

Romance / Sex

Two characters kiss. Two different characters kiss goodbye. Innocent exploration into first love—holding hands, flirting, and one kiss.

Language

A character uses words like "poppycock", "pish-posh", and "fiddlesticks" when she is frustrated. A character is verbally abused by another character.

Consumerism

Characters purchase magic hourglasses.

Drinking, Drugs, and Smoking

None.

What is the story?

Glinda is the rebellious teenage daughter of a sorceress. She wants freedom from the life she has. She refuses to conform to her parents' plan, which disrupts everything, and destroys everything that Glinda knew. She runs for her life and finds friends to stand beside her. The Wicked Witches want control over all the land. Glinda and her friends stand against the armies of the Witches and fight for freedom. They fail, time and again, but they keep working for what they believe is right. Glinda and Oscar make a clever plan to fight against the Witches and end this war, once and for all. Through their efforts, they learn the consequences of both action and inaction. Glinda's broken promises change her life, and she vows to become a better person. They establish two havens of freedom in Oz: one is The Emerald City, and other is in the South. The Witches divide the other parts of Oz among themselves, taking East, West, and North. Glinda rules in the South, and Oscar becomes the Wizard in the Emerald City.

Is it any good?

Glinda has a good life, but she feels like she is a slave. She refuses to cooperate with her parents, and runs away from her responsibilities. As a result, enemies of her family put their plan into action, and Glinda loses her parents and her home. Now she has the freedom she wanted. She comes to realize that all she has is what is inside of her. She makes friends and finds courage to stand against the Wicked Witches. She makes promises, but doesn't follow through, hurting other characters. She learns from her mistakes. She learns to be responsible. However, she still keeps her rebellious attitude as a way of holding on to her independence.

Families can talk about

Parents may wish to discuss the idea of slavery. What types of slavery are there? (economic, ignorance, addiction, physical) What is the difference between feeling like a slave, and actually being in slavery?

Parents may wish to talk about keeping promises. Glinda makes promises, but she does not follow through immediately. What are the results of her procrastination?

Glinda acts in opposition to what she is asked to do. What are the results of her actions? Why is it important to recognize that all actions have consequences?

At the beginning of the story, Glinda wants freedom from her life. What events provide her this "freedom"? How is this freedom different from the freedom and liberty that Oscar talks about?

Oscar quotes Benjamin Franklin in saying that the United States of America was *"A republic, if you can keep it."* How does liberty require responsibility? What is the difference between being ruled by a king, and the people ruling themselves? Why is it important to recognize that you are responsible for your own freedom?

The characters talk about freedom and choosing their own destiny. What is the difference between talking about ideas, and actually working to accomplish them?

Nobody in Oz dreams. Then Oscar comes to Oz, and he is a dreamer. His dreams literally change the land and other things around him. The people believe he is a great wizard. Oscar doesn't believe that he is anything special, but his friends, and other people do. Why is it important to be honest with others? Why is it important to be honest with ourselves? Have you ever experienced something that other people did not understand? Did they believe you when you told them? What was the result of being honest?

Book Details

Author	Tarl Telford
Genre	Fantasy, Adventure
Topics	Freedom, Slavery, Loyalty, Honesty, Keeping Promises, Friendship, Adventure, Magic
Book Type	Fiction
Publisher	Emerald Engine Studios
Publication Date	July 11, 2012
Number of pages	275
Publisher's recommended ages	10 and up
Available on (platforms)	Paperback, Kindle, other digital

ON THE WEB

The Hidden History of Oz blog
http://hiddenhistoryofoz.wordpress.com

Contact the author
Oz@tarltelford.com

Also available
The Hidden History of Oz, Book Two: Crown of the Dreamer
Available in both paperback and Kindle versions.

ABOUT THE AUTHOR

Tarl Telford is a technical writer, versed in taking the words of others, discovering overall meaning, then weaving them into a clearly understandable finished product. He annotated *The Wonderful Wizard of Oz*, and discovered many stories that required this type of technical analysis to complete. This project became the genesis of The Hidden History of Oz saga.

He is a student of history and a proponent of freedom and individual responsibility. These themes resonate in all his works.

The Hidden History of Oz, Book One: The Witch Queens, is his first published novel.

Tarl keeps a dream journal, which he adds to daily. He lives in Texas with his red-haired wife.

Lightning Source UK Ltd.
Milton Keynes UK
UKOW02f2000100916

282698UK00001B/84/P

9 780615 667874